The Perfect Suicide

The Perfect Suicide

Lotte Worth

Winchester, UK
Washington, USA

First published by Sassy Books, 2013
Sassy Books is an imprint of John Hunt Publishing Ltd., Laurel House, Station Approach,
Alresford, Hants, SO24 9JH, UK
office1@jhpbooks.net
www.johnhuntpublishing.com
www.sassy-books.com

For distributor details and how to order please visit the 'Ordering' section on our website.

Text copyright: Lotte Worth 2012

ISBN: 978 1 78099 726 1

All rights reserved. Except for brief quotations in critical articles or reviews, no part of this book may be reproduced in any manner without prior written permission from the publishers.

The rights of Lotte Worth as author have been asserted in accordance with the Copyright, Designs and Patents Act 1988.

A CIP catalogue record for this book is available from the British Library.

Design: Stuart Davies

Printed in the USA by Edwards Brothers Malloy

We operate a distinctive and ethical publishing philosophy in all areas of our business, from our global network of authors to production and worldwide distribution.

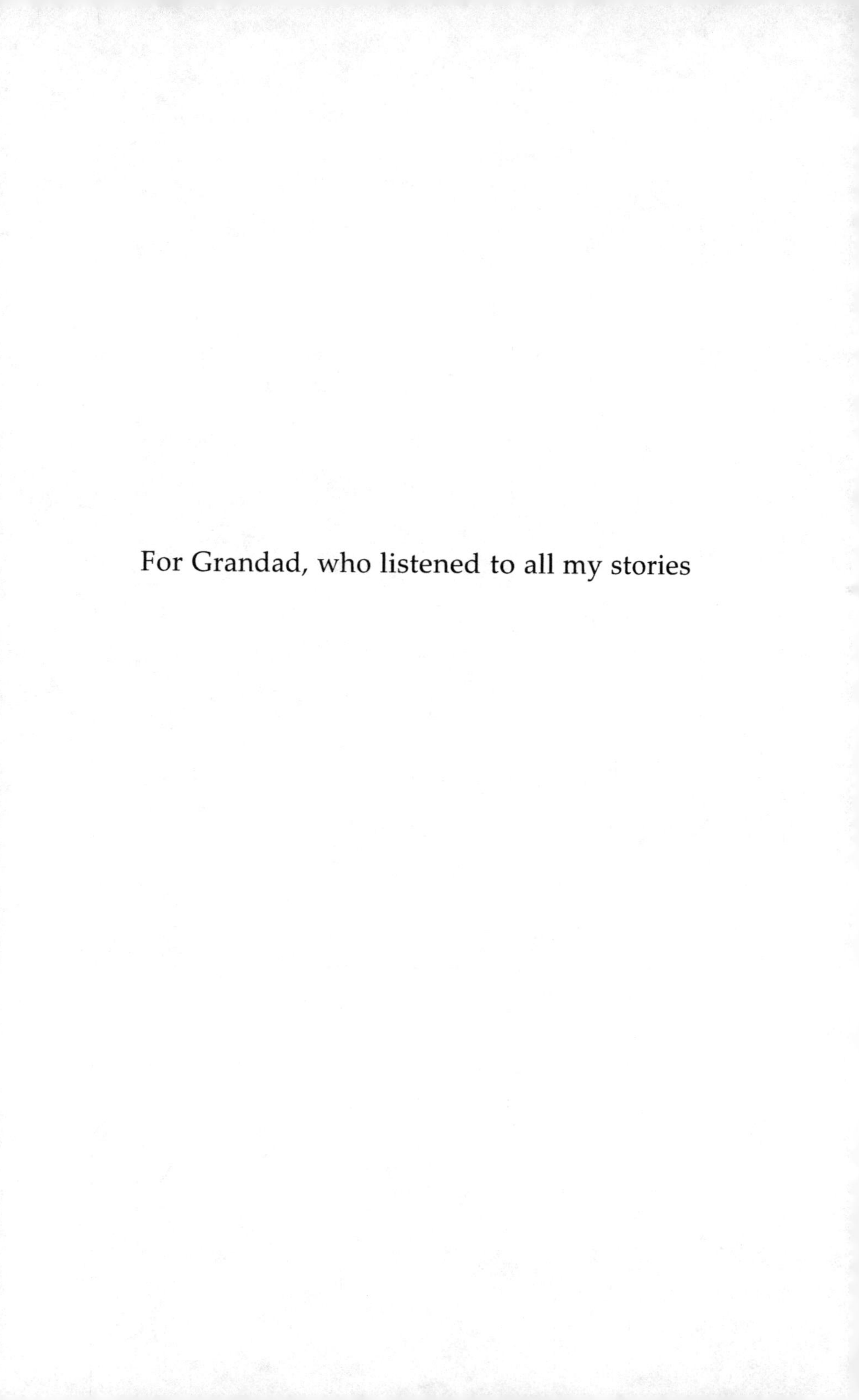

For Grandad, who listened to all my stories

Odi et amo. Quare id faciam, fortasse requiris.
Nescio, sed fieri sentio et excrucior.

I hate and I love. Why do I do this, perhaps you ask.
I do not know, but I feel it, and I am in torment.

Catullus, 85

Prologue

Pete, February 1999

They were looking for crystals. As always, it was a competition. Last time she had collected more than him, and now, by rights, it was his turn to win. The beach was a gigantic stretch of opportunity, and with his new spectacles, he was sure he was unbeatable.

'You don't understand Lucy. These glasses are part of my arsenal,' he boasted as they walked down to the beach, the brittle wind turning the tips of his ears and nose first pink and then blue. He knew Lucy wouldn't understand what arsenal meant. He'd heard the word last week on *Doctor Who* and she didn't have a television at her house. 'So I'll win this time, you wait and see.'

She laughed at him, tugging at her shabby school kilt, unsuccessfully attempting to pull it down over her knees. 'Not if you couldn't see properly in the first place! Now you'll just see the same as me, not better.'

He stuck his tongue out at her. Why was she always one step ahead of him, always that little bit smarter? But at least it took the shame away from previous defeats. *Astigmatic,* that's what the optician in Ashington had said, before handing him a lollipop – a sort of fake Chupa Chup – and cuffing him under the chin. It made him feel special and he decided it didn't matter that the lollipop was missing a corner and that it was a strawberry one, when cola was his favourite.

He didn't often feel special. Noticed. Last time they'd played this, he'd run home to his parents, red-faced with glee to show them his spoils, and his father had merely grunted.

'Just ruddy bits of glass you bloomin' eejit. Crystals!'

Peter had stared down at the tiny pieces in his hand, their once-jagged edges now smooth – sparkling lots of colours: brown, green, blue but mostly clear. The clear ones he believed were diamonds, those things his mam was always going on about wanting, like rich southern people had. He tried to polish one of them up to give to her as a present, but no matter how hard he'd rubbed it with bits of sandpaper stolen from the battered cupboard in the fish house, it wouldn't gleam like he wanted it to.

That didn't matter anymore though, not now the game was in force. All he cared about was winning. He watched Lucy running along the beach. Every now and then she bent down, sometimes leaping back up with a smile, other times hauling herself to her feet, disappointed. He liked watching Lucy, even though she was annoying and she was a girl. She was his best friend and she never got mad with him, no matter what he did or said. Not like his dad.

But she was being stupid now – they had covered that part of the beach last week. He headed off in the opposite direction.

At the far end were lots of rocks. He had to climb around them to get to the other side but he didn't mind. As usual, there was no one else about and in his head he was an adventurer, discovering new territory. The sea was a frightening grey mass that he'd learnt to ignore.

Scrambling over the biggest rock, he found himself in a clearing. He had always loved the perfect vanilla-yellow sand. He walked slowly up and down, methodically scouring the ground, and after only ten minutes, he had six crystals in his pocket. And then, closer to the sea, he spotted a real rarity – a deep red one, the colour of blood, reflecting up at him. He grabbed it in triumph. No one had ever found a red one before. The colour made him think of his mam's rosary ring – it was gold with a deep red stone in the middle, and lots of gold bumps all around the outside. Each one was for a Hail Mary, and the big red stone at the front was for a Hail Mary, Glory Be and the Lord's Prayer all at once. He spat on his discovery and rubbed it clean. Carefully, he pocketed it. His mam would love it.

'Boo!'

He felt his collar yanked and a handful of wet sand trickle down his back. Turning, he discovered Lucy grinning at him.

'Hey!' he shouted. 'What did you do that for?'

'Got you!' she taunted, doing a series of cartwheels. 'Time's up. How many did you get?'

He wriggled, trying to shake the sand out of his clothes. But he was laughing too now.

'The sand is so cold! I'll get you back for that, you wait and see. I got loads this time actually, more than you I bet. And I got a special blood crystal too.'

'Let's see. Show me, show me!'

He reached into his pocket and pulled out the handfuls of glass pebbles. There it was, the deep red gem. His booty. Lucy reached out to grab it.

'Wow,' she gasped, holding it up to the sky, where a pale sun was attempting to break through. 'That's amazing. Wow.'

'Give it back! It's for me Mam.'

'If you want it, you'll have to come and get it,' Lucy shouted, running off.

Instinctively he took off after her, knowing it was a race he would win. He picked up pace, leaping across the sand, his Start-rite school shoes leaving zig-zag tracks behind him. Then, he saw Lucy had stopped running. He squinted, trying to see what she was looking at, the low February sun confusing his vision. He reached her and stopped too. This was the furthest along the beach he'd ever been.

They were both panting as they gazed down at the word 'sorry' carved into the sand in front of them. A pile of folded clothes and some sensible black shoes lay next to the letters. Placed carefully on top of a red jumper was a gold rosary ring, with a ruby *paternoster*. It glinted up at them.

Grains of sand were still trickling down his back.

'I don't understand,' he said, frowning as he turned his head towards the churning sea. 'Mam can't swim.'

PART ONE

Chapter One

Emma, September 2010

They were all there, looking down at me.

The people who cared about me. The people to whom I was significant. They were all watching me from behind frozen eyes.

Heather's face appeared several times. Posing against Bowerman's Nose, camping on the moor, on holiday at Tencreek Caravan Park in Looe. And then there were my friends in the beer garden at the Runner – a gaggle of cider-induced grins at the summer of freedom ahead. There was one of me and Ben, his arm around my waist, head peeping above my shoulder. There were family pictures too: on holiday in Spain, Mum's face glowing bright red from the sun and sangria; Matt playing on his Playstation, eyes slanted sideways in a sarcastic glance; dear darling Granddad, confused yet smiling at the birthday cake before him: 88 that day.

But the people in the pictures were far away now, and on the other side of the plywood door were four complete strangers, a narrow corridor and a communal kitchen. I was thirsty. It was time to venture out. I briefly wondered what would happen if I never left the room. Would anyone come and knock on the door to see if I was OK?

Probably not.

I could die in here and no one would know.

I was being ridiculous. I looked again at the mosaic of photographs. This time, I saw only lies. I would never forget Ben's last phone call, full of excuses about how events had changed me, about the difficulties of long-distance relationships. Heather was far away; working as an au pair in Metz, too busy mopping up after babies for our usual hour-long Facebook chats. The rest of my friends were scattered across the country, waiting for their new lives to start, just like me. Matt had grown bored of his Playstation, and Granddad was in a nursing home, unaware of who or where he was.

And I was in Leeds. In this small, dark room, with its paisley curtains and pine furniture. I walked to the window. There might as well have been a piece of grey cardboard behind it, because all I saw was grey concrete, industrial buildings and a depressed autumn sky – thick, threatening clouds suffocating the feeble sunlight. From my first few hours, it looked like Leeds was little more than an extension of the monotonous M1 that had brought me here.

But it didn't matter. It might be grey, and rainy, but Leeds was a whole new world, far from them, far from everything I'd been so desperate to leave behind. There was another life out there, beyond this grey car park, just waiting to be discovered. I felt a fresh tingle of anticipation – the same feeling I'd had last night, when I couldn't get to sleep and lay there wondering what was in store for me, like a child on Christmas eve.

I pulled the curtains back as far as they would go, and it was then that I noticed it on the windowsill, tucked into the corner. Mum had hidden it behind the folds of fabric.

I picked up the silver frame. It was a shot I recognised – my father and I, sitting on a beach in Barbados, our fair hair tousled by the sea breeze. My swimsuit had been neon, garish and multi-coloured, but years spent on the dining room sideboard opposite the large bay window had faded it. In the photo I'd once had an impressive tan, the result of a ten-year-old's fortnight of sun worshipping, snorkeling and swimming. But now, my skin was pale, bleached back by the same sun that had once coloured me.

Seven months ago this photo had vanished, along with every other trace of him, during the fit of anger that lasted about a week. I thought Mum had thrown everything away. She must have put it in here while I was in the toilet – there definitely hadn't been any other opportunity as we'd unpacked everything together. She'd flicked through my collection of pictures, carefully chosen in advance to decorate the expected magnolia wall, smiling with the memories. She knew I hadn't brought any of him, and rightly so. I gripped the frame tightly. I wouldn't let him ruin my new optimism. Not today. Yellowing silver polish had collected around the edges of the glass. I scraped it off with my nail and smeared it over his face.

I couldn't understand why it was OK for her to hide away from him, but insist that I keep a place for him in my heart and on my windowsill. He had let me down too, and devastated the last few months of my life just as much. Possibly more, although she didn't know it.

Well, he wouldn't any longer. I opened the window. It was stiff at first but eventually gave way. There was no wind, so I hardly felt the fresh air as it slowly seeped into the room.

Flat P8 was on the top floor, up five flights of stairs. I leaned out of the window and dropped the frame, watching it fall.

It landed face down, in a mass of brambles that grew unchecked against the iron railings of the student compound. The blue velvet backing was still visible among the twisted branches, but a couple of days' growth after an inevitable downpour would see to that.

I had my story ready, in case anyone asked; he had died from cancer, when I was a child. Not that I expected anyone to take an interest. The last seven months had taught me people weren't as observant as you'd expect.

Edging closer to the door, I could hear muffled voices and someone laughing, which meant the other inhabitants of P8 had already met.

I checked my reflection. The excitement and anticipation had brought colour to my cheeks and the ends of my hair were falling in the right direction for once. I gave myself a bright smile. I'd cried a little when Mum left, but the truth was most of my tears came from relief. It felt as though the tension and stress of the last few months were leaving with her, and up here, where nobody knew me; I could have a life again. A normal life, like I'd had before, like any other 18-year-old starting a degree. Up here, I was safe. I'd no longer have to try to avoid contact with the person I loved more than anyone else but could no longer look in the eye. And of course, there would be no more contact with the person I had once loved – yes, I had loved her – but whose presence now made my skin shrink with disgust.

It was a new start and I was ready.

I took a deep breath and opened the door.

I came face-to-face with the tallest man I had ever seen. Behind steel-framed glasses, kind eyes peered at me. I looked down, a little embarrassed. He was wearing orange socks. When I looked back up, he smiled at me and I relaxed.

'Hullo,' he said, running his hand through a mop of chestnut hair then holding it out to shake mine. 'I'm Pete.'

~

'I'm just going to the loo,' I said, pushing my chair back and wincing at the scraping sound.

Pete looked up. The others didn't, they were too busy discussing one of their cousins – Samuel's, the skinny one with short, spiky hair – who coincidentally went to school with one of the other ones, Maria. It really was a small world.

Four cups of tea in three hours was obviously my limit. There hadn't been a suitable time to interrupt before but desperation had overcome me. They were all so animated and friendly already. It wasn't like me to be quiet, but I'd hardly said a word, answered the questions I was asked and tried to keep up. My bottom was numb from sitting down for so long and I wiggled my toes as I walked to my room.

I went into the tiny en suite and stared in the mirror, trying to imagine how the others would see me. As usual, my self-assessment boiled down to: not great, but not ugly. I was on a par with Maria, the freckled redhead. The other girl – Amelia or something, she'd said her name so fast I'd nearly missed it – she was very pretty, with charcoal hair and gleaming gingerbread-coloured skin. But she was short. I had height on my side at least.

Amelia, Maria and Sam were all doing the same course: Pharmacology. Pete was studying Economics and Statistics, which meant they were all doing BSCs, and were all frighteningly clever. Someone had once told me that people who were good at music were often very mathematical, but that sadly hadn't applied to me.

I walked to the window. It was drizzling, the sun setting behind the foggy clouds. I could still make out the streak of blue velvet under my window. He was still there. He always would be, of course, and perhaps it was too naive of me to think it could be any other way. I looked out further. There really wasn't much of a view: just a large empty car park, with arbitrary puddles of rainwater scattered across it. Out of the corner of my eye, I could make out the canal Maria had mentioned. She said the towpath alongside it lead you straight to the city centre. I leant on the windowsill, lingering. For some reason, I really didn't feel like going back in the kitchen. It wasn't that I didn't have anything to say, it's just that everyone else seemed to have more and to be able to express it so much better.

I didn't want to talk about Dad. I didn't, and yet, after months of talking about nothing else, it seemed I had run out of normal conversation.

Amelia, Maria, Pete and Sam were all from the north. Thanks to their gap years, they were all older than me too. I was a little in awe of them. They'd all done so much already: travelling around the world, helping save the rainforests, building hospitals for gorillas and mud huts for Mexican peasants. The only one who hadn't been saving the planet on his year off was Pete. He said his gap year had been used for the 'wholly self-centred purpose of working to save up money to come to uni'. I think he'd said it to make me feel better, but I couldn't be sure.

My pondering was interrupted by a knock on my door. I opened it to find Amelia, the small one with dark hair. She smiled, revealing perfectly white, perfectly straight teeth.

'Emma,' she said. 'We're off to the bar. Want to come?'

Behind her I could see Maria and Sam grinning at me, but there was no sign of Pete.

'Sure,' I said. 'Hang on, I'll just get my bag.'

Chapter Two

Emma, September 2010

The bus turned a corner sharply and I fell into Maria, head-butting her into a brief silence.

'Sorry,' I said, gripping the seat in front to pull myself back upright.

'Steady there,' she said, smiling at me. 'See, snowboarding, that's all about balance too.'

I hadn't really noticed just how attractive she was before. She was rugged and healthy-looking, not overweight but muscly, with freckly skin, a wide smile and narrow yet piercing eyes. I'd known her for a week now, long enough to learn that she was always slightly red, and that it wasn't thanks to a furtive jogging obsession.

Maria was very excited about joining the snowboarding club. For the entire ten minutes we'd been on the bus, she'd been talking about it. Apparently, she'd learnt the full range of snow-related sports as a child: skiing, ice-skating, sledging...you name it, she'd done it.

'I can't believe you've never been Emma,' she was saying. 'It's just fantastic. The biggest adrenalin rush. I'll have to take you one day. You can come up to Spean Bridge – that's where my grand-parents live and where I learnt – and I'll take you up Ben Nevis. You'll love it.'

I nodded, not sure what to say, part of me wishing I'd stayed behind like Pete. But Amelia had been so persuasive, saying there was bound to be a club for me at the Freshers' Fair, despite me flicking through the handbook and not really finding anything.

'So what sports *do* you like?' she asked, flicking an elastic band off her wrist and tying her bushy red hair back.

'Well, I've never been that sporty,' I said. Her face fell. 'I mean, I like swimming.'

'Fantastic aerobic exercise,' she said, nodding seriously. 'Brilliant for you. Works all parts of your body without putting stress on your joints. We'll definitely have to go swimming one day. So,' she said, dropping her voice. 'What do you think of our men?' She jerked her thumb in Sam's direction. 'He's a bit scrawny for me, bless him. But Pete's handsome, don't you think? There's something about him. He's so private. But funny and sweet too.'

I felt myself blush, memories of a wholly unexpected dream I'd had the previous night flooding back to me.

'Yes, he's lovely,' I said.

She picked up on my honesty.

'I thought you liked him,' she said. 'Amelia and I were talking about it this morning. Last night, he was watching you, you know. I reckon you're in with a chance there.'

I smiled, wondering if she was right. I couldn't tell – I'd always been rubbish at working out whether people liked me or not.

'What about you?' I asked.

She sighed, looking down. 'Well, there are a couple of good-looking men in P7, but to be honest, I'm still not really over my ex. We only broke up three weeks ago.'

There was an awkward pause. I didn't know what to say – I found it really difficult to feel pity for practically anyone now, not after what had happened. Their problems always seemed so trivial in comparison to mine. But there was no way to explain that to Maria, not without explaining everything, and I was relieved that seconds later we arrived at the uni, which let me off the hook.

The Freshers' Fair wasn't what I was expecting at all. It was more like a car boot sale. Behind each stand, enthusiastic older students were handing out leaflets, chatting and luring prospective members to their tables with lollipops and sweets.

I trailed after Amelia, Sam and Maria, wondering whether

there was a music society. The ski and snowboarding club was at the end of the first row and Maria eagerly approached the tanned guy behind the table. They tried to persuade Amelia to join. Sam had recognised someone from his school and wandered off so I listened to Amelia deciding whether she was keen enough on him and his tan to part with £25.

It turned out she was, although her hair flicking and fluttering eyelashes didn't get her a discount. In the end, I think it was the details of the infamous weekly 'Otley Run' pub-crawl – with photographic evidence – that convinced her. Opposite the ski and snowboarding stall was a girl sitting on her own, behind a rather bare stand. No sweets, no crowds. I stepped forward to look closer. The French society.

Finally, something I could join. I'd done French A level and it would make Mum happy. She was still going on about how much more useful a modern language degree would be.

I approached the girl. She was sitting on a portable stool reading, a heavy chocolate-brown fringe hanging in front of her eyes. She was so engrossed in her book she didn't notice me.

I gave a small cough. She looked up, and smiled.

'Oh hello,' she said, pushing her hair back from her forehead with the back of her hand. Her eyes were exactly the same colour as her hair. 'Didn't see you there. You really snuck up on me.'

'Oh, sorry,' I said.

'Don't be silly. Are you interested in joining?' She fiddled with some of the leaflets on the table in front of her. 'Let me tell you what the French Soc does…'

She told me about the weekly nights at the Firkin, the exchange trips, the French cinema evenings and various other advantages of membership. None of it mattered; I'd already made my mind up.

'What do I need to do?' I asked.

'Oh, just fill in your details here,' she said, handing me a chewed biro and a clipboard. There was a form attached to it, with only two signatures so far. 'I'll get you a membership card.'

I started to fill in the form while she fumbled around with a carrier bag under the stand.

'Let's see,' she said, craning her neck to read where I'd written my name. 'Emma Dewberry.' She copied it onto a small card. 'Good to have you in the group. Where are you living? Oooh, Clarence Dock, nice. I was in Lupton in my first year – you wouldn't want to board your dog there.'

'Lupton?' I asked. 'That was my second choice.'

'Really? You had a lucky escape then. God, that place was a dump. Mind you, great location for Headingley. Stumbling distance from The Original Oak.'

'The Original Oak? Is that a pub?' I made a mental note to suggest it to the others later.

'Don't tell me you haven't been there yet! I think it was the first place I went when I got here. It's a Leeds institution …' She smiled, eyeing me curiously. 'Mind you, I suppose it's a bit of a trek from Clarence Dock.'

I beamed at her. This girl must be a third year or even a postgrad, and yet here she was, chatting away to me. After all, we had something in common. I had something in common with everyone in this room. I felt another tinge of excitement at the future as I continued filling in the form. The final column asked me whether I was doing a BA Single or Joint Honours in French. There didn't seem to be space to put any other subject.

'Um,' I said. The girl was laminating the little membership card, smoothing down the sticky plastic carefully. I was impressed with her technique; there wasn't a single air bubble. 'I'm not actually doing French, I'm doing Music. Is there somewhere I can fill that in?'

'You're not studying French?' she asked. Her eyebrows moved towards one another.

'No,' I said. 'Does that matter?'

'Um, well, you can't join the French society unless you're a

French student.' She looked at me as though I was mad. 'I'm not sure why you'd want to…?' Her voice tailed off.

'Oh, I'm so sorry. How stupid of me.' My voice came out in a weird croak. I crossed through where I'd written my name and address, several times, pushing the pen down with force. She threw my little membership card into a carrier bag on the floor – it landed on a half-eaten sandwich. 'Sorry, I'm so stupid.'

'Don't worry,' she said, but this time her smile was pitying. 'I'm sorry we can't have you. It's only for people studying French you see. Otherwise the group would get too big. I'm sure there's a music society or something though. Why don't you go and have a look?'

'Yes, I…I will. Sorry for wasting your time.'

I handed the clipboard back, staring down at it, and nodded. I imagined her laughing about this at the inaugural meeting for new members. *You don't know how lucky you lot are to be here! This group was so popular; we even had some sad music student try to wheedle her way in!*

But she didn't reply, she'd already sat down and re-opened her book.

I turned and walked away, not thinking where I was going. Before I knew it, I was back at the entrance. Where would the others be? Probably still at the snowboard club table, wondering where I had gone. I hesitated, peering down the different rows. There were so many people – all in groups or pairs, all smiling – and every single one looked happy and relaxed. My chest began to tighten, and a low humming sound started somewhere in my head. I felt hot and dizzy, and if I had thought it possible, I would have said the inside of my ears were sweating.

I began to pace up and down the rows, scanning the crowds, squeezing past people, but I didn't spot anyone familiar. After a few minutes, with my head starting to pound, I decided to get some air.

I stepped out into the main square. Compared with the stuffy, packed hall, the courtyard was a haven. I sat on the first bench I came to, and tried to catch my breath.

What had happened to me? I wanted to cry. I stared at my feet. A pigeon landed next to me, cocked its head sideways, and flew off again.

Even the pigeons didn't want to know me.

I tried to compose myself, digging at the inside of my palms with my fingernails, until the sharp pain brought my thoughts back into focus. The best thing to do would be to go back to the flat. There was no point in walking around the huge campus searching for them. Something told me they weren't going to miss me. I got up.

As I was walking in what I hoped was the direction of Woodhouse Lane, I passed a large building with immense windows. Inside, there were lots of tables and multi-coloured chairs, with people sitting around drinking from polystyrene cups. My eyes fixed on a group in the corner. Even from a fair distance, there was something familiar about them – the colour of their clothes, their hairstyles perhaps. And then, when I came within a few feet of their table, I realised who they were.

I stood stock-still for a few seconds, staring at them. Amelia was talking animatedly, her eyes and arms dancing around, lips moving furiously. Maria was red-faced with hilarity. Sam had one hand in front of his mouth and the other clutching at his stomach in surrender.

I moved closer to the window, watching their faces. How strange that I could see them but they didn't know I was there.

And then, without warning, Amelia looked up and saw me.

Her eyes locked onto mine. I smiled weakly. But her expression wasn't one of joy at recognising a friend. It wasn't even confusion. It was the look of someone who has been caught out. Her mouth hung open slightly as her eyes widened against mine.

Then I realised: they had been laughing at me.

I turned and ran, thinking only that I wanted to get away. I hated the uni and I hated Amelia and Sam and Maria and I hated whatever it was about myself they were laughing at.

I ran all the way down the hundreds of steps to the entrance of the campus, not caring whether the other students in their Leeds University jumpers and trendy jeans saw me pelting past and thought I was weird.

In my pocket, my phone began to vibrate. That was all I needed. She wasn't taking the hint. I knew she'd leave a voicemail, a plea for me to return the call...another helping of guilt.

On the main street, I scoured the road for buses. Which bus would take me home? No 11? No 28? I couldn't remember. I should have written it down.

Then, there was a voice behind me.

'Emma?'

I turned. It was Pete. He smiled at me, his wax jacket draped over one arm.

'Hi,' I said, suddenly wondering what I looked like. I rubbed at my cheeks, imagining with dread how shiny they would be.

'What on earth have you been doing?' he asked. 'Running? You're bright red. You'd make a tomato look pale.'

A laugh of relief escaped me.

'Something like that,' I said. 'I…just…'

'Come on,' he said, taking my arm and linking it through his. 'Let's get a drink and you can tell me all about it.'

~

I was relieved he hadn't taken me back to the union, but instead to a ship that had been plonked in the middle of a central reservation and transformed into a bar. It was called the Dry Dock, and bottles of Bacardi Breezer were only £1.50.

We sat at a table near the window. I was still hot from running so I took off my jacket.

'So,' Pete said, taking a sip of his pint. 'What were you up to?'

I wasn't a good enough liar to come up with a plausible story.

'Oh it's silly really,' I said, fiddling with my hair. 'I just lost the others, and began to panic a bit. I thought I was lost. It's all quite overwhelming.'

'It's a big campus isn't it? I haven't explored much myself yet. I think I read somewhere that it's the biggest in the country. Easy to get lost anyway.'

'Yes,' I replied, the sickly pineapple taste of my drink sticking in my throat. 'And I went to such a small school. It's just a bit different I suppose.'

'Where are you from again?' he asked. 'Somewhere south west wasn't it?'

'Yes. Devon. Paignton. We moved there eight years ago, after my dad...'

Stupid mouth, always running away with me. I dug my fingers into my palm again.

'...got into a bit of trouble. Financially. He thought he'd make a fresh start in the west country. Thought it would be easier.'

I gave a bitter laugh and stared down at the Bacardi Breezer bottle. If Heather hadn't told me it was common knowledge that peeling labels off bottles meant you were sexually frustrated, I would have done it now.

'Oh,' he said. I glanced up and noticed Pete was looking at me strangely, his eyes hard with curiosity. 'So, did it help?'

'Not exactly.' I breathed deeply. It was too late now. 'Um. He died earlier this year. But I don't really want to talk about it, if that's OK. Anyway, I lived in Guildford before that. In Surrey. So, really, I grew up there.'

So much for my story. Tears pricked at the backs of my eyes. I willed Pete to fill the silence before I lost it completely.

'Oh,' he said again. 'I see.'

'And you?' I asked, staring down at the table, wondering why he hadn't offered any condolences.

'My dad's still alive and kicking,' he said. 'More's the pity.'

I frowned.

'Oh Emma, sorry, that wasn't very sensitive of me was it?' he said, slapping himself on the side of the head. 'What am I like? I'm so sorry. It must be dreadful for you to have lost your father. I can't imagine what it would be like.'

'It wasn't great,' I said, feeling strangely disengaged from the conversation suddenly. Perhaps there was no need to keep it quiet after all. No one would suspect my involvement. Perhaps I should tell people he killed himself after getting into debt, seeing as that was what everyone at home believed anyway. 'But anyway, I meant where are you from? I've never heard anyone who speaks like you before.'

'Well you wouldn't do, being from down there. They're all in-bred down them there parts, don't you know?' he said, in a surprisingly effective Cornish accent.

I smiled. The humour was unexpected but welcome.

'Hey! I just told you, I'm from Surrey originally,' I said, resisting the temptation to playfully whack his arm. 'But really, where are you from?'

'Oh a long way away from Devon. Deepest darkest Northumberland.' He raised his eyebrows.

'Right,' I said, nodding although I was none the wiser.

'It's half the world away, it really is,' he said, taking another sip of his pint. 'But listen, I'm really sorry about your father.'

Chapter Three

Pete, February 1999

They wouldn't let him go to the funeral. His aunt Matilda had arrived, a tall, harsh woman who looked too much like his father for Peter to believe that she really was a woman and not a man in disguise. He sat at the top of the stairs, the place where he felt invisible, and listened to Matilda phone Lucy's mam.

Don't think it's appropriate for him to go, considering the circumstances, he heard her say. *Not the boy's fault after all. He should be spared the humiliation. Imagine, a cremation! Such an embarrassment. So you'll have him. Good. I'm glad you agree it's for the best. The vigil is tonight, so I'll drop him off before. Well, we're only having one because Father Gerry made an exception. It's at Bert's. Wasn't appropriate to hold it in the church. Oh it's all such a mess. And Peter's a canny lad, there are bound to be questions. Don't know what Bert will tell him. Not my problem. He should never have married such a weakling in the first place.*

Peter didn't know why he wasn't being allowed to go to the funeral but he didn't want to go anyway. He'd been to his grandmother's funeral the year before and it was the longest mass ever. The night before they'd had some special service at the church, and they'd done the rosary all together and lots of other strange prayers. At the proper mass the next day, he was horrified to see the coffin in the middle of the aisle and couldn't stop thinking about his grandmother all rotten and smelly inside it. He'd started to cry, wishing it wasn't so close to him. And everyone from the village had fussed over him and told him how sorry they were, when he didn't really care about her being dead, he just didn't want to be in the same room as her body.

This was different though. Everyone seemed cross at his mam. Especially his da. Probably for being so stupid and going in the sea when she couldn't even swim. Which actually, now he thought about it, was really stupid and even he was a bit cross about that. No one was crying. Peter tried not to cry but he did wonder if her body was all bloated. He'd seen enough dead fish to know that they swelled up when they were left in the water after they'd died. And his mam had been in the sea for a week. She must have got huge.

When the time came for Aunt Matilda to take him next door, he started to cry for the first time. She told him to be good and to stop sniveling, because Ruth was being very kind looking after him for the night and had enough on her plate without having to put up with his whining too.

'She was good for nothing your Mam. Selfish, inconsiderate woman. Remember that. Your poor pa, left without a wife, with a young boy to bring up. No need to shed a tear for her,' Aunt Matilda said as they waited for Ruth to come to the door. He nodded mutely and didn't look up at her. *Evil hag*, he thought, remembering the time when Lucy had dressed in that witch costume her dad had found thrown out when he was working for the council. *Look!* Lucy's muffled voice had called out behind the grotesque rubbery mask, complete with warts and green teeth. *I'm your Auntie Matilda!*

He smiled at the memory, on the verge of an amused snort, and then the cold enormous truth came back to him: *Mam was dead*. As dead as the fish he had to pick out of the tanks each morning, floating on their sides, half eaten by their brothers and sisters. *Dead and swollen up. Never coming back.* After a few minutes, the door opened, and Lucy stood there, her face blotchy from crying. She held out her arms.

'Where's your mother?' Matilda said.

'She's coming,' Lucy said. 'Peter. Peter, I...'

Matilda tutted and pushed Peter forward.

'I can't be waiting around all day. Here're his things.' She placed a small bag at Lucy's feet. 'Tell your mother I'll come and get him tomorrow. About tea time.'

Peter failed to stop a large sob from escaping.

'There, there,' Matilda said, bending down to face him, her tone softer. 'Don't cry. I know you feel badly for your father. But life's full of hardships you know. And boys don't cry. Keep it inside. Good boy. I'll see you tomorrow.'

She patted him on the head and walked away. Lucy was still staring at him, arms outstretched, her eyes wide and red.

'I'm alright Luce,' he said. It was too much for him, seeing Lucy so upset. He would have to stay strong. Be a man. He shrugged and stepped into the warm, welcoming hallway.

Chapter Four

Emma, October 2010

All the dresses Amelia was picking out were too short. She was making a special effort with me, and had done ever since the awkward moment when I'd caught her making fun of me. We had never talked about it, I didn't even know if she had told the others that I'd seen them. But ever since then, she'd been really kind, making time to talk, and show she was interested. I could tell she'd made me her little project.

'Here,' she said, flinging a satin fuchsia-pink mini-dress at me. 'This would really suit your colouring.'

I looked at it.

'I don't know...' I said. 'It's a bit bright.'

'Emma,' she said, standing in front of me with her hands on her hips, dresses draped over each of her arms. 'For god's sake. You need something bright. You're so bloody pale. I mean, no offence though. But you've got great legs, so why not show them off? You're never going to get a boyfriend at this rate.'

'Well, I'm not sure that I really want a boyfriend actually,' I said but then I laughed and she smiled. We both knew I was lying.

'You might not want a boyfriend, but everyone wants an admirer...or two...or three...or three hundred.' She wandered off, deeper into the depths of Topshop, like a foolhardy explorer.

There was a shriek.

'Oh god!' Her tiny form was jumping up and down a few rails ahead. I walked towards her.

'This is it!' she said, clutching a tiny silver metallic number. It looked as though it was made of plastic chainmail. 'This is my dress. This is my dress! Oooooh it's perfect.'

'It's lovely,' I said.

'I'm trying it on. Come on. You've got lots haven't you? We are going to be THE best looking girls at the freshers' ball…'

She started humming *Girls Just Wanna Have Fun*, and pushed her way through the people and the clothes rails, until we got to the changing rooms. There was a queue for the individual booths. She tutted.

'Oh bloody hell! I can't be bothered to wait. Come on, let's go in the communal area, you don't mind, do you?'

'Er, no,' I said, even though I did. 'OK then.'

We squeezed past the queue and into a tiny corner of the changing room. I turned around; it was as I had suspected – the curtain hanging between us and the rest of the store was less than sufficient. Anybody walking past would be able to see us getting undressed. I stood for a few seconds, clutching the multi-coloured dresses to me. Amelia stripped off quickly and efficiently. I stared at her beautiful black and pink lacy bra and matching pants. It was impossible not to. There was something so comforting about the sight of her curvy brown body. No visible bones. I ran my fingers up and down my own ribs, through the thin fabric of my t-shirt, feeling the bump and curve of each one. Horrible. Especially the long one across my shoulders – a constant reminder of how I was nothing more than a great big mixture of bone and skin that somehow had the ability to walk around.

She wriggled into the chainmail dress and stood on her tiptoes, putting one hand on her hip, like a filmstar posing for the cameras. The dress fitted her perfectly, hugging her shape.

'Hmmm,' she said, trying different angles: tipping her chin upwards, tilting her head to one side, flicking her long curly black hair behind her shoulders. Her facial expressions varied between satisfaction and mild irritation at her reflection.

'I think I'm going to get it. It's gorge isn't it Emma?' she said.

She turned to me. I immediately started to fiddle with the pink dress, undoing the zip.

'Why haven't you put it on yet?' she asked.

'Sorry, I was just...' I said, fumbling about with the little tags inside. 'That looks great, by the way.'

She stood back slightly and crossed her arms.

'Yes, it does, doesn't it?'

Eventually I got the dress off the hanger and took my top off, holding it up in front of my dreadfully greyed bra, while I stuck my head through what I presumed was the neckline of the dress. I wriggled and squirmed but couldn't seem to get my arms in the right holes.

Amelia laughed.

'Emma, you're so funny. Hang on, let me give you a hand. No, that's the arm hole not the neck one, go back up...yes that's right put your head through that one. Oh hang on, the electronic taggy thing's got stuck.'

My heart rate increased and I felt a furious urge to rip the thing off my head and hurl it on the floor, but finally I got my head and arms in the right holes, and smoothed the dress down over my jeans. Amelia zipped me up before I even asked her if she would mind.

She was right about the colour. It suited my fair hair and pale skin. Gave me a boost. I ran my fingers through the static strands of hair sticking out at amusing angles and smiled at my reflection.

'Take your jeans off,' Amelia said, tugging at them.

I did as I was told. Only the grey socks ruined the outfit now.

'And your socks! Stand on your tiptoes, so we can get a look at your legs!'

I followed her instructions, surprising myself at how unconcerned I was when I noticed that the few other people in the changing rooms were looking at me. They were smiling, looking approving.

'Oooh yes, you look fucking fabulous! You have to get that one.'

Amelia put her arm around my shoulders and made a pouty-kissing face at herself in the mirror. With almost five inches height difference between us, we made a comical-looking couple.

'Aren't we hot?' she said, laughing and flicking her hair. 'We are going to have those boys on their knees this Saturday.'

~

'Ah, participants in the vicious circle of retail therapy. Let me take those bags from you ladies, you both look fit to collapse.' Pete un-burdened my aching arms.

He peeped inside the Topshop bag, where my brave pink dress was nestled in tissue paper. £65. It was twice what I would normally spend on a dress.

'Hmmm, Emma,' he said, peeling back the layers of tissue paper. 'This doesn't look very you. I hope Amelia's not been leading you astray.'

'I need a cup of tea,' Amelia declared, pushing her way past us both into the kitchen.

Pete laid the bags carefully down by the door to my room and turned to face me.

'Spent a fair bit of your loan today then,' he said.

'Yes. Amelia was really helpful. She picked out lots of different things – stuff I wouldn't usually choose. The dress – the pink one – that's what I'm going to wear to the freshers' ball on Saturday.'

'Oh, I see.' He was staring down at the shopping bags.

'Didn't you like it?' I asked. He wouldn't meet my eye.

'What? Oh yes, it was very...what's the right word? Colourful.' He raised his eyebrows.

'Oh,' I replied. So he thought it was tarty. But then, he was right. And he hadn't even seen how short it was yet. Perhaps if I wore my white cardigan too...

'Just a shame I won't be able to see you in it, that's all,' he said, finally directing his eyes at mine.

'Oh,' I said, again. I hadn't expected that. 'Why not?'

'I'm not going to the ball.'

'Really? Why not? I, er, I thought everybody went.' The slight tremor in my voice belied my conversational tone.

'Not my sort of thing really. All that drinking and debauchery.'

'I'm sure it won't be like that,' I said. What was I trying to do? Persuade him to change his mind? As if I had any influence over his decisions.

'Well maybe not,' he said. He looked thoughtful. 'But in any case, my girlfriend Lucy is coming to stay, so I will be in other ways disposed.'

He cast his eyes down at the Topshop bag, rolled them comically and went into his room.

His girlfriend Lucy. The decisive click as his door shut behind him struck me as a fitting allegory to the depressed thud of my heart.

~

It was *so* pink.

Half past five. I still had a few hours to work up the courage. There was a knock on my door, but before I could say anything Amelia had barged in and handed me a tumbler of bright orange liquid.

'Half vodka, half Irn Bru. I promise, you won't be able to taste the vodka with this stuff in it, it's really distinctive,' she said, before turning swiftly on her heel and heading back to the kitchen.

I sipped. What I'm sure she actually meant to say, was 'really disgusting'. But a little Dutch courage might be what I needed to wear the dress in public. Ever since Pete's reaction, I'd had my doubts about it. I held it up against myself and looked in the mirror. I so wanted to fit in tonight, to prove to them that I wasn't some friendless weirdo, that I was normal, just like them. But it was *so* short. I sipped the drink as I stared at my reflection. The more I drank, the less inappropriate the dress seemed. Finally, I slipped it on. The fabric felt reassuring against my skin.

I curled the ends of my hair under, put some make-up on and rubbed moisturiser into my legs. Apparently tights were forbidden, as they would ruin the look and annoy me when the temperature rose on the dancefloor, or so Amelia said. My legs were deathly pale but smooth, and in the dimming light, I could see that no one would be able to tell they were naked.

'Amelia,' I called, tiptoeing my way into the kitchen. Those two pairs of heels she'd picked out for me – one white and one a sort of metallic silver – we hadn't really discussed which would look best. I pushed open the door to the kitchen. Empty. The table was cluttered with glasses, bottles and bags of Doritos. Without thinking, I picked up one of the half-drunk glasses and finished it.

The floor was cold under my bare feet. Back in the hallway, I knocked on Amelia's door. When there was no reply, I tried the handle, but it was locked. The flat was silent.

And then I remembered. They had all been invited to a pre-ball party by another Pharmacology student, at another halls. Henry Price or something. I probably missed their shouts of goodbye when I was drying my hair.

Feeling silly standing in the hallway all alone, I knocked on Pete's door. I would prove to him I could look attractive, yet respectable. So what if he had a girlfriend?

'Hello Emma,' he said. There was nothing in his expression that told me what he thought of my outfit. 'What's up?'

'Can I come in?' I asked, trying my best to look coy. Every few seconds, another tiny bubble of Irn Bru seemed to travel up from my stomach to my throat. That drink from the kitchen probably wasn't a good idea.

'I thought you were going out with the others,' he said.

I wished I didn't feel quite so wobbly.

'I am,' I insisted. 'I just wanted to see if I could persuade you to come.'

Pete smiled and shook his head in mock regret, kissing me lightly on the cheek before shutting the door. I stood there. Indignant but determined. Sod him then.

Back in my room, I tried to locate my shoes. The silvery ones would probably look best. They were still in their box, at the back of the wardrobe. I sat on the floor to put them on, and then it hit me: I was really, really drunk. It had been so long since I'd even been tipsy, it felt as though it was the first time.

How irritating! I'd regressed to having the hand-eye coordination of a three-year-old. In my dizzy-headed state, the shoes were beyond me. I couldn't get the strap thing in the buckle properly.

'Come on Emma,' I said out loud.

After a few minutes wrestling with the strap and buckle, it suddenly dawned on me that my efforts were being impeded by the fact I was sitting in the dark. I reached over and switched on my bedside lamp. The shoe problem was solved in seconds.

I hauled myself to my feet and grabbed my bag. Pausing at the mirror behind the door, I added a little more eyeliner. Amelia had mentioned the smoky-look was in at the moment. On the way out, I knocked on Pete's door again.

'I'm still here,' I giggled, when he answered.

'So I see. You seem slightly worse for wear,' he said. 'Perhaps you should give it a miss. Or have a coffee.'

'Don't be stupid Pete,' I said. 'I'm fine, I'm really happy and I can't wait to go out.' I started a dance in the corridor – an attempt to convince him of how 'up for it' I really was. As I wriggled about, the ten per cent of my brain that was still sober kept one hand on the back of my dress, to guard against knicker-flashing.

'If you can't wait to go out, then why are you still here?' he said. 'Seriously Emma, how much have you had already? You've got eyeliner all over your cheek. You'll just end up being sick if you go out.'

Who did he think he was? My bloody dad? Not that my dad had ever paid much attention to what I got up to. He'd always had other things on his mind.

'I'm fine,' I said. 'I just think you should come out too! Instead of being a moody-old-loner. Don't you like my dress? It's not tarty is it, see?'

'No, it's lovely. OK, go and have a good time. Just be careful.' He paused, looking at me with suspicion. 'Hang on, your shoe's undone.' He knelt down and did the buckle up. Then he looked up at me. He was magnificent. Refusing to go to the Freshers' Ball! Imagine having that kind of self-confidence, that strength. The courage to go against the behaviour of the masses. Deep down, I didn't really want to go. But I could never have admitted that to anyone else. Not going had never seemed like an option. But Pete... he was strong, brave, self-sufficient, happy to go against the grain and follow his own path. Amazing. I gazed down at him, thinking how much I wanted to tell him I fancied him, but I wasn't quite that drunk.

'Anyway,' he said. 'I'm not being a... what did you call me? A moody-old-loner. I'm staying in because Lucy's coming tonight, as I told you. Be careful Em. What are you like?'

He stood up and smiled again. I tossed my head, turned on my heel and toddled down the corridor.

'I don't need anyone to look after me!' I shouted triumphantly, as I opened the front door and fell out into the stairwell.

~

The bus journey was torture. Every speed bump necessitated an exhausting degree of control over my gag reflex. Other students on the bus were all in groups, chattering excitedly. Occasionally they even broke out into song. My drunken euphoria had been replaced with nausea and the beginnings of a headache. Finally, we arrived at the union, and the bus emptied.

There was already a long queue. I scanned the faces, looking unsuccessfully for the familiar, and joined the end. The girls all wore similar outfits – too tight, too revealing and wholly inadequate against the cold night air. Their legs were blue, like defrosting sausages, but their faces were bright orange thanks to lashings of bronzer. I pulled my pink dress down; no longer convinced this was something I wanted to aspire to. The boys looked younger than the girls. Matching 'deliberately scruffy' hair, jeans and Abercrombie t-shirts. For some reason, I'd thought they would be wearing suits.

The queue moved quickly, and before long I was near the front. A bored girl in a bikini top, a cowboy hat and riding chaps handed out small plastic test tubes.

'What is it?' I asked, as she handed one to me.

'Tequila,' she said.

I sniffed it. The vodka from earlier had worn off and I downed it, reasoning if nothing else, it would warm me up a bit.

I climbed the steps to the union entrance, reaching in my shabby black handbag for my purse. I glanced at the bouncers flanking the door.

'Ticket,' one of them said to my legs.

'Sorry?' I said. 'How much is it?'

'No ticket, no entry,' he said. 'Move aside please.'

'What? I don't understand. I want to buy a ticket.'

He made a noise. I suppose it was a laugh.

'Do we look like a box office? You have to buy tickets in advance love. Didn't you read the posters? If you haven't got a ticket, you can't come in. Now, please, move aside.'

I stared at him for a few seconds then walked back down the steps and stood on the pavement.

How could I have been so stupid? Why didn't I know about the ticket? Why had I spent £65 on a tarty dress but not even bought a ticket?

I started to walk, away from the union and back in the direction of Woodhouse Lane. It was the exact same walk I'd done a few days before, after everyone laughed at me in the refectory. What was wrong with me? No one had mentioned buying a ticket to me. Not even Amelia. It didn't make sense. I hadn't heard anyone in the flat discuss buying tickets once.

They didn't want me to come at all. That's why they'd all gone off together, and said they'd meet me there. They knew I didn't have a ticket, and they didn't want to watch my humiliation at the entrance. This was the easiest way. Pass it all off as a mistake – my mistake. How silly of me. How silly of them to assume I knew I had to get one in advance!

It was obvious now. The shopping trip with Amelia was just another ploy to make it look like they genuinely wanted to be friends with me, when, in reality, they wanted to avoid me as much as possible. I was tainted, freakish, and it showed. I remembered Sam's reaction when I'd revealed I was studying music, the way he'd sniggered and hid his mouth. Then he'd made some comment about all musicians being a bit weird. When I'd questioned him, he'd tried to backtrack – saying he just meant creative people were wired up differently from others.

I walked fast. I didn't care whether the stupid short dress blew up in the wind anymore. I glared at every passer-by, narrowing my eyes, hoping bystanders could see how angry I was.

I so wanted to call Mum. To sob down the phone to her, tell her what had happened to me, listen to her soothing words of comfort. But of course, I couldn't. I couldn't heap any more misery on her. She had enough to cope with and now there was no one, nobody in the world, who I could rely on for support. He had alienated them all from me with his selfishness. It had been the ultimate punishment for the most menial of crimes. Did I really deserve this?

My last scribbled postcard to Mum sprang to mind. It was full of lies, full of ridiculous exclamation marks mocking us both with their insincerity. Thanks to him, and her, I would live a lie for the rest of my life.

It began to drizzle. I marched towards home, too angry to stop and work out which bus would take me back. I knew the way now and walking made me feel better, like I had a purpose. As I carried on, the soles of my strappy shoes started to feel slippery.

Outside the station, I fell. My ankle folded over, making me shriek and collapse.

I got to my feet, but my right shoe was no longer attached to my foot properly, and when I tried to put weight on it, the sharp pain outweighed my disgust at treading on the muddy pavement. I stared around. There were no benches in sight, and nothing to lean on except a bin near the taxi rank a few yards away. I hobbled over to it. Every bit of pressure I put on my toes felt wrong and my body didn't hold back from telling me so.

I leant on the bin and tried to put my shoe back on. The sole of my foot was bleeding, and all my previous strength left me. I started to cry; big fat sobs.

'Are you OK?'

I turned to face the voice. A girl peered at me, concern in her eyes. She had the kind of complexion you dream about: flawless. She pushed her hair out of her face with one hand, the other clutched the handle of a small suitcase.

'Sorry, I just thought you looked like you were in a bit of trouble,' she said when I didn't reply.

I smiled, blinking away my tears.

'I'm fine,' I lied. 'Thanks. I fell over. It's these stupid shoes you see. I think I've sprained my ankle and I must've stood on some broken glass or something, because I've cut my foot.'

'Oh crikey, you poor thing,' she said. 'Come on it'll be OK. Let me help. Why don't you sit on my suitcase – take the weight off your feet?'

I stared at it doubtfully.

'Here, hold on to my arm, you can hop on the other foot can't you?' she asked. 'How deep is it? Maybe you need stitches, does it hurt much?'

'Only when I put weight on it.' I said, holding her hand and sitting down on the case. 'It's strange, the cut hardly hurts at all.'

'I'm sure it just looks worse than it is. Here, let me.' She fished about in her handbag and pulled out a packet of wet wipes. 'I always have these when I travel. Yes, I don't think it's very deep. It's just the blood. Enough to make anyone feel queasy. Where do you live? I expect you've sprained your ankle but if you go home and rest it, I'm sure it'll be better in the morning. It doesn't look swollen, which is good.'

I watched her crouching on the ground in front of me, wiping my feet gently. To my surprise and embarrassment, more tears came.

'Thank you,' I said, swallowing a little. 'You're so nice.'

'Don't be silly, it's nothing. Now, where do you live? I'll get a taxi for you, just wait here.'

'I'm a student,' I said, unnecessarily. 'I live in halls. Clarence Dock.'

Her face broke out into a smile, emphasising the width of her mouth and her perfect white teeth. Had it been on a less attractive girl's face, it would have given her an ungraceful horse-like quality, but on her, it was breathtaking.

'I'm going there too! Great, we can share a taxi. Even better. Now I can get you right to your front door.'

'Are you a student?'

'No, no, I'm going to visit my boyfriend. He lives there. I'm Lucy, by the way.'

It didn't register at first. I hadn't seen a picture of her, and Pete had never described her to me as anything other than stunning. I didn't know what to say. It could be a different one, of course.

'I'm Emma,' I said, sniffing and wiping away the residue of my tears. 'Nice to meet you.'

She threw her arms around me.

'Nice to meet you too!' she said, and kissed me on the cheek. 'Now hold on to me, do you think you can hop to the taxi rank?'

Once we were safely in the warmth of the cab, I asked her.

'Um, this might sound a little strange, but is your boyfriend called Pete by any chance?'

There was a pause, and in the dark, I couldn't measure her expression. When she didn't reply, I blundered on.

'It's just, I've got a flat mate called Pete and his girlfriend's called Lucy, and she's coming to stay…I thought perhaps...'

'Emma,' she said, slowly. 'Yes of course! He's mentioned you. From Devon aren't you? Sorry, I'm not used to hearing him called Pete, we call him Peter at home. Funny. I wonder why he started that.'

'I don't know,' I said. Listening to her voice, it was clear she was from the same area of the country as Pete. Her accent wasn't as defined as his, but it still had that soft, lilting quality I found so soothing.

'Well, I think there are higher powers at work here. It's meant to be, obviously, us bumping into each other like that,' she said, staring out of the window. Haphazard lines of rainwater ran down the glass, illuminated by the oranges and reds of the street lamps. She was wearing a gold necklace. From it hung two pendants: one a small medallion, the other a cross. They glinted in the watery light.

'So, why didn't Pete come and meet you at the station then?'

'Oh there's no point in him coming all the way down here. Just to come straight back again. I'm a big girl.'

'It isn't far,' I pointed out.

'No,' she said, turning away from me. 'I suppose he could have come.'

She didn't say any more for a few minutes, but continued

staring out of the window as we whizzed through the grey city centre. The meter clicked up to £6.20. After a while, she turned back to me.

'What have you been up to this evening? Have you been to a party? It's quite early to be coming home, isn't it?'

I explained about the ball, about Amelia and about the non-existent ticket. She listened, and at the end she reached out, patted my hand and told me how awful it must have been for me.

We arrived at the flat. Lucy insisted on paying for the taxi, saying she would have had to even if we hadn't bumped into each other, so it made no difference. I thanked her, and leant on her arm, climbing the stairs to flat P8, pain coursing through my ankle with each step. My stomach turned at the thought of Pete's reaction to the two of us together.

'Look who I found,' Lucy said, as Pete opened the door. I hung back, but smiled when he met my eyes.

He kissed Lucy on the cheek. I couldn't help thinking it was the type of kiss you would give an aunt.

'Well, well, well. Emma. Back so soon?'

'Long story,' I said, determined not to share the details with him.

'Emma fell over and twisted her ankle,' Lucy said. 'She didn't have a ticket, so they wouldn't let her in to this fresh ball, or whatever it's called. Isn't that mean? Anyway I saw her by the station, so we shared a cab back together.'

'Must have been her guardian angel at work,' Pete said.

In the kitchen, Lucy made a big fuss, propping up my foot on one a chair, putting frozen peas on my ankle and hunting down painkillers. She made us all hot chocolates and finally sat down too. I wanted to get changed out of the ridiculous dress. I felt exposed and humiliated, my long pasty legs dominating the space: one raised on a chair, the other tucked meekly under it.

'Well, it's lovely to see where you live Peter,' Lucy said,

tucking her hair behind her ears.

'It's not bad,' he murmured.

'Oh I think it's great,' Lucy said. 'I didn't expect it to be this nice. I thought it would be all grotty, but it's so new.'

'It's further out than the other halls, but I agree,' I said. 'It's a lot nicer than I had expected too. So, where do you live, Lucy?'

Pete shifted in his seat. He looked over our heads, out of the kitchen window to the car park.

'I live at home with my family,' she said. 'Back in Cresswell. Peter and I live next door to one another. We always have, ever since we were born. But my place is a bit of a mess. There're so many of us.'

'Really?' I said. Pete was fidgeting in his chair, his eyes darting around the room.

'Yes, I've got seven younger brothers and sisters, would you believe. So it's quite a handful.'

'Wow, it must be. What do you do?'

Pete let out a loud cough.

'Peter! It's OK, I don't mind.' Lucy turned back to me. 'I don't do anything. I mean, I don't work. I help my mam with my brothers and sisters. Where we live, well, there's not much work to be had anyway, and Mam's been ill. I'd like to work with children one day. You know, teach primary school. But at the moment, it's not really possible.'

'Oh,' I said. 'Sorry to hear that. Horrible, having your dreams put on hold. And,' I paused and glanced at Pete, 'you must miss Pete.'

She laughed, and fiddled with her hair. 'Well, yes, I do. But I don't think of it as horrible. Not really. There's a lot to be gained from putting others first, you know, Emma. A lot. Putting your own desires aside, and instead making those you love happy. Really it's no hardship at all, when you think of it like that, is it?'

Making those you love happy. Who was she kidding – it was the greatest hardship of my life. 'No I suppose not,' I insisted, 'but still, you must get fed up sometimes.'

Lucy put her mug down and turned to me. Gazing at me intently, her head cocked, she was an annoying vision of loveliness.

'Trust me, there is nothing but pleasure to be gained in sacrificing things for others. All you have to do is offer that sacrifice up, and you...'

'Alright Lucy,' Pete said, roughly, standing up and stepping in between us. 'That's enough, I'm sure Emma doesn't want to hear all this.'

'It's OK...' I said.

'Sorry Peter, of course. You're right. Silly me. I do go on a bit I know.' She fiddled with the cross and medal hanging round her neck, twisting them between her fingers.

Feeling awkward and superfluous, I finished the rest of my hot chocolate, made my excuses and limped back to my room.

The peas had worked and my ankle had improved, but I felt a low fog of depression as I took off the now-crumpled pink dress. Unsure what to do with it, I left it on the floor instead of hanging it up. I was sure I'd never wear it again. I climbed into bed and lay in the darkness. As I drifted, I dreamt of Lucy and Pete standing over me laughing as I lay on the pavement, my legs sprawled in opposite, inelegant directions.

'Oh dear,' Lucy was saying. 'Poor thing. She really shouldn't have drunk so much. What a silly little girl...'

~

I awoke again a little later and the clock told me it was 11.15pm. My throat was dry with thirst so I limped to the kitchen. The others were obviously still at the ball. Pete's door, for the first time, was ajar. Lucy was laughing softly and Pete was murmuring something. Intrigued, I peered in. Through the crack I could just make out the scene: Pete sitting on his bed, and at his feet, Lucy, cross-legged. She had her back to me, her face tilted up to him, with her long brown hair almost touching the floor. Pete was staring down at her. His hands rhythmically stroked her face, her hair. It was making her laugh. I watched them. Watched him, watching her. Whispering words I was unable to hear. The expression on his face was pure, unadulterated love. After a while, she rose to her knees, pushing her body towards him. She lifted her arms up, cupping his face with her hands and just as he leaned down to kiss her, his eyes flickered upwards towards the door and met mine.

I gasped, frozen in shame. But he didn't move, he carried on staring at me. His eyes on mine as he kissed her, with that same overpowering expression. I stared back, my heart racing, until their kiss ended. The spell was broken, and I escaped to my room.

Leaning against my shut door, I was aware for the first time of the dampness in my underwear. He felt the same way. He must have done.

But then, the way he had been looking at her, before he noticed me, was as though she was the only other person in the world.

Suddenly there were no magical feelings, and instead only an incessant pounding in my head. And an overwhelming determination to sleep, to erase the image of him engaged in that most potent declaration of longing.

A longing not for me, but for Lucy.

Chapter Five

Emma, October 2010

'Never again,' Maria groaned, her head bent low over a cup of coffee.

'You have only yourself to blame Missy,' Sam said. He was smearing a thick coating of peanut butter over the top of the strawberry jam on his toast.

She groaned again. 'Alright. No need to gloat. Emma, do you have to have tuna for lunch? The smell of it is going to make me sick again.'

Putting down the tin I'd just taken from my cupboard, I turned to look at her.

'It's not Emma's fault that it's half past one and you're still in your dressing gown,' Sam said.

'I don't understand,' she moaned. 'I didn't even drink that much.'

Exploring the depths of my cupboard revealed the expected: tuna was all I had left. Pete would probably have some baked beans. There hadn't been any sign of him that morning though, so I couldn't ask. He'd probably taken Lucy somewhere romantic. Shopping perhaps, to buy her something extravagant and beautiful as a thank you from tearing herself away from her ill mother and thousands of siblings. I glared at the tuna tin.

'Go and get dressed you slag,' Sam said, sitting next to Maria. 'You'll feel better.'

'Murgggh,' Maria said, slumping off, one hand clutching the coffee mug as though it were a life-support machine.

No one had mentioned my absence from the ball. Perhaps they had all had such a fantastic time they hadn't even noticed. Or perhaps they were just too embarrassed. Sam had said something about the man Amelia had sloped off with – she was half his height and the ideal size to indulge his 'BJ' fantasies. It took me a while to work out what he meant.

Sam and I stayed in the kitchen, eating our respective meals in an honest silence. He was reading the Observer, his face concentrated in a frown as he pored over every page. I chewed my tuna pasta numbly, watching the drizzle settling again in the car park, and wondered where Pete and Lucy were.

After a while, I went back to my room, filled a bin-liner with my washing, took it down to the launderette and waited and watched as it spun around in the machines.

When I returned, Pete was in the kitchen, cleaning. Wearing Marigolds – the pink ones my mum had packed for me.

'Hello,' Pete said, scrubbing at the draining board.

'Hello,' I replied, taking a seat. 'What are you doing?'

'What does it look like? Although I'm probably wasting my time. The smell of the bins alone is enough to make anyone want to kill themselves. What are you up to?'

I glanced at my watch. Half past four. My plans for the rest of the afternoon amounted to precisely nothing.

'Er, I was going to make some notes from some books I got out of the library…for an essay,' I lied.

'Oh, never mind then. I was going to suggest we go for a walk in a minute. Have a chat. But no worries.'

'No!' I said, too eagerly. 'A walk would be great. I mean, you're right, the bins do stink and it would be lovely to have a chat. But, where's Lucy?' I looked around, as though she might pop out from behind the fridge.

'Lucy? Oh, she's gone. Just dropped her off at the station,' he said.

'Already?'

'Yes, afraid so. She had to get back to her mam. She said to say goodbye though.'

'Oh,' I said, searching for significance where there likely wasn't any.

'Give me five tics, Em, and we can go.'

We walked down the towpath along the canal. The temperature must have plummeted overnight because it felt much colder. I'd forgotten my gloves and my hands were soon numb.

'So, your foot's all better then,' Pete said as we strolled along, eventually arriving at a park I'd never been to before. The sky was clear above us.

'Er, yes,' I replied. 'I mean, it's still a bit sore. But my ankle doesn't hurt anymore.'

'Healed quickly didn't it? Must have been Lucy's magic touch.'

'It was nothing. I was fine. I was just a bit annoyed that no one had told me…never mind. Serves me right for getting so drunk.'

'It was pretty thoughtless of them not to remind you about the ticket, but I'm sure they didn't mean it.'

'No, I suppose not.'

'I'm sure it wasn't deliberate. And they do all see each other a lot more, you have to remember that. After all, they do the same course. We're *l'etrangers*.'

'What?'

He stopped walking suddenly, and turned to face me. The smell of his Barbour jacket tickled my nostrils. *Farmer Pete,* Sam had called him, laughing about how only old men wore waxed jackets. He'd taken it all in his stride.

'The outsiders. Don't you know your Camus? Anyway we'll have to stick together. The non-pharma geeks of Flat P2.'

'Oi. Speak for yourself,' I said, smiling. 'I could have done Pharmacology!'

'Really?' Pete said, grinning. 'Reeeeaaally, Emma?!'

I laughed.

'Yes,' I said, sticking my chin out. 'My dad always said you could do anything you want to, if you put your mind to it.' He'd certainly proved that.

'You're right of course,' Pete said, suddenly thoughtful. 'And so was your dad.'

We continued walking until we reached a children's playground – a run-down affair with a few swings and a rusty slide. I sat on one of the swings, and Pete pushed me. I felt like a child again, protected and cared for. But my Good Samaritan was at the back of my mind, with her perfect white skin and beautiful face.

'I haven't been on a swing since I was a kid,' I said.

'So last week then?' he said.

'Very funny. It's good to get some fresh air actually, I don't feel like I get outside enough these days. But it's always so cold. At home it always feels so much warmer. And we've got a garden, and a dog, I miss taking her for walks.'

'What's her name?'

'Promise you won't laugh?'

'Promise.'

'She's called Lassie. I was just a kid…I had a right tantrum when my parents tried to persuade me to call her something less, er, obvious. I really miss her. Stupid huh?'

'Not at all,' he replied. 'Do you miss home a lot? It's been a month now. I can't quite believe it. Tempus fugit and all that.'

His use of Latin caught me unawares. Maybe he had studied it at school too.

'I haven't really thought about it much,' I lied. Was he probing me for more details about my dad? I didn't want to tell him anything else. I missed home, yet not having to see either of them was still such a relief. I'd been sleeping relatively well for the first time in ages. 'But yes, I suppose I miss my mum, and my friends. Mostly my best friend Heather. You know, just having someone to talk to who really understands you. Especially after... I mean, the others are lovely, but obviously…' I paused. 'I don't know. It just seems to be taking me a bit longer than most people to make friends.'

'I know what you mean. It must be tough for you. I mean, it's not even been a year yet has it? Since your father passed away?'

'No,' I said, sharply. 'Just seven months.'

'Seven months is no time at all,' Pete said. 'The pain must be very raw.'

I wished he'd shut up.

'But we get on well don't we?' he said. 'You can always talk to me if you're feeling down. Can't guarantee I'll listen mind, especially not if there's a game on, but you women just like to sound off anyway don't you? It's not like you actually care whether the other person is paying attention.'

'Hey,' I said. 'Stop stereotyping!'

He smiled. 'Seriously though, I know what you mean. Of course, it's very strange, being in this foreign city without anyone close to turn to. I've had a few low moments myself. I really miss Lucy,' he said.

'Of course you do,' I said quietly, dragging my feet to stop the swing and getting off.

'You'll have to come and see my fish tank sometime,' Pete said. His breath was visible in the air. 'Not quite as responsive as dogs, to be fair, but I find watching them really soothing.'

'An invitation to venture into your room? I don't believe it. I thought it was forbidden territory. I had no idea you even had a fish tank.'

'Ah well, I was keeping it a secret you see. Couldn't take the risk of you all wanting to come in my room for a gawp – that rotting corpse is a bugger to hide.'

I laughed and my teeth began to chatter.

'Is that your phone?' Pete asked, pointing at my bag, from which a faint buzzing emanated.

'Er, nope, no, not mine,' I lied, stamping my feet to drown out the sound. It would be her, again, the persistent nightmare. I certainly wasn't going to speak to her in front of Pete.

'Oh,' he said, looking puzzled. 'Anyway, come on, you're freezing aren't you? Let's go and get a cup of coffee.'

He took my hand and we walked like that, hand in hand, his

thumb rubbing my palm every now and then. We kept walking until we found a small café near the Corn Exchange. It was almost deserted. Across Leeds, my fellow students would be cooking their fish-finger sandwiches and deciding where to go to get drunk that evening.

After our coffees, we walked back along the canal in silence. My thoughts returned to Lucy. OK, so he missed her. But that was all he'd said. He was holding *my* hand. And being with him felt so natural, so easy. So surely, despite his past with her, there was something there.

No man has that amount of self-control. It was only a matter of time. I was here, with him everyday, she wasn't. He was only 20, there was no way that he could say with certainty Lucy was 'the one' for him.

I just needed patience and perseverance. It would be my turn soon, surely.

'I've always believed people get an equal amount of happiness in life,' I said, as we reached the front door. 'You know, some people will be incredibly rich, but have poor health. Others will be healthy but worried about money. It all adds up to the same amount of happiness in the end.'

Pete stared at me.

'You are so like Lucy,' he said. 'I'm not convinced your opinions aren't a little simplistic, but she feels the same way. She believes that the world is inherently good. I'm not so sure. Speaking of which, this is for you.'

He turned my hand over, palm up, and pressed a small envelope into it. It had a single word on the front, *Emma,* written in tiny, perfect handwriting with pink ink. The handwriting looked familiar although I knew I had never seen it before. Pete turned the key in the lock and walked ahead of me into the flat.

The bins still stunk.

~

Amelia came bounding down the corridor as soon as she saw us.

'Oh my god! Where have you two been? The most exciting thing ever has happened!'

'We've been for a walk,' I replied. 'Why, what's the matter?'

Her cheeks hadn't been this flushed since she discovered that the Vodka night at the union sold shots for only £1.

'I always knew he was a bit, you know, well different. Always dressed so well for a start. Sophisticated. Not like Farmer Pete here. And anyway, now Maria's caught him, and..oh it's so exciting!'

'What on earth are you talking about?' I said.

'It's Sam. He's gay!'

'What? Seriously?'

I glanced up at Pete. His face remained impassive as always.

'Yes, seriously! Maria caught him last night! It just came back to her…as she was leaving she saw Sam in the distance, holding hands with what she thought was a girl. Anyway she ran up to him to see who it was. And as she got closer she realised it wasn't a girl but a guy! He tried to deny it but she was having none of it, she knew what she had seen, and anyway he's come out now and told us. I always wondered why he loved Kylie so much.'

'Wow,' I said.

'I'm going for a lie-down,' said Pete, abruptly. 'See you later Emma.'

'But wait!' I said, to his bedroom door as he shut it. 'What about the fish…?'

'What's the matter with him?' said Amelia. 'Grumpy sod. Come on, Emma, we're all in here.'

I followed her into the kitchen.

'Hey babes,' said Maria as I sat down beside her. 'How are you?'

'I'm OK,' I said. The letter was getting hot and sticky in my hand.

'Of course she's bloody OK!' said Amelia. 'She's just been on a romantic walk with Farmer Pete.'

'It wasn't romantic. We're just friends.'

'Yeah, whatever! Anyway aren't you going to say anything to Sam about his news?'

I glanced over at him. 'Er, congratulations,' I said. He rolled his eyes and laughed.

'Congratulations? Jeez. It's not an *achievement*.'

'No, I know…' I began.

'We were just discussing how he should tell his parents,' Maria interrupted. 'I mean, I think he should tell them sooner rather than later, don't you? No point in putting it off.'

'I'm not sure I'm ready to open that can of worms yet, Maria,' Sam said.

'Well, you just need to be prepared, that's all. Go in there, be really mature about it. Not emotional. Try to anticipate what questions they might come up with and prepare rational answers. That way they can't dismiss it as a phase or anything.' Maria was flapping her hands up and down as she spoke.

'I don't think my parents would try to talk me out of it,' he said. 'I just don't think I can cope with the look of disappointment on my mum's face. She's always wanted me to have a big white wedding like my sister.'

'A big white wedding like your sister? Pah!' said Amelia. 'She's more likely to get you into a big white dress now she knows you're a poof!'

Sam threw a cushion at Amelia's head and laughed.

'Shut it bitch! Anyway can we stop talking about my love life now please? It's getting boring. Come on, I think it's time we grilled these two.'

'Yes,' I agreed. 'So…'

'Where did you stay last night?' Sam interrupted.

Amelia went quiet. 'Yes, well actually, he turned out to be a bit of a wanker. Only after one thing.'

'And you're telling me he didn't get it?' he said.

'No he didn't! I'm not some sort of slag you know.'

'No of course not,' he laughed. 'You're the Virgin Mary.'

'Alright, enough already! Bastard basically threw me out of his room when he realised that I wouldn't sleep with him.'

'Yes, we know babes,' said Maria. 'He sounds horrible, but just be grateful he didn't rape you or anything. Anyway, Emma, how about you? What happened to you last night? How come you didn't come to the ball?'

I stared at her. She couldn't have been bluffing. No one would be this brazen. Perhaps they really had just forgotten to tell me about the ticket. I was becoming so paranoid, so insecure, it no longer occurred to me that people might make genuine mistakes. I searched for the double meaning in everything.

'I didn't have a ticket,' I said, quietly. I watched their faces for signs of discomfort, and found none. They really had just forgotten. 'They wouldn't let me in.'

'Oh Emma,' Amelia cried. 'You daft bat. We thought you'd decided you'd rather hang around with Farmer Pete and his girlfriend. You know, suss out the situation – get to know your enemy and all that. I can't believe you forgot to get a ticket! I'm sure we talked about it last week. Did no one on your course remind you?'

I thought of my course mates. I couldn't name a single one of them. My first lecture had been a disaster – I'd got lost in the labyrinth of the Roger Stevens Building and mistakenly ended up in a civil engineering lecture. I still didn't know how I had sat through ten minutes of it before noticing that it wasn't, in fact, the Introduction to the Psychology of Music, but something rather less appealing related to soil mechanics. When I'd finally realised, I'd felt paralysed, unable to leave for fear the lecturer might think I found him boring. I only managed to slip away when he finally turned from his podium to write something on the board. And then, I'd hurried to theatre number 6, not 9, and finally burst in on my first music lecture half an hour late, red-faced with shame. By which time, it seemed, the group had already bonded.

Maria took my silence as embarrassment and interrupted. 'How are things with Pete anyway? I know you were hoping that things would develop. But obviously this thing with Lucy is relatively serious...'

'I know!' I said. 'We're just friends. Seriously. That's all.'

'Yes, but you never know, him and Lucy, it's a long-distance thing, so it might still end. It's very hard to keep these things going sometimes. Especially at uni.'

'What about you then Maria? How's your love life?' I said, changing the subject.

She stared straight back at me.

'My love-life is non-existent,' she stated proudly. 'And that's the way I like it. I'm far too busy. I've just joined the animal rights group at the union, and it seems we're going to have quite a few things coming up over the next...'

Amelia let out a large snort. 'Ha! Too busy! That's right! Tell Emma what you will be doing outside that bank next week.'

Maria went even redder.

'Alright, I know you think it's funny. But you wouldn't if you saw the way those poor animals suffer.'

'Get this, Emma,' Amelia said. 'Maria's got to dress up as a beagle and stand outside a bank handing out flyers and trying to stop students from going in! It's bloody hilarious! A beagle!'

'Why?'

'Because they support Huntingdon Life Sciences, which is the biggest animal testing lab in Europe.'

'But why do you have to dress up as a beagle?' I could hear Amelia giggling softly to herself.

'For impact,' said Maria. 'I might look a bit stupid but it's for a good cause and that's the main thing.'

'Yeah blah blah blah!' laughed Amelia. 'It's hilarious. We'll all have to come down and take pictures of you. Ha!'

'You do that,' said Maria. 'It would be a big help actually. We're hoping to get some exposure in the paper and online so some publicity shots would be great.'

We lapsed into silence. After a while, the others dispersed and I went back to my room

What a mess. I pushed my three pillows up against the head of my bed, sat down and opened the letter. Inside was a small, white card, with a silver edge. It was difficult to read the pink writing.

Dear Emma

I hope you don't mind me writing to you. It was lovely to meet you, and I was so surprised when I found out that you shared a flat with Peter. He tells me the two of you are good friends, and it doesn't surprise me. I can tell you are the sort of girl Peter would get along with. It's a comfort to me that he has you there to keep him company – I do worry about him sometimes.

I hope your cuts heal quickly and that you don't take any more tumbles! It would be so lovely if we could be friends. I feel somehow that the three of us have more in common than most people our age. I hope to see you again soon.

Best wishes, Lucy

The last time I'd received a letter so unexpected, my whole body had convulsed with shock at its contents. But there was nothing in this letter to hurt me – this thoughtful message made no demands of me whatsoever. Lucy's attention and kindness were flattering.

But at the same time, I felt slightly sick. The way she had called him Peter not Pete set herself apart.

A subtle way of reminding me that he was hers.

Chapter Six

Emma, October 2010

The room didn't smell as I had hoped it would. No manly fragrance, no lingering scent of aftershave. Instead, the pleasant smell of Dove soap filled the air, making it seem cleaner and fresher than my own room.

Of course, the rest was laid out exactly the same as mine. They were perfect reflections: directly opposite each other and divided only by the thin strip of corridor and utilitarian brown carpet. So as I walked in, it already felt familiar. Directly in front of me was the window, with its thin nylon curtains hanging limply either side. Pete's room was at the front of the building, so where mine looked out onto the Royal Armouries car park, his faced into our little commune. He had a perfect view of the bar, just like Maria, who was next door.

Opposite the door to his en suite was his large pine wardrobe – on top stood one large, black suitcase, as unremarkable as it was functional. Then, at the far end of the room was his desk. He had a large dictionary, a few books on philosophy but no computer. On the floor by the desk was a large cactus – the biggest I had ever seen, with small pink flowers adorning the ends of tentacles, like tiny Iced Gems. Behind the desk stood his bed with a simple white duvet, uncrumpled and immaculate. Unlike the rest of us, Pete hadn't put anything on the walls – no posters, nothing. On the windowsill stood a large, creamy-yellow sculpture of a man crouching, his arms wrapped around his legs, his limbs elongated and distorted, his backbone sticking out. His face looked up at me, devoid of features. A perfect flat surface. The sculpture and the cactus seemed to be the only sources of decoration in the room. Except for, of course, the fish.

Pete had turned his bedside table on its side, and on top stood the tank, which was smaller than I imagined. Two pieces of gnarled wood rested on the floor of the enclosure, and around them darted numerous tiny fish, each one with a minuscule spark near its tail. In one corner, a larger, opalescent fish, with a broad fin and tail, and bluey-grey scales regarded me solemnly. Barely moving in the water, it kept itself in more or less the same position with simple, sporadic flaps of one fin.

'That's a gourami,' said Pete. 'Neil. He's probably thinking how ugly you are too.'

'I wasn't thinking that,' I replied. 'I was thinking the opposite, how beautiful he is. Now I'm thinking what a weird name Neil is for a fish.'

Pete smiled. 'It's not weird. It's perfect. Gouramis are all Neils! Solid, dependable. Not like the tetras. They can't keep still, poor buggers. If one moves, the whole lot has to go with him. They can't make a decision on their own… their idea of hell is to be left in a tank alone. They can actually drive themselves crazy trying to find the rest of the shoal.'

'They're very pretty,' I conceded. 'Just flecks of light rushing around. But they're so small. Do they have names too?'

'Don't be ridiculous. How could I name all the tetras? There are fifteen of them, and I can't tell them apart.'

Pete's body stiffened. I sat down on his bed, messing up the perfect duvet, and stared up at him, wondering why he was suddenly cross. I thought of my father's mood swings, of the way an off-the-cuff remark could have him red-faced with rage in seconds. Stress, my mother always blamed it on. What a convenient excuse it had been. I recently pondered on whether the debt had been deliberate, a handy tool to cover his tracks.

Pete stood at the window, gazing down at the early birds making their way to the bar. He was very thin and always wore baggy clothes, perhaps in an effort to hide his lanky body. His nickname was really quite apt. Farmer Pete. Only his pallid complexion disagreed.

'Why don't you have any posters up?' I asked, in an attempt

to pull him back from his introspective musings.

'There's nothing I want to look at every day,' he murmured, without bothering to turn from the window.

He leant down to open the window, stuck his head outside and inhaled deeply. My call to leave presumably. A photograph of Lucy on his desk caught my eye. It was propped up in front of a pile of books, unframed, and the edges were frayed and tattered. Without any conscious thought I walked over to the picture and picked it up.

Lucy was sitting on a beach, a beautiful, empty sandy beach that seemed to stretch for miles. The sea was barely visible – just a thin blue strip across the top of the picture. Her hair was billowing behind her. Some of it had blown in front of her face, and she was laughing, trying to find the direction of the camera's lens behind the strands impeding her vision.

'That's nice,' I said.

Pete turned and looked at me, as if he'd finally remembered I was in the room too.

'That's Cresswell,' he said, softly. 'It's where the two of us grew up.'

'I thought you were from Newcastle.'

'Well, no one has ever heard of Cresswell. It's a tiny hamlet north of Newcastle.'

'But you grew up by the sea? That must have been amazing. It looks so peaceful.'

'It's like nowhere else on earth.'

'How long have you lived there?'

'I've known Lucy my whole life,' he replied. 'Didn't I tell you that before? Her family lives next door to mine, they always have done and probably always will do. She was born a week after me, we played together as toddlers, we went to the same primary school, the same middle school, the same high school. She's always been there.' He took the picture out of my hands and stared down at it. 'And she always will be.' His demeanour changed, he replaced the picture and turned to face me, holding my elbows with his hands.

'I hope you find someone who deserves you,' he said. 'I'll pray for it.'

I laughed. 'Pray for it?' I said, sarcastically, seizing the opportunity for dry wit. 'I didn't realise you were the religious ty...'

Just as I was saying the words, my eyes fell on a large, important feature on the wall. Something I hadn't noticed before, having been so preoccupied with the fish tank, Neil the dependable gourami and the fifteen indistinguishable tetras. There, above the tank, breaking up the monotony of magnolia wall, was a crucifix.

The wood of the cross was dark, almost black, and heavily varnished, giving it a sheen. It looked wet, as though it were coated in blood. And nailed to the black slimy cross was an orange clay Jesus, his ribs protruding hideously from his chest, his stomach hollow, his legs and arms thin and feeble. His head was slumped to one side, resting on his shoulder, but unlike the sculpture on the windowsill with its reassuring lack of character, Jesus's face was detailed – bearing a contorted, twisted expression. A crude representation of the pain he was in. His crown of thorns was highly defined too, each spike ground firmly into his skull. Above his hanging head was another piece of clay, shaped to represent a piece of parchment nailed to the top of the cross. It bore the letters 'INRI'.

As a child, I'd been told it was a glorious thing. Jesus sacrificing his life to save our sins. Pete's crucifix was anything but glorious. I shuddered.

Pete was watching me. He took a step back and let go of my elbows.

'It wasn't pretty was it?' he said. 'The way our Lord died. It was miserable, painful, degrading, messy, bloody. He was in agony for hours. That's why he looks so horrible Emma. That's why his face is all screwed up and his chest broken and mutilated. He was dying.'

'So this is why you never let anyone come into your room,' I said.

'Of course. The others – they wouldn't understand. That there's more to life than self-satisfaction. That there are more important things than indulging yourself every day in every way.'

'So,' I began. 'Why did you let me come in? I don't even believe in God.'

'Maybe not,' he said, a little softer now. 'But you're different. Like me. You expect more from life than others. You see depths to life that others miss. Maybe you don't have faith, not yet, but you will. One day.'

'I don't know.'

'Don't look so horrified. We can agree to disagree. Anyway, there's no need to discuss this now. Religion is just one part of my life. But I didn't want the others coming in here, seeing the crucifix and writing me off as a religious nutter. But you, I knew you were more sensitive than that. More understanding. That's why I've always found you such good company Emma.'

Despite his kind words, sadness and disappointment overwhelmed me. The picture I'd had in my mind of Pete, my Ideal Man, didn't include God, or an ugly Jesus dying a slow painful death on a slimy cross.

But maybe that was why I thought so much of him. Without realising that he was religious, I'd seen the benefits that faith can bring. Pete was kind, caring, loyal, and dutiful.

And Lucy… she must have had some sort of faith too. It would explain the cross around her neck, the letter she had written to me, the way she had helped me in the street, even though I was a complete stranger.

That was why they were so special. That was why they had both impressed me so much. Faith, the belief in a higher power, an inherent drive to be good – concepts that had become so alien to me in the last year, they were what defined them.

I knew it wasn't for me, but it didn't really matter. There was no harm in it. Christians were good people, weren't they? Kind people.

Chapter Seven

Pete, February 1999

He would have been happy to stay at Lucy's forever, even though he had to sleep on the floor in Lucy and Joe's room. Lucy's mam was chubby, red-faced and happy, despite all the children she had to look after. She kept saying she never got a moment's rest, but she was always laughing when she said it, and Peter knew she wouldn't have it any other way.

He was there for two whole weeks in the end. He saw his dad at mass, but he didn't even bother to say hello, which made Peter feel sad. He got the bus back home with Lucy after school every day like normal, but instead of going home, he would go back with Lucy and Ruth would let them have one and a half digestive biscuits each and a glass of milk before they started their homework. His father never had biscuits in the house, except at Christmas and even then, he made such a big show of giving Peter one he wasn't even sure he wanted it. He wondered what Christmas would be like without his mam, and whether or not his dad would even remember to get him a present. He thought he might. If his Auntie Matilda reminded him.

It made him feel good to help Lucy with her homework – she had lots of trouble with her spellings and maths especially. He worried because he knew that once he was back home, she wouldn't have anyone around to help her anymore. She wasn't stupid, she just wasn't very good at maths or spelling. Her brother Joe was pretty smart but he was always off doing something else. Lucy's mam called Joe a 'flibbertigibbet', which Peter thought was ridiculous.

After their homework was done, Lucy and Peter would go and do a jigsaw puzzle together, or play with the puppies, until it was time to go to bed. They didn't go down to the beach anymore. He didn't want to because of his mam, and when Lucy suggested it he noticed Ruth gave her a 'look' and said they weren't allowed because it was too cold. He thought it was nice of Ruth not to mention the real reason. There was no TV at Lucy's house and Peter was surprised that he didn't really miss it. When Lucy was around, there was no need for television.

Anyway, he was happy to just play with the puppies before bedtime. Lucy's dog Bear had had five of them just a couple of months before.

'What does litter mean?' she said, when he asked if this was Bear's first.

'I don't know really,' Peter replied. 'Just, all the puppies together, they're a litter. When you have puppies, you have a litter. All at once.'

Lucy looked at him thoughtfully.

'Yes, then. This is Bear's first litter.'

Peter thought Bear was a stupid name for a dog, but he didn't tell Lucy that. The puppies were very cute and all out of proportion – their paws and heads too big for their bodies. Lucy's father said that they were collies, and Peter was pretty sure that this meant that they were black and white striped. There were four puppies in total – Ruth told him the fifth was only a wee mite and had gone to heaven the day after he'd been born.

'What's going to happen to them all?' he asked Lucy, as he stroked the smallest one, who was making squeaking noises like a baby.

'Dad's going to sell them,' Lucy said, dangling a knotted piece of rope and watching one of them try to catch it with its paws, like a cat would.

'I wish I could have one. I'd call him Brutus,' Peter said.

'Get away! Your dad would never let you have one and you know it!'

He felt angry when she said that, even though it was true. Lucy knew all about Peter's dad being mean, and how he sometimes hit him and his mam with a belt when he got mad. She knew about how his mam used to cry a lot, practically every day, and how Peter had to take care of her because she'd just sit in the corner, staring into space otherwise, and they wouldn't have any tea.

Sometimes, he was happy that Lucy knew these things because it was like she was on his side. But other times, he wished she didn't, so that he could dream that things were different, without her spoiling it.

Chapter Eight

Emma, October 2010

I flicked through the pages of my music books. Bach's Allegro from the Sonata in D. That's what I would play. I knew it off by heart, it was cheerful and I'd got top marks for it in my grade six. I wondered what level the other people auditioning would be. I looked around at them. There were at least fifty others there, all assembling their various instruments, smiling confidently at each other. They were probably all grade eight.

I took my flute out from its case and screwed it together. It was cold in the rehearsal hall, and when I tentatively blew into the mouthpiece the note came out flat. I wondered if I'd have the opportunity to tune up. There was a piano pushed into one corner. Someone could play an A for me, but I'd probably have to ask. I couldn't work out exactly where the auditions would be held. There didn't seem to be any obvious side rooms.

I looked down at the leaflet in my hand.

Chamber Orchestra is a high-standard, auditioned orchestra of around 40 players. We welcome music students and non-music students into an enthusiastic, friendly and hardworking group of instrumentalists. We enjoy playing a wide range of repertoire that has previously included such works as Walton's viola concerto, Prokofiev's violin concerto, Mendelssohn's Hebrides overture and Beethoven symphonies one, three and seven. Each semester, students are invited to audition for the opportunity to perform a concerto. Rehearsals for chamber orchestra are every Wednesday, 5-7pm, followed by an important trip to the Eldon pub.

High standard. Who was I trying to kid? I wasn't high standard. I might have been at home, where I was a big fish in a small pond, but here I was at uni, among people who probably had grade eight on seven different instruments. I thought of the text message from Mum earlier, wishing me luck. I needed more than luck. I needed a miracle.

I sat down on one of the plastic chairs, cradling my flute, hoping I wouldn't have to wait long before it was my turn. A woman with short bobbed hair and an ankle-length skirt walked past me towards the front of the hall. She was carrying a music stand, and had a clipboard tucked under one arm. After placing the stand near the piano, she turned to face everyone.

It was then I realised. The auditions would be held in here. In front of everybody.

'Can I have Michael Chan first please?' she said, reading from the clipboard. 'We're starting with the flautists. Those of you who are playing other instruments and want to come back later, it'll be about half an hour judging by how many people we have to get through.'

There was a collective groan, and several people started to pack their instruments away. Others remained, relieved grins on their faces that they weren't Michael Chan, and didn't have to go first but could sit and watch the competition. I stayed seated, frozen. Surely, surely, I wouldn't have to play in front of all these people?

I couldn't do it. It wasn't possible. I'd squeak, over-blow, mess up my fingering. There was no way I could play in front of all these people, especially not without accompaniment.

Michael Chan placed his music on the stand and played some long notes into his flute to warm up. Why was I putting myself through this? It wasn't necessary. I didn't have to join any type of group or ensemble just because I was studying music. It wasn't worth the worry. I was a pianist anyway. Solo piano. That was me. Better to excel at one instrument than be mediocre on two. I started to take my flute apart as Michael Chan began his piece. The sound rang out, sweet and clear. His pitch was immaculate, his face plastered with a frown of concentration. I didn't recognise what he was playing, but it was fast and complicated and far more difficult than my poxy Allegro. If this was the standard I was competing against, I was wasting my time anyway. I would never get in.

I hurried towards the exit at the back of the hall. Several people watched me as I left, smirking as they realised I'd decided I wasn't good enough after hearing just one person play. As I left the hall, my phone began to vibrate. I ignored it. It would be her of course – she still wasn't getting the message. I paused in the corridor outside, catching my breath, feeling my cheeks burn with humiliation. The music coming from the hall had stopped, and after a pause, I heard the woman's voice call out.

'Emma Dewberry?' she was saying. 'Have we got an Emma Dewberry here?'

I turned and fled. My phone vibrated again. I grabbed it from my pocket in irritation, wondering why she had such difficulty understanding that I wanted to be left alone. But it wasn't her this time. It was Pete.

~

I must have walked past St Anne's Cathedral dozens of times on my way through the town centre up the hill to uni, and I'd never noticed it, not specifically. Not like the concrete monstrosity that was Morrisons supermarket on Woodhouse Lane – every time I walked past it, I felt pangs of revulsion. Leeds Student had called it the 'ugliest building in the city, if not the country'. Perhaps it had been a landmark building when it was built – those curved cement panels must once have been considered the height of modern design. But the cathedral, if someone had asked me about it, I wouldn't even have known it was there.

We walked up Woodhouse Lane. Pete chose the route and I followed, treading carefully for fear of slipping over on the pavements coated in indigenous drizzle. The rain was dusting its way down, so light, I couldn't feel it land on me, yet I was aware of my hair gaining weight as it absorbed the minuscule droplets of water. We passed Morrisons. At 5.30 on a Saturday evening, the bus stop outside the shop was crammed full of students, spilling out into the road, all clutching those green and yellow bags, waiting impatiently for a First bus. They were in our way. Pete stared at his feet as he meandered a path around them, deep in thought.

'Nearly there,' Pete said. 'It's a left up here.'

We crossed the busy road and took a left down a small side street, walking past a tramp sitting on the pavement. He had a hood over his head masking his face and was fiddling with something in his lap. We got closer: a mobile phone. So much for abject poverty. A pitiful, skinny mongrel sat next to him and looked up at me, wide-eyed and hopeful as we came nearer. I spotted the faintest flicker of movement from his tail. But when he realised we weren't going to stop, his head dropped back onto his paws and his tail flopped.

'Hang on Pete,' I said, reaching into my bag for my purse.

'What?' he said. 'You're not going to give him any money are you?'

'For the dog…' I explained, opening my purse to discover I only had 60p in change.

'Emma, I wouldn't. Honestly. He'll likely spend it on drugs not the dog. Or phone credit.' He raised an eyebrow. 'Anyway, save your change, there's a collection box at the end of mass.'

On the way up from Clarence Dock, he'd given up his seat on the bus to an old lady. Yet here he was, instructing me not to be charitable.

'OK,' I said. 'It's just, you know, the big eyes. Makes my heart melt.'

'It's just a trick! Where do you think the expression hang-dog came from? You're so generous but no need to feel guilty. Look, he's fine.'

The dog yawned and licked his own nose. Pete was right, he was fine. And anyway the tramp had chosen a good spot – fellow worshippers were dropping pennies into his lap as they walked by.

The cathedral loomed ahead of us.

From the road, it was hard to tell much about the building except that it was big, because you couldn't stand far enough back from it to get a good view. It was hemmed in on all sides by a mish-mash of buildings, all from different eras. But it was certainly the oldest, largest and grandest building on the street. I swallowed.

'I won't have to talk to anyone will I?' I said, tugging on Pete's sleeve.

'No, just do what I do. Don't worry Emma.' He squeezed my hand. 'Look around, isn't it wonderful?'

Inside was only a few degrees warmer. As we entered, I remembered the last time I'd been inside a religious building. It came back in a rush: the agonisingly slow car journey there, the mumbled hymns, the choked readings, the speech the priest gave – bland eulogising about a man he'd never met. A proud father, he'd called him. Proud, loving, devastated by the knowledge he had let his family down, convinced he no longer deserved them. That priest had no idea just how much my father had let me down. Mum had stared straight ahead, unblinking, her eyes clear. I had fought alternating emotions – deadening guilt, bitter hatred, and inexorable grief. That day at least, the grief had won. After the priest's euphemistic speech, I wept my soul out for my dad. The rest of the service had been a blur.

But this was a different time, a different church. Not even a church: a cathedral. And it lived up to its superior moniker – it was far grander, with an ornate series of paintings forming a backdrop to the altar at the far end, decorated with gold leaf. Pete quickly and efficiently went down on one knee for a second, as if proposing, in the middle of the aisle. Rows of backs clothed in heavy winter coats faced me as I sat down. The bench was hard. We sat there for a few minutes, Pete staring down at his feet, me at the magnificent domed ceiling and the rest of the congregation. There was a real mix of ages, from teenage to OAP. Quite a few of them could have been students.

After a few minutes, an organ began to play. The astonishing sound came out of nowhere, making people shuffle to their feet. Then, from behind me, the priest, in long robes, walked slowly up the aisle, swinging what looked like a giant pendant. Smoke was leeching out of it, softly and slowly curling its way up to the top of the cathedral, leaving behind a pungent yet pleasant smell. Incense. He was followed by two boys, wearing similar robes and bright red collars and each carrying a large, lit candle.

Once the procession had reached the altar, the boys placed a candle at each end and stood on one side of it, and the priest handed the pendant thing to a blue-suited lady. It continued to smoke for a few minutes before dying out. Then, turning his attention to us, the priest raised his hands in the air. They were red and slightly swollen, as was his face, contrasting with the white of his hair. He looked a bit drunk.

'In the name of the Father,' he boomed, touching himself on his head, the shoulders and the chest. 'the Son, and the Holy Spirit.'

The congregation spoke as one to reply, 'Amen'.

The sound sent shivers down my spine and a tear down my left cheek.

~

Afterwards, most people left quickly, without any hanging around or chatting. Pete, however, was talking to an unattractive girl with crazy curly hair, who'd smiled and waved at him as we stood to leave. At first sight, she looked like one of those people who would have stood on the sidelines in the school playground. It was the hair – the bullies would have loved it. Pete was saying something about confession.

'I don't think Father Michael is doing them after Mass on Saturdays anymore,' the girl said. Her accent reminded me of Lucy. 'You'll have to come back tomorrow afternoon. Didn't you go last week anyway?'

'No, there was a huge queue,' Pete was scanning the church and wouldn't look at the girl. 'Oh well, I guess I will have to come back tomorrow. How irritating, I really wanted to go...'

'Why, what have you been up to? Must have been bad if it can't wait one day.'

It must have a rhetorical question or a joke because he didn't reply and the girl then turned to me.

'Hi there,' she said, holding out her hand. 'I'm Mary. Pete's so rude, he should have introduced us. I haven't seen you here before, where do you normally go?'

'Er, I don't,' I replied, flushing. 'It's my first time. My name's Emma, I share a flat with Pete. I sort of just, well, came along to see what it's all about.'

Her eyes flicked briefly over to meet Pete's, who responded with a look I couldn't interpret.

'Yes, sorry, sorry,' Pete said. 'I should have done the introductions. This is Emma, she's been wondering where I disappear to every Saturday night. So I told her to come along and see for herself.'

'Well Emma, it's a pleasure to meet you,' Mary said. 'I hope you enjoyed the service, Father Michael is one of my favourite priests. Really *thought-provoking, traditional* sermons. None of this liberal nonsense. But enough about all that, how about we all go for a cup of tea and a chat? It's freeeezing out there.' She rubbed her hands together and grinned.

Pete nodded in agreement.

'Great idea,' he said. 'I know a place round the corner.'

We passed a Christian bookshop on the way, and they paused briefly, taking in the books on display in the window. They both tutted softly, clearly unimpressed. In the café, Mary insisted on getting the drinks for both of us as well as paying for them. She went up to the counter leaving Pete and I alone.

'So,' he said. 'How did you find it? Incredible huh? Did you feel moved?'

'It was amazing,' I said, truthfully. 'Beautiful. Especially the music. I mean, I've studied ecclesiastical music before of course, but it was always out of context. And the hymns... hearing the organ play, and all the singing.... the people really sang. Sang their hearts out. It was amazing. Thank you for taking me.'

I reached out and touched his hand. He continued smiling as he grasped mine and squeezed it.

'That's great Em, it really is. I knew you'd enjoy it. Nothing like it for lifting the spirits, eh? But there's more to it than music. Really, it's what takes place that's important. The moment the bread and wine become the body and blood of Christ – well...that's a *miracle moment*. This evening, you've witnessed a *miracle* Emma.'

'It's very humbling,' I said. It was the best I could offer.

'So,' said Mary, placing three Styrofoam cups of horribly milky tea in front of us. 'What's going on here then?' She nodded at our joined hands.

Pete retracted his. 'Nothing. Mary is Lucy's cousin by the way Emma.'

'One of them,' Mary laughed. 'We're from a big family. My mam and Lucy's mam are sisters, and they have eight other siblings too, so that's a lot of cousins. Have you met Lucy?' She glanced at Pete.

'Yes,' I said. 'Only once, but she's written to me. She's so sweet. I hope she comes and visits Pete again soon, it would be good to get to know her better.'

'She won't be down for a while actually,' Pete said. 'There's so much for her to do up there with Ruth being ill.' He sighed.

'Oh sweetie. You poor thing. It must be so hard. I know Lucy misses you terribly.' Mary turned to me. 'Lucy and Pete, they've been together forever you know. Known each other their whole lives. This is the first time they've been apart. To be honest with you Emma, I wouldn't be surprised if there wasn't a wedding around the corner.' She nudged me – an uncomfortable gesture of familiarity. I wasn't her friend. Not yet anyway.

Pete looked up. 'It's possible,' he said, 'that Lucy and I will get engaged soon, yes. But her family really needs her at the moment. And I have my degree here. I couldn't provide for her properly yet. But we'll see.'

'It will happen,' Mary said. 'The doctors think her mam's going to be in remission again by the New Year. Then she'll move down here, don't you worry about it.'

I looked down at my fingernails, pushing the cuticles back hard on my left hand. Their wedding. I saw them on the day: Pete looking uncomfortable in a suit, Lucy luminous with joy. Perhaps they would ask me to play *Clair de Lune* as she floated up the aisle. At the reception afterwards, I would sit at a table surrounded by members of Lucy's comically large family. They would all peer at me, wondering who I was, until several glasses of wine later they felt emboldened enough to ask. *You're not a member of the family are you?* they'd say. *What are you doing here?*

'Yes, let's hope so,' Pete said, his words cutting through my daydreams.

'What about you Mary? Have you got a boyfriend?' I asked.

She laughed loudly and her hair began to vibrate. 'No, no, no! That's not for me Emma. I've got other callings in life. Nope, I am young, free and unattainable. And happy that way too, I might add.'

'Oh,' I replied. I wanted to ask her what 'unattainable' meant but wasn't sure I'd like the answer. 'So, are you at Leeds uni too, then?'

'Oh no. I'm not a student. I'm a PA. I actually live in Manchester. I've just taken some time off work to come down here and give some talks to the uni students down here. It's something I do a lot back home.'

'Talks? What about?'

'Well, you know, religion. The place of religion in society these days. How students can seek spiritual fulfillment. That sort of thing.' She stared down at her cup as if it was a secret she shouldn't have let out so soon.

'You'd think she'd be really boring,' Pete said, 'but she's not. And there are biscuits. You should come along to one of the talks Em. There's one on Tuesday afternoon. I'm going. You can come with me.'

Mary playfully punched him on the arm. 'Oh, thanks very much Pete. That's charming! Boring indeed!'

'I have a piano tutorial on Tuesday afternoon,' I said, a little too quickly. 'But thanks anyway.'

'Suit yourself,' Pete said, draining the last drops of tea from his cup. 'I'll just have to eat your biscuits for you.'

Chapter Nine

Emma, November 2010

I clutched my last tin of Morrisons multi-pack tuna, sighing at the thought of lugging home another batch on the bus.

'Amelia, I'm sorry. But really, I'm not well,' I said, pouring the tuna over the pasta I'd just drained.

'But you've got to come! It's gonna be amazing. We've been planning it all week. So you've got a tummy ache...big deal – what is it, time of the month? I can get you some Anadin.' Amelia tossed her freshly washed hair in my direction.

I felt my face grow hot. 'No, it's not that,' I said. 'I just feel really sick...and you know, I'm having problems at the other end too.'

Amelia snorted. 'No wonder you feel sick. All you ever eat is bloody tuna. You're only supposed to have it twice a week you know, cos it's got loads of mercury in it or something, and you have it practically every day. You've got to learn to cook, Dewberry,' She stared at me, raising one immaculate eyebrow. 'Otherwise, how are you ever going to become that perfect housewife you want to be?'

She stood up and carried her plate to the sink. There was nothing left of her gourmet meal. Haddock kedgeree. I added some ready-grated cheddar to my plate of pasta and tuna and pushed the concoction around with my fork.

'Well if I can't change your mind,' she said, grinning as a new idea occurred to her. 'I know a man who can. Pete! Pete! Come in here will you?'

'Oh Amelia, please,' I said. 'Give it a rest.'

Pete strolled in, glancing sideways at me. 'You smell good Amelia. Had a shower for once? What can I do for you?'

Amelia giggled and put her arms around his waist. They both looked at me. What were they expecting? Did they want me to scream in jealous protest? I never understood this side of Pete. It was so unnatural, so forced and a blatant attempt to fit in. It was weak of him. I carried my plate to the table and began to eat. The pasta was undercooked and the tuna was still cold.

'It's Emma,' she said, stepping back. 'She won't come to the bonfire, 'cos she's got a bad tummy or something. But Sam's bought some cider and we're going to relive our teenage years. Play truth or dare. Maria's bought some crappy fireworks too, and afterwards we're going to go to that dodgy abandoned warehouse opposite to let them off. It won't be the same without Emma. Make her come Pete. She listens to you.'

Pete picked up the kettle and filled it from the tap. 'Stop whining,' he said. 'If Emma doesn't want to come, she doesn't want to come. I'm sorry, that's just the way it is. You can't make her.'

Before I could stop it, a huge smile broke across my face. I carried on eating. Amelia frowned.

'OK fine,' she said, crossing her arms. 'I thought it would be nice that's all. I'm so sorry I wanted Emma to share something fun with us. She's hardly been out since she got here…'

'What about the ball?' Pete interrupted.

'What?'

'The ball. You forgot to remind her she needed a ticket.'

Amelia looked at her feet. 'That's not fair. I thought she knew. It wasn't deliberate. Look, we've already discussed that, it was a misunderstanding.'

I should speak, say something. But my voice seemed to have disappeared.

'Well, you can hardly expect her to jump the next time you click your fingers after that can you?'

'Look, I'm sorry, OK? But there's no point in her sitting in her room alone at night or spending every waking hour in the practice rooms playing the bloody piano. She might as well be a nun. I mean, how is she going to meet anyone like this?'

It had finally happened. I had become invisible. They were having an argument about me, in front of me, and they didn't even care.

'Maybe she doesn't want to meet anyone,' Pete said. 'Did that occur to you? Or maybe she's already met the person she wants.'

He turned his head and winked at me. Amelia's frustration rose. It was filling the room, like a thick, hot smoke.

'Oh you two are just bloody weirdos,' she fumed. 'Why don't you just get together and put us all out of our misery? For god's sake! You're two of the most sexually frustrated people I've ever met. And you,' she said, rounding on Pete, waving a small tanned finger at him. At only 5ft 1, she was nevertheless intimidating when incensed. 'You are completely out of line. You're supposed to have a girlfriend you love and adore. Princess Lucy. But you treat her like CRAP. How can you sit here flirting with Emma knowing that poor girl is at home thinking you love her? And Emma, you need to get a bloody life. Pete's just messing you about. It's pathetic, the way you follow him around like a bloody puppy, hoping he'll throw you some crappy bone. It's not going to happen.'

Her words brought stinging tears to my eyelids. I was shocked. Shocked at how accurate Amelia had been, and that she'd actually come right out and said it.

'I...don't...' I started, before abandoning the effort, knowing that attempting to speak would just make me cry even more.

Pete stirred his cup of tea. 'Girls, girls,' he said. 'Please, there's no need to fight over me. I'm sorry that I upset you, Amelia. I was only messing around with Emma, and she knows that. As for Lucy, well, she's known me for a lot longer than you have, and has never yet had a problem with my sense of humour. Also you should probably know that Emma and Lucy have become friends, and don't seem to have any problems with each other.'

'What?' Amelia sniffed. Perhaps she was crying too. 'Lucy and Emma are friends? What are you talking about?'

I found my voice. 'She's been writing to me,' I said slowly, feeling the hot, wet smudges trickle down my face. 'She's been very kind. She's lonely, up there, you know, she looks after her whole family. Six little kids. With no one her own age to talk to. We sort of, well, have a mutual interest in things.' As I thought of her, I smiled.

'What?' Amelia said. 'Don't you think that's just a little bit fucked up? There you are, writing to this girl, pretending to be her friend, at the same time as trying to steal her boyfriend?'

'Amelia don't be ridiculous. I'm not trying to steal her boyfriend. Pete's my friend. Just a friend. I really like Lucy. She's so sweet, she texts me when I have recitals to wish me luck. You know, she *remembers* things.' I stared at my yellow dinner plate, subconsciously counting the chips in its edges over and over again, watching the tears fall onto the congealed shells of pasta, avoiding looking at Pete. I wanted to bring up my dad now, shame her into shutting up. It was the ultimate trump card. But it was sick, and wrong, and I couldn't do it, especially not in front of Pete.

'Of course she does.' Pete's arms appeared from nowhere, wrapping around me, pulling me close. 'Don't cry. Amelia just doesn't understand, that's all.'

He turned his head away from me. 'Don't you understand? Emma is vulnerable. Think about what she's gone through this year. Have some consideration for goodness sake. She doesn't need you to set her up with some immature idiot who's only after one thing.'

There were footsteps, then a silence that lasted a few minutes, and then I knew Amelia had left the room. I imagined her storming out, wide-eyed, open-mouthed and aghast, then relaying the whole conversation to Maria. But I didn't care; things weren't *that* bad, but at least he'd stuck up for me. He was on my side. I wondered how Amelia knew about my dad. Pete must have told her because I'd never mentioned it. I should have felt angry with him for telling her without asking first, but I felt strangely touched instead. Even if neither of them knew the whole story.

Eventually, he yanked out a plastic black chair from under the table and sat down next to me. He drank his tea. The mug said 'World's Best Boyfriend'. Obviously Lucy had bought it for him, but it didn't matter, they were both my friends now.

'So,' he said. 'Why didn't you want to go tonight? You don't really like Amelia do you? I mean, she's not your sort of person. Just like she's not *my* sort of person.'

'It's not that. It's just,' I began. I couldn't tell him the truth, that it would be the first firework night since dad had gone, and that every year, he'd put on a display in our garden that the professionals would be proud of. And once we'd moved down to Devon, they'd come to stay with us every November, to watch the fireworks… It was Dad's thing. One of the few times he excelled as a father. But I didn't want to explain it to Pete. 'Well, I just don't like fireworks. All those loud bangs. And if I told her the truth, she'd just take the mickey.' I stared down at the dirty kitchen table, scratching at a dried-on food stain with my fingernail. To my satisfaction, it came off easily.

'Not too fussed about fireworks myself either to be honest. As for the cider – well, they're just kids really aren't they? Not my scene either. Don't you worry; we'll just have a night to ourselves, shall we? Just you and me? What do you want to do?'

~

Dear Emma

Peter tells me that you two went bowling the other night. He loves bowling, even though as I'm sure you discovered he's not too good at it! I have to tell you again how grateful I am that you have been spending time with him. He's not very sociable so it's good to know he doesn't spend all his time in his room with the fish.

In your last letter you asked me why Peter is so interested in fish!

You could have asked him yourself – it's not a secret. His father breeds tropical fish, and used to run a shop selling them. Peter grew up with fish around. He knows so much about them. His father wanted Peter to take over the shop, but I know he's destined for greater things. Not that there's anything wrong with running a shop of course.

Things are the same as always for me. My second-youngest sister, Bernadette, is settling in well at her first year of school. It's good for me that now most of my siblings are at school during the day. I only have Martha to worry about, and it frees up time for me to help my mother. She has finished her most recent course of chemotherapy, and is almost back to her normal self.

As you can see, I've enclosed a present for you. You're probably wondering what it is. It's called a "scapular medal" and you can wear it on a chain around your neck or carry in your purse. I wear mine on a chain. Don't look upon it as a "charm" but rather a comforting reminder of God's mercy and Our Lady's motherly concern for all her children. I've had it blessed by a priest. I hope you find it a source of strength.

Peter is coming home to visit me next weekend, and we were discussing it, and we would very much love for you to come too, if you would like it? His father has plenty of room in his house. Let us know what you think.

Hopefully see you soon.

Your friend Lucy xxx

I placed the letter on my desk, its pink ink now a familiar source of comfort. I turned the medal over in my hand. It was silver and oval-shaped and in the middle was an etching of woman, holding out her arms, with a long veil caught in her fingertips behind her.

She didn't look like Pete's ugly Jesus did. She was smiling. She looked kind and motherly. Around the outside of the medal were the words "O Mary conceived without sin, pray for us who have recourse to thee". For some reason, I lifted it up to my nose and sniffed it. I could have sworn it smelt of roses.

Chapter Ten

Emma, November 2010

The afternoon before we were due to leave for Newcastle, Maria came home early. Being a conscientious student, she usually attended all her lectures, so it was strange to see her come in after lunch. She looked pale for once, behind her spattering of freckles, but then I suppose we all did – two months under predominantly grey skies had seen to that. I smiled at her as she slipped into her bedroom, but unusually she didn't smile back. Perhaps being cooped up with four virtual strangers was getting her down too. Whatever was wrong with her, I was probably the last person she wanted to confide in. Best left to Amelia to cheer her up.

I couldn't decide what to take. Lucy had called earlier and told me that the most important things were warm jumpers and comfortable shoes. My trainers would do, and all my jumpers were warm anyway. Staring down at the piles of clothes on the bed, half-heartedly folded and ready for packing, I was dismayed at how unglamorous they all were. Black cotton knickers from M&S that I'd had since forever, white, black and skin-coloured T-shirt bras with elastic straps that betrayed their hours spent in the tumble-dryer, two pairs of skinny jeans with faded knees and backsides and three mandatory woolly jumpers – red, green and a multi-coloured striped monstrosity that I'd bought in an attempt to look 'fun'. Tragic, more like.

Still, it didn't really matter. My jumpers probably wouldn't get a public viewing. Lately, I had been wearing my coat indoors most of the time anyway. My requests to turn the heating up had met with derision – apparently, seeing as we were now students, it was a budgetary impossibility. All those jokes Pete had made about how I must have cold blood, like a fish, and that was why he understood me so well, were getting boring.

Amelia's voice came from the corridor. 'So. Off on a long, romantic weekend with Fish Farmer Pete are we? Is that what you're taking? Nice pants. Bloody hell Dewberry, pull out all the stops why don't you?'

I found her breeziness disquieting – she'd still never mentioned the row in the kitchen. Her ability to forget so easily was probably representative of how insignificant I was to her.

'I know. I just don't have any nice clothes for cold weather. Pete says it might snow. Anyway, never mind. I'd rather be warm than pretty.'

Amelia sat on the edge of my bed and stared out of the window at the ever-present rain falling on the car park, which I now knew belonged to the Royal Armouries museum. It must have been the most under-visited tourist attraction in the UK. Even at weekends, the car park was empty, a depressing grey triangle framed by those ghastly paisley curtains. I should take a photograph and title it 'The World's Worst View'. I'd probably win some huge photographic prize or something. Amelia began to re-arrange the coloured tealights on my windowsill.

'I shouldn't tell you this, but...Maria's pregnant,' she said, lining up all the pink candles next to each other. 'Poor cow.'

'What? Maria?' I sat down.

'Yep. Maria. With child.'

'I didn't even know she had a boyfriend! I thought they broke up before she came to Leeds.'

'They did. She's three months gone already. I can't believe it. Stupid cow.'

'What's she going to do?' I asked.

'Get rid of it I expect. Dunno yet. My best friend Jess – you've must've heard me talk about her before – had an abortion last year. I don't think the actual procedure's so bad, but the hormones really fuck you up. And you know, there's the whole delayed guilt thing. A little bit of bleeding and a sore tummy – anyone can cope with that. I think it's what happens later that makes it so bloody awful. You know, seeing little kids in the park or whatever, imagining what yours would have looked like. Head fuck.'

'I suppose she wouldn't want to keep it. She wouldn't want to mess up her degree.'

'Hmmm. I told her to call the wanker that got her in this situation. Should be a joint problem after all. At least she can offload on him a bit. Serves him right. You know, it's funny. I've only known Maria for what, two months? But it feels like ages. And you too, Emma. I guess we're like a big substitute family for each other.'

I was touched. She cared about me. I'd misjudged her. She was volatile, she spoke her mind, but it was only because she cared. She stood up and ran a neatly manicured finger over my scary striped jumper, raising an eyebrow almost imperceptibly.

'Be careful this weekend Emma, yeah? Don't get your hopes up. Maybe I'm being a suspicious old bag. I dunno. Just don't want to see you get hurt. Take care of yourself.' She reached forwards and put her arms around me.

'OK Amelia. I will,' I hugged her back and the scent of Hugo Boss Woman tickled my nostrils. 'Good luck with Maria.'

~

The 16.27 GNER train from Leeds to Newcastle was packed, and we didn't get a seat until it arrived at Darlington. After half an hour standing, I sat on the floor next to the luggage shelves, while Pete stood by the door, gazing out as we whizzed along. It grew dark within a few minutes of leaving Leeds, but he didn't move. He was like a fish in a tank himself, always staring out. So much for our time alone together. He was lost in his own thoughts, which he chose not to share.

The arrival at Newcastle was quite exhilarating. We crossed over a bridge on the train, the city's twinkling lights reflected in the still waters of the Tyne. Lucy didn't meet us at the station as I had assumed she would, and after arriving, we instead walked immediately to a cold bus shelter. Pete stayed quiet as we trudged through the busy streets. It was a long half an hour's wait for the bus.

'It will only take us as far as Ashington,' Pete said eventually, once my teeth had started chattering. My 'duvet coat' was proving inadequate.

'Oh, right.'

'Then my dad will have to pick us up from there. I can't be bothered waiting for another bus once we get there. The old git can come and get us.'

'What about your mum? I bet she'll be excited to see you.' I said, unsure of how to react to Pete's insulting his father. They clearly weren't close.

'My mam won't be there,' Pete said quietly. 'She's in a better place.'

His tone told me not to press him further. I couldn't believe it. His mother must be dead, but why wouldn't he have told me? Especially after I'd told him. We were equals, both demi-orphans. It was significant. Someone should have told me. If not Pete, then Lucy.

But then, perhaps his mother had left Pete's dad and run off with another man or something, and that was why he didn't want to talk about her. I could certainly understand that.

'Ashington's a bit of a dive, just so you know. But hopefully we won't be there long.'

I looked around. A teenage couple alternated between snogging and arguing the whole time we waited. Their accents were so thick I couldn't really understand their shouts. Several middle-aged, overweight women clutched shopping bags with one hand while they puffed on cigarettes with the other. A handful of teenage mothers pushed prams and pushchairs containing babies and toddlers, all mostly wearing black and white stripy football shirts. Everyone looked cold.

The X18 was small and slightly battered but the driver smiled at me as I boarded. He spent the rest of the journey chatting away to one of the middle-aged women about the bargains she'd picked up in TK Maxx. The only item I recognised was a pair of Calvin Klein boxer shorts she'd bought for her son Callum, and that was only because she got them out of the box and flapped them around for the driver to see.

'Talk aboot a bargain pet!' she squawked. 'I cannae see the point in paying more. Just as canny as those in proper shops.'

I stared out of the window, bewildered by the number of huge industrial buildings and factories we drove past. Halfway through the journey, Pete rang Lucy and told her we were nearly there and even the rumbling diesel engine of the bus couldn't drown out her squeals on the other end of the line.

'She won't be able to see us till tomorrow,' Pete said, once he'd finished speaking to her. 'She's got to pick up one of her sisters from a friend's house in Morpeth later tonight.'

I tried to hide my disappointment. My unexpected disappointment. After all, Pete was the one I wanted to spend time with, and this meant spending the whole evening alone with him. Didn't sound as though Pete was terribly excited about seeing his dad, so it would be just him and me. Maybe he'd take me for a walk along that beautiful beach I'd seen in the picture. Then I remembered it was about 3ºC outside.

'Are you hungry?' Pete asked, as we clambered off the bus. 'Thought maybe we could pick up some fish and chips now. There won't be anything at home. My dad lives off Findus Crispy Pancakes and whatever else happens to be on offer in Asda's frozen section.'

'I wouldn't mind some chips,' I replied, thinking about the ones Callum's mum had been eating.

'Follow me then. Looks like my dad's late anyway. No great surprise there.'

'What exactly is the issue with your dad?' I asked, as we made our way along a dimly lit row of terraced houses, punctuated by the odd newsagent and a Working Men's Club.

'Nothing really. We're just not best friends like some fathers and sons, that's all. He's not an educated man himself you see, and he doesn't really like the fact that I've gone to university and left him behind. After me mam went, he lost touch with...well, everyone really and now he doesn't get out much. So his only entertainment is making life that little bit harder for me. But that's OK, 'cos I make his life just as difficult in return.'

He winked at me as he pushed open the door to the fish and chip shop, letting me go in first. Must have been a joke. After all, Christian teachings dictated that you honour your mother and father.

Pete ordered a battered sausage – which looked appropriately revolting – with his chips and we walked back to the bus shelter while eating. The chips were hot and salty, singeing the inside of my mouth. Eventually, an old silver Volvo appeared, and Pete got to his feet.

'Here he is,' he said, taking my hand. 'Don't take any notice of him. His bark is worse than his bite.'

We walked towards the car, Pete carrying both our bags and tossing the empty chip cartons to the floor. I tutted instinctively, but looked around and there were no obvious bins nearby. His dad didn't look at us as we clambered in the back of the car.

'Bus early then?' Pete's dad said, his accent as strong as the TK Maxx woman.

'No. You were late. Doesn't matter, we got some chips while we waited.' Pete reached over and squeezed my hand, which had gone numb.

'Aye, thought ya maght have eaten, so I didne bother getting any food in for tonight. Thought the lass can sleep in the den. Wouldn't like her going upstairs.'

'It's very kind of you to have me,' I said, sounding completely out of place. 'I hope it's not too much trouble.'

'Trouble!? Wha would it be? You ganna cause trouble?' Pete's father laughed. He was driving unbearably slowly. How long would it take to get there?

'No, er, I just meant...'

'Only messin' lass.'

'Right Mr Field. Sorry.' Why didn't Pete say something?

'Mr Field! None of that. Call me Bert if you want an answer.'

Leeds and the emptiest car park in Britain began to look very attractive.

Chapter Eleven

Emma, November 2010

I woke to the sound of a car starting outside the window. My face was cold but I ventured out of bed, keeping the sheet and blanket wrapped around me as I peered out at the driveway, which stretched along the side of the stone house. Pete was sitting in the driver's seat of the Volvo, tapping the steering wheel. His father appeared and got into the car too, and the pair of them drove off. Leaving me, I presumed, alone.

I must have overslept. I found my watch abandoned on a windowsill in the adjoining shower room. It was ten past eight. Where were they going, and why hadn't Pete told me he was off somewhere? I sat back down on the bed, tucking my feet up under my bottom to keep them warm, and my eyes rested on a small, silver crucifix hung above the bedhead. Then I realised: Pete and his dad must have gone to church.

It had been a surprise to learn on bonfire night that Pete actually went to mass every day, not just on Saturday evenings as he'd first said. When I asked him why, all I got in response was that he went because he wanted to. Clearly his father was also religious; the crucifix pinned to the faded green wallpaper was just one sign. Propped up on the low stone windowsills were books covering a range of topics – from football to bird watching, but interspersed at regular intervals with copies of the Bible, and at least three books entitled *A Concise Catechism of the Catholic Church.* Medieval-looking paintings on gold-leaf backgrounds adorned the walls, along with a particularly graphic painting of Jesus, his chest ripped open to reveal a huge glowing heart, one hand pointing upwards as if reprimanding the viewer. His heart pulsated slap-bang in the middle of his chest... I shivered. Beneath him, a cross-stitch cushion on an ageing velvet armchair declared: '*Blessed are the meek, for they shall inherit the earth.*' At least there was something in store for me.

I made use of this time alone to get ready, and showered, dressed and did my hair. Once satisfied, and feeling hungry, I ventured into the kitchen. It was a typical 'farmhouse' affair: pine wooden cupboards, a butler sink and a beautiful old dresser, adorned with blue and white crockery. A large black Aga sat reassuringly beneath the chimneybreast, but it was covered with dust. The gleaming silver microwave oven on one of the counters opposite was clearly preferred. After searching through some cupboards and unearthing a box of cornflakes, I opened the fridge to get some milk. There wasn't much in there: a half-drunk bottle of wine, a few milk bottles, a jar of beetroot and some butter, and the sides of the fridge were covered in speckled mould. I couldn't find anything to drink, so I poured myself a glass of water from the tap. Holding it up to the light, I noticed it was cloudy but it tasted OK.

I walked through into the large lounge area. It was huge, feeling spacious despite the low ceiling and long, dramatic beams. Where it was visible, it was obvious that the carpet had seen better days. It was mainly covered by a mish-mash of rugs – some Chinese-style wool, others woven, and others jute or hessian – which, although shabby, gave the room an unintentional charm. There wasn't even a sofa, just a collection of mismatched armchairs, and a simple table surrounded by ladderback chairs. And in one corner of the room, a huge pile of empty fish tanks of varying sizes, standing out like alien vessels, and coated in varying degrees of filmy dust. The room's neglected feel reminded me of a garage.

But the view from the French doors at the back of the room was something else. It overlooked the biggest garden I'd ever seen, an immaculate lawn wrapped in a veil of crisp frost. I walked towards the window, touching the icy pane. I couldn't see any fence or boundary marking the garden's end. Pete would have played in this garden when he was a child; tree-climbing, hide-and-seek among the many shrubs and bushes. It was hard to imagine him young and carefree somehow.

I caught the sound of a key turning just in time. They were back. I quickly placed my cornflake bowl and glass in the deep ceramic sink and was standing in the middle of the kitchen when Lucy and Pete walked in.

'Emma!' Lucy cried, throwing her arms around me. Her face was cold as she pressed it against mine. 'So good to see you. How are you? You look very well.'

'I'm great thanks,' I replied. 'How are you?'

She laughed. 'I've just been telling Pete, I feel completely run-ragged. One of the little ones – Martha – you'll get to meet her soon. Well, she's at that stage, you know, and she's just so sulky. Always whining about something. She threw a huge tantrum when I told her I would get a lift back from church with Pete, instead of going with her and Mam.'

'Martha's just jealous,' Pete said, opening the fridge and frowning at its lack of contents. 'She wanted a lift back with me too, of course.'

Lucy ignored his joke. She rubbed her hands together.

'Brrr. It isn't half cold in here. Your dad, Peter, honestly, I come over at least once a week and tell him to put the heating on but he just won't have it. It's ridiculous. Insists on burning a fire in the evenings but that's all. Poor Emma, you must be frozen. Don't you worry, we'll go over to my house in a bit.'

'I am freezing actually. But I slept OK.'

'Sorry,' Pete said. 'He's a tight-wad, the old man. I'll put the heating on now.'

'Where is your dad, Pete?' I asked, peering to see if he was somewhere in the corridor.

'He's gone off to check on the fish. See those big warehouses over there?' Pete said, nodding towards some buildings opposite the driveway at the front of the house. 'That's where he keeps the breeding tanks. He'll be there for most of the day now.'

'Yes,' Lucy said, laughing again. 'And you can bet your life that it's as warm as toast in there. So long as the fish are OK, who cares about the rest of us!'

'Sorry you were cold,' Pete said again. 'Did you manage to find anything to eat? I think there's some cereal if you're hungry, or I could make you some toast?'

'Thanks, it's fine, I had some cornflakes. I couldn't find any tea bags though, would be great to have a cup.'

'Of course it would,' Lucy said, pushing Pete out of the way. 'I'll make us all some tea shall I? You two go and sit in the living room, at least it gets the sun in there, should be a bit warmer.'

'Thanks,' Pete said, kissing her on the cheek.

Pete and I walked through to the living room, and sat facing each other on two of the unhappy-looking armchairs. I crossed my legs underneath me to allow the warmth of my own body to heat up my feet. The garden still looked glorious.

'Sorry to rush off like that this morning,' Pete said after a while. 'I didn't want to wake you. Thought you might appreciate the lie-in. Hope you didn't feel abandoned.'

'Not at all,' I said.

'Good. What do you fancy doing today? Lucy and I thought we should take you for a walk around Cresswell, show you the sights. Although there aren't too many. But you can see the beach of course. And the tower. And then we can go back to Lucy's for some lunch. Her mam's better now and she's a great cook.'

'Sounds good.' I said, truthfully. I breathed deeply. It was so peaceful – Cresswell was miles from anywhere. No noise, no traffic, just the sound of the wind moving slowly through the trees.

Lucy came in, perilously balancing three mugs between her hands. She sat on the rug at Pete's feet and rubbed his knee.

'And this evening,' Pete said slowly. 'We thought maybe, just if you felt like it, we could go and visit Father Gerry. He's a great friend of ours, and you'll like him too. He's dying to meet you.'

Dying to meet me. So they must have told him all about me. They had had a discussion about me. I was one of their subjects of conversation. With people who never even met me.

'Sounds great.' I said.

'We told him lots about you,' Lucy added, and there was something in her smile – something over-eager and unnatural – that made me look away.

~

It was just a short walk to the beach. We passed a few children playing football on the grass verges that surrounded the main road through Cresswell but apart from them, the tiny hamlet was deserted. There were only a few cars parked along the road and an ice cream shop, which was closed.

We were all silent as we negotiated the icy pavements. There was something about the quiet little village that made you feel like you should be quiet too. But when we eventually stepped onto the sand, I was amazed. The tide was high and the waves came crashing onto the sand with alarming force.

'Pretty spectacular isn't it?' Pete said, raising his voice above the din.

'It's beautiful,' I replied. 'I recognise it from the photos. I've never seen such an empty beach. The sand's so… yellow. It's like the Caribbean or something!' I thought back to the years of luxury holidays I'd had as a child. How utterly hollow the memories felt now.

'Come on,' Lucy said, tugging at my arm. 'Let's go a little bit further along and sit on those rocks, the view is amazing.'

I followed her as she marched ahead but Pete hung back slightly, turning his head every now and then to look back down the other end of the beach. He looked as though he was concentrating on something. Lucy chattered away.

'I love the beach,' she said. 'It's the one thing I would really miss if I were to move away. It's so peaceful here, and really safe too. I don't know how you and Peter cope over there in Leeds. All that rushing around, all the traffic.'

'I know,' I said. 'I don't really like big cities either.'

'What's your home town like then Emma?' she asked, scrambling to a top of rock and wrapping her arms around her legs, bringing her knees up to her chin.

'It's a little fishing town. Very quaint and pretty, but packed with people. Tourists mostly.'

She reached down to give me a hand as I attempted to clamber up the rock.

'Do you miss it?' she asked.

I paused. Did I miss it? I wasn't sure that I did. What was there to miss, anyway? The poky garden flat we'd moved into several months before, that would never feel like home despite my grandmother's trite attempts to cheer the place up? My mother's incessant 'brave face' before strangers and the sound of her softly crying once she thought we were both asleep?

'Yes,' I replied. Of course I missed it. Despite the relief I felt at not having to face her every day, aware that she didn't know the whole story, that her assumptions were useless, based on half-truths. Despite that pain, I missed it. 'Yes, I really do actually. I miss my mum, and my dog. And I even miss my annoying little brother sometimes.'

'But not your dad?'

My mouth fell open. How could Pete not have told her?

'No. I mean, yes, but... my dad died earlier this year.'

Her face fell. 'Oh, I'm so sorry. You poor thing.'

'I'm surprised Pete didn't tell you.'

She looked confused, pushing a heavy curtain of hair from her face. 'No, he didn't mention it.'

There was a silence. Just the same as when I had told Pete about my father. For some reason, I felt angry.

'He killed himself,' I blurted out. My tone of voice was hard, intended to shock her, but as soon as I spoke the words, I was on the verge of tears.

'Oh!' She looked genuinely horrified. I felt a pang of guilt, regret at my outburst. I hated watching people try to figure out what to say.

'Don't worry. It's fine. He'd been depressed for ages, it wasn't much of a shock.' The lies tumbled out of me, sounding so convincing it surprised me. 'But… it is strange Pete didn't tell you. There's no reason why he wouldn't. Maybe he thought I wouldn't want you to know.'

'That's why he feels so close to you,' she said, so quietly I could barely hear.

'Um…' I said. The lies dried up, and I had nothing to say. As usual. Another critical moment in conversation, and I collapsed in a silent heap.

'You see,' she said, eventually, turning to me. 'His mam killed herself too. So you have something in common.'

'Really?' I said, staring down. 'I knew she… I thought she must have died. I didn't know she killed herself.'

'Yes. It was a long time ago though, we were just children. It was very hard for him. If there's anything I can do, any support you need, you know you only have to ask. Please.'

She reached out and laid her hand on my arm.

'Thank you,' I said.

We fell into silence. The waves pounded back and forth.

'Oh!' Lucy said suddenly, pointing at my throat. 'You're wearing it!'

I glanced down. The scapular medal glinted back up at me, having worked its way outside of my coat. I grabbed it, turning the engraved face around between my fingers, rubbing them over the now familiar outline of Mary.

'Yes,' I said. 'It's lovely. Thank you for sending it to me.'

'I'm so glad you wear it. I hope you find it helps you. Mary is always looking out for you, you know. Keeping an eye on you, just like any mother would. And of course, now, more than ever.' She paused, rubbing at the rock with her thumb. 'Can I ask you a favour? Would you mind if we prayed the rosary together? Only I haven't done it yet today and this might be my last bit of peace.'

'Um. No, of course not,' I said. 'But – where's Pete?'

She didn't look around.

'Peter? He's probably gone for a walk. He likes to go up the other end of the beach. It reminds him of his mam. Don't worry, he'll come and find us.'

'What happened to her? How did she die?'

'She drowned,' she said, after a pause. My heart beat a little bit faster. 'A bit further up the beach, behind those rocks you can see in the distance. Her body washed up a week later, at the north of Druridge Bay, near Amble. Peter was only eight. And we...we were on the beach the day it happened. That's why he gets a bit depressed coming home, and it's hard for him to come down here.'

'That's terrible,' I said.

'Yes. It was a tragedy,' she said.

'But isn't there a grave he can visit? Somewhere more peaceful?'

I thought of the cemetery and how mum had wept for the first time at his headstone. The ridiculous oversized headstone. It seemed so big, when I knew nothing remained of my father but a handful of ash. I hated the tombstone. My father had been a bear of a man. He'd been disfigured beyond recognition when he died, burnt up in the crematorium, funneled into a small pot the size of his fist and then buried under a gigantic slab of stone. I knew my mother felt the same; she'd rather have had his ashes scattered somewhere beautiful. But Grandma had insisted, red-faced and puffy-eyed, on the burial, and the stupid pompous headstone. I'd almost wanted to shout out how he didn't deserve it, how he didn't deserve any sort of memorial after the way he'd behaved, but of course I couldn't.

'No, he can't visit the grave, sadly,' Lucy said, without elaborating further. 'How about we pray the rosary together, for Peter's mam, and for your father? Let's pray together that they're happy where they are, that they're close to God and that they're looking down on us all.'

'Well, OK,' I said. It would make her happy, I could tell. 'I don't know how though.'

'It's alright. You don't need to do anything, just say Amen when it's appropriate. I'll do all the talking. Here, I've got my rosary in my pocket.' She pulled out a long chain of black beads with a heavy silver cross on the end.

It seemed to take forever, with Lucy repeating the same prayer, mumbling the words almost incoherently, so that I could only hear snippets, something about 'the fruit of the womb'. Who would have thought, a month ago, that I would be sitting on a rock in the far north of England, overlooking the most beautiful isolated beach, praying the rosary? Everyone was right about uni changing your life. My previous experiences began to look superficial, pointless, childish. Selfish.

'Hail, holy Queen, Mother of Mercy, our life, our sweetness and our hope. To thee do we cry, poor banished children of Eve; to thee do we send up our sighs, mourning and weeping in this vale of tears. Turn then, most gracious advocate, thine eyes of mercy toward us; and after this our exile, show unto us the blessed fruit of thy womb, Jesus. O clement, O loving, O sweet Virgin Mary. Pray for us O holy Mother of God, that we may be worthy of the promises of Christ.'

She made the sign of the cross, then looked up at me and smiled.

'How do you feel now?' she asked. 'It's long I know, but the rosary is one of the most helpful prayers.'

'It's beautiful,' I said, looking down at my fingernails. They were blue. Perhaps I should have prayed for my Mum, after he'd died. Perhaps it would have helped. The words were hypnotically comforting, even if I didn't exactly understand them. The inside of my ears began to burn with the cold. 'Should we go back?'

'Of course! Sorry, you're not used to this ferocious weather. Let's go back to mine, and you can meet my mam and all the little ones. Come on, I'm sure we'll find Peter somewhere on the way.'

Chapter Twelve

Emma, November 2010

It was delightfully warm in Lucy's mother's kitchen. She too, had an Aga, but this one was in full use, the star attraction of the rather shabby kitchen, pouring out heat into the room. I stood next to it, enjoying the satisfying pang of pain in my face and my hands as they slowly defrosted. The house was tiny in comparison to Pete's, and couldn't have been more different. It was packed to the rafters with things; people, children and animals. Lucy's mum was small and plump but her smile was just like Lucy's – wide and genuine with no agenda.

'Mam,' said Lucy, 'this is my friend Emma, that I was telling you about. You remember? She's at university with Peter.'

'Oh Emma. Hello. I'm Ruth.' She grabbed my hands and pressed them between hers.

'Lordy aren't you cold? You poor lass. Lucy shouldn't have kept you out in this weather. I'll make you a cup of tea, that'll warm you up.'

'Thank you. We've been on the beach. It's beautiful,' I said.

'Oh listen to that accent! Like the newsreaders. Now I know how you southerners take your tea. All weak and milky. But that's no good in weather like this. You need a strong cup, that'll see you right.'

She beetled around the kitchen, using an old-fashioned kettle that she heated up on the Aga like a saucepan. It even whistled when it was ready, steam rising up from its spout and settling on the windows. I cradled the chipped mug in my hand, its faded strawberry pattern only adding to its charm, and surveyed the ensuing chaos.

I had no idea which children belonged to Lucy's family and which were friends or neighbours. They all had similar sandy coloured hair and paid me no attention as they came in from outside, the boys kicking a football through the kitchen, chased excitedly by another dog, that leapt up at me as it passed, leaving muddy paw prints on my jeans. A baby was sitting contentedly in a high chair in the corner of the room, dribbling slightly, while at a small round table in the other corner, two young girls looked as though they were trying to do their homework. A toddler staggered around, her cute pigtails bouncing up and down as she wobbled from one leg to the other. Martha. Lucy picked her up and planted a huge kiss on her face, which made the girl giggle. A tall teenage boy, who looked so much like Lucy my heart skipped a beat, came in and grabbed a handful of Hobnobs from a big biscuit barrel on the windowsill. He stopped when he saw me.

'Hello,' he said, his voice as delicious as Pete's. 'I'm Joe.'

'Hi, I'm Emma.'

He nodded at me, a slight tinge of colour rising to his cheeks. The Hobnobs started to disintegrate slightly.

'Joe's my favourite brother,' Lucy said. 'He's the most handsome boy in all of Cresswell.'

'Not much of a compliment that really is it Luce?' he said, before leaving the room.

'He's only 17,' Lucy said, noticing me watching his departing back.

He didn't look it. He looked older than Pete.

'Can I do anything to help?' I asked. I was in the way, I could tell, but there didn't seem to be anywhere suitable for me to go.

'Aw pet, that's kind of you,' Ruth replied. 'Here, can you take the baby, and give him his bottle. I'm still a bit sore, you know, after the operation,' her voice lowered to a whisper. 'No, he's not mine! I'm looking after him while his mammy goes off to the Metro centre. Late night shopping – run up to Christmas.'

She handed him to me, smiling at his chubby face.

'Ah, wee John, he's going to be a handsome one,' she said, gazing at him.

I held him in my arms, trying to imitate the way I'd seen people hold babies on television. He was surprisingly heavy, but he took the milk eagerly and contentedly, slurping away with his eyes fixated on my scapular medal. What was Maria going to do? She couldn't have a baby.

'He likes you,' Ruth said. 'You're a natural. My husband will be home in a minute and we'll be eating soon. You must be hungry. We're having chicken pie. Home made, and by me, not Lucy for once! My husband, he works on the playgrounds, you know, doing maintenance and that, setting up climbing frames for the kiddies. They get vandalised something terrible though. Has to do lots of emergency call-outs. That's why he's working on a Saturday. Busiest day of the week for playgrounds you see. Don't want the littl'uns seeing them all messed up. It upsets them.'

I smiled back at her, the tantalizing smell of baking pastry stirring my appetite, and wished I could stay in the warm kitchen, with the happy baby in my arms, forever.

~

'My dad said it's OK to borrow the car,' Pete called to us, as he walked out of one of the large outbuildings outside his father's home. I thought it was the one with all the fish tanks in, but I'd still not been inside.

'Great,' Lucy said, opening the front passenger seat door. 'Come on Emma, get in.'

Pete drove much faster than his father, and within half an hour or so we pulled up outside a terraced house with a huge bay window. I wondered if Lucy had told Pete yet that my dad had committed suicide. It didn't seem likely; there hadn't been time. I was nervous, unsure what this Father Gerry would ask me.

'He lives with his sister,' Lucy explained as she rang the doorbell. 'She's a widow.'

'Oh right,' I replied. 'Really? I always thought priests lived in the church or something.'

'Oh Emma,' Lucy laughed. 'You are funny.'

A stick-thin lady with wispy reddish hair came to the door and peered at us suspiciously.

'Hello Ann, we're here to see Father Gerry,' Lucy said. She moved aside and ushered us into the front room. It was eerily silent, except for a ticking grandfather clock in one corner, and it was more like a study than a living room, with a green leather chesterfield sofa filling the bay window, facing a big, dark desk. A serious desk for serious matters. The large crucifix on the wall failed to disturb me this time: I was getting used to seeing Jesus, his body distorted by pain.

'Hello, hello, hello,' said a red-faced man dressed in a long black coat, a perfect white square at his throat. He got up from behind the desk and held his arms out as he came towards Pete and Lucy, offering them a sort of half-embrace. He must have been about forty, younger than I expected, and his hair was short and flecked with grey. He wore black-rimmed glasses, which looked too trendy for him somehow. I liked him instantly.

'And who is this young lady?' he said, looking me up and down.

'This is Emma, Father Gerry, she's visiting us this weekend.'

'Ah Emma,' he said, a look of recognition spreading across his face. 'Of course. Lucy has filled me in. Lovely to meet you.'

'You too.'

'So, you're after some classes I presume? Lucy and Peter, when he can, both come to me for formation. They said you might find it helpful. After losing your father so recently, I'm sure it would help.'

'Um, I...'

'Sit down, sit down,' he said, gesturing towards the chesterfield. I did as I was told. Lucy perched on the corner of the desk while Pete remained standing.

'Let's start at the beginning, shall we?' he said. 'So, now, without putting too fine a point on it, do you believe in God?'

I smiled nervously. 'Er, yes, I suppose so. Well, I don't really know to be honest.'

'Let's make it a bit easier then. Have you ever thought about Him?'

'Yes, a bit. My dad…he was religious. Sort of, anyway.' He'd insisted he married Mum in a church; she'd wanted something quick and simple at the registry office. I remembered her laughing about it when she told me.

'But you personally, you've come to no firm conclusions on whether you believe in His existence?'

'No, I suppose not.' There was a pause. 'It's a bit difficult to believe in something when there's no proof. It's like believing in ghosts.'

'So you're not sure if there is a God or if there isn't, and you're content with that state of mind – not knowing either way?'

'I suppose so.'

'Forgive me, but from what Lucy has told me; you're not an ignorant person. You're intelligent. You think things through; you make decisions based on reasoned judgments. So, am I to believe, that you have chosen to simply *not bother to decide* for yourself whether or not God exists? One of the *most important questions* in life, you've chosen to completely ignore?' His friendly tone and smile were confusing.

'I…well, I haven't ignored it exactly…' I said, quietly.

'So you're agnostic?'

'Yes, I suppose you could say that.'

'You don't know whether or not God exists?'

'No. No I don't.'

'And you're happy, to go through life, not knowing either way?'

'Well, I would rather know I suppose, but I mean, how can I? There's no way of knowing.'

'You're right. There's no way of knowing. Not for sure. And as I'm sure you've worked out, that's why it's called faith. But have you ever prayed for His help? Prayed for Him to give you faith?'

'No.' He looked a bit annoyed. 'I suppose it would feel a bit silly, praying to something I'm not even sure is there.'

'Of course it would. But if you prayed and asked God to give you faith, you'd have nothing to lose, right?'

'I suppose not.'

'So the truth is, you're lazy. Forgive me Emma, if this comes out harshly, but since the answer isn't readily available, you've decided to ignore the whole issue. Turn a blind eye, pretend the matter doesn't even exist. Emma, this might sound a bit brutal, but I would have more respect for you if you told me you were an atheist.'

I was speechless. I looked over at Pete. He was frowning. But Father Gerry had a point – I had been lazy. It was only since I'd met Pete and Lucy that I'd really thought about religion at all. Mum had never talked about it. Dad sometimes mentioned the man upstairs not smiling on him much, but that was as far as it ever went. At school, I'd sung hymns perfectly in tune without the faintest idea what I was singing about.

'But,' I said. I didn't want him to think that I didn't care, that I didn't want to try. 'What can I do about it? I mean, it's not my fault, it's never come up before.'

'Of course not. It's no one's fault. But come now, you're, what? Eighteen? Old enough to drink and to drive, and to vote. And certainly old enough to start to explore the spiritual side of your life.'

'Yes, I suppose so.'

'Lucy tells me you study music. You're a pianist aren't you? But, the first time you saw a piano, did you know how to play it?'

'No.'

'Did you know whether you would enjoy playing it?'

'No.'

'Did you even know whether you would be any good at playing it?'

'No,' I replied. I felt tired, suddenly.

'Exactly. You didn't know. So how did you find out? You took lessons, you read books, you *learnt* about it. And you discovered that, lo and behold, you had a talent for it. A vocation, you could say.'

'Yes.'

'So, I ask you Emma, what's the only way we can discover whether something is right for us? By learning about it. By opening our ears and eyes to the possibilities. It's simple, and the same goes for God.'

'It isn't Emma's fault,' Lucy said, patting me on the knee. 'She hasn't had a religious upbringing. You don't even know anyone religious do you Em? Except for us.'

'Lucy,' Pete said suddenly. 'And Father Gerry. Do you think that I could have a few words with Emma alone? I don't want to be rude, but I'd like to talk to her quickly, just one-to-one.'

'That's a good idea,' Lucy said, standing up. 'I'll make some tea for us all shall I? Father Gerry?'

'Yes, splendid idea. Now Emma you must forgive me for my bullishness, but sometimes it takes strong words to make people face up to themselves, as it were. To help people really understand where they are going wrong. Come on Lucy, I'll show you where the kitchen is. I hear your mother is feeling better.'

The two of them left the room, leaving Pete and I sitting on the sofa.

'Em,' he said, turning to face me. 'I'm sorry about all this. I had no idea that Lucy was planning to unleash him on you like this. I thought we were just going to have a nice, light-hearted chat. He's not normally so take-no-prisoners. I really didn't want you to feel under pressure.'

'Well, he has got a point,' I said. 'I never realised that it was such a bad thing but... I have been lazy, haven't I? I never gave religion a second thought. I've lived selfishly, just worrying about the trivial things...never looking beneath the surface...'

I might cry. It was so easy these days, the tears were so quick to come.

'You haven't done anything wrong. He was hard on you. You're just beginning to realise there's more to life that's all. But I promise you don't have to do anything you don't want to do. If you want to leave, we can. I don't want you to feel pushed into anything. That's not what it's about at all. I'll tell Lucy that you want to leave, and we can go now.'

I smiled at him, grateful for his thoughtfulness.

'No it's fine,' I said. 'I feel better to be honest. All of you are right, it's time I made some decisions about these sorts of things. It's time I grew up a bit.'

Pete's face lit up.

'Would you like to find out more? Do you think that would help? Father Gerry can be a bit brusque but he's great. Really in touch with people, you know, forward-thinking and contemporary. I realise religion probably seems like just a load of rules about how to live your life, but it's not like that. Really. I get out a lot more than I put in. And Lucy and I both know that sometimes, please don't take this the wrong way, but, sometimes you lack inner strength, and it's because you have no relationship with God. Lucy and I, well, we just want to help you, that's all. But please don't feel railroaded into it.'

There was something infectious about the enthusiasm they all shared. I wanted a piece of it too. They were right – there was no harm in it. It could only enrich my life, like learning about anything would. And if it wasn't for me, then fair enough. But it would mean I would be part of their lives. Their beliefs. Everything. I would be included. People would say to me, *Where do you go on Saturday evenings?* and I would say *To mass* and they wouldn't understand. They couldn't. They would be intrigued.

And, perhaps, just perhaps, it would even help resolve the

endless repetition of one question in my mind: was it my fault?

'I'd like to hear more,' I said. 'I don't feel railroaded.'

'Great,' he said, beaming at me.

As if on cue Lucy came back in, followed shortly by Father Gerry, who presented me with my third cup of tea of the day.

'Emma and I have had a chat,' Pete said. 'She was a bit overwhelmed before but she'd like to hear more. Wouldn't you?'

I nodded.

'Good stuff,' said Father Gerry, rubbing his hands together. 'Right, well, I think I should begin by saying that you've made the right decision. You want to live a fulfilling, selfless life, and be rewarded by the richness of heaven.'

I nodded and smiled again.

'Well, the Church is here to help you do that. For today, I think we should talk about the examination of conscience. One of the fundamental parts of being a good Catholic, is knowledge of oneself. You need to look objectively at yourself, and examine your actions and thoughts. Each one of us was born to sin…even me, can you believe?' He gave a carefree wink, before shifting his face back into concentration. 'And we all face a daily struggle to keep those sins to a minimum. So Emma, every night, before you go to bed, I want you to ask yourself this: how have I behaved today? Have I been critical of others? Did I make good use of my time? Did I try to make life pleasant for other people?'

I nodded again, feeling a little like a puppet with all this prompting.

'It's the most important thing. To be aware of yourself, and how the way you behave affects others. Here,' he said, handing me a small red book, which had *Handbook of Prayers* written on the cover in gold letters. 'Take this. There are plenty of prayers in there. To begin with, how about you find one you like, one whose words seem to mean something to you, and say it every night before you go to bed. Concentrate on the words as you read, what they really mean. It'll help. Especially with your grief. And remember, Emma, your father has gone on to a better place. Undoubtedly.'

He smiled encouragingly. He knew nothing about my grief, but I appreciated his efforts.

'Wherever he is now, he'll be looking down, watching you, loving you still. I know you might not believe it at the moment, I know the pain is still raw, but it's true, I promise you.'

'Thank you.' I took the book from him. He did believe it, I could tell.

How wonderful it must be to have that certainty.

Chapter Thirteen

Pete, February 1999

It was the day Peter was going home, and his father was standing on the doorstep waiting for him to get his stuff together, having refused Ruth's offer of a cup of tea. Peter wished his father wasn't so rude. Ruth was rambling on, filling the silence, asking after his health, saying how they were all thinking of him, how Peter had been no trouble at all, and that if he ever needed some time to himself, Peter would be welcome to come and stay again. His dad didn't even say thank you, or smile, like anyone polite would have done. He just grunted and said there would be no need, that the lad would be fine back with him.

Lucy hugged him goodbye, and gave him a picture of the puppies that she'd drawn especially for him. It was a very good drawing and Peter told her so. She smiled bashfully and said she'd see him at mass on Sunday, and then she ran off. So now, it was just him, Ruth and his dad, standing at the doorway. He was going home.

'Bye Ruth,' he mumbled, staring at her waist.

'What kind of gratitude is that, boy?' Bert said, shoving Peter towards Ruth. 'Thank the lady properly.'

'Thank you Ruth. For taking care of me,' Peter said, looking up at her and finding to his surprise she was crying a little.

'Aw pet, that's alright. We've loved having you. Now give me a big hug, and here's some gingerbread for you.'

Pete felt himself squashed against her bosom. She smelt of bread, but he liked it.

On the short walk back to his house, Peter's dad seemed nervous.

'Now lad, listen to me. Things will be different without your mam, of course. So you're going to have to be good, and not give me any trouble. I'm getting Mrs Wilkes from Newbiggin to come in every day, she'll be sorting all the things in the house out, but you're going to have to do your fair share of chores. And I don't want any nonsense.'

'Yes Dad,' Peter said, sniffing the paper towel that enclosed the gingerbread men. They were still warm. He broke the head off one of them and ate it as they walked, but folded the paper back around the rest. He wasn't going to eat them all straight away.

When they got home, Peter was surprised to find that his dad had made him fish fingers and potato waffles. There were no peas though, and he knew his mam wouldn't have been happy about that. She always made a big fuss of him eating his vegetables. But he didn't say anything – he hadn't even known that his father could cook, and he didn't want to mention the peas in case it made him angry. His dad was obviously trying to make an effort. He even asked him if he wanted ketchup or HP.

He didn't know what to say. He'd already had dinner at Lucy's house and he was stuffed. He looked at the fish fingers. They were a bit burnt, but he didn't mind that. Better burnt than soggy. But he knew he couldn't eat it. His tummy was still full of a mammoth portion of shepherd's pie.

'Well, what you sitting there staring at it for? Eat it you soft lad. Before it goes cold.' His dad was on the verge of angry, but not there yet. Peter could tell. He and his mam had had a scale for his father's anger. Points out of five. At the moment, Peter reckoned he was on a 2.

'Dad, I ate already,' Peter said, his voice small.

'What?' The tone of voice told Peter he'd gone up to a 2.5.

'I'm not hungry.'

'You ungrateful.... Where is it?' The tips of his dad's ears were going pink. That was a 3.

'What?'

'The gingerbread the fat woman next door gave you. Where is it? Give it to me!'

'No Dad, you don't understand, it wasn't the gingerbread...'

'Don't you talk back. Give it to me!' Peter wished his mother was there to intervene and calm his dad down.

But it was just the two of them now. Peter passed the small parcel to his father, who snatched it out of his hand and marched straight to the bin, throwing it in with a force that made the bin wobble.

'That'll teach you to spoil your appetite with sweets and cakes. What would Jesus say? How dare you turn your nose up at a perfectly good meal?'

'Dad, I'm sorry, it's just I already...' Peter felt the tears begin, and the anger with himself for crying was only outweighed by the fear of his father's temper.

His dad didn't say anymore, but strode towards him, large and red-faced. For a second, Peter thought he was going to get walloped, but his dad simply gripped the back of Peter's head and pushed it down into the plate, shaking it from side to side until Peter's nose and eyes were full of hot, mushed-up fish and potato. He felt the skin on his face burning, and when he tried to scream, his dad let him up for air.

'Now say Grace,' he shouted.

Peter shook, but somehow found the words. 'Bless us, O Lord, and these thy gifts which we are about to receive from thy bounty, through Christ our Lord. Amen.'

His dad paused for a few minutes, and then picked up great handfuls of the mashed-up food and pushed them into Peter's mouth.

'Swallow!' he commanded, and Peter did as he was told.

Chapter Fourteen

Emma, December 2010

It was the fourth lecture in a row in which he'd sat next to me, which meant it was definitely more than pure coincidence. He must have *chosen* to sit there. The lecture theatre was big; it could easily seat sixty people, yet there were only eighteen in this group. He could have had an entire row to himself, if he'd wanted. Most people chose to sit at the back, as though sitting as far from the tutor as possible offered them some sort of street cred. It amused me. A group of about eight of them clearly knew each other well now, and they tittered and giggled their way through each lecture. Maybe they'd been housed together and that was why they were so close. Not for the first time, I wondered who had chosen to lump me in with Maria and Amelia and Sam. Clearly someone with a perverse sense of humour.

I looked over at him. He had a notebook on the desk, and was jotting something down in it, but he didn't really look as though he was listening. Every now and then, he rested his forehead on his palm, rubbing his fingers into his dark hair. I'd only ever caught his eye once, and had noticed the wideness of his nose – something that marked him a few notches down from handsome. There were two spare seats between us. Perhaps he thought sitting right next to me would have been an invasion of my personal space. We were the two losers in the third row. We had to write our names down on a piece of paper at the beginning of the lecture – some kind of futile record of attendance – but it had always been me that handed it to him. So although he knew mine, I had no idea what his was.

I should say something. Anything. Hello even. What was the worst that could happen? It was becoming embarrassing. I'd been at uni for nearly three months, yet I still hadn't spoken to a single person on my course. I'd never imagined it would be this hard to make friends. No one else seemed to be having the same trouble.

Professor Ryan droned on, clearly as bored as we were. It must have been so depressing for him, spouting out the same old crap year in, year out, to a bunch of first years who knew it didn't really matter if they did no work at all this year, provided they scraped through their exams.

At the end of the lecture, I gathered my things together. My phone was lit up as usual. Three missed calls, only one voicemail this time. I decided to say something to the boy with dark hair. He wouldn't ignore me, no one would be that rude. Even a quick 'Hello' would be progress. As soon as the whispering crowd at the back had left the lecture theatre, I would make my move. I looked over at him. He was still scribbling in his notebook. Maybe he had been listening after all. I didn't want to interrupt him at full flow. I lingered for a few minutes, fiddling with my pencil case.

'Hey Emma,' a voice called. I looked up. Pete was standing near the podium at the front of the theatre.

'Pete,' I said, confused. When had he come in?

'I was just leaving my lecture in number 18 and saw you through the window. What you up to now? Do you fancy getting a drink?'

I glanced across at the boy. He was packing up now. Our eyes met briefly. His lips twitched into a tiny smile of understanding, and then he quickly left the room.

'Not up to anything,' I said to Pete. Everyone else had left. It didn't matter; I didn't need friends on my course anyway. I had Pete. It was quality not quantity that counted. 'Let's get a drink.'

~

We wandered to the Old Bar, as usual. I didn't like it much. It was eponymously old, of course, and smelly, and windowless, being in the basement of the Union. A Leeds institution apparently. Stuffed with fruit machines, rickety stools and televisions in every corner, blasting out endless boring live sports, invariably football. I wondered why everyone at the uni seemed so proud of it. Another part of celebrated Leeds uni life that I just couldn't understand.

'So how are you?' Pete asked when he returned from the bar with a Coke for me and a pint of something for him.

'Good thanks,' I replied, vaguely.

'How's the preparation been going?'

He meant for my upcoming baptism. I'd been studying morning, noon and night for it. Far harder than I'd worked on any of my coursework. There was a surprising amount of work involved in finding the Lord.

'Yeah, OK, I think,' I said. 'Lots to learn. It's very interesting though.' I didn't want to let him down.

'Just a week to go, and you'll be a Catholic. I'm excited for you.'

'Thanks,' I replied. 'Me too.'

'Have you told the others?'

I looked down at the heavily varnished table. Someone had carved 'CD ARM' into the wood. Romantic vandalism.

'No,' I said. 'I haven't mentioned it yet. Do you think I should?'

'Well...' He stared across at me, trying to gauge my thoughts. He mustn't think I was ashamed of it, that I wasn't sincere.

'The thing is, Maria's pregnant, so everyone is...' I blurted out. Bugger. Was it a secret? Shame at my lack of discretion descended on me.

Pete's eyes widened.

'Goodness, poor girl. Who's the father? We've only been at uni for three months.'

'I know. It's her ex-boyfriend's. The one she broke up with just before she came to Leeds.'

'Poor Maria. What's she going to do? Move back to her parents'?'

I frowned. 'No. I think she's going to have an abortion. At least, Amelia seems to think she will. You know Maria's really bright. I think she's decided it's the best thing to do. Instead of messing up her course.'

'Well, it's very brave of her,' Pete said. 'It's a horrible thing to have to do.'

'I know.'

'Makes me a bit uneasy to be honest. Imagine the guilt you'd feel afterwards. Knowing that you'd prevented the child from its chance to live. It doesn't seem like Maria, somehow. Not when she's so passionate about animal rights and everything. I just can't see her doing it.'

I thought of Maria, in her beagle costume and resisted the urge to laugh. It wasn't funny. 'When you put it like that, it is a bit weird.'

'I just feel sorry for them both. The baby especially I guess. It didn't ask to be created. It's just sitting there, growing away, waiting to be born. Seems unfair, somehow.'

'I suppose. But there's not much we can do about it, is there?'

Pete reached across the table for my hand. 'Probably not. But you know what? We can try.'

~

My first communion. The wafer didn't taste of anything. It disintegrated quickly on my tongue in a rather underwhelming manner. It was meant to be the body of Christ. As I bowed my head to receive it, it struck me that I still didn't believe in the concept of, what was it called again? Transubstantiation. Not really. I wanted to though. My faith was still young, Pete kept telling me. It would strengthen with time, and, presumably, with many more communion wafers. I took the tiniest sip of wine –

there were lots of us getting confirmed that day and it didn't seem as though there was much in the heavy silver chalice to go round. It tasted of Ribena – sweet, thick and sickly, like cough syrup. There was something uncomfortably unhygienic about drinking from the same cup as all these people. The priest especially, whose bottom lip had an unattractive tendency to hang down, wet and slimy, wobbling as he boomed the sacred words, filling the church, bouncing off the icons, statues and thick columns. This is the cup of my blood, the blood of the new and everlasting covenant, which will be shed for you and for others, so that sins may be forgiven. Out of the corner of my eye, I could see Lucy and Pete in the front row behind me. If I turned around right now, would they wave? I suppressed a giggle. This was a serious situation. I was becoming one of them.

I would now *belong*.

I smiled. It had all happened so quickly. I thought the process would take years. But Pete and Lucy knew people in high places and it was only a matter of weeks before I was a full Catholic. At the back of my mind, disloyal doubts that I had gone through the procedure properly surfaced. Maybe if I had, I would have really believed that the wafer and wine were fragments of the Lord's body. Maybe. Or maybe it just took time. Did it matter if I truly believed anyway? Wasn't it enough that I wanted to?

After the service, people I didn't know smiled and congratulated me – even the priest. Lucy hugged me tight, for such a long time I could have taken a nap on her shoulder. She smelt of apples: I couldn't tell whether it was her shampoo or her perfume. Pete hung back as the others crowded around me, but eventually handed me a small box, inside which I discovered a long rosary. The stones were black and shiny. They reminded me of a necklace I had once bought from Topshop but I didn't tell him that. I thanked him and promised I would use it.

As we left the church, walking down the aisle to greet the heavy snow outside, I heard the heavy chords of the middle of

Chopin's Raindrop Prelude playing somewhere in the vicinity. It irritated me. They were dark, melancholy notes, fitting in with each step I took towards the exit, entirely inappropriate for what was meant to be a glorious occasion. I turned around. In the corner of the church, at the small battered upright, a man was hammering out each chord. Thumping them out, with no respect for the subtleties of the piece's dynamics. What was he doing? Playing Chopin in a church? So soon after mass. And so badly!

I frowned at him, but he was engrossed and did not notice.

~

'Where have you three been?' Sam asked as we piled through the door to our flat. My hands were so cold they ached. I giggled as I cupped them in front of my mouth and blew on them to try to warm them up.

'Emma?' Sam asked. 'Are you...*drunk*?'

'No!' I said. I was happy. Not drunk. It amused me that Sam might confuse the two, and I giggled a bit more.

'She is a little,' Lucy replied. 'We've been out celebrating. Hello, I don't think we've met properly, have we? I'm Lucy, Peter's girlfriend.

'Well, hello,' Sam said, taking her hand. He glanced sideways at Pete, who as usual was doing his best job of subtly ignoring him. I wondered if Sam had picked up on the fact that Pete couldn't stand him. Probably not. He was even more self-assured than Amelia. 'I've heard so much about you, Miss Lucy. Pete's a lucky man.'

Lucy smiled. 'Well, I wouldn't say that.' She put her arm around Pete's waist and beamed up at him. Pete stared ahead, at the kitchen door. 'I think I'm the lucky one.'

'Hmmm,' Sam said. There was something about the noise; something that gave away everything yet nothing at the same time. Perhaps I was wrong, perhaps he knew only too well what

Pete thought of him. 'So, what have you been celebrating exactly?'

'Let's go and make some tea,' Pete interrupted.

'Emma's baptism!' Lucy cried, turning to squeeze me round the waist too.

Sam raised an eyebrow. There was an excruciating pause.

'Her...*baptism*?' The word was loaded with sarcasm. I looked helplessly at Pete, who frowned at me unfairly. It wasn't my fault. I hadn't blabbed. It was Lucy. Why wasn't he frowning at her?

'Yes,' Lucy said, happily. She was so stupid. How could she be so utterly oblivious to the tension between us all?

'Well.' Sam seemed lost for words but I knew he wasn't. This was pure gold for him. Perhaps I should just slip away to my bedroom now. I looked at my watch. It was quarter past five, which in student land meant it was the perfect time for a nap.

'I might just...' I began, but my window of opportunity was slammed shut.

'Emma's baptism indeed!' Sam said, loudly, pulling me towards him by the wrist. 'Well, well, well. I must tell the others. Come on, let's go and share the good news with Maria and Amelia.'

'Yes,' Lucy smiled. 'Why not? I'm sure they'll be pleased for Emma too.' I caught Pete's eye again. He wasn't frowning any more; he just looked resigned. Fed up. Bored, even. Lucy might have been beautiful, kind and gentle, but she was clueless and irritating too. A little voice in my head whispered: *Emma – one, Lucy – nil.*

Sam strode off down the corridor, into the kitchen and we trailed behind him. Maria was sitting at the table, her chin propped up with one hand, Amelia, next to her, rubbing her back. Sam didn't seem to care that he'd interrupted them in the middle of a heart-to-heart.

'Great news, girls!' he exclaimed, pulling up a chair beside them and sitting on it the wrong way round, like he always did. Maria frowned. She wasn't crying, but she looked unhappy. The way Sam had blundered in made it clear he had no idea about her pregnancy. So Amelia had chosen to tell me, but not him. There was some significance there, but my brain was too focused on trying to prevent the imminent car crash to work out what it was.

'What, Sam?' Amelia asked.

'Emma's just come back from church! She's seen the light! Been baptised! Would you believe? I told you Pete was determined to help our Emma.' His voice slowed to a drawl. 'Told you he had her *best interests at heart*.'

'What?' Amelia looked at me searchingly.

'Er, yes,' I replied. 'But let's not go into...'

Sam began to make the sign of the cross. 'In the name of the Father, the Son...'

'That's enough thanks Sam,' Pete said, shooting him a look of measured fury.

Lucy looked a bit puzzled.

'It's a wonderful thing,' she said, quietly. 'Not something to mock.'

Sam looked sheepish for a second, then indignant. 'Of course it is. I wouldn't *dream* of mocking something like that. I'm Catholic myself, you see.'

Lucy's face relaxed. 'Really?'

'Oh yes,' he replied. 'Catholic born and bred. Half Irish in fact.'

'Sam, shut up,' Amelia snapped.

'I am,' he insisted. 'I was even a choir boy at school. I tell you what, those priests, they aren't half...'

'Sam, for fuck's sake,' Amelia shouted.

Pete grabbed Lucy's arm. 'Come on,' he said. 'Let's leave them to it.'

She looked as though she might cry.

'See you later then Emma,' she said, following him out of the kitchen.

'Sam you're an arsehole,' Amelia hissed once the door had shut behind them.

'What?' he said, holding his hands up in feigned innocence.

'You're a bloody wanker,' she said. 'For fuck's sake.'

'I honestly don't know what you're talking about,' he replied.

Maria sniffed. 'Is it true?' she said, looking straight at me.

'Yes,' I replied. My head started to hurt. I felt abandoned, weak, unable to defend the controversial decision I'd made. I hated Pete for leaving me here with them all. For taking his precious Lucy away from the cynical stares, leaving me to diffuse them on my own.

'But why?' Amelia asked. 'Why Em?'

'Because,' I answered, pathetically. 'Just, because OK? Because it made sense to me. So stop judging me.'

'It won't help you win him over you know,' Amelia said. Her voice was gentle: sympathetic without being patronising. 'I hope that's not why you did it. Those two… they're meant for each other.'

'Can we change the subject?' I snapped.

Sam started to flick through a copy of the previous week's *Leeds Student*. He'd had his fun, he was bored now. At that moment, I hated him almost as much as I hated my father.

'Yes,' Amelia replied. 'But…seriously, it seems a bit…drastic. To change your religion. You're sure he didn't force you into it?'

'No!' I said, loudly. 'Of course not. What do you take me for? It was my decision. Honestly. Anyway, I think we should talk about something else.'

'OK, OK,' Amelia said. She looked a bit sad. 'So long as you're sure.'

She got up and switched the kettle on. I looked down at the back of Sam's head and pondered whether it was immaturity or a problem-free life that made everything a joke to him. For a brief moment, I wished we could trade places.

Then, without warning, Maria stood up, walked towards me and put her arms around my shoulders, silently pulling me towards her in a hug. I had no idea what the gesture meant, but I hugged her back all the same.

Chapter Fifteen

Emma, December 2010

Beethoven's Moonlight Sonata was probably his most overplayed, but it didn't stop it from being my favourite. The third movement at least: for me, playing it was the equivalent of smashing a whole dinner service against a wall. I'd first learnt it when I was about 13, and played it incessantly after Dad's death, much to Mum's distress. *Try something more cheerful,* she would implore me, but I didn't care. There was something about the *Presto agitato* that enthralled me, and I never got bored of playing it, trying each time to get the arpeggios even faster. I would play it until the tips of my fingers were bruised and my wrists ached. It was the only way I could feel any kind of release from the confusion in my head.

She had called me three times that morning, left three messages imploring me to get in touch. The final one had included a brief mention of their cat being recently diagnosed with cancer, which enraged me. It was a low-handed attempt at guilt-tripping me into returning the call. In response I marched straight to the practice rooms and let rip on the small Japanese Kawai upright in the practice room. I didn't need the music; the notes were indelibly inscribed on the tips of my fingers. I played the piece over and over; noticing with amusement bewildered other students peering through the window at me, probably wondering if it was the only thing I could play. I glared back, completely immersed in the anger of the piece, my body swaying with the aggression of the music.

I was midway through the trill on the last page when I glanced up and spotted him. Standing outside the room, his face close to the window, watching me. I carried on playing the last few bars, although my concentration was lost and the arpeggios were stilted and overplayed. As I lifted my hands from the final chord – played far too loudly – I noticed that I was shaking.

'Bravo!' Pete cried, clapping his hands. 'I'm impressed Emma. That was incredible. You really are talented.'

'That was terrible actually,' I said, panting slightly and staring down at the keys. 'My tutor would have been horrified. I murdered the last page.'

'Well I'm no musician, but I thought it was wonderful. The emotion on your face as you played it, well, it took my breath away.'

I smiled.

'I don't want to disturb you. I just came to give you this.'

He handed me a dark green carrier bag. Reaching inside, my hands closed around a something plastic and oval shaped. I pulled it out. A tiny plastic baby sat neatly in the palm of my hand, its head almost as large as the rest of its body, its legs and arms curled up around it. On one side of the head was a minute, black eye, staring up at me.

'What is it?' I asked.

'It's a plastic foetus. The same size as the one Maria wants to abort.'

'Why are you giving it to me?' I said, stuffing it back in the bag and handing it back to him. 'What am I meant to do with it?'

He wouldn't take the bag from me. 'I don't know. I just thought it would help. I think she might be making a mistake…I know it's none of our business, but I just think it might help. You know, get her to think about the other side of the story. About the baby's point of view. I thought maybe you could leave it outside her room.'

'Pete,' I said quietly, shaking my head. 'I can't. It's awful. You do it. If it means so much to you, you do it.'

'She won't know it was you. You could just put it outside her room, or plant it in her handbag or wherever she'll be likely to find it. She won't know who put it there.'

'Well if she won't know, what difference does it make if I do it or if you do it?'

He was silent for a while.

'OK,' he said. 'You're right. I'm sorry. It's alright, I'll do it. I'll talk to her. Just forget I ever mentioned it.'

Reverse psychology. Did he think I was stupid?

I looked again inside the bag. Maria's face came to my mind. I couldn't let her see this freak baby. It was too cruel. Pete was passionate, trying to do the right thing. I admired his dedication but this was going too far. It wasn't his place to try to influence her on something like this. He shouldn't have even known about it – it was only because of my big mouth that he did.

'No,' I said. 'It's OK. I'll do it.'

That's great,' he said. 'I'm proud of you. Now, I'll leave you to your music.'

With that he walked away, turning to smile again through the glass in the door as he left. I waited till he was out of sight, then scanned the tiny room for a bin. There wasn't one, so I carefully placed the baby in the bag into my rucksack, determined to dispose of it as soon as possible.

~

It was dinner time, and for the first time in a while we were all in the kitchen, except for Pete, who I suspected was at Mass. Amelia was being her usual coquettish self.

'So how are we all?' she chirped, tucking into some Marmite on toast and resting her feet on the chair next to her. She was so cute. Like a tiny Russian doll.

Ferociously, I attempted to scour some burnt pasta from my one and only saucepan, destroying the washing-up sponge in the process.

'Fine,' I muttered. 'If only I could get this pasta off. Urgggh, it's – so – tough.'

Amelia laughed. 'Don't bother, if it's that hard to remove, it's hardly likely to come off when you next cook in it is it? Leave it! It'll add to the flavour.'

Sam threw one of his prawn cocktail crisps at Amelia's pretty round face.

'Did anyone ever tell you, Amelia, that you are a minger?' he said. 'With a capital 'M''

She poked her tongue out at him. 'Oh sod off you big poof!'

'Anyway,' he continued, scrunching up the packet and throwing it at the overflowing bin, missing it completely. 'I've got some gossip actually.'

'Oh yes?' Amelia said, her eyes lighting up in anticipation. 'Spill!'

'Well, I'm not sure I should to be honest with you. Don't want to upset the washerwoman.'

I turned round to check. Yes, he was referring to me.

'Emma?' Amelia snorted. 'Why, it's not gossip about Pete is it? Can't be very interesting if it is.'

'What is it?' I asked, shaking my head to flick my hair out of my eyes, my hands still immersed in soapsuds.

'Well,' he said, drawing it out for as long as possible. 'Last night, I went to a rather fantastic night actually, at the Underground – have you been there? Wicked crowd.'

'Have I been there?' Amelia rolled her eyes. 'Of course I've bloody been there. Only like six times. It's got really low ceilings. Sweat dripping off the walls and all that. I don't think, actually, that there is a single nightclub in Leeds that I haven't been to.'

'Ooh get you. You're just SO popular and cool. Loser,' he said, grinning. 'Anyway, while I was there, I got chatting to a very nice young lady.'

'I keep reminding you darling, you're gay. That means you're supposed to chat to very nice young men, not women,' said Amelia.

Over in the corner of the kitchen, neatly slicing an apple, Maria giggled. I stamped my foot with impatience.

'Sam,' I said.

'OK, OK. Anyway it turns out that this lovely young lady, Laura her name was, is in her first year of Economics and Statistics.'

'Big deal,' Amelia said. 'So she does the same course as Pete. Wow. How fascinating. Write to *Heat* magazine, I'm sure they'll put it on this week's cover.'

My phone started to ring. Amelia picked it up and looked at the screen. 'Emma,' she said, 'it's your mum again.'

'Ignore it, I'll call her later,' I lied, turning round. She frowned at me but put it back on the table. Mum was making me look pathetic by calling all the time.

'Anyway,' Sam continued, 'as I was saying...Laura bumped into Pete in town the other day.'

'And?' Amelia interrupted. 'Get on with it!'

'And...he was shopping. For a ring. An engagement ring.'

'Seriously?' Amelia giggled. 'Oh my god. He's going to ask Lucy to marry him! Jesus! What's *wrong* with them? Don't they like being young and responsibility free? Weirdos!' Then, she remembered me, and a look of guilty sympathy crossed her face. The others noticed, but said nothing.

I turned back to my saucepan with its tar-like coating. Bits of sponge came away in my hand. The silence was unbearable. They were all sitting there, feeling sorry for me. So Pete and Lucy were going to get engaged. It wasn't exactly a surprise. Why didn't one of them say something? I suppose they expected me to run out of the room in tears.

Someone coughed. Amelia stood up and carried her plate to the bin.

'While I've got you all here,' she said, staring down at the mixture of carrot and potato peelings stuffed in between takeaway pizza boxes, coke cans, beer cans and empty bottles of Barcardi Breezer. 'This is disgusting! Can we please get some kind of rota or something going? Not only does the bin smell really bad, it's also dead annoying that it always seems to be me that can't stuff my rubbish in it because it's overflowing.'

She pointed to a large empty Crunchy Nut Cornflake packet that someone had left by the side of the bin, now itself jammed full of apple cores, dried-up tea bags and KitKat wrappers.

'And this! This, is NOT a bin! What is the point of putting things *next* to the bloody bin! Not IN the bin! SO lazy. Fold up the cardboard! Are you all trying to create some group of weird mini bins? I know what happens, tomorrow someone else will finish their box of Sugar Puffs or whatever and leave that one by the bin too. And then, someone will start filling that up with crap as well! And eventually, they'll take over the world! Used-up cereal boxes full of toxic waste. Urggh. And don't you lot laugh at me, it's NOT funny.'

'Fair point,' Maria said, coming to her side. 'It is gross. Here, I'll help you, let's get a binliner.'

'Thanks,' Amelia said.

I gave up on the saucepan and tore off the Marigolds. Water had found its way inside them and my hands were itchy.

'What's this?'

Turning around, I saw Maria holding the plastic baby in the air by its bottom, onion peelings hanging off it like shedding skin.

'God, what is it?' Amelia said, peering in for a closer look and flicking off the onion. 'Urggh, it looks like some kind of creepy doll, with a big head. Like an alien. Weird.'

Panic rose within me. 'Oh. You weren't meant to...' I blurted out. I reached forward to grab it from her, but Maria held on to it.

'It's yours?' Maria asked. She looked confused for a second, then hurt.

'I'm sorry...I thought it was...'

'What?' she asked. Her right hand was wrapped firmly around the baby's body, one scarily long fingernail digging into its eye.

'It's...' I stopped. There was no explanation. They all stared at me.

'Yours?' Maria repeated.

'Yes. No, it was...'

'What's it for?' Sam asked. He looked mystified. I imagined his opinion of me as an utter weirdo fortifying.

'It's... Look, you weren't meant to find it,' I said, feebly. My eyes flicked over to Amelia, but she was looking at her feet.

'Why did you have it?' Maria asked. 'And why's it in the kitchen bin?'

'I thought it was squashed down enough. You weren't meant to find it.' My voice was small, pathetic.

'Oh really?' Maria asked. She spoke over me. Her sarcastic tone was unfamiliar. 'I wasn't meant to find it. What did you have it for then? If I wasn't meant to find it?'

'I thought... It wasn't my...'

'You bitch,' she hissed.

'Hey Maria,' Sam said. 'Calm down. What is it anyway?'

'I'll tell you what it is,' Maria shouted, rounding on Sam. 'It's a model of a foetus. That's right isn't it Emma?'

'Um...'

'Why did you get it Emma? For me, right?'

'Yes... But I changed my...'

'A model of a foetus?' Sam interrupted.

'Yes,' Maria replied. 'It's a sick tool anti-abortionists use. Look.'

She threw it at the table. It skidded and came to a halt next to Sam's mug, leaving a trail of brown slime in its wake.

'It's got miniature feet and legs and a great big, out-of-proportion head just to remind you what your unwanted baby actually looks like.'

'Yuck,' Sam said, wrinkling up his nose. 'That's just bloody weird. God it's looking at me. Take it away.'

'It's not funny,' Amelia said, putting her arms around Maria.

'Emma, how could you? It's so insensitive.'

'Look, I threw it away. I didn't want her to find it. Honestly,' I said. I didn't move though.

'I can't have this baby,' Maria was crying. 'I can't.'

'Just get lost Emma,' Amelia said, hugging Maria even tighter. 'Seriously. Go away.'

I left the room, picking my phone up from the table on the way out, feeling ashamed and embarrassed. But to my surprise, my feelings of shame didn't last long, and as I sat in my room, staring down at the grey car park, I began to feel something else. Pride. The way she had burst into tears…it was obvious she still had doubts. Perhaps I had actually got through to her.

That night, before I fell asleep, a wave of satisfaction rippled through me. My actions, inadvertent though they were, might have helped save a life, to replace the one I'd destroyed. That would leave me quits. It felt like fate, my destiny. And Pete and Lucy would be so impressed if Maria kept the baby. Was it the sort of thing I could bring up in confession? Probably best not to boast about these things.

The next morning, I left my room with my head held high. As I walked towards the front door, Maria came out of her room. She had swollen, bloodshot eyes and an angry red nose.

'Going to uni?' she asked, sniffing slightly.

I nodded, a little frightened. The pride I'd felt the night before evaporated at the sight of her face, so different from the carefree one I'd shared a bus ride with during freshers' week.

'Have a good day,' she said.

I started to walk onwards but she reached out her hand to stop me.

'Oh and Emma,' she said, smiling through gritted teeth. Her eyes were dark with anger. 'Seeing as you decided it was your business, perhaps you'd like to know… I'm having the abortion today. I just wanted to thank you for making the most traumatic experience of my life even worse.'

Chapter Sixteen

Emma, December 2010

It turned unseasonably warm in the last week of term. It was 13°C on the day that Lucy came down to Leeds for the last weekend before Christmas. Pete attributed the mild weather to Lucy's presence.

'You always bring good weather with you Luce,' he said, pressing his face against her shiny hair on the crowded platform at Leeds station. 'I reckon it's all thanks to your name. Lucy, bringer of light.'

'It's hardly tropical,' I said. Was it the physical affection or the ring secreted in the inside pocket of his coat that was inflaming my jealousy? This was depression at its most bitter. I was an outsider, a hanger-on. Should I simply vanish into thin air, at that point, neither of them would notice.

'Warmer than home though,' Lucy said, characteristically positive. She put her arms around me and I responded with a hug flavoured with regret at my snideness. It wasn't her fault I had a crush on her boyfriend, after all.

We went straight to the cathedral church for Saturday evening Mass. We were early and Lucy went to speak to the priest. It was the second week of advent and I was surprised when, midway through the service, she got up and lit the second candle on the wreath. Pete wore a lazy smile on his face as he watched her make her way up the aisle to the altar and as the wick was illuminated, his face glowed with a possessive pride. He was like a proud father watching his child play the lead role in a school production.

It was Lucy's idea to go to TGI Friday's after – and since it was just outside the centre of town, we took a taxi to the ubiquitous restaurant as a treat. Lucy was inordinately excited about going there.

'I'm going to have a burger, with cheese and bacon,' she said, sounding about six years old. 'And a chocolate milkshake. I love TGI Fridays. I suppose having dinner there is the closest I'll ever get to America.'

'I've been to America,' I said, staring out of the window of the taxi.

'Have you?' Lucy said, leaning forward to make eye contact with me over Pete, who was sandwiched between the two of us in the back of the cab. 'You're so lucky. Whereabouts?'

'Florida. When I was about 14. We went to Disney World and all that. It was good. My dad was obsessed with foreign holidays. We went everywhere. Shame he wasn't quite so keen on saving up enough money to pay for them though.'

She ignored my comment. 'If I have children, I'll definitely take them to Disney World,' Lucy said.

I glanced up at Pete, but he didn't appear to be listening.

Pete insisted on a table by the window even though the view was only of the busy car park, and we sat in silence for a few minutes, each staring at the garish menus in front of us.

'Can you order the barbecue chicken for me, and a Coke?' I asked. 'I'm just going to the toilet.'

I stared at myself in the toilet mirror. Would Lucy be more sympathetic about the plastic baby incident? Pete kept telling me it was all part of a Catholic's struggle – people not understanding you. He said I should stop worrying about myself, that Maria would forgive me eventually. She'd been refusing to talk to me and Amelia, while still her usual chirpy self, had obviously re-assessed her opinion of me. I was no longer a friend, merely an acquaintance – a burden of a flatmate to be endured. It was a relief to be in the company of people who didn't think I was mad, or evil. I smiled at my reflection, my heart lifting ever-so-slightly at the thought of sharing my pain with a sympathetic ear.

I walked towards the table. The menus were gone and Pete and Lucy were talking quietly, their heads and their hands pushed together, as if they were leaning on one another.

'What's the big secret?' I asked as I sat down, grabbing my napkin from the wine glass and almost knocking it over in the process.

'We wanted to tell you together...' Lucy said. 'It's so exciting and you're such a good friend to us both. It's, well, the best news in the world. We're engaged!'

'I asked Lucy over the phone last night,' Pete said. 'After speaking to her father first of course.'

Lucy waved her left hand in front of my face. Something sparkled. It was moving too quickly for me to be sure, but it didn't look very big.

'You asked her over the phone?' I asked Pete. It was the first thought that had come to me.

'Oh I know what you're thinking. Not the most romantic of ways,' Lucy said, beaming. 'But I don't care how he asked me! I'm so happy. Aren't you happy for us?'

'Yes,' I said. 'Congratulations! I'm sorry. I wasn't expecting that. I'm...a bit distracted, sorry. That's, er, fantastic news.'

'We're going to get married on the third of January, before Peter has to come back to uni. You'll come to the wedding won't you? It's going to be in the church in Cresswell of course, and then we'll have a small party back at my house. Or maybe Peter's, if his dad will let us.'

I made some brief calculations in my head. 'But that's only three weeks away!' I said. 'Why the rush? Surely it's not possible to organise a wedding that quickly?'

'I know, I know. We should really have marriage classes first. We won't have much time for them, but Father Gerry's fine about it. He's going to give us three days' intense teaching just before Christmas. It's so good of him. I know he's busy at this time of year too, but he's a close friend and I think he's really happy to help us out. We just didn't want to wait, did we Peter? Well, Peter didn't want to wait. He's always in a hurry. So impatient, aren't you?'

Bile rose in my throat. And there was no way out – a huge plate of chicken wings and chips had just arrived.

'I didn't mean that it wasn't enough time to have marriage classes or whatever,' I said. 'I meant...three weeks? To organise a wedding? What about your dress? The rings? All that stuff?'

'Oh I'm not worried about all that. It's sweet of you to be concerned. It doesn't matter what I wear does it? I'll go into Newcastle with my mam next week and have a look for something. And we're going to choose the wedding rings tomorrow. Want to come with us? I know you shouldn't really go shopping on a Sunday but I think God would let us off for this one.'

'I can't,' I said, staring numbly at the greasy lumps of chicken in front of me. 'I've got some things I need to sort out before I go home next week.'

'Cheer up Emma,' Pete said, reaching over and taking one of my chips. 'We rather fancy you with Joe, don't we Luce?'

'Oh Peter, stop it. Leave her alone. Emma's OK, she's happy as she is. Aren't you?'

'I guess so,' I replied.

There was no point in continuing to stare at them. They weren't about to tell me it had all been a joke, that really it was me and Pete getting married. And the question I really wanted the answer to: *Why now?*, I was too scared to ask.

I cut a small sliver of brown meat from one of the chicken wings, and put it in my mouth. It was hot, and burnt the insides of my cheeks, but I continued chewing until it disappeared.

PART TWO

Chapter Seventeen

Pete, March 1999

By the time Peter had been home for a week, he'd learnt how to handle his father. The most important thing, he realised, was not to get in his way, and the best way of doing that was by avoiding him as much as possible. Peter would come home from school, eat his dinner with his dad while the six o'clock news was on, and then go and do his homework and then go to bed. In the three hours between coming home from school and going to bed, Peter didn't really need to speak to his father at all, except to thank him for dinner, and to ask him if there were any chores that needed doing. On the nights that he wet the bed, Peter made sure he had the sheets washed and hung up to dry before his father had a chance to notice. That way, his father never got above a two on the anger scale.

Peter found it strange how it was easier to get along with his father now his mother had gone. It was as though her presence was what infuriated him in the first place, and Peter had just got in the way. He missed his mam though, and he missed telling her about his day. She used to sit him up on the stool in the kitchen and listen to him talk about Lucy or his teachers or his lessons while she cooked dinner. He missed that. But other than that, he was relieved that life had been bearable since the fish-fingers-in-his-face incident.

One windy Thursday, he came home in a very good mood, because his teacher had singled his last essay out as being the best in the class. It was about his favourite season – autumn – and he didn't actually think it was very good himself, but that didn't matter, because he wasn't the teacher. He'd had to read it out to the rest of the class, and Lucy had watched him, clearly entranced by his story of a baby squirrel asking his mother why the leaves had fallen from the trees, and he'd felt proud of his cleverness.

He was in such a good mood, he was humming when he came in the front door, and he didn't even realise it. He was shocked, therefore, to find his father sitting on the bottom of the stairs in the hall, frowning and holding a small black box in his hands.

'He...hello Dad,' he stammered, hanging his coat up on the iron hooks by the door.

'Singing?' his father asked.

'Um, sorry.' Peter wondered if he could just walk straight past his dad and go into the kitchen, or whether he should ask him if he was alright or something.

'Do you know what this is?' his dad asked, shaking the box at him. His voice was low, lower than usual. More like a growl.

'Er, no, Dad. No I don't.'

'This,' he said, with a pause, 'this... is your mam.'

Peter thought for a second that his father had lost his mind. There was something about the way he was looking at him. He wondered what he wanted him to say.

'My...my mam?' That was all he could think of.

'Yes, your useless, pathetic, weak mother.' He tossed the box into the air and caught it. He did it again. Peter didn't understand.

'What shall we do with her?' he asked Peter.

'I don't understand Dad,' Peter said, feeling the urge to go to the toilet.

'Well, I'm sure she doesn't want to be kept in this tiny little box. Shall we set her free? That's what she always wanted you know. To be free. Free of me. And you.'

'I don't understand. How can Mam be in that box? She's dead.' He surprised himself with his own boldness.

'What's left of her. Idiot. Her ashes. What's left of her now her body has been burnt and ground up into dust.'

Peter's mouth fell open.

'Not much to her, is there?' His father laughed. 'She always was a skinny little mare.'

Peter began to jig from one foot to the other; scared his bladder might let him down.

'What's the matter with you?' his dad said. 'Need the toilet? Alright then.'

He stood up, grabbed Peter by the arm, and dragged him outside to the garden.

'Her precious bloody garden,' he hissed, looking around. 'Let's put her in her precious garden.'

It was cold, and Peter's arm hurt where his father was yanking it. He pulled Peter along to the back of the garden, in amongst the shrubs, where the compost heap was hidden. There was a pile of fresh manure on the top, deposited there a few days ago by the farmer whose land bordered their garden, and it stank.

'Here we go,' Peter's dad said, stopping just beside it. 'Perfect place for her.'

He opened the box and tipped the contents on top of the manure.

'She'll feel right at home there, among the rest of the rubbish.'

Peter began to cry. He knew this was wrong, very wrong.

'Still need to go?' his dad asked.

Peter nodded through his tears. Perhaps if he kept quiet, and didn't make a fuss, his dad would let him run back to the house, where he could try to forget about what had just happened.

'Right then.' His father grabbed Peter's trousers and pulled them down, along with his underwear, exposing his willy. Peter felt humiliated and terrified. 'Go on, then. What are you waiting for? Take your piss. Here. On top of your stupid, wretched, bitch of a mother.'

'Dad!' he cried, staring at the small pile of light grey dust that had landed on the side of the compost.

'Do it, or I'll smack your backside so hard, you'll never be able to sit down again.'

He closed his eyes, and as he urinated, he repeated in his head what the mammy squirrel had told the baby squirrel about the bare trees: *It won't always be like this. It won't always be like this.*

Chapter Eighteen

Emma, January 2011

The night before the wedding, I dreamt it was me getting married. I glided up the aisle wearing a white dress that completely covered my feet, giving the impression that I was walking on air. My hair fell across my shoulders in immaculate golden ringlets. In the dream, it was long, almost reaching my waist – far longer than my hair in reality. A single child's voice rang out across the church, pure and clear. I felt weightless and beautiful as I made my way towards Pete, heads turned as I passed them, and I absorbed the guests' adoration and envy in the whispers and wide eyes. When I reached the altar, I kneeled, in one precise fluid movement, and turned to face my future husband. I closed my eyes as he reached over to kiss me on the lips. His kiss was gentle and my whole body responded to its call. I opened my eyes and drew back and it was then that I saw her.

Lucy.

Not Pete. Lucy was in front of me, her deep blue eyes boring into my heart, her amber hair falling in natural, uncontrolled waves. Her lips were red, the colour of ripe strawberries, splayed into a half-smile. It was Lucy's lips I had kissed.

Not Pete's. Lucy's.

~

Lucy and her mother were having an argument. Three hours before Lucy was due to marry Pete, Ruth had chosen to ponder on whether her daughter might be rushing into things.

'Mam,' Lucy said, ferociously dabbing cream blusher onto her cheeks. 'What's the problem? Really? You like Peter don't you? Why are you saying this now? You know how much I love him.

You love him! He's like a son to you.'

There were at least ten people squashed into Lucy's bedroom, most of whom were under eight. Lucy had introduced me to all the children and some of the round-faced adults but I couldn't remember who was who. It was a relief to be among all these people, to be in a room so full of life and excitement after my shadow of a Christmas back at home in Devon. It was difficult to imagine a greater contrast than the excited buzz here and the depressive atmosphere of our living room in Paignton. I'd only been home for a week, which was the shortest amount of time I could get away with. I'd spent most of it alone in my bedroom, reading, staring at the wall, taking out the note and unfolding and refolding it repeatedly. My mother had made an effort of course, there were Lebkuchen and a magnificent chocolate roulade and a tree covered in glass decorations, but no amount of papering over could ever conceal the cracks he had created in our relationship. They weren't just cracks anyway, they were chasms.

I drew comfort from the joy in this home. It was alive with anticipation. And the wedding was a secret: no one else at Clarence Dock knew about it. Pete had made me promise to keep my mouth shut until after the event. He hadn't wanted to risk everyone spoiling it for them with their mickey-taking, like they had when I'd been baptised. Despite my sadness at the knowledge I was losing Pete for good, it was exciting to be part of their rebellion. Pete was a year older than me, but he was still only 20. Lucy was just 19. Their marriage was so nonconformist, like most things about them. Amelia would be so jealous that she hadn't been let in on it too.

My task, however, helping three-year-old Martha put her dress on – was proving impossible. She was going to be a flower girl, and had a puffy pink creation to wear. But the heat in the little room was overwhelming and she screwed her face up every time I attempted to put the dress over her head.

'Don't waaaaannnnaaaaa weeeeaaaar it,' she shouted. Her

cries went unnoticed by everyone but me.

'Please Martha, there's a good girl. You want to look pretty for Lucy don't you?'

'No,' she screamed, pelting me with one of her pink ballet shoes and running off out the door.

'I just dunna know why it's all so sudden,' Ruth was saying as I laid the ruffly pink dress to one side and sighed. 'I just thought you were ganna wait until Peter had finished his degree. You're still so young.'

'Mam please. We know what we're doing. We just wanted to wait until you had the all clear, and now you're better, we have nothing holding us back do we? I've told you already that we'll visit every other weekend. It'll be fine. Emma, would you open a window for me? It's getting so hot in here.'

I ploughed my way through the children and pushed the crittal window outwards. A rush of icy air hit me. Lucy's brother, Joe, was walking up the pathway to the front door, his brown hair tousled and messy.

'Martha won't put her dress on,' I said, to nobody in particular, watching Joe's figure slip inside the house. 'She's run off.'

'Oh she's a little devil,' Mary said, pinning her hair up as she crouched down to look in a tiny mirror on the dressing table. 'Don't worry, I'll get that minx sorted. She listens to me. You don't have much experience with kids do you? Not from a big family like the rest of us?'

'No,' I replied, glaring at the back of her frizzy head.

'Knock knock,' Joe said, leaning his head round the corner of the door. 'Can I come in, or is it women only?'

Lucy pushed past her mum who was entangled in some long piece of fabric – it might have been the veil – and marched straight up to Joe.

'How's the church?' she said. 'Is it ready? And Peter? Is he OK?' She turned to me. 'Joe's the best man. Did I tell you that

Emma?'

'No. You didn't.' Joe's eyes looked like liquid pools of dark blue ink. Was I blushing? I couldn't tell. I had to get a grip: he was only seventeen.

'Pete's fine Luce. He's just talking to Father Gerry. God knows about what though. Bit too late to change his mind now.'

No it's not, I thought.

'That'll be the end of your blaspheming please Joseph,' Ruth interrupted.

'Give it a rest Mam,' Joe said. 'Anyway Luce, what I came to tell you is that you've got a delivery. Huge box of flowers just arrived at the church. Lilies. From some woman – Sylvia Hart think her name was. What do you want me to do with them? All the Christmas stuff is still up there. Ferns and that kind of thing.'

'Oh Mrs Hart,' Lucy said, clutching her hands to her chest. Her intricately pinned hair and flattering make-up were only let down by the baggy jumper she was wearing. 'How kind of her. She's one of the old ladies up at the hospice. I can't believe she even remembered that I was getting married. She must be about ninety.'

'Lilies?' Ruth said. 'Lilies are for funerals!'

'Well, they might not er, actually be lilies,' Joe said quietly. 'But they look like lilies.'

Lucy sighed. 'Don't panic. Emma, would you mind going up the church for me and sorting it out? Sorry to be a pain. Ask the priest if he's got any ideas on where they could go. Maybe he could hide the Christmas flowers in the vestry. Joe, be a love and go with Emma won't you?'

'Of course,' he said. 'But I'm only taking orders from you because it's your wedding day.'

'OK,' I said. 'But Martha still needs to put her dress on. She wouldn't do it for me. I think Mary said she was going to do it.'

'Coming, coming!' Mary called in a sing-song voice, smoothing her hands down the front of her outfit and casting me a sideways glance. 'What would you do without me?'

She was jealous of me! Suddenly, it was clear. She had obviously known Lucy all her life – they were cousins – and probably didn't quite understand why I was also one of Lucy's bridesmaids. I'd only known her for three months after all. The more I thought about it, the stranger it seemed. Where *were* Lucy's friends? The only bridesmaids were me, Mary and three of Lucy's little sisters. What about the girls she went to school with? Surely there must be other people in her life. Then it hit me. Everyone crammed into that tiny terraced cottage – bustling about and helping to organise the wedding – was related to Lucy.

Everyone, except me.

Maybe her friends would be coming to the church later on. After all, I was only there because I lived so far away and had stayed at Pete's the night before. Perhaps my imagination was getting the better of me. Lucy was a lovely girl – kind, caring, funny, and good company. There was no reason why she wouldn't have other friends.

Joe and I began the walk to the church in silence. It was cold and grey, and my breath was visible in the dry air. It didn't feel like the right weather for a wedding. Joe walked in funny disjointed strides. Perhaps he was nervous.

'Got your speech prepared?' I asked, dodging patches of black ice on the pavement.

'Yep,' he said.

'Is it full of revelations then? About Pete?'

'No. I don't know much about the guy to be honest with you. He only really talks to Luce. I'm just doing it as a favour to her. She wanted him to have a best man. As it's traditional.'

'But you've known him your whole life, haven't you?'

'Yes we mucked about together as kids. Built sandcastles and all that. But I don't really *know him*. You know, he doesn't really make much effort with people. Keeps himself to himself. That's why we were all surprised when he suddenly came out saying he'd met you. We couldn't believe that he'd made a friend, and also that it was a girl. Thought he'd had a personality transplant or something.'

'I can't believe that. Pete's really outgoing,' I said. 'He's got lots of friends at uni.' I paused. I guess he didn't really. Not that I knew. 'Well, most of our flat mates love him. And it's not surprising he's a little bit withdrawn. After all, his mother…well, I lost my father recently and it's certainly affected me.'

'I heard, I'm sorry. Lucy uses that as an excuse for Peter's behaviour all the time too. But if he's so outgoing, why is his future wife's brother the only person he can find to be his best man?'

He had a point, but my loyalty was fierce.

'Perhaps Lucy thought it would be nice. You know, keep it in the family.'

'Hmm. Mary thinks you're after him for yourself you know. Us Catholics can't understand platonic relationships. It's not in our genes,' he said, pushing open the large oak door to the church.

'That's rubbish,' I said, hoping the inevitable colour of my cheeks could be blamed on the temperature.

The church was small and quaint: a picture-postcard place to get married. As Joe had said, the back wall was decorated with typical Christmas foliage in varying shades of red and green, with a few bits of gold thrown in. All that was needed to complete the scene was a dusting of snow on the steps outside. But that day, there was no snow, only ice, and a foreboding grey sky that offered neither charm nor warmth.

'Here they are,' Joe said, leaning down and picking up two long and thin cardboard boxes. Lifting the lid of one, he revealed a beautiful bouquet of pink lilies interspersed with roses and some other pretty white flowers that I didn't know the name of. 'Bit more appropriate than the other stuff isn't it?'

'They're beautiful,' I said. 'We should put them in water.

Where's the priest?'

'Doesn't seem to be around,' Joe said, peering over my shoulder down the aisle of the empty church. His accent echoed around the cavernous space. 'The old fart doesn't like me much though. Apparently I don't go to confession often enough for him. Personally, I don't think God's too interested in my sins. They're not very original.'

I laughed.

'What about you?' he said. 'Done anything naughty recently?'

'Wouldn't you like to know?' I said instinctively, raising an eyebrow.

'Well yes, actually, I would. That's why I asked. You know what they say about the chief bridesmaid and the best man, don't you?'

I opened my mouth to reply and stopped. This was wrong. It was inappropriate and probably a sin in itself. We were mocking the holy rite of confession. That must be forbidden. Most things were. It was very *hard* being a Catholic sometimes.

'Would you mind going to find the priest, please?' I replied blandly, a small part of me wishing I could carry on being silly.

Joe frowned slightly and walked off down the aisle and through a small door at the side of the church. I looked down at the lilies, their petals and leaves tinged with tiny crystals of frozen water that sparkled in the dull light. Joe. He obviously didn't think much of Pete. What did he mean about him not having anyone to ask to be his best man?

I heard the sound of someone smacking their hands together loudly behind me and turned to see the groom marching towards me.

'Well, well, well,' Pete said, kissing me on the cheek. 'What have we here? Flowers from one of Lucy's secret admirers? I'm going to have to keep tabs on my new wife aren't I?'

'Don't be silly, they're from one of the old ladies Lucy used to visit in the hospice.' I stood back slightly. He looked amazing.

Clean-shaven for once, his curly brown hair teased into a wave across the top of his head. The image of Lucy back at the house, transforming her milky face into the epitome of an English Rose with peach-coloured blusher and soft pink lipstick, floated into my head. They were going to make an annoyingly attractive couple.

Joe ambled up behind him, looking like a poor relation next to Pete. But where Pete's skin was pale and slightly grey, Joe's face was ruddy with health. Like Maria's had been before...well, before the incident.

'What about these then?' he said, handing over two large vases. 'Father G says we can put one each side of the altar. We'll have to put them on stools or something though, because they'd look a bit stupid on the floor.'

I sighed and took them from him. 'I guess they'll have to do.'

'I'm sure you can work your magic with them. She's a star, isn't she Joe? And doesn't she scrub up well.'

'Yes,' he said, looking puzzled.

It was then I realised: Pete was caught between two worlds here, with both of us present.

It all started to make sense. In Cresswell, he was one of those nice men who never got in anyone's way and never got anyone's back up. The kind of man whose presence goes unnoticed, whose talents and flaws are overlooked. He was like one of those men who one day go out and murder a classroom of school children for no particular reason. *Such a shock, he was such a quiet man. Kept himself to himself,* the neighbours always say afterwards. Not that I thought Pete was a serial killer of course.

But then, it wasn't only the quiet ones who surprised the world with their unexpected, devastating actions. Dad had been loud, cheerful, everyone's friend, and the last person you would ever expect to kill himself. He was the quintessential family man, an adoring husband, father, son. But of course, if it hadn't been for me, he wouldn't have killed himself. And not a single soul suspected the part that I had played. It seemed there was nothing you could trust about a person's external character. You just never knew the truth. Or even if you did, you were probably better off pretending you didn't.

I walked up the aisle but unlike my dream the previous night, I felt anything but weightless. I was fat and frumpy in my blue skirt and flowery top. Lucy had just told me to wear something blue. There had been no official 'bridesmaid's outfit' shopping trip and the top was one I'd borrowed from my mother, which made the whole thing even more pathetic. The vases were heavy and unwieldy. As I clambered up towards the altar, not a hint of grace or elegance apparent, I saw the 'Order of Service' sheets on the pews.

St Bartholomew's Church, Cresswell

The marriage of Lucy Nichols & Peter Field

January 3, 1999 at 12 noon

They'd obviously been photocopied on a machine in need of a service, and the ink was faded in parts, with smudged blobs dotted over the pages. It was all rather pitiful. This was the most important day of Lucy and Pete's lives, and everything was second-rate. The wilting flowers would be propped up in dirty, mismatching vases on stools by the altar, in front of a clashing array of Christmas decorations. The weather could only be described as miserable.

And the chief bridesmaid was wearing one of her mother's tops.

~

'How long have I got?' Lucy whispered.

We were alone in her bedroom. Everyone else was downstairs or already at the church. Lucy's mother was busy putting the finishing touches to the wedding feast she'd prepared for after the service. This was to be my first Catholic wedding, and apparently, the service would be even longer than a usual mass. Ruth had complained that noon was such an awkward time to get married, as people's stomachs were bound to be rumbling midway through the Lamb of God litany.

'About twenty minutes. Unless you want to be late of course. It's traditional.' I was frantically brushing my hair, trying to inject some life into it, but it was full of static and looked thin and flyaway.

'Oh no,' Lucy said. She was sitting at the dressing table gazing at her reflection in the small mirror. 'I don't want to be late. Peter would worry. Have you seen him? Was he at the church?'

'Yes he was at the church. He was there when I was doing the flowers. He looked lovely Lucy. And really happy.'

'Really?' she asked, her eyes shining.

'Yes. And you…you look lovely too. I was thinking earlier, you are going to make such a beautiful couple.'

'Thank you.' She reached forward and grabbed my hands. 'You know, I don't know what I'd have done without your help over the last few weeks.'

I flopped onto the bed next to her, dislodging a fat tabby who hissed at me and slinked off.

'Don't be silly. I've loved helping you out.' I paused. 'But, I can't help wondering. Why me? Why did you ask me to be your maid of honour? Surely…surely you must…'

'Have other friends?' she said.

'Well, yes I guess so. What about people from school?'

'Oh they're all long gone. I wasn't that popular. You see how we all live here. My mam and dad, they did their best, but they had nine children and no money. I couldn't go out with the other girls in my year. They all lived in Morpeth or Ashington. But I always had Peter, so that was OK.'

'Were you bullied?'

She looked down and fiddled with her shoes. 'Not really. Teased a bit perhaps. Well, you know how it is.' She straightened up. 'But that's all in the past now. Peter always said I'd find a really good, true best friend one day. And look, here you are!'

I looked at Lucy, her Debenhams wedding dress hugging her tiny frame. She was like a little girl who had wished for a fairy as a friend, and lo and behold, one had appeared before her. Perhaps the reason I felt so close to her was that deep down she was as insecure as I was. She wanted friends, she wanted to be loved. And Pete, he loved her so much; he'd gone out and found her what she wanted. A loner who was just as insecure, to adore her, to care for her, to listen to her. He couldn't have his little princess without a maid of honour could he? Without a best friend to help her do her make up on the most important day of her life. So he'd gone and found her one. Me.

I'd been recruited.

I began to breathe heavily.

Had he manipulated me ever since the day we'd met, just to find his precious Lucy a friend?

'Do you know what I think is strange?' I asked.

'What?'

'Joe. I spoke to Joe. He doesn't really know Pete. But he's his best man. So where's Pete's best friend? You've got me. But who has Pete got? Why has he asked your brother to be his best man?'

'Oh Emma,' Lucy said, fixing me with her wide smile. 'You don't want to take too much notice of Joe. He's probably just pulling your leg. They're like brothers. After Peter's mam died, my mam practically brought him up.'

'Lucy!' a voice shouted from downstairs. 'Are you coming? Get down here so I can sort the veil out!'

'Come on Emma, my mam's probably having kittens. Let's go.' She paused in the doorway and looked back at her reflection one last time. 'Oh Emma. I'm so excited. I really do look quite special today don't I?'

Her smile made me feel sick.

Chapter Nineteen

Emma, January 2011

Despite the large number of people in Lucy's family, it looked as though there were only about fifty people in the church as I walked up the aisle behind the bride. Pete didn't seem to have any relations there apart from his father and a bewildered-looking old lady I presumed to be his grandmother. Everyone just sat where they liked. As I scanned the pews, Lucy's assertion that their two families were already as good as entwined, thanks to her mother looking after Pete so much as a baby, didn't ring true. And there was no sign of Pete's relations on his mother's side.

My reading went relatively well considering I'd only been given it the night before. As I evangelised about love not being jealous or selfish, about love rejoicing in the truth, I watched Pete's face. It was impassive as ever. Lucy was sniffing, that infuriating smile so wide she looked as though her face might crack in two.

After the ceremony we all trudged back to the house. It had started to drizzle. Again I found myself walking alongside Joe, who grabbed my arm when I almost slipped over on some ice. Cresswell must be completely different in the summer. Better than this. Lucy and Pete were walking arm-in-arm in front of me, the bottom of her dress black and wet with the rainwater from the ground. But she was oblivious.

'Where are all of Pete's family?' I asked Joe in a hushed voice.

'Oh he doesn't keep in touch with them. After his mam died I think her sisters had some kind of problem with the way his dad handled the funeral. Anyway they all fell out. And I don't think his dad's got any family, except his older sister, and she's seventy and losing it.'

'Poor Pete.'

'Hmmm. I don't think it's ever bothered him too much.'

The party progressed as expected; my time spent making polite conversation with various people who all seemed to be related to Lucy in some way or another. None of them seemed particularly religious, surprisingly. Like Joe, many of them were lapsed Catholics, who muttered to me indiscreetly that they thought Lucy was too young to get married and that Pete took his religion a little too seriously. Mary took control of proceedings, dictating when people were allowed to come and help themselves to the extensive buffet that Lucy's mother had prepared. At 3pm she put on a CD called 'Wedding Party Classics' and the younger children jived in the crowded living room beneath an explosion of cheap decorations.

I was looking for a means of escape from a particularly boring middle-aged aunt when the bride herself came over and tapped me on the arm.

'Emma, would you come upstairs for a minute?' she said. Her eyeliner was smudged, and I resisted the urge to lean over and wipe it off.

'Yes of course. Excuse me,' I said, turning to the aunt, whose eyes were now fixed on the blushing bride.

'Isn't she a picture?' she said, as I got up to follow Lucy.

Upstairs and alone, Lucy threw her arms around my neck and kissed me on both cheeks.

'I've had such a lovely day. Thank you so much, for everything. It's all gone perfectly.'

'I'm glad you've enjoyed it,' I said.

'Peter and I wanted to give you something. Come here, sit down. I know we should give it to you in front of everyone but Peter didn't want to do a speech – he gets a bit embarrassed – so he asked me to give it to you. Here, and thanks. Thanks for everything.'

She handed me a small, red jewellery box. I opened it. Inside was a silver ring, with a red stone in the middle. I knew at once that it was a rosary ring. I took it out and turned it around in my fingers. The bumps around it weren't quite evenly spaced.

'It's like mine,' she said, holding out her right hand. On her middle finger was the beautiful gold ring, with a larger ruby set into the middle that I'd admired on several occasions.

'Thank you,' I said, putting my ring on. It was a bit too big.

'The jeweller said that it can be adjusted,' Lucy said, looking anxious. 'It's too big. Oh that's such a shame. But we'll get it sorted. Do you like it? I know it's not gold, but it's solid silver. And it's a real ruby in the middle like mine.'

'It's beautiful. Thank you.'

'It's much easier to use a rosary ring than a proper rosary. You will use it, won't you? Pete and I had it made up especially for you. It's a one-off.'

'Of course I will.' It was my turn to hug her.

'I'm so glad you like it. Come on, let's get back to the party. I don't know about you but I could do with some more of that fizzy wine.'

~

Where was Pete? I couldn't stand being stuck in that room with Lucy's relations any longer. A quick search of the tiny house turned up no one except Martha, who was hiding in the airing cupboard.

'Lucy,' I said. 'Have you any idea where Pete might be? I wanted to thank him too.'

She was swaying slightly and reached forward to lean on one of my shoulders. 'Oh, isn't he here? I saw him a while ago. If he's not here he's probably gone back to the house. I think he's a bit cross with me for having too much too drink.' She giggled.

I walked off without replying. In that state she wouldn't remember my rudeness the next day. Lucy and Pete might even have a row over her drunkenness. Not the most promising start to married life.

Despite that, there was no doubting that Lucy still knew him best. She was right, he'd gone home. He was sitting in his father's living room, in the semi-darkness, just one dusty table lamp on in the corner. At first I thought he was asleep, but as I approached I saw that he had his eyes open, and was just staring into space.

'Have you had enough too?' he asked.

The depression in his voice confounded me. I took a seat next to him. 'You could say that. I'm really tired. It was a long train journey up here yesterday and all the excitement…well, it's got to me. What about you though? What are you doing here? You should be celebrating.'

'I think I've done enough celebrating. Just wanted some time to myself.'

'I need to talk to you,' I said, remembering why I had come. 'I was talking to Lucy before the wedding. Because, well, to be honest, I couldn't understand why she wanted me as her maid of honour. Nice as it was to be asked, I wondered why she didn't have any other friends to ask – school friends, people she grew up with.'

'Lucy and I are like lone ships. On our very own crusade.' He chuckled. 'We don't have friends.'

'What are you talking about?' I said.

My hands shook. He raised an eyebrow at me.

'Just be straight with me,' I continued. 'You've used me. Haven't you? You recruited me, to be a best friend for your bride. You saw that I was lonely. That night after the Freshers' Ball… you knew you could control me, make me into what you wanted – a friend for Lucy. A good, Catholic friend. And I did it. I was obedient. I converted for you. I helped her get ready on her big day, told her she looked beautiful...'

'You don't think she ever did anything for you in return?' He was still sitting in the same position, his eyes now half-closed. His apathy enraged me.

'That's not the point! You used me. Lucy practically admitted it. You never cared about me at all.'

Pete stood up and stared at me straight in the eyes.

'Come with me,' he said. In the half-light, he looked more attractive than ever, his collar and tie undone, revealing a glimpse of smooth skin.

'Why? Where are you going?'

He took my hand and pulled me towards the door.

'Let's go to the beach. I need to talk to you but I don't want to risk anyone else hearing.'

'Are you mad? It's freezing out there.'

We reached the hall and he grabbed a padded wax jacket from the banister at the bottom of the stairs.

'Here,' he said, placing it around my shoulders.

It was so hard to stay angry when he was so calm.

We walked the short path down to the beach. He was still clutching my hand. It was dark except for the two flickering streetlights on the road outside the ice-cream shop, but the full moon provided enough light for us to find our way. I turned my head back. Lucy's little house, ablaze with noise and lights, stood out like a beacon in the silent hamlet.

Once we got onto the beach itself, my high-heeled shoes sank into the sand as I walked and my toes began to freeze. Pete led me up to the end of the beach I had never been to before, and soon, we reached some grey rocks that blocked our way. In the moonlight, they glistened. I couldn't see the sea, but I could hear it, a gentle lapping more appropriate for a hot summer's afternoon than a lifeless night in January.

'I'll help you,' Pete said.

He lifted me up with a strength I hadn't expected and I climbed to the top of the rock, stood and waited for a few moments, then fell into his arms on the other side.

His breath was hot on my face.

'Emma,' he said, holding me tightly, speaking into my hair.

My cheeks were burning with the cold. 'There's so much you don't understand.'

Even though I knew it was coming, it was still a shock when he cupped my face in his hands and kissed me, his mouth full on mine. It was only a few seconds, but it seemed to last for much longer. For so long that I stopped feeling the cold; that I stopped feeling everything but the pressure of his lips against mine.

'Come with me,' he said, pulling away and taking my hand again.

We reached another clearing and Pete stopped, turned to me and held both my hands in his.

'OK,' he said. 'This might sound crazy but I love you. I'm not one for big displays of emotion but there you have it. I love you. And I have since... It's been a nightmare. Everything I ever believed about my life, my future. It all changed the first time I saw you.'

He dropped my hands and started to pace up and down. When he turned to face me, the moon shone full on his face and his eyes glistened like the rocks, dark holes with a silver sheen.

'Don't you understand?' he said. He was angry now and I wanted to cry. The volume of his voice startled me and I stumbled backwards. 'Everything I ever believed. It all changed. Lucy. She was meant for me. I was meant for her. It was what my mother wanted. It was what everyone wanted. But you came along...'

'What…' I began, but he wasn't listening.

'It was the only way I could prevent it. Do you think I wanted to get married this young? It was the only way. I didn't trust myself, living in that tiny flat, seeing you every day. In the morning, with that stupid towelling band round your head, at lunchtimes, clearing up other people's mess in the kitchen, in the evenings, staring out of the window while the others talked, fiddling with your hair. Every day, I saw you and every day I... And I knew you felt it too.'

'Pete…what…'

'You have to understand. I didn't recruit you for Lucy. It was the other way round. It was the only thing I could think of. To give the power back to you. If you got to know Lucy, if you two became close, I knew you wouldn't betray her trust. It was the only solution.'

'We could have been together,' I said desperately. 'You didn't need to…it doesn't make sense.'

'You weren't even Catholic! And anyway, I told you, it was my duty to be with Lucy. It was what my mam wanted.'

'Pete, your duty? To marry a girl you don't love? Are you crazy?'

His eyes were cold as he met mine.

'I do love her,' he said, softly. 'It's not about love. Of course I love her. Why wouldn't I? But you…'

'But you don't love me?' I interrupted.

For a second I thought he was going to hit me, he came towards me so aggressively. But instead, he grabbed me round the waist and pulled me back towards him.

I could smell the aftershave Lucy had given him for a wedding present, diluted and insignificant against the crisp night air. This time, I kissed him back. And as we made love on the freezing sand, my senses grew used to the smell of the aftershave, until I could smell it no more and for the first time since I met her, Lucy's shadow faded from my consciousness.

~

There was a knock on my door. I shivered under the cold blankets, staring dimly at the faded curtains. Behind them, a light shone through. I could hear the low murmur of people chatting excitedly outside, the stamping of feet to keep warm, the dull purr of an engine. They were leaving. The knock was repeated, louder this time. I hugged myself tighter.

'Emma?' a voice called softly from the other side of the door. 'I'm coming in, OK?'

I shut my eyes and pretended to sleep. The door creaked open and I heard someone enter. Joe.

He walked over to the bed and shook my shoulder gently.

'Emma, are you awake?' he whispered.

He clearly wasn't going to leave me to it. I rolled over as sleepily as I could manage, and peered up at him. The remnants of a party popper were wrapped around his ears.

'Sorry,' he said. 'I didn't mean to wake you up. But they're leaving now. The taxi's outside. I thought maybe you'd want to say goodbye. Lucy was wondering where you were, she wanted to see you before she left.'

I shifted onto my elbows and sat up. Joe sat down at the other end of the bed and smiled, the corners of his eyes crinkling up.

'You look so funny,' he said. 'Your headband thing's gone all wonky and you're sporting a rather fetching afro.'

I frowned and patted my hair.

He blushed. 'Sorry, didn't mean to be rude.'

'That's OK,' I said. 'You don't look too clever yourself, with that bunting stuff around your ears.'

'I don't dare pull it off, Martha put it there, she thinks it's absolutely hilarious. So how come you're up here? Had a few too many gin and tonics?'

'Something like that,' I replied, staring right through him. Did that really happen, out there on the beach? 'I'm just shattered. I've had such a long day and it's what…' I looked over at the clock radio in the corner of the room. '1.30? Way past my bedtime. Sorry to be a party pooper.'

'I'm knackered too. But anyway looks like things are winding up now. So come on Ugly Sister, brush your hair out, stick some clothes on and come down and say goodbye. They'll be in Rothbury for a week you know.'

He got up and walked to the door. 'Lucy will miss you,' he

said. 'I'm sure Pete will too.'

I started to un-pin my hair.

'See you down there. Be quick,' Joe said, and left the room.

Wrapping the blanket and sheet around me, I stood up, my legs a bit wobbly, and walked to the window. Pulling back the curtain slightly, I saw the village green stretch before me. People were huddled around the taxi, like ghosts in the misty light. Someone was singing *Here Comes the Bride*, their voice rising up above the muffled chattering. I stood at the window and stared. Eventually Lucy and Pete appeared at the doorway. A cry broke out and people started to clap and cheer.

The top of Lucy's bronze head glinted up at me before she climbed into the taxi. Pete walked around the other side of the car, people slapping him on the back as he went. He paused for a moment, one hand on the car door, and scanned the crowd. His eyes rose back up to the house, higher and higher, until he found me at the window, half-hidden by the curtain. His head jerked back slightly and despite the dark and fog, I could see his eyes clearly. He stared at me, just for a second, before getting in the taxi.

The car drove to the green, back around and then off, down the only road that let into and away from Cresswell. As the taxi's red taillights disappeared into the darkness, the crowd dispersed.

They were gone.

Chapter Twenty

Pete, April 2006

Now he was older, he didn't mind his Aunt Matilda so much. He went to stay with her occasionally, especially during the school holidays, and though she was never particularly kind to him and never let him talk about his mother, she was always interested in what was going on in his life. He told her about school, and his success in the rugby team and she helped him to decide what to study for his GCSEs. He appreciated her interest, because his father had made it perfectly clear he wasn't in the slightest bit bothered what Peter did with his life, so long as he went to church once a week and didn't bring any more shame on the family. His Aunt Matilda was a live-in housekeeper for a wealthy doctor's widow, who lived in Morpeth. The house Matilda looked after was large and grand, and she had the whole of the basement as her own flat. When Peter went to stay, he slept in the spare room, and he was the only one who ever used it, so after a while, it began to feel like his own. He left books there, including his tatty copy of the Bible, a toothbrush, a flannel and a few jumpers and t-shirts. He considered asking his father if he would mind if he went to live with Matilda permanently, because her house was just a few minutes' walk from the town centre, and he wanted to get a job in the summer holidays. But then he realised that he'd miss Lucy too much.

Matilda was a good cook, and her homemade meals made a welcome change from Peter's father's reheated frozen-food dinners. After they ate, Peter would do the dishes and clean up the kitchen, and then the two of them would sit by the small gas fire in the front room, and take it in turns to read from the Bible. Matilda was very religious, even more so than his dad. She gave Peter endless lessons on the Catechism, made him repeat the Apostles' Creed five times before going to bed, and even though he was learning it at school, gave him extra Latin lessons. She told him stories of how she had once wanted to join a convent, but had had her heart broken during the war by an American soldier, and then felt too ashamed and too old to start her postulancy. The stories of her teenage years in the war reminded him of just how old she was. And of just how old his father was too. He was Matilda's younger brother but even so he was ancient in comparison with all his school friends' parents. Peter liked to use that as an excuse as to why his father was so strict – he was simply from a different era.

When he was staying with Matilda, Peter went to mass every evening, instead of just on Sundays. He found this immersion in religion comforting and started to wonder whether he should become a priest. One night, while they were eating steak and kidney pie, with green beans from the large garden, he asked Matilda what she thought.

'A priest?' she said.

'Yes,' Peter said. His palms felt clammy. He hadn't even mentioned the idea to Lucy yet.

'How old are you again?' she asked, even though she knew his age.

'14, Aunt Matilda,' he replied, shovelling a large forkful of pie into his mouth.

'Bit young to be making these decisions, don't you think?' she said.

'Well, I'm quite mature for my age,' he said. 'I feel that it's my calling almost. To be a priest, and to serve God all my life.'

'Interesting,' she said.

'What do you mean?'

'Nothing, nothing. Just considering what happened to your *mother*,' she spat the word out, 'perhaps you're feeling the urge to pay something back on her behalf?'

'I don't understand,' Peter said, surprised at Matilda mentioning his mam. She never spoke about her. 'Pay something back for what?'

'Well, her suicide of course,' Matilda replied, staring straight ahead. 'Make amends for her sins. Not that you can do that really. Sin isn't transferable from one family member to another. But I know how devoted you are to her. I've seen the picture you keep by your bed.'

'Her suicide?' Peter let his fork fall to the plate with a clatter. 'You're saying my mam killed herself?'

'Well of course she did, what did you think?' The sneer in her voice reminded him of his father. When she was being nasty like this, she looked like him too.

'Nothing,' Peter replied, determined not to give her the satisfaction of realising the bombshell she had just dropped.

But she pressed on. 'Did you think she drowned? That it was an accident? Did nobody tell you?' She laughed. 'Well, that's Bert all over I suppose. Didn't want to admit it even to his son.'

Peter stabbed the remaining beans on his plate and didn't look up.

'She was doolally, your mother. Completely insane. The trouble your father had trying to keep her under control. She once went down to the beach in just her underwear you know. In the middle of the day! Imagine how humiliating that was for him. She knew what a mortal sin was. She knew that killing herself was the most selfish, evil act she could possibly commit. But she did it just the same. Your poor father. The shame in not even being able to bury his wife in consecrated ground. Having to have her cremated, like a heathen!'

She leaned in closer, and forced Peter's eyes to meet hers. He remembered why Lucy used to refer to her as a witch.

'Your mam destroyed your father's good name. She had the devil in her, and don't you ever forget it.'

Chapter Twenty-one

Emma, January 2011

'Married?' Sam's tone was incredulous. He let out a shriek, clapped his hands. 'Oh that's just brilliant!'

'Are you serious?' Amelia asked me.

'Yes. Two weeks ago. On the third. I was a bridesmaid.'

'A bridesmaid?' Sam's grin widened.

'I don't know why you're so surprised,' I said, failing to contain the aggression in my voice. 'You knew they were engaged.'

I looked around for a means of escape. I hardly ever came into the union these days. It was just my luck that I'd ended up bumping into Amelia and Sam today. Toilet roll. That was all I came in for. Not the Spanish Inquisition. I knew it was only a matter of time before they found me and grilled me about Pete's whereabouts. For the past two weeks I'd managed to avoid them all, restricting my exchanges with them to shouts of hello and goodbye in the corridor. Every evening, I'd eaten my dinner in my room, under the pretense that I was reading stuff for my course at the same time. No one had bothered checking up on me or asking if I was OK.

'Where did they get married?' Amelia asked. She was disguising her opinion of my revelation well, trying to glean more information before delivering her assessment. Sam was still sniggering away. It was hard to understand why Amelia liked him so much. He was a dick.

'Back in their home town.'

'And you went up there for the wedding?' Amelia let her rucksack fall to the floor with a thud. A thick textbook with an orange cover poked out of the top.

'Yes. It was a lovely day,' I said. Was it a lovely day? For me, for Lucy, for Pete? I had no idea. Since it happened, I'd tried not to think about it at all. Tried and mostly succeeded. I hadn't heard a thing from Pete. Lucy had been pestering me with texts; friendly, excited, looking forward to sharing her honeymoon photos. There was nobody in the world I could talk to. Pete wouldn't be coming back to Clarence Dock. I didn't know where he was, but his room only had a single bed. Lucy had mentioned she would definitely be moving to Leeds to be with him after the wedding, so they'd have to find somewhere new. But where?

'So Pete's not coming back to the flat?' Amelia asked, reading my mind. 'I'd wondered where he'd got to. Where's he going to live now then?'

'I'm not sure,' I replied. 'I haven't heard from him. They went on their honeymoon...I don't know if they're back yet.'

'They must be,' she replied. 'Lectures started last week. Pete wouldn't want to miss any.'

'Wouldn't he?' I asked, but the question was rhetorical. Who knew what Pete would do? Nothing seemed to make sense anymore.

'Are you OK Emma?' Amelia said. 'I know how much you... Look, Sam, why don't you run on and get us a table, I'll catch you up. I just want to have a word with Emma.'

'Sure,' he replied. He paused for a second, looking as though he was about to say something to me, but thought better of it, and walked off, towards the Refectory.

'Listen, tell me to mind my own business, if you like,' she began, 'but, nothing happened, did it? Between you and Pete?'

I pulled my best 'shocked' face. 'No, of course not.' Perhaps I wasn't such a bad liar after all. What a guiltily comforting thought: I'd inherited something useful from my father. 'What makes you say that?'

'It's just... odd. That Pete and Lucy would get married in such a hurry. They only got engaged at the end of the year didn't they? Don't you think it's a bit strange? What was the rush? They're so young.'

Before the wedding, before the incident on the beach, Pete had taken me to one side and told me what to say to the others when I was asked this question. It was a question I'd asked him myself. He'd explained it all so methodically and I'd believed it then, but now it seemed wrong, immoral almost, when I knew the real reason he'd brought the wedding forward. But I wouldn't let him down. I couldn't, even if I wanted to. Amelia would hate me if she knew. I didn't have the strength to cope with that.

'It was because Lucy's mother had been given the all clear,' I said, delivering my lines like a pro. 'She'd been ill – cancer – but she went into remission at the end of December, so they decided she'd be well enough. And Pete…' I paused. It was hard to speak with conviction when my heart was torn to pieces. 'Pete missed Lucy in the first term more than he thought he would. He didn't want to be without her any longer.'

My eyes began to water. More than anything, I was angry at the injustice of it all. This was Pete's dirty work, why should I have to do it?

'Oh Em,' Amelia said. 'It's OK, you know, you don't have to pretend. I know how much you liked him. He's been a real bastard to you, hasn't he? Led you on. Don't look so horrified. It's true. I saw the way he was with you, all flirty, making you believe there was hope. It was totally out of order. And to expect you to be bridesmaid at his wedding! Bloody wanker. You wait till I see him again.'

'No Amelia,' I pleaded. 'It's OK, honestly. It's not his fault. I shouldn't have got my hopes up.'

'No, you shouldn't.' She smiled at me sadly. 'But you're only human. Listen, Sam and I are about to go for lunch if you fancy coming? Take your mind off it?'

'Thanks,' I sniffed. 'But to be honest, I just feel like being on my own at the moment. If that's OK.'

'Sure,' she said. 'Are you off home now?'

I nodded, pushed my hair back behind my ears.

'Cool. But listen...Maria, she's not mad at you anymore. I promise. You don't have to avoid her. I know it was all a bit...weird...last term, but it's in the past yeah? All forgiven and forgotten. Let's put it all behind us shall we? New term, new start eh?'

I nodded again.

She slung her rucksack back over one shoulder.

'You never know, we might even get someone new in the flat! In Pete's room. Someone better looking! Ha ha. If not, we can make it into a TV room or something. It'll be OK, you'll see.'

'Thanks Amelia.'

'Alright, well, catch you later then.' With that, she patted me on the arm and walked away.

~

Distractions. That's what would get me through this. Work. I would work hard. That's what I was here for anyway. The government wasn't lending me £1,100 a term to have a good time. I was supposed to be studying. There was so much for me to learn. For one thing, I could practise the piano every day. Get the Fantaisie-Impromptu nailed. Three hours a day hammering away at its awful semi-quavers versus triplets cross-rhythms and I'd have it perfected. That would be an achievement – something I'd tried and failed in the past. It would make me happy.

I'd begin today, with a trip to the library. I'd seen how many books were on our reading list for this term. If I borrowed them now, I'd be well ahead of the game. No one else would be worrying about their reading yet.

I walked across the union courtyard towards the Edward Boyle library. I'd only been inside a few times before, to use the computers. Where would the music books be? I logged into a machine on the ground floor and searched for the first book on the list. Level 9. It took me several minutes to work out that I was already on level 9. Why did they call it level 9 when it was actually the ground floor? Another little trick to confuse freshers.

The books were shelved by subject, alphabetically – at least that was logical. There were surprisingly few music ones, just two shelves' worth. As I approached, I noticed the dark-haired boy from my lectures, crouched down, thumbing through some titles on the bottom shelf. I hesitated. The book I wanted was right in front of him. Should I wait for him to finish or just reach forward and grab it?

I lingered for a few seconds. He must have sensed my presence, because he looked up.

'Hello,' he said, staring straight at me.

Instinctively, I glanced down at what I was wearing. The duvet coat, of course, but also my nice scarf, the pink one I'd been given for Christmas that suited my colouring. My pale jeans, finished off with battered old trainers. Nike, but not Air. I put my bag down on top of them, hoping he hadn't seen.

'Hello,' I replied. 'Sorry, I didn't mean to interrupt.'

'It's OK,' he said, smiling. Where was he from? The north, definitely, but east or west? It wasn't Manchester or Birmingham, but he didn't sound like Pete either. 'It's Emma, isn't it? I've seen your name on the attendance sheet.'

'Yes,' I replied, puzzling over his background. His accent was thick, nebulous, making him speak as though his mouth were full of cotton wool.

'Daniel,' he said, holding out his hand. 'Nice to meet you finally.'

I smiled, took his hand. 'Yes.'

'What were you after then?'

'Oh...just that one on Elgar.' I pointed to it. He reached down, picked it up and handed it to me.

'You play piano, don't you?' he asked. 'I've seen you in the practice rooms.'

'Yes. And flute. Although I'm not very good at either.'

'I wouldn't say that.' He smiled. 'I'm a violinist myself. I play piano too, but violin's my forte.'

'Really? How wonderful.' I scratched the side of my head, as ever, pathetically unable to think of anything else to say.

'Well,' he said, gathering several books together. 'I'll leave you to it. See you around.'

'Yes. Bye then.'

He walked away, leaving me to sigh at his retreating back. It was a start, I supposed. At least I knew his name now, which would make it easier next time I saw him. Perhaps we could go for a drink after our next lecture or something. Although it was difficult to know how to ask without making it sound like a proposition. He played piano too, so at least we would be able to discuss that. I looked down at the book he'd handed me. It all seemed like such a huge effort. I didn't know if I had the energy.

I walked back towards the counter. As I made my way along the rows of desks and chairs, occupied with students making notes – probably third years, no freshers would look so keen, so desperate, so focused – I felt as though I was being watched. I reached the last desk and looked back. In the far corner, a shadowy figure was observing me. I squinted, cursing my short-sightness. He was too far away for me to be 100% certain, but I was sure it was Pete.

The panic I felt was illogical but overwhelming. I abandoned the book on a shelf labelled 'Anatomical Sciences' and hurried for the exit.

~

'Emma!' she cried. I could almost hear the tears springing to her eyes.

'Hi Mum,' I replied, pressing my ear hard against my mobile.

Everything made her cry these days. Perhaps that was why I had avoided her for so long. It was only a phone call, yet I knew what would happen: there would be gentle sobs, and then she would repeat how proud she was of me, how brave I was, how she wished she could be as strong as me and my brother. She would tell me yet again that we had taken after Dad with our strength, and it made me angry the way she revered him now. Since Christmas, her feelings had made a complete U-turn. Now, he was a hero. Her recent incessant placing of the mediocre Martin Dewberry on a pedestal made me furious. I had dreams where I saw him perched on a rocky hill, trying to climb down from it, insisting he wasn't worthy. But my mother's hand, looming larger than life, would simply pick him up by the shoulders and place him back on the top, like a decorative figurine on a cake.

It wasn't only him she admired now. She'd also decided my quietness and my lack of demonstrable grief were some kind of huge achievement, to be admired and mentioned at every available opportunity. Of course, she didn't know the true reason behind my reticence, and like her, I was proud of my ability to keep my mouth firmly shut, albeit for different reasons. I hadn't told a single person, which was most unlike me. In my more romantic, whimsical moments, I reminded myself that I had a secret with the dead. I tried to make it something to be excited about, something to bolster my self-worth. It didn't work, of course. It was an ugly, dirty secret, not a glorious one.

'Where are you?' Mum said. 'It's noisy.'

'Sorry, I'm just leaving the lecture hall. I'll be outside in a few minutes. How're things?'

I walked down the red route, away from my final lecture of the day.

'Oh well, alright really,' she lied. 'Not great. But what about you? Your letters…they keep me...I'm so glad for you. So glad that you're having the time of your life up there. Too busy to phone your mum though of course.' She gave a short laugh.

She was so pathetic, I could almost believe she had driven my father to it. It had been ten months since he'd died. Ten months was long enough to have a baby, and definitely long enough to get over a man as unremarkable as my father.

'Yes,' I said. 'Things are good here.' Whenever I spoke to her, I became a robot, spouting pre-programmed stock answers on repeat.

'And your little friend – what was her name? The one that got married to your flatmate. Is she all settled in now?'

'Lucy. Yes. Lucy and Pete. Yes, everything's great with them.' It didn't feel like a lie.

'Good, good.'

I reached the library, and turned and walked back the way I had come. This time, I walked outside, parallel to the corridor I had just exited. I could see the pond in front of the Roger Stevens Building ahead of me. Students hurried past. It was cold but bright, the sky completely blue except for a scattering of pale grey clouds. I reached the shallow pond, a concrete square filled with muddy water and rubbish, and sat on the edge, staring at my muted reflection in the water. People said the pond was toxic. I'd heard of drunks stripping off and jumping in. There had also been rumours of ducks living in it once. Both seemed unlikely.

'Tell me about when you met,' I said.

'What?' Mum asked. 'When I met who?'

'Dad. Tell me about when you met Dad.'

There was a pause. My question had thrown her. It was probably the first time I'd mentioned him since the funeral.

'Why?' she asked, suspicious suddenly.

'I just wanted to know.'

'I thought you did already,' she said, still confused. 'I've told you before, surely?'

'Tell me again,' I insisted. 'Please.'

'Oh, I'm not sure...it's very hard for me you know.'

'As much as you can manage Mum. Please.'

'Emma...have you...you know what we talked about, before

you went to Leeds? Matt's got through it now, he's done his...grieving. But you... You being so quiet, going on like nothing happened. It's not *normal,* my darling.' Her voice dropped to a whisper. My cheek was sweaty against the mobile phone.

'It would help me to hear about you and Dad,' I said, my voice monotone. 'Perhaps it would help me...work through the grief, or whatever that counsellor woman called it.'

'I don't see...it's not relevant is it?' She sighed. 'Anyway you know how I met Dad. I met him through your Auntie Mae.'

'She's not my auntie,' I said quietly.

'What? I can't hear you, you're breaking up.'

'Nothing,' I said. 'Carry on.'

'At a party, at your Auntie Mae's. That's where we met. Mae had done some bookkeeping for him...she thought he seemed lonely. She introduced us at the party.'

'Yes.'

'We just hit it off. Had the same interests, the same outlook. Not quite love at first sight though.' Mum gave a tiny laugh. 'He was awfully podgy when we first met. You must have seen some of the pictures. Hair down to his shoulders, and a healthy appetite for beer.'

'Can't imagine what you ever saw in him.' My mother was skinny, she always had been, and when she wasn't tear-stained and blotchy, she was beautiful.

'Don't say things like that. Your father was, and still is, the most charming man I've ever met.'

'You need to get out more.'

'Emma.' Her voice was full of reproach. Guilt stabbed me.

'I'm sorry Mum. I better go.'

'I thought everything was OK with you,' she said. 'I'm worried now, this doesn't sound like you. All bitter...'

'I'm sorry. Perhaps I'm not ready to hear about Dad after all. It doesn't matter anyway. I'm fine honestly. Listen, I'd better go, my bus has just arrived.'

It was a lie; I was still staring into the pond.

'But I'll speak to you again soon. I promise.'

~

All the practice rooms were full. Four in the afternoon seemed to be peak time, which made sense when you thought about it. It was that awkward hour after your final lecture and before Neighbours – the perfect time to let out a bit of emotional angst on a cheap, out-of-tune piano. I wandered up and down the corridor, staring through the small windows in each door, wondering if anyone was nearly done.

Through the final window, I saw him. He was frowning with concentration like the rest of them. It was difficult to make out what he was playing from the muffled sound. I leaned closer to the door. Impressionist. Debussy perhaps. A few bars later, I recognised it: Doctor Gradus ad Parnassum. I smiled. He was clearly being honest when he said violin was his forte; I'd learnt this when I was about twelve. Although the fingering was tricky and he was playing it fast, and from what I could hear, flawlessly.

I stood and watched him. His hair was almost black. It kept flopping in front of his eyes and he shook his head impatiently as his hands made their way up and down the keyboard.

Dad had hated Debussy. He insisted none of his pieces had a melody. *You know me, Emma, I like a good tune. Something that starts at A and goes to B. Logically. None of this aimless meandering up and down the notes.* I couldn't stand Dad when he was flippant like that – when he failed to appreciate the beauty in something subtle and restrained, or something that made you work to understand it. It was a chilling prediction of just how shallow he was, and it had disappointed me.

Daniel finished playing. He didn't look up, but off to the

middle distance, as though contemplating what to play next. I paused for a few seconds before swinging the door open. Thinking of my father had flooded by body with adrenalin and it spurred me on. Carpe diem and all that. We could bond over Debussy.

'Hello,' I said. My voice sounded loud and almost raucous in this tiny room that seconds before had been flooded with gentle music.

He looked up in surprise. A shadow passed over his face, for a brief moment, and then he gave a spurious smile.

'Emma,' he said. His voice was still thick – I now thought maybe Cumbrian – but there was a new hardness to it.

'Doctor Gradus ad Parnassum?' I babbled. 'Tricky fingering on those right-hand semi-quavers from what I remember. And keeping the left-hand crotchets nice and light is always a challenge.'

'Er, yes,' he said. He was looking at me as though I was completely mad.

'Sorry,' I mumbled, glancing at the floor. 'I shouldn't have barged in like that.'

'No,' he said, reaching forward and taking his music from the stand. 'No, it's fine, I'm done. You can have the room.'

'Oh,' I said. 'Thanks.'

He smiled nervously at me as he pushed the sheets of music into his rucksack. Some of it caught on the zip as he forced it in, ripping the corner from one page. He tutted but continued stuffing it into the bag. What was the hurry? It was as though I was diseased or something.

'Er, are you OK?' I asked. 'You're not ill or anything?' I realised how stupid my question sounded the second after I asked it, but it was too late.

He paused, gave another smile. This one was nervy but seemed genuine. 'Sorry, it's just. No offence or anything but that lad you hang around with – he told me about it. And, you know, it's just not my kind of thing.'

'What isn't?' I had no idea what he was talking about.

'Well, you know, religion. Bible-bashers. They make me a bit nervous. Totally no offence. Each to their own and all that. Whatever works for you huh? Anyway, see you later.'

With that devastating explanation, he grabbed his rucksack by the strap and swept out of the room before my mouth had time to hang open in disbelief.

Chapter Twenty-two

Emma, February 2011

The picture often painted of Elgar is of the social outsider, a devout Catholic, snubbed by the English musical establishment but eventually, through the force of his music, reaching the pinnacle of British society and close friendship with royalty...

Over on my bed, my phone began to ring but I ignored it and continued reading. How ironic that I'd chosen to write my essay for the *Music in History and Culture* module on how Elgar's personality manifests in his compositions. I'd never known before he was a lapsed Catholic who was shy among strangers. Was there anyone I admired that wasn't a Catholic? I checked my watch. 4.45pm. Great. I'd managed to write about two hundred words, and I only had half an hour before I'd have to leave for Mass. So much for finishing the essay today.

I continued to read. The face of the twenty-pound note seemed to be as enigmatic as his work. My phone rang again. How could I write an essay on Elgar with the third movement of Vivaldi's Summer trilling away in the background? It was February anyway. Winter not Summer. Definitely time to change the ring tone. I picked the phone up. For once, it wasn't Mum, or her. As I pressed the green button, I realised with a shock it was a Northumberland number.

'Hello?' I said.

'Hi Emma, it's Joe. Joe Nichols,'

'Joe! Hi. How are you?'

'Good, thanks. I just...well...wondered how you were. So what you up to? Back at uni? Er...'

He coughed. I could almost hear his cheeks burning up. Or was that my cheeks? I wondered how he'd got hold of my number.

'Yes, I'm, um, in the middle of writing an essay actually. About

Elgar. But I think it's nearly time for Mass.' Holding my phone rendered me unable to see my watch. I flicked my eyes across to my bedside clock radio, but it was obscured by the pyjama top I'd flung on top of earlier.

'It's five o'clock,' Joe said. 'What time is Mass? You could always be naughty and miss it.'

'And spend all day tomorrow reciting Hail Marys?' I said. It was so easy to talk to Joe, to become this confident, sarcastic person who was almost like my old self. 'I don't think so. It's at half-past. Don't worry; I don't have to go yet. So how are you? It's a surprise to hear from you to be honest.'

'Well, I was a bit bored. Just thought it would be nice to catch up. I'm meant to be revising for one of my mocks tomorrow, but I think I've got it nailed.'

Mocks. His Mock A levels. His confidence was justified though – both Lucy and Ruth had gone on about how smart he was. He intended on studying medicine at Durham and no one seemed to think there was any question of him not getting the marks he needed.

'Oh, good luck. I'm sure you'll be fine.'

'Thanks. So how are things? We miss Luce here. Have you been over to their new place? It doesn't sound like much. Leaking toilet and everything.'

'No I haven't been round yet actually,' I replied. The four unanswered text messages from Lucy on my phone came to mind.

'OK um, this is awkward but...well, what's the point beating around the bush, as my mam would say. The reason I'm ringing – it's Lucy. She asked me to. She hasn't heard from you for a while and I think she's a bit hurt. I know you've just had your exams and all that but they must have been over a couple of weeks ago now, and surely you've got time to just stick your head round the door and say hello? And I am sure Pete would like to see you too – after all, you used to live together didn't you? Luce said she's tried to call you as well, but you don't pick up.'

I was momentarily floored. There was nothing in his tone to suggest he was suspicious of anything but I didn't know what to say to him. I was surprised by such an unexpected tactic from Lucy – getting Joe to call me just didn't feel like her style.

'Oh that's silly,' I said, unconvincingly. 'I just wanted to give them some space, you know, since they're newly married and everything…'

'But…' Joe said. 'Sorry to sound accusatory and you know I couldn't give a flying fart, but, you haven't even been to Mass have you? Lucy and Peter have been looking out for you and they say you haven't been. Not even on Sundays.'

'Yes I have!' I said. 'I've just been going to a different church. One that's nearer me. I really have been going, honestly. Every weekend, and to confession every fortnight.'

My confessions had been a joke. The most heinous crime I'd admitted to was plagiarising large amounts of *The Companion to Music* – an out-of-print book that my antiquarian grandfather had found me.

'I really couldn't care less whether you've been having an affair with the priest. I'm just doing Lucy a favour. Give her a call, will you? Just to say hello. She doesn't know anyone in Leeds and Peter's tied up with his studying, so it would be nice for her to see a friendly face.'

'OK, I'll call her after Mass. I have to go now.'

'Sure. Take care then. Hope you'll come up and see us soon. Good luck with Egman or whatever he was called.'

I laughed. 'Bye.'

I hung up and flicked through the messages in my phone. There were five in a row, all from Lucy.

Hello Emma! We're back! Missed you but had a fab time. When can we meet? Our new address is 9 Royal Park Terrace. Come anytime. Lucy xxx

Hi Em, Married life is great so far. Got our photos from the honeymoon back, can't wait to show you. When can you come over? Mrs Field xx

Emma, did you get my last message? Hope you are well. I'm not pregnant yet! Come over soon, love Lucy xxx

Em, it's Lucy again. I'm just checking to see your phone number's right. Haven't heard from you. Call me if you get this. Lx

OK Emma what's up? Getting worried about you now! Peter and I haven't heard from you in ages. Are you OK? Amelia says this is definitely the right number for you. Hope you are alright and exams went well. Lucy xx

I started to write a new message but couldn't think what to say. I stood for a few minutes staring at my phone.

Hello Lucy, it's Emma, I'm fine.

What could I add? I slept with your husband? I'm in love with your husband? I never want to see you or him again?

Just been busy with uni work that's all. I'll come and see you soon. Em x

I sent the message and looked around for my handbag, which I uncovered beneath a pile of washing on my bed. Just as I was reaching to tuck my phone into my bag, it started to ring. It was Lucy. I couldn't ignore it this time. If I didn't answer, she might turn up at the flat.

The strains of Vivaldi were rapidly hurtling towards the first perfect cadence, leaving me hardly any time before the call went to voicemail. I hesitated for another second, then pressed the green button again.

'Hi!' I said. 'Lucy. Thanks for calling but it's just not a great time at the moment. I have to go, sorry, I'm just on my way to Mass. I'll call you straight after, I promise. But I'm already running late.'

'It's me,' Pete's voice said.

My knees gave way and I sank down onto the heap of washing on my bed.

'Pete.'

'Look, I knew you'd be off to Mass, I'm about to go too. Just tell me where you're going now. Which church? I'll meet you there. There are a few things I have to talk to you about. Lucy's not coming with me, she's just leaving to visit Mary in Manchester for a few days. So we can have a talk OK? Which church?'

'Our Lady of the Sacred Heart,' I replied robotically.

'Right. See you there,' Pete said, and hung up.

~

He arrived late, as I knew he would. The church was the furthest one in the city from his new flat with Lucy, which was why I had been going there. He would have to change buses twice. This church was nothing like as grand as the city cathedral, and on weekday services was usually practically empty, with only a little old woman and a handful of students attending. The priest performed mass with the least amount of charisma and enthusiasm I had ever seen, his voice monotone enough for his words to wash over me, leaving no indent.

Pete must have crept quietly, because he startled me when he suddenly appeared at my side in the pew. The carrier bag he held rustled as he tucked it under the bench in front. He arrived just in time for the first reading and muttered the response so quietly I wondered if he was saying anything at all. Maybe he was having a crisis of faith too. I certainly was.

The problem with being a Catholic was that so much was expected of you. You had to live up to this ideal of the perfect person. There were so many things you couldn't and shouldn't do. And it was just impossible. Truly impossible, to be a perfect Catholic. Sometimes I wondered why I bothered. No one could attempt to live a Catholic life and not fail. Even priests must do hundreds of things wrong every day. But there was something that kept me coming back, some belief that my hours spent in devotion and contrition would eventually wash away my guilt. And some days, I simply prayed for him, because Dad believed in God, and I wanted him to know how much I loved him, despite everything.

Sitting next to Pete, during Mass, although I expected everything to feel different, it didn't. It was the first time I had seen him since we'd slept together. He didn't look different, behave differently or even look sheepish. But then neither did I. We looked like two old friends, sitting beside each other and literally singing from the same hymn sheet.

Afterwards, I wordlessly followed Pete out of the church. It was snowing but not heavily enough to settle. Snowflakes gently landed on my face, but they were so small they felt like droplets of icy rain.

'Pete, it's cold, please, I don't want to stand out here.'

'OK,' he said. 'Come on, let's go to that pub,' pointing to a pebble-dashed building at the end of the street. A faded sign pronounced it as The Clarence Inn.

The pub was smoky inside with a roaring fire in one corner. I sat on a wobbly stool near the chimneybreast, and Pete went to get some drinks. He left the carrier bag propped up by his stool and I peered in it. Inside was a small black cardboard box, half the size of a shoebox. Whatever was inside was definitely not a piece of jewellery.

He came back with a pint of brown liquid for himself and a lemonade for me. Sitting down, he took a great gulp from his glass, swept his hand across his mouth and let out a sigh.

'Needed that,' he said.

I sipped my drink and nodded.

'So how have you been?' I asked.

'Great,' he said. 'And wretched.' He laughed.

'Really? No wedded bliss then?'

'I've missed you, I really have. It's been hard. Moving out so quickly, I didn't even get a chance to tell you. I had no idea the university was so accommodating to married couples, but it seems I'm not the only student to get married. It was the best idea, of course, for us to get a place of our own. I thought it was important that Lucy branch away a bit, you know? She's always been stuck up in Cresswell, never really seen the world. I'm hoping she'll get some work soon, that would really help her make some friends so she doesn't feel so isolated while I'm studying.'

'Oh yes. Of course. A nice little part time job.'

He ignored me. 'I'm sorry I haven't had a chance to speak to you until now Emma. Lucy's really missed you. Of course, I understand why you might not want to see her at the moment, but she's your best friend…'

'Excuse me?' I interrupted.

'Sorry, sorry, I'm tired. Slip of the tongue. I meant you're her best friend. She needs you, you know.'

'Oh well, Lucy's needs must be met of course. How selfish of me. I must go to her at once.' I picked up my bag and half rose to my feet. My own bitterness came as a surprise. It wasn't Lucy's fault. Just like it wasn't Mum's fault. It was mine.

'Please,' Pete said quietly, gently tugging my arm until I sat back down. 'I'm trying to do the right thing.'

'What about me?' I said. 'What about what I need?'

'All the time, you know, I've been thinking of you. For these last few weeks, I can't stop thinking of you. What happened.' He reached forward and held my hand. His fingers were warm against mine. 'I love you. I really do.'

'But what are we going to do?' I asked, softly.

Pete dropped my hand and leaned back in his chair.

'Nothing. We can't. I'm married. I can't have what I want. I'm sorry. It was unbelievably, utterly wrong. You should never have met me. I've ruined you. We've ruined each other.'

'Pete,' I implored. 'You're over-reacting. Please...' I felt tears welling up but I didn't brush them away. 'Lucy will understand.'

'That's not the point. I made a promise. In God's eyes, Lucy and I are the same person now. There's no way back.'

He stared at me for a few moments, and I was silent, tugging at the crucifix around my neck, staring at him.

'Emma,' he began, after a while. He looked concerned. 'Have you confessed it? I saw you take communion.'

'No,' I said, staring at the table. 'Of course I haven't. I can't tell some priest that I've had sex with my friend's husband.'

'You must. If something happened to you… as I am sure you know, sex before marriage…it's a mortal sin. I know it's awful but the priest will have heard worse. You'll feel so much better for it.'

Pete sighed and rested his elbows on the table, holding my hands in his. I tried to twist them free, looking everywhere except at him, but he held on tight.

'I'm so sorry. Please, look at me.' I stared at him. 'We need to make the best out of a bad situation.'

'What's in the bag?' I said. I didn't want to hear any more.

'Bag?' He looked confused for a few seconds and then our eyes rested on the carrier bag with its box inside.

'In the bag,' I said, gesturing towards it with my eyebrows. 'Present for me?'

'I was coming to that,' he said. 'But since you're so determined not to listen to anything I have to say, why don't you have a look?'

I hesitated. I didn't want to know what was inside now.

'All I want to do is help you. I know I've let you down, and I'm trying to make amends. But perhaps you don't understand. I'm no good at explaining these things. You should speak to someone older.'

I reached towards the bag and pulled out the box. It was light. I placed it on the table in front of us and looked up at Pete. Without speaking, he motioned for me to open it and I lifted off the lid.

For a second, I couldn't comprehend what I was looking at. Inside, curled among a frayed piece of tissue paper, was a long piece of knotted black leather, like a piece of thick rope. I pushed the tissue paper aside to get a better look. Rolled up into a coil, the object looked like a bit like a belt. The leather was old and slightly worn, and there were patches showing through the dye. One end of it was thicker and smooth. A handle.

It wasn't a belt.

'Is this some kind of joke?' I said.

Pete reached forward and lifted it out. All around the sides of the handle, images I'd seen time and time again over the last few months were inscribed into the leather. Mary, Jesus, the cross, all embossed in the smooth leather.

'It was made in Mexico,' Pete said, quietly. 'The craftsmanship is beautiful. Look Emma, can you see the detail?'

I nodded numbly.

'But Pete,' I said, already knowing the answer to the question I was about to ask. 'What is it for?'

Chapter Twenty-three

Emma, February 2011

Amelia always picked the worst possible moment to knock on my door.

'Em,' she called, in her 'friendly' voice. 'I've got a cuppa for you. What you up to in there?' She tried the handle but for once, thankfully, I was one step ahead and had locked the door.

'Hang on,' I said, getting back on my feet and flinging the thing underneath my bed. I was holding my *Handbook of Prayers* – the one Father Gerry had given me on my first trip to Cresswell. I paused for a second, examining its red cover. It looked worn and old now. I flicked through the creamy yellow pages, several of which had corners turned down.

My favourite prayer – the one I had been about to recite as I flagellated myself – was the Mea Culpa:

I confess to Almighty God, to blessed Mary ever Virgin, to blessed Michael the Archangel, to blessed John the Baptist, to the holy Apostles Peter and Paul, to all the Saints and to you, brothers (and to you Father), that I have sinned exceedingly, in thought, word and deed: through my fault, through my fault, through my most grievous fault. Therefore I beseech the blessed Mary, ever Virgin, blessed Michael the Archangel, blessed John the Baptist, the holy Apostles Peter and Paul, all the Saints, and you, brothers (and you Father), to pray to the Lord our God for me. Amen.

Perhaps this prayer appealed because I felt permanently guilty, and I would do, forever, because whatever I did, my father's death would always be my fault. Perhaps it was because I liked the idea of admitting that I wasn't perfect. Perhaps it was because Pete had gone through it with me on several occasions.

Or perhaps it was because I recognized it from *Gone with the Wind*, which had always been one of my favourite films. In any case, I said it nightly, before I went to sleep, as part of my examination of conscience. I knew it off by heart and found it helpful. I liked the idea of apologising for my crimes, especially the ones that no one knew about. I shut the book and put it on my desk, covering it with *Elgar – Child of Dreams* by a chap called Jerrold Northrop Moore, which was a suitably eccentric name for an Elgar-fancier.

'Amelia,' I said, as I let her in. 'Thanks, that's really kind of you.'

'No problem,' she replied, her eyes narrowing in suspicion as she cast them about my cluttered room. She restrained herself from asking why I'd locked my door in the middle of the afternoon, and pushed her way past me, cradling her own mug in her hands, wiggling her bottom into a space on my bed. A Twix stuck out of one of her jeans' back pockets. Each of her fingernails was painted a different colour, ranging from orange to deep red, but they were all exactly the same length. I waited for a few moments, then turned my desk chair round and sat opposite her.

'Is it cold out? I haven't left the flat all day,' I asked.

'Yes, it's bloody freezing. Even worse than yesterday. Didn't you have lectures today?' She looked down at her pink socks as she spoke, circling her feet at the ankles.

'I had one, this afternoon, and I should really have gone to the practice rooms too, but I was trying to get this essay done.' I glanced at the notebooks, textbooks and sheets of paper scattered across my desk. Amelia peered at my laptop and smirked. I'd only written the title and my name so far.

'Em, it's four o' clock in the afternoon,' she said. 'Is that all you've done?'

The infuriating thing about Amelia was that despite appearing to do very little actual work, she had done amazingly well in her exams. She'd managed to get comfortable 2:1s in every single one, which made her one of those annoying secret studiers. But she never talked about it. I only knew her exam results because I'd asked her, and she'd reluctantly revealed them with a shrug and a speedy change of subject.

'I've been making notes,' I protested weakly. Amelia's reticence was beginning to worry me. It was almost as though she was building up to telling me something horrible, like she'd got together with Maria and Sam and they'd decided as a group that I should move out. Now Pete wasn't there, they didn't think I had any friends in the flat and it was best I found somewhere else to live. Or she'd found out about Pete and me, and wanted to give me a piece of her mind. Amelia was very passionate about cheats. My adrenalin levels climbed as I tried to read her body language. She wasn't giving anything away.

'Hmm,' she said. She continued wiggling her feet. After a further pause, she finally looked up at me and met my eyes. 'Do you know what? You haven't been out with us once this term. You should be ashamed missy.'

The sparkle came back to her eyes and I relaxed. Perhaps she was the one feeling insecure. Maybe she thought I'd been avoiding her. I'd continued being anti-social, holed up in my room for the majority of the time since Pete had left, and had hardly chatted in the kitchen, preferring instead to listen, laugh, nod and smile at appropriate moments. I was paranoid that Maria kept a voodoo doll of me in her bedroom, and that was why my shoulder seemed to ache permanently, and it was actually nothing to do with the bag stuffed full of textbooks I lugged into uni every day.

Amelia wasn't so bad really. We just didn't have a lot in common.

'I know,' I said. 'I haven't really got a good excuse.'

'Well, it's either one thing or another,' Amelia replied, breaking her Twix in half and offering me a piece. 'It's either cos you're still paranoid that Maria hates you – which as I told you already isn't the case – or you're busy mourning the loss of the great Mr Field. In any case, it's high time you came out with us. We were discussing it earlier, and it's decided. This evening. No arguments or excuses allowed.'

Perhaps it would take my mind off things. 'OK,' I said. 'If I've no choice.'

'None whatsoever. Fab. We'll be leaving at about eight. So pull out your best outfit and highest shoes. We are going to get wrecked.' She sprang neatly off the bed and walked to the door.

'Amelia?' I said.

'Yes?'

'Where are we going?'

'Ask me no questions, and I'll tell you no lies. It's a surprise. All I'll say is, be prepared for the night of your life.' She winked at me over her shoulder and left.

I stared over at the thing, the end of which had come unfurled and was poking out menacingly from underneath the valance. The contrast between the normal conversation I'd just had with Amelia and what I had been about to do to myself ten minutes before was staggering. What was wrong with me? It was as though I was possessed. My normal, rational mind had been poisoned, hijacked, stolen from me and replaced with that of a fanatic.

Whipping myself was not going to help anybody. It wouldn't bring my father back, and it wouldn't erase what had happened the night of Lucy and Pete's wedding.

It was the first time Amelia had been in my room this term, and the first time since I'd slept with Pete. In the intervening weeks, I'd turned into someone else.

I thought of Daniel, of the horror in his eyes when I'd burst in on him. He'd been warned off me. Someone must have told him I was a Catholic, and I reckoned it must have been Sam. It was exactly the sort of thing he would do, although I wondered when he had seen me with Daniel. Sam would've found it hilarious. He must have told him I was some kind of religious zealot, who went round trying to convert people.

I walked to the mirror, depressed at how tired I looked. My

hair was tied up, a habit I'd recently adopted out of laziness. I pulled my hair band out and let it fall down around my shoulders. The colour wasn't bright anymore. I used to highlight it myself, but I hadn't done it since last summer. I tugged my fingers through my hair and smoothed it down. It was almost brown.

I suppose I was lovesick. I'd been happy when Pete and I had spent time together, just me and him, and I'd been able to listen to him, to draw strength from his utter, unwavering strength in his own convictions. I'd hoped that I could adopt these too, and enjoy the same security he did. But it didn't work like that.

I missed him. She had him, and now, I had nothing, and I didn't know where I belonged.

A surge of aggression took hold of me and I pinched my cheeks, harder and harder, until they glowed red and blotchy. I walked over to the underused wardrobe, opened the doors, and there they were: my party clothes. Shiny and glittery and gorgeous. I pulled out the first hanger. It was the red top Amelia had made me buy on that shopping trip at the beginning of the year. It was tight, shiny satin, with boning like a corset but little spaghetti straps. Teamed with my boot-cut black trousers, it made me look tall and thin. I stared at it, trying to remember when I'd last worn it, and then it struck me. I hadn't worn it at all.

I would wear it tonight. I turned to put it on, excitement and anticipation building, when something caught my eye.

Stuck to the inside of the wardrobe I hadn't opened for so long was a poster.

An angelic Victorian girl in a cute little bonnet smiled at me serenely. Above her head were written the words:

Good girls go to heaven. Bad girls go… everywhere

~

It had been too long since I'd drunk any alcohol. Walking to the toilet, that familiar unsteadiness brought my mother's words back to me as I tried not to trip over: *Head up straight, stick your bust out and push your shoulders back.* I made it and plonked myself down heavily on the seat.

We were in a new nightclub that had opened up over the Christmas break. Heaven and Hell. 'Heaven' was on the top floor, all white painted clouds and cherubs, playing the kind of cheesy pop I found myself able to quite happily jig around to, but Amelia, Sam and Maria couldn't endure. 'Purgatory' was on the middle floor, a rather bland bar playing R'n'B. 'Hell' was in the basement and was predictably painted in red and black, with the bar staff all wearing devil horns. The music was what Amelia called 'hardcore'.

We were in Hell.

It was still early. Amelia hadn't yet got into one of the podium cages but I'd left everyone doing tequila shots, so it wasn't going to be long. It was too warm in the toilets. Drizzles of sweat ran down the bright red walls. My eye make-up had begun to settle in the corners of each eye, and underneath all the blusher my skin was almost transparent. I reached into the tiny handbag I'd borrowed from Amelia to find some lipgloss, and noticed that my phone was lit up with a new message. I clicked to read it.

What are you doing this evening? I think we should talk some more. Lucy is away, so why don't you come over. I need to see you. Px

I also had a missed call from him. I paused for a second but decided not to reply, and shoved my phone back into my bag. I would see this evening through no matter what.

When I sat back down, there was some kind of alcoholic shot sitting in front of me.

'Come on Em,' shouted Amelia. 'We know your trick, disappearing to the toilet at appropriate moments! You didn't think you were going to get away with it did you?'

'It's red,' I moaned. 'What is it?'

'Ask me no questions…' Amelia began, then started up into a fit of giggles, followed immediately by Maria and then Sam.

'Drink it!' Sam shouted, slamming his palms down on the wobbly table, and then laughing yet again in disgust as his hands stuck to it.

The red liquid looked evil. Drips of it trickled down the outside of the sticky shot glass. Pete's face appeared in my mind. *Why are you such a sheep Emma? Don't follow the crowd. Be your own person.*

I picked up the glass and sniffed its contents. Aniseed. The three of them were grinning at me expectantly.

'Come on!' Maria shouted, smiling at me. 'Go on, just open up and swallow!'

I did it for her. Or at least, that's what I told myself. Maria's smile, which surely meant I was forgiven… that smile meant so much to me, I would have done anything for it.

~

Three hours later, I'd ascended to Heaven, having persuaded Sam to come with me. And there I was, swaying away to Kylie's *Spinning Around*, bumping my bottom against Sam's periodically. I couldn't remember a night I'd had more fun. The three text messages I'd received from Pete pleading with me to speak to him didn't seem important. I was powerful and attractive, convinced all the men in the club had noticed me in my red top. As I span around, I caught the eye of one particularly handsome gentleman watching me from beside the bar. He was tall with the most perfect hair I'd ever seen. It was deep brown, coiffed at the front into an understated sweeping curl. He wore a coat and had a maroon scarf around his neck, but he held a pint glass and didn't look as though he was preparing to leave. He continued watching me until a large shadowy female walked in front of him. When she moved out of the way, I looked again but he had turned back to the bar.

I tried to work out how to get his attention. Perhaps I should march over to the bar, align myself next to him or at least in his field of vision and order another drink. Water this time though. Nothing alcoholic.

'I'm just going to get a drink,' I shouted to Sam. 'Do you want one?'

He shook his head.

I cast my eyes around for a convenient gap, finding one and squeezing into it. Out of the corner of my eye, I could see Mr Maroon Scarf. Eventually, one of the barmen decided it was my turn and raised his fingers as a way of asking what I wanted.

'Just a glass of water!' I shouted.

He nodded. As he bent down to fish out a glass, I noticed the back of a girl's head opposite me. Even in the dim light I could see her hair was gloriously thick and shiny. It flicked about when she moved her head, as though she was looking for someone. The longer I admired it, the more I knew whose hair it was. What could she be doing here?

I shrank back behind the person next to me and continued to watch as she turned around. My drunken brain struggled to process the situation. I couldn't think of a single reason that Lucy would be in a nightclub.

She was alone, still in her coat and scanning the dancefloor. I had to get away. There was no way I wanted to see Lucy like this. Not dressed in this top! She'd think I was a tart, with my ridiculous cleavage, hoiked up as high as possible. There was no way she was seeing me like this. I grabbed the glass of water the unsmiling barman had placed in front of me and turned to go, finding myself face-to-face with Him. Or His Chest at least. I looked up.

He leant down and spoke straight into my ear.

'Where are you going with that?' he said.

'To the dancefloor, where my friend is,' I replied, hoping that my back wasn't as familiar as Lucy's and that she wasn't staring at it in recognition as I had been with hers a few minutes before.

'Mind if I join you?' he said, moving out of the way so I could get past.

'Er, no, I suppose not.'

He followed me back to the stage area where Sam was dancing. I stood at the edge of the dancefloor, looking at Sam, not sure what to do. The man stood beside me. I wished he'd go away. There was no sign of Lucy anymore. I glanced at my watch – it was just after midnight and the place was heaving.

'So why are you wearing a scarf?' I asked. It was the only thing I could think of.

'Oh, you know, to stand out from the crowd. Make myself a bit more appealing to the girls. Does it work?'

Sleazy. Urggh. 'Um, yes, I suppose so. Although you must be very sweaty underneath it.'

He put his arm around my waist and put his face close to mine. 'Would you like to see?'

I moved away quickly. What a creep. Amelia and Maria appeared, weaving their way through the throng and I waved at them.

'Sorry, my friends are coming back,' I said, turning to walk away, but he put his arm around me forcefully, pulled me towards him and began to kiss my neck. I squirmed, but he wouldn't let go.

'Emma! What are you doing?' Amelia's voice rang out clear over the music.

I disentangled myself from the man and turned to see Amelia and Maria both staring at me, their mouths open.

'What?' I said, confused, looking back at the man, who let go of me.

'Maria!' he said loudly, giving a nervous laugh and looking

straight at her.

Amelia's face fell. 'Oh Emma…' she began, but Maria had turned away and stormed off and Amelia went to follow her. I didn't understand. I looked around at Sam, who was also gazing at me disapprovingly. He came down from the stage and the man disappeared into the crowd.

'What?' I asked Sam, starting to panic. Maria's frown was imbedded in my mind's eye like the flash from a camera. The lines across her freckly forehead were so deep that she resembled one of those strange-looking puppies with all that extra skin. That horrible frown, directed at me. Again.

'I didn't realise,' Sam said. 'Of course, I should have guessed from the scarf. Oh Emma you dopey thing. That was Maria's new man.'

'What? I don't understand. Maria's new man? Since when?'

'We were talking about him only the other night. Don't you remember, in the kitchen? You were there for god's sake! She met him a couple of weeks ago at one of those animal cruelty prevention meetings. She's been besotted with him ever since.'

'I don't remember…'

'Come on you must do. He's got a big birthmark across his neck, that's why he wears a scarf all the time – one of those cravat things. She's been banging on about him every night for the last two weeks. You must remember!'

'How was I to know it was him? It could have been anyone.'

'Come on,' Sam said. 'How many 20-year-old men do you know that wear silk scarves? It's not rocket science.'

'Oh…'

Maria came towards me again, her face expanded with rage. Amelia was trying to drag her backwards.

And then it hit me, full in the face. Cider, laced with black-currant cordial.

'You bitch!' Maria screamed. I blinked furiously to get the sticky liquid out of my eyes. 'What is your problem? Seriously

Emma! Just can't keep your hands off other people's men can you? Well fuck you! You stupid horrible sad bitch!'

'Maria,' Amelia pleaded, tugging at her arm. 'Come on, you're drunk, let's go.'

Maria burst into angry sobs and Amelia led her away, glancing at me. Her expression said '*sorry but you did bring it upon yourself*'. Pushing my tangled, saturated hair out my eyes, I looked at Sam.

'Come on Emma,' he said. 'Let's go to the toilet and get you cleaned up.'

His kindness was wasted on me. There was no point. My beautiful red top was ruined. I pushed him away and walked off.

Outside, there were no taxis so I walked in the direction of home, checking my phone as I dragged my feet along in misery. I had two messages.

Hi Em, you won't believe it but I'm in Heaven and Hell. Amelia said you were coming here tonight. I hope you don't think I'm stalking you or anything but I so want to see you. And you know what they say about Mohammed and the Mountain. Anyway if you get this, text me. Lx

Please call me. Pete x

What had Lucy told Pete? He said she'd gone away for the night. It made no sense, he'd never let her go to a nightclub, which means she must have lied to him, and made up some excuse so she could come looking for me. But why? Why couldn't she just leave me alone?

I pressed Pete's number into my phone.

My heart pounded in the certainty that it was wrong, but I was a sinner's daughter after all, and the surprise and elation in his voice when he answered reassured me I should go to him.

Chapter Twenty-four

Emma, February 2011

As I contemplated the cracks in the ceiling above their bed, I found myself irritatingly worried about Lucy. As far as I knew, she didn't have any friends in Leeds. So where was she? She must have had some kind of plan for her foray into the seedy world of student discos. Pete maintained she was in Manchester, as he kissed my face and neck, and I didn't correct him. The idea that Lucy had lied to him was very strange. She'd never lied about anything.

Pete was in the shower, washing me off, as I lay there wondering whose side of the bed I had slept on. The pillow smelt of rosewater, and smoke from my hair. On the tiny bedside table was a photo of Lucy and Pete on their wedding day, a crucifix, a small teddy bear and a book called *The Furrow*. I sat up. It had been dark when I'd arrived at about 1am last night, and in my drunken haze, all I could remember was throwing myself at Pete, quite literally, and the passionate embrace that ended up with us in bed. I understood now why it was so easy for us to 'land' in bed – it was about two foot from the front door.

I hadn't seen a studio flat before. It was basically just a large front room of an Edwardian terrace. The bed was pushed up against the opposite wall to the window, at which hung stained blinds, one on each pane. The room was warm and condensation had gathered around the corners of each window, sticking the thin calico to them with a sweaty glue.

There were very few things in there that made me think of Lucy. The room was perfectly tidy but the walls were covered in bumpy wallpaper that looked as though it had ants trapped underneath it, and the carpet was horribly scratchy underfoot, as I discovered when I stood up.

Pete came out of the bathroom.

'Morning,' he said standing in front of me with a towel around his waist and nothing else. Just like our episode on the beach, the situation started to feel like a dream: unreal, unsettling. All the truths in the world had been turned on their heads.

'Hi,' I said, and quickly got back into the bed, covering my legs with the duvet.

'Would you like a cup of tea?' he asked, filling the kettle up.

'Yes please. I need the toilet though; do you...have any trousers I could borrow? Mine are all sticky.' My crumpled heap of clothes lay on the floor at the side of the bed, the red top flung open like it had exploded. I remembered him undoing all the buttons in frustration and his excitement at discovering me braless underneath.

He opened a drawer in his bedside table, pulling out a pair of grey jogging bottoms. 'Here you go,' he said, throwing them at my head. 'Although it's a little too late for modesty isn't it?'

I smiled but didn't answer. I felt awkward and uncomfortable, trying to work out what had happened to Pete, the most religious man on the planet, whose conscience followed him wherever he went.

I crept into the bathroom and shut the door. In here, there was more evidence of Lucy's existence. A pink fluffy exfoliating sponge hung from the shower taps, wet from Pete's shower, the bath was cluttered with various shampoos, conditioners and shower gels, and on the shelf above the tiny basin were a couple of perfume bottles. Impulsively, I picked one of them up and sprayed it into the steamy air in front of me. It smelt the same as the pillow. I ran to the toilet and retched.

I was consumed with guilt. I had to leave.

Pete was dressed when I went back into the main room, sitting at his desk reading. 'Your tea's on the table,' he said, without looking up.

'I have to go.' I rummaged around on the floor for my things. Why hadn't I worn a coat last night? Now I had to creep back to

Clarence Dock, which was miles away, wearing my stained, night-before clothes.

'Emma?' he said, turning around. 'Are you OK?'

'No, not really,' I said. My nose flooded. 'I've got to get out of here.'

'Don't cry.' He didn't get up and put his arms around me.

'Can I borrow a jumper?' I said, battling inside with the tears, one of which won and rolled happily down my cheek and straight into my mouth.

'Yes of course.' He handed me the jumper that he was sitting on: a grey fleece, fluffy and worn. I pulled it on over the top of his t-shirt. 'But don't cry, please.'

'What's going on?' I sank down on the bed and stared up at him. 'I'm so confused.'

'You're so tired and hungover, that's what you are.' He knelt down on the floor in front of me. 'I tell you what. You sit here, wrap the blanket around you, and have your cup of tea and I'll nip down to the Day and Night and get some bacon and eggs.'

I nodded. He kissed me on the cheek, grabbed his wallet, jacket and shoes and left. I drank the tea. I didn't have the energy to do a runner, but Lucy would surely be back soon. I kicked at my trousers, still lying by the bed, and unearthed Amelia's tiny handbag. My phone had started to beep mournfully to alert me to its low battery. I checked my messages, almost certain there would be one from Lucy, but there wasn't. There were none from Sam either.

It was 9.30am. Perhaps no one in the flat was awake yet and they thought I was in my room. It was doubtful any of them would bother to knock and see if I was OK. Maybe Amelia would, if there was nothing more important occupying her head. My initial terror of dying in my room and laying undiscovered for days, until people realized the stench wasn't the bins after all, flooded back to me. It really was possible. You could disappear and your three-month-old friends wouldn't even notice you were gone. It was all so fake, the way we'd told each other we loved each other last night after the first few rounds of tequila kicked in. What a load of crap. We didn't love each other, we were just united in our displacement.

But where the hell was Lucy? I had to find out. I walked slowly around the room. Inside the wardrobe was a mix of her and Pete's clothes. She couldn't have taken much. Her shoes were neatly lined up underneath the window, alongside Pete's only other pair. I turned to the bed. The bedside cabinets were full of books and on Pete's side, there was another photograph of him and Lucy on their wedding day. They were standing on the beach, the grey January sky aggressive above them. Behind the photograph was a black metal box, with a sticker on the lid, tattered at the edges, that read *Elizabeth M Field* in faded, sloped handwriting. I'd only seen one before, and it had been far more ornate than this, but I instantly knew it was an urn. I shuddered, finding it hard to believe Pete would keep his mother's ashes with him. I didn't remember seeing them in his room at Clarence Dock. Shaking, I took the lid off. Thankfully, there were no ashes inside. Instead, I found a handwritten order of service, clearly the work of a child. On the front of the folded piece of paper was a large, wonky cross, drawn in black crayon, and inside, there were several lines listing hymns. *In memry of Mam.* I smiled. There were photographs in the box too, a tall young woman standing by a Christmas tree, with a toddler standing between her legs. Pete and his mother. I paused for a while, examining her image. The photo was blurry but I was struck by how much she resembled me. The same dirty blonde hair, the same angular jawline. I shut the box and replaced it behind the wedding picture, wondering where the ashes had ended up. Perhaps they were under a big slab of stone, like my father's, or scattered somewhere beautiful.

I continued my snooping. A stack of books about marriage

occupied one corner of the desk, with Pete's laptop and a pile of papers the only other things on it. I rummaged through the papers. They all seemed to be related to Pete's course, except for the one at the bottom. It was a letter from Leeds General Infirmary's Reproductive Medicine Unit relating to the referral of patient Mrs Lucy Fields, giving details of her appointment with a specialist. The appointment was three days before. Although Lucy was obsessed with getting pregnant, it was strange she would be seeing a specialist already. They'd only been married for six weeks.

Maybe there was something wrong with her. Maybe that's why she'd been trying to get in touch with me. Perhaps she was seriously ill, and that's why she had even asked Joe to call me. Without thinking, I grabbed my phone and searched for her number. It rang three times before she picked up.

'Hello? Emma?'

'Lucy,' I said. 'Where...'

There was a pathetic beep and then the line went dead. My phone, running low on fuel like its owner, had given up on our friendship.

'Brilliant timing,' I shouted, chucking it onto the bed.

'Why thank you. My timing has always been perfect. Just like the rest of me.' I looked up to see Pete making his way through the door, letting in a blast of freezing air with him. 'Damn it's cold out there! Honestly Emma, I don't know how you managed to go out last night wearing nothing but that top.'

'What's going on? Please! Talk to me, I don't understand what's happening here. Last night. I don't understand.'

He carried the shopping bags over to the tiny kitchen worktop and put them down.

'Another cup of tea?' he said, over his shoulder.

'Don't ignore me!'

Still silence. He filled the kettle and switched it on.

'Pete!'

I ran towards him and pulled him round so that he was facing me. He wouldn't look me in the face but hung his head like a cowed puppy.

'Pete?'

'I can't do this anymore,' he said.

'Just talk to me. I want to understand. I want to help. Before, you seemed so sure, nothing could ever happen between us. But now...'

'What have I done?'

'I don't know, you have to tell me. What have you done?'

'I shouldn't have married her. I shouldn't have done. But I did, didn't I? I did?' His face had gone bright red.

I took his hands and we sat on the bed together. His red-rimmed eyes bored into mine.

'Yes, you did. You married her.'

'I can't stay away from you. I'm too weak. I married her, but I didn't have a choice. That's always been the problem. I thought what she wanted was what I wanted but it wasn't.'

He got to his feet – pushing me aside as he stood up – and started to pace up and down in the room.

'I've been so selfish. Just like he always said.'

He seemed to have got bigger somehow. It felt as though he was filling the entire room, striding up and down, his arms outstretched, flapping about in frustration.

'So bloody selfish,' he whispered. 'So weak.'

I should disappear somehow, and leave him to his thoughts. I didn't belong here, in his private world. It was nothing to do with me.

Pete,' I said, but he didn't seem to hear me. I stood up and gathered my things together. 'I'm going to go. I'm sorry, I didn't mean to upset you. I'm sorry.'

I walked to the door but he stopped me.

'Don't go. Forgive me.' He spoke very slowly. 'I haven't been able to sleep lately. Listen, don't go, let's eat. I got you bacon and eggs. Come on, sit down, please.'

'What about Lucy?'

'Listen to me. I want you to listen to me. I'm sorry for last night. You know how deeply I care about you, and how strongly I'm physically attracted to you. You're beautiful. And you're everything I could ever want in a woman – strong, independent, high-spirited, intelligent. But you know, I'm married to Lucy. And that's it. I wish that it wasn't that way, but it is and I can't do anything about it.'

He was wrong. I was hollow, defeated, and spiritless. The exact opposite of how he had just described me. If I was independent, it was only because my father had forced me to be. He didn't understand me at all.

'Is it because…because… Lucy's ill?' I asked.

He looked surprised. 'Ill?' He shook his head. 'No, she's not ill. Why would you say that?'

I was caught. What would he say if he knew I'd been rifling around on his desk?

'Well, you know, her mother's been ill. I thought perhaps she had the same thing.'

'No. Lucy's not ill.' He drew me towards him in a hug. 'Perhaps there's some way…I don't know… we can see each other. Perhaps, if it doesn't get physical…it wouldn't be wrong. I don't know. I'm so tired. But I don't want to be without you. You know that, don't you? Even if it's just as a friend. So long as you know that. Now, let me get you some bacon and eggs.'

It made no sense. But I was hungry and weak, so I let him cook for me.

~

When I finally got home, Amelia was waiting for me in the kitchen. She didn't ask me where I'd been but her eyes gleamed with disapproval.

'Pete's wife stayed in your room last night,' she said before I had the chance to speak. 'Hope that's OK. Since you were staying in hers I don't suppose you have any right to complain.'

'Lucy was here?' I asked.

'Yes. She waited for you to come back until about lunchtime but then she had to go. She said you called her earlier and then hung up when she answered. I told her I didn't know where you were.'

'Thanks.'

'Don't mention it.' The tinge of sarcasm was painful. 'Anyway, she left you a letter.' She passed me an envelope.

'Thanks,' I said again, taking it from her.

'I don't know what you're doing but be careful. You're going to get a reputation if you carry on like this.' She left the room. I so wanted explain to her that the whole thing with Maria's man was a total mistake, and that even I didn't understand what was going on with Pete, but that we really cared about each other and that he had only married Lucy because of some misguided obligation towards her. But even if I'd managed to find a way to put it into words that made sense, it wouldn't make any difference. She'd already written me off. The irony of it all was beginning to dawn on me, and I felt ashamed. I'd had no right to judge my father, no right at all. Fragments of our last conversation came back to me, taunting me with their self-righteous hypocrisy. *You disgust me…traitor…you're sick…I hate you…how could you?* – and, worst of all – *you're dead to me now*. And here I was, just as deeply flawed.

I took Lucy's letter into my room and sat on the bed to read it. Something had changed. Lucy had tidied up, put all my clothes away and left me a bunch of daffodils on the windowsill. The tiny ones that smelt intoxicating. Lucy always smelt of flowers, and for a moment it was as though she was in the room with me.

I curled my legs up underneath me and leaned back against my pillows to read the letter.

Dear Emma
First of all, I hope you are OK. Amelia told me what happened in the club last night. She said you drunk a little too much and ended up in a compromising position with a man Maria is involved with. I know you wouldn't have done this on purpose, and I told Amelia as much, but I think you might have to convince Maria that you had no intention of hurting her.

I don't know where you went last night, but I have my suspicions. I hope Peter looked after you. It's funny isn't it? I stayed in your room and you stayed in mine.

I'm not stupid Emma, and I know that ever since the wedding you have been avoiding me. I'm so sorry that you're in this situation. It's not your fault and it's not Peter's fault. It is just 'one of those things'. I know Peter cares about you in a way that really isn't appropriate. But I also know that he is a loyal, loving husband. I hope that with time you can come to accept that you and he will only ever be friends. It hurts me to think that perhaps Peter would prefer to be with you but I know that he is unselfish to the end, and so this will never be the case.

I am sorry for this Emma, but more importantly I'm sad that we are losing our friendship over it. You mean so much to me, and I can't bear the idea that we will no longer be friends. As you know, you're my only real friend in Leeds.

Please call me when you get this. I'm sorry it's hard for you, but I hope it's not so hard that you can't separate your feelings from Pete from your friendship with me. We need each other.

All my love, your, Lucy xxx

I read it three times over, and each time more tears came. The tears grew into sobs, until I felt I might explode with misery. I reached down underneath the valance of my bed and took out the discipline.

The handle was cool and smooth in my grip. With each hit, as the searing pain rippled across my legs, I felt calmer and calmer, until my heart and my mind were finally still.

Chapter Twenty-five

Pete, April 2006

'Hello Peter,' Ruth said, holding open the door. 'I thought you were staying with your aunt.'

'Is she in?' he said, pushing past her. His voice sounded aggressive, like his father's, but he didn't care.

'Yes she is,' Ruth said, crossing her arms. 'But I don't care for your tone young man.' He ignored her and stormed off up the creaky stairs, marching straight into Lucy's bedroom. She was lying on her bed, writing in a book with a pink pen. A fluffy feather was attached to one end. He despised how girly she was sometimes. So childish.

'Did you know?' he shouted.

'Peter?' She sprang to her feet, surprised.

'Did you know? About my mother?'

'What?'

He reached forward and grabbed her shoulders. He shook her as he spoke, spitting his words at her. 'Did you know about my mother killing herself? Did you know that she didn't drown? That she killed herself, on purpose?'

'Who told you?' she asked. She'd gone white. He wanted to reach forward and snap her stupid neck.

'So you did. You knew. I can't believe you didn't tell me!' he shouted, his arms flailing, tugging at his unruly hair.

'You're scaring me. Sit down. Please. This isn't like you.'

There was a pause. He sat on the chair at her tiny desk and she sat beside him on the bed.

'Why didn't you tell me?' He was calmer now, almost plaintive.

'I'm... I'm sorry... I didn't know how to. I didn't want to upset you. Your dad thought it was for the best.'

'You listened to my father?'

'I'm so sorry, I was only little myself. I did what I was told. Everyone said it was for the best.'

'So what else don't I know?' he said, his voice rising again.

'Nothing. Nothing. Don't be silly. I'm sorry.'

'So you're telling me that my mother, my mother, went down to the beach that day, and drowned herself in the sea? On purpose.' He let out great gasps of air between each phrase.

'Yes. I'm sorry. She was depressed. You knew that.' Lucy began to look around nervously, as if she wished someone would come and rescue her.

'Is that why she wasn't buried?' Peter asked. 'Is that why she was cremated? Is that why her remains ended up on the compost heap in my garden?'

She shrugged. 'I'm so sorry Peter. I don't know. You have to ask your father. You know that suicide is a mortal sin. Perhaps the priest wouldn't allow it.'

'Why would she do that?' He cradled his head in his hands. 'She loved me. She should have stayed alive for me. She was my mother. The only person who ever gave a damn about me.'

Lucy took his hands in hers. 'I'm sure she had her reasons. What do we know about her life? We were just kids. I don't think she was well, you can't blame her.'

'I thought she drowned. I thought it was an accident.' He was hissing at her now. 'All those years, that's what they let me believe. That's what you let me believe.'

'I know. I know.' She tried to sound soothing, but he exploded.

'You don't know anything!' he shouted, standing up again. 'It's alright for you. You with your perfect family, and your millions of brothers and sisters, and your friendly father and your happy mother who bakes! You haven't got a clue what it's like to be me!'

She stood up too and raised her chin. 'Don't speak to me like that,' she said, as calmly as possible. 'It's not my fault. I'm sorry you're upset. I'm sorry you feel this way. I never wanted you to find out any of this. There was no need.'

Without warning, and from somewhere deep inside him, he drew up his hand and slapped her across the face so hard she fell back towards the bed. She let out a shocked cry.

'I will never forgive you for this,' he said, his voice low with fury. 'And you'll regret this betrayal. I thought you were the one person in the world I could trust. But you're just like everyone else. I'll never forgive you.'

He pushed past her crumpled body and strode out into the hall, coming face to face with Joe, who was lingering just outside the room.

He knew that the expression on his face as he glared at Joe was not one of his, but his father's.

Ugly, twisted, and rotten to the core.

Chapter Twenty-six

Emma, March 2011

Amelia handed me my post in the kitchen. I knew they speculated why I received so many letters. Of course, there had been the notes from Lucy last term, but now she was up in Leeds, there was no need for her to write. Today, I received two cards, and a letter. If I was honest, I had expected more. Heather hadn't been in touch for weeks now. Out of sight, out of mind, clearly. It hurt.

'Not your birthday, is it?' Amelia said. She was trying to forgive me, and I was grateful to her for that. Sometimes I even thought about telling her everything, soliciting her help through the mess of my life. She seemed so grounded, so principled and sure of herself. But I couldn't. The truth was, any friendship between us died the second she had gone after Maria in the nightclub, and I didn't blame her. They had a natural affinity with one another – they clicked, their friendship came easily. Like mine and Pete's.

'No,' I said, quietly. 'It's not my birthday.'

I took my post into my bedroom. The letter was from the university's wind band, suggesting I join. Apparently, they were a non-auditioning group. Maybe they'd heard about my disastrous retreat from the chamber orchestra auditions in the first term and taken pity on me. Or maybe they were such a terrible group that even someone of my low standard would be an asset. Whatever the reason, I tucked the leaflet behind my bedside lamp, thinking that I might even consider it.

I looked at the cards. It seemed a senseless practice – the sending of remembrance cards. Our living room last year had been packed with them. And flowers: so many pointless flowers. We only had two vases, which we put the biggest bouquets in. The rest wilted their lives away in an assortment of soft drink bottles. Mum had arranged them in front of the fireplace. The flowers made Lassie sneeze, which was amusing, but none of us ever laughed about it.

I wondered if I would receive remembrance cards for the rest of my life. Perhaps it was just because I'd refused to go home for the anniversary. Maybe it was a way of making me feel guilty, of preventing me from avoiding the memory – which made it a cruel rather than thoughtful gesture.

I opened the first one, even though I knew it was from my mother. A vapid watercolour of a field sprinkled with poppies stared up at me. Another ridiculous association in her mind. He hadn't died in battle, for goodness' sake. I read inside.

Thinking of you. Hope you're OK up there. Mum x

What mattered more was that she was OK. She had sounded surprisingly chirpy the last time I'd spoken to her. Maybe time really was healing. I propped it up on my desk and looked at the other card. The handwriting wasn't familiar, and as I opened it, I wondered if it was from an old schoolteacher. They'd made a dreadful fuss of us after his death.

I wouldn't have believed it possible, but this card was even worse. A picture of a sepia Mary, her head bowed, beneath the words 'May God Comfort You in Your Time of Sorrow'. The card was thin and cheap-looking, the type that come in packs of ten. I had no idea who it was from. Only Mum knew I'd converted to Catholicism, and judging by her reaction when I'd told her, I couldn't see her spreading the news around our friends and relatives with pride. I opened the card.

The scrawled text was spidery and difficult to read and my eyes immediately fell to the name printed at the bottom. Mae.

~

I left my room with the card scrunched up tightly in my hand. It was mild outside, for once, and my heavy winter coat made me sweat as I stormed along the canalside. I refused to accept, after a year of devastation, confusion, guilt, agony, that I wasn't the only person who knew the whole truth after all. Was that the reason for the phone calls? It couldn't be. She didn't know, she couldn't have done. She hadn't seen me there.

Had he left her a note too? Asking her to keep an eye on me, telling her I knew everything? It didn't make sense. Those desperate few days after his death, Mae had comforted me the way she always had, whether it be after my disappointing Merit grade in my last piano exam, or the time I'd seen Ben kissing Sophie outside the pub. If Dad had told her what I knew, the tension between us would have been palpable.

There hadn't been any weirdness there. Not on her part anyway, and if there had been I would have sensed it. My intuition had been at its most heightened then, when my brain was a raging jumble of emotions. But perhaps I'd been so wrapped up in my own anger and self-condemnation, I'd been unable to interpret what was going on around me accurately.

No. I was sure of it. She hadn't known, he hadn't told her, which meant she must have started to work it out on her own. The suddenness of his death, the unfortunate timing, just one day before Matt's 15th, my taciturnity…she had put two and two together. And now, she was pretty sure she knew, but she couldn't come right out with it, just in case. So here she was, sounding me out. Pathetic.

I paused at the end of the towpath, panting slightly. I looked again at the card, crushed and crumpled in my palm.

Emma,
Just a little note to say I hope that you're alright up in Leeds. We haven't spoken for ages. I know your mum says you're busy with all your college work. Still, I hope I haven't done anything to upset you. I wish you'd tell me if I had. I tried calling you many times but your

mobile always went to the answer machine. Anyway, I hope you're not too sad today and you're remembering how proud your dad was of you.

Love Auntie Mae x

If this was a genuine letter of concern, then it should have been signed by Uncle Rog too. Auntie Mae and Uncle Rog did everything together. Their childlessness had kept them young, and they were fun to be around, even when we were moody teenagers. They weren't really my aunt and uncle of course, although Mum insisted they were better than the biological equivalent. Mae and Mum had been best friends at school, just like me and Heather. Best friends – it used to mean something. But Heather had forgotten all about the anniversary of my father's death, so perhaps it meant nothing at all. Perhaps the truth was that everyone was out for themselves, and other people could either come along for the ride or get out of the way.

Mum still went on about what a rock Mae had been after Dad died, about how she couldn't have coped without her. Mae had stayed with us for one painful, drawn-out month, having left Uncle Rog back in Surrey. Perversely, I was glad Mum had her. It was small comfort, a minimal compensation, but at least it was someone else she could weep all over. Someone else to stay up with her late at night and trawl through All the Reasons Why. Someone else to take care of the funeral arrangements with the detached manner of an outsider.

I was glad Mae had to go through all that, because, surely, that was the bitterest price to pay. It was the ultimate punishment.

To attend the funeral of the man you loved as nothing more than a friend of his wife.

PART THREE

Chapter Twenty-seven

Emma, May 2011

I sipped my cup of tea slowly and waited for Pete to arrive. The café was empty. It was unlike him to be late, and I hoped there hadn't been a problem. Often there were: mini-crises in our risky, immoral lives – Lucy finding receipts, Lucy wondering why his phone had been switched off, Lucy bumping into the friend he was supposedly with. He explained them all away so easily, and we both felt ashamed. Sometimes it made it even worse. She was so trusting, so determined to see only the good in people.

He arrived, panting slightly, his cheeks rosy.

'Sorry Em,' he said, reaching down to kiss me. 'I missed my bus. Happy birthday!'

I smiled. 'Thanks. I got you a coffee. So what's the big mystery? Tell me.'

He didn't say anything but reached into the pocket of his jacket and took out an envelope. Inside was a card – a pencil drawing of a young girl staring across an open field, looking contemplative but determined. Opening it, I read his words: *To my Odette, this will be your year. Love always, your Siegfried.* Then he told me to follow him, and we walked around the corner, arriving within a few minutes outside The Grand's imposing Romanesque entrance. Swan Lake. When I saw the tickets, I couldn't believe he'd bought such good seats – the fourth row of the stalls. They must have cost a small fortune.

'Thank you!' I gasped, and for a second it was as though we were a normal couple.

'And how about a gin and tonic before the show starts?' He said, opening the door for me.

'Yes please,' I replied.

I'd only been to the ballet once before. Heather and I saw Sleeping Beauty at the Royal Opera House in Covent Garden after we finished our A levels. We even stayed in a hotel afterwards. Her parents had paid – people were absurdly generous towards Matt and me in the months after dad's death. I suppose it made them feel better, like they were helping. It had been amazing, and I hadn't even wanted to blink while watching the graceful ballerinas twisting their lean bodies into bizarre but beautiful positions, just in case I missed something.

I gulped my gin and tonic down quickly and Pete squeezed my hand in amusement. It was a Thursday evening but the theatre was packed. The curtain came up and the show began, and I recognised the strains of each movement precisely. Pete wore a look of awe on his face as the graceful lead ballerina performed, resplendent in a diaphanous white tutu. He seemed to know the storyline.

During the interval, he bought me a chocolate ice cream while I was in the toilet and put his arm around me as I ate it.

'Are you enjoying it?' he asked.

'It's absolutely fantastic. Thank you so much.'

The second half began and we took our seats again. It felt as though Lucy had never even existed. At least it did until the part when the prince is blinded by the black swan's beauty, resulting in him being unfaithful to Odette. As the prince span around the stage in tormented guilt at his betrayal of the angelic Odette, I could see the evil black swan far in the shadows at the corner of the stage. It was like my life re-enacted for me. Who was Pete trying to kid? I wasn't Odette, the beautiful, innocent princess. I was the black, evil, sorcerer, trying to spoil their love. My gratitude turned to fury at Pete's lack of sensitivity. We were seated in the middle of a long row, and I was stuck, forced to watch the lovers reunited as the black swan perished alone and miserable.

I was quiet when we left the theatre, but Pete continued jabbering away at how much he'd enjoyed it and didn't notice. We walked automatically to the bus stop. As we stopped to say goodbye, he took me by the shoulders and kissed me.

'I meant what I said in the card,' he whispered in my ear. 'I promise you. Things are going to change.'

Hollow words, as usual. I didn't believe any of it. My bus pulled up.

'It's stupid,' I said, bitterly.

'What is?' he replied.

'Nothing.' I felt tired.

Pete sighed and pushed against his forehead with one hand.

'You better get on, or it'll leave without you.'

I didn't even say goodbye before clambering up to the top deck. I watched him through the steamy windows as the bus left to take me back to Clarence Dock. His bus would arrive soon, to take him to his studio room in Headingley, and his home with Lucy. I'd only been there again once, when she was visiting her parents, but unlike the time I'd been drunk and turned up covered in snakebite and black, I'd found I couldn't stand it. Sobriety made Lucy's possessions – her shoes, her coats hanging on the back of the door, the mug with her name on it – leap out at me. Pete understood, and so now he only came over to see me.

She was stupid if she didn't suspect him. We had a well-established routine. He came over after uni every weekday, and would stay for an hour, sometimes two, before leaving in time for dinner at home with his wife. Maria, Amelia and Sam knew, of course, but they never said anything about it. They'd washed their hands of me entirely.

I wondered if it was like this for Mae and Dad. I knew now that our move to Devon had been his last pathetic attempt to escape her. He had tried to resist, to stay faithful to Mum. But they came to stay so often, and Dad worked all over the country... obviously the pull was too strong. I could understand it now, ironically, but I wondered about their remorse. Mae had shown none, whereas I repented every day. After Pete left my flat, I would spend twenty minutes apologising to God for our infidelity, and another five wearing minutes using the discipline on my back and thighs.

She had him at the weekends anyway. If the other members of the university wind band knew I'd only joined to keep myself busy, they would have found it hilarious. I was second flute, which meant I was always passed over for the melody. Their surprise that I never missed a rehearsal was justified given that I was hardly a crucial member.

The whole thing was ridiculous. This was my birthday, and I would remember it all my life. Lucy now had a job working in the Brotherton library, which meant there was no escaping her. She still insisted we have a coffee and a chat once a week, so she could her talk about her wonderful life with him.

But my tantrums got me nowhere. No matter how much I cried and begged Pete to leave Lucy and be with me properly, he was always calm and logical, explaining it was the way it had to be, that we had no alternative and that we should be grateful that we had each other in our lives at all. And I always agreed with him eventually, because he was right. I would never find any other man who made me feel the way Pete did. There was no point in settling for second best. Our relationship was complicated and unfulfilling – for one thing, we rarely had sex – but perhaps it had begun to suit me.

I couldn't imagine being without him. It was pathetic, but he was my soulmate.

~

The day after Swan Lake, I met Lucy in the cheap little coffee shop in the union. It was the first time I'd seen her in weeks because of my exams, but now they were all over, except for a few pieces of composition and an essay, and I had run out of excuses.

I walked towards the coffee shop and within seconds spotted her in a table at the corner. The sight of her shiny, swingy bob always surprised me. Her long glossy hair had been the thing I most envied and I couldn't get used to this new, more mature style.

She beamed at me as I approached the table. An overflowing mug of hot chocolate, with marshmallows, and my present, beautifully gift-wrapped, greeted me.

'Happy birthday!' she said, leaning over the table to kiss me on the cheek.

'Thanks,' I said, taking my seat. 'Thanks for the hot chocolate too – you read my mind. I'm not late am I?'

'No, no, I was early. Oh it's so lovely to see you. We've got loads to talk about. Anyway, come on, open your present.'

I looked at the box. The only presents I'd ever had from Lucy were religious ones – medals, rosaries, books, crucifixes, but this didn't look like it fitted into any of these categories.

'What is it?' I undid the ribbon and carefully opened the corners of the wrapping paper, but Lucy started ripping at the sides.

'Don't worry about the paper! Get stuck in!'

Inside, a cardboard box held a beautiful green handbag, with cream stitching around the edges, and decorative but pointless little pockets on the front and sides.

'I don't know what to say,' I said.

'It's leather, if you're wondering. You do like it don't you? If you don't you can say so. I've got the receipt.'

'Like it? Yes it's beautiful. Thank you. But… it's too much, it really is.'

'Don't be silly. Anyway, it's not just from me, it's from Peter too.'

I swallowed hard and stared at the bag. This must have been

how Mae felt, whenever Mum bought her a present. Unless it amused her. How many birthdays had they celebrated together, with Mae laughing behind Mum's back? Maybe she still laughing, revelling in her good fortune that she was never found out.

'Of course,' she continued, taking a sip of her tea, 'He didn't help me choose it or anything, but he put some money towards it. He wanted me to get you something special. He still thinks of you, even though you two don't see each other much. I hope you like it. It's nice and big.'

I reached across the table and held both of her arms. 'Thank you,' I said. 'Thank you very much.'

'You're welcome. I'll tell Peter you liked it; he'll be so pleased. Anyway how was your birthday? Did you do anything special?'

'Yes. Well, I went for drinks with some of the girls from the band.' I couldn't be bothered to elaborate further.

'So you didn't go home then?'

'No.'

She paused. 'You haven't been home since Christmas have you?'

'Nope,' I said, trying to sound as though it was completely insignificant.

'You're so brave,' she said, smiling at me. 'I get so homesick down here. Still, I'm sure your mum sent you a nice present?'

'Yes. She sent me some money.'

Lucy was staring at me, her face radiating positivity.

'Lucky you. Hope you got something nice with it,' she said, blithely. 'Anyway I've got the most fantastic news.'

'Really? What?' She was wriggling around in her chair and her cheeks were flushed. 'Tell me.'

'Oh I don't know how to. It's just so exciting! Sorry, you'll be the first person I've told.'

With those words I knew what was to come.

'I'm pregnant! Three months and a week today. Can you tell?'

She half got up and hovered over the table, her stomach in my face.

'Wow…' I began. 'I don't know what to say.'

It didn't matter, she wasn't interested in what I wanted to say anyway.

'It's so exciting. In October I'll be a mum! If it's a girl, we're going to call her Margaret. I really hope it's a girl. Peter doesn't mind of course, he'd be happy with a boy or a girl. I'm just so excited. Peter is beside himself too, he's going to make a wonderful father, don't you think? I still can't quite believe it.'

Neither could I. The night before he hadn't mentioned a thing. What did he think he was playing at? Did he just hope I wouldn't find out? How could he have not told me?

I'd always assumed they didn't sleep together, which was stupid of course.

Before I could say a word, Lucy had started rummaging around in her bag.

'Look!' she said, handing me one of those black and white scan photos of the baby. 'Isn't she adorable? Look at the size of her head. It's huge, she's clearly going to take after her father and be a real brainbox.'

I nodded numbly and looked at the blurry image in the picture. There it was, in all its glory: the official end to my and Pete's relationship. I'd pictured this day in my mind hundreds of times, but it hadn't been anything like this in my sombre daydreams. The end came with Pete's death usually, and in that ending, the irony of attending his funeral as nothing more than a distant friend destroyed me. That was how our relationship ended in my fantasies. Not with a baby. This ending was too huge, too powerful, too catastrophic for me to ever have imagined.

From now on, this grey, blurry child would come first. It would come before Lucy and certainly before me.

A huge fat tear dropped onto the picture, landing slap-bang in the middle of the baby's head. Lucy noticed and put her arms around me awkwardly across the table.

'Don't cry, Em. You'll set me off too.'

I wiped away the tear on the picture, smudging the ink. The baby's head now looked huge, like some kind of monster, which was what it was of course: a monster that had come to destroy my life. My vision blurred behind the wetness in my eyes and the picture became 3D, getting bigger and bigger. I was being consumed by it. Lucy noticed the smudge and snatched the picture back.

'Oh…' she said, staring at it. 'Never mind, I'm having another scan next week, I'll get a new picture.'

'Sorry,' I said, without conviction. I struggled to compose myself. 'Listen, please don't take this the wrong way, I'm… very happy for you, but I'm afraid I've got to go now.' I stood up to leave.

Lucy grabbed my arms and frowned at me. Her voice changed and she sounded the closest to cross I'd ever heard. 'Why? What's the matter? I'm not stupid; I can tell you're upset. You know how much we've longed for a baby. Don't spoil it for me, please.'

We've longed for a baby. The words sliced through me like scissors through an umbilical cord. They'd only been married five minutes. 'I'm not trying to spoil it for you,' I said slowly. 'Please, I've just got to go.'

'What's wrong?' She stared right into my eyes, a direct hit. There was a pause and then her face began to soften, like wax melting. 'You're not pregnant are you?'

The ridiculousness of it almost made me laugh. I sat down again, my misery diluted. 'No of course not,' I said.

There was a pause and neither of us said anything. I stirred the remainder of my hot chocolate while Lucy stared at me, her eyes digging around for clues.

After a while she spoke. 'I'm sorry,' she said. 'I realise that this must be hard for you. I know how much you would like a boyfriend. I'm being so selfish. I just got so carried away, I didn't stop to think about how it must be for you. That you might be slightly, well, *envious…*'

'I am happy for you,' I said. She had thrown me a lifeline in her accurate interpretation. 'I suppose you're right, perhaps it's just made me more aware of the fact I'm alone in the world. I'm sorry, I really am. It's just a bit of a shock that's all.'

She smiled sympathetically, and her although her pity stung, my tears dried up. *It wasn't my Pete. It wasn't my Pete.* That baby had nothing to do with me. I finished my hot chocolate.

'Let's talk about something else,' she said, uneasily. 'How were your exams? Have you finished them all now?'

'Yes, thanks, they were fine. I won't know until I get the results I guess. But I think I did well. But then, it's only the first year, so it doesn't really matter what I get.'

'Of course. And do you have anything left now? I remember you saying something about coursework, some composition?'

'Yes. Just one more piece to complete.'

'I'd love to hear it sometime. Is it piano?'

'Yes, it's a piano duet actually.'

'Wow, sounds great. You are clever. So talented. I wish I could play an instrument.'

I smiled and raised my eyebrows. She began to rub her stomach gently and her eyes fixated on a spot above my head.

'Any thoughts on what you might do in the summer?' she asked.

'No,' I lied. 'Just see what happens I guess.'

All I knew was that I wasn't going back to Paignton. I hadn't found anywhere to live, but that could be sorted in a weekend, and I could stay at Clarence Dock until the end of June, or even longer if I applied for an extension. I'd wanted to find myself a temping job. It had seemed unthinkable that I might spend the summer apart from Pete, but this would probably all change now.

I suddenly felt overwhelmingly tired. My brain was pulsating with conflicting thoughts and feelings.

If I'd had a big, fat hammer in my hand, I'm not sure I would have been able to resist the urge to smash my head in, then and there, on the horrible red-checked plastic tablecloth in this crowded student café.

'Listen Lucy, I'm sorry, I shouldn't have got upset before. I am happy for you. I've just been tired, and stressed with the exams and everything, I really am just so tired.' I leant my elbows on the table and held my head in them, looking down at the sludgy remnants of hot chocolate in my mug. 'Please don't hate me, but I really have to go now. Congratulations.'

I stood up, gathered the handbag and the wrapping paper into the box, gave her one last pathetic smile and walked away. She didn't try to stop me.

Chapter Twenty-eight

Emma, May 2011

I would have to wait until Monday. Back in my room, I collapsed in front of the tiny television I'd bought with my birthday money and attempted to lose myself in other people's fictional worlds.

I slept badly that night. The next morning in the shower, the picture of the tiny baby with the huge head came flooding back to me, and I broke down, the soap suds and my tears combining and collecting at my feet. More than anything, I was furious that he hadn't told me. Did I really mean so little that I didn't even deserve that? I tried to convince myself it was just didn't want to spoil my birthday, but he must have known for such a long time.

He texted me a few times over the weekend, cheery texts about how relieved he would feel once his final exam that following Monday was over. His nonchalance threw me, as he must have known that Lucy had told me. He must have known how miserable I was feeling, yet he didn't mention it at all. It was as though nothing had happened.

Perhaps he was in denial. Perhaps he didn't believe it. Perhaps she'd had miscarriages in the past and he expected the same thing to happen again. Perhaps he was as depressed about the situation as me, and was trying to pretend it wasn't happening. He loved me. I played 'our song' over and over again: *True Love Ways* by Buddy Holly. Often, we'd sit in silence on the bed together, content to be in each other's arms and he'd gently start to hum the tune. His humming would build up and up until he leapt to his feet and gave me a loud, slightly out-of-tune rendition of the song, lyrics included. I knew he loved me. There was no doubt about that. All that remained to be discovered was how he felt about the baby.

God was no use to me. I prayed for comfort and guidance but my prayers were ignored. So I tried praying to Mary instead. In truth, I'd never really believed praying worked, but thinking of her gave me some sort of calmness of mind, and I didn't cry again all weekend. I sat there, thinking and wondering and hoping. Although I wanted to see Pete, to have the whole issue resolved, perhaps his resolutions wouldn't be ones I could bear. In some ways it was nice to sit and reflect, and Pete's final exam was his most important, so I didn't feel brave enough to disturb his last day of revision.

He was coming over for lunch after his exam, when the others were out celebrating, and I would have all the answers I ever wanted, as well as those I didn't.

~

He was late again, and I sat there nervously, my stomach turning over as I checked my phone again. I'd texted him 'Good luck' that morning, but he hadn't replied. He might have already turned his phone off by the time I sent it.

By quarter past one, there was still no sign of him. I didn't want to call him, so I sat in my room, staring blankly out of the window, waiting for his tall silhouette to appear along the towpath. I was making jacket potatoes with cheese and beans – his favourite – and now it was quarter past one, they were already ready, but what if he had forgotten? I didn't know what to do.

Eventually, at about half one, he rang. I picked up but couldn't find my voice to even say 'hello'. Wherever he was, it was very noisy. There was loud music playing and the murmur of a crowded place, but he couldn't have been in a pub. Not Pete.

'Emma?' he shouted.

'Yes,' I said. He sounded a bit tipsy.

'How are you?' he said.

'I'm fine. Where are you Pete? You're meant to be coming over for lunch.'

'Sorry. We went for a quick pint after the exam. Just leaving now.'

I was infuriated, which actually made a welcome change from feeling sick with nerves. 'You went for a pint?'

'Can't hear you Em. Sorry, I'm leaving now, will be with you soon. Looking forward to lunch, I'm starving.'

I didn't know what to say.

'OK see you then,' he said, hanging up.

I went into the kitchen, watched the potatoes burn and waited. Forty-five minutes later, he arrived. When I answered the door to him, he was grinning. I'd never seen him look so happy, and it made me want to slap him across the face.

'Why so glum?' he said, marching into the corridor. He frowned slightly, clearly listening for evidence that any of the others were in.

'They're all at the Old Bar. You're really late. The potatoes are burnt.'

'Sorry. They'll be alright in the middle. Anyway I like them crispy. Come on, let's eat.' He wandered into the kitchen, knelt down in front of the oven and started to pull the plate out of the tiny oven with his bare hands.

'Ouch!' he shouted, dropping the potatoes to the floor. 'Bloody hell. That hurt.' He walked to the tap and ran his fingers under the cold water. 'Sorry Em,' he said, looking round at me sheepishly. 'Pick them up, quickly, they'll be alright.'

I started to cry; fat tears rolled down my cheeks and I began to howl.

'Emma,' he said. 'What's the matter? What's happened?' He didn't look at me, but put on my spotty oven gloves and bent down to pick up the potatoes from the floor. He looked so ridiculous.

'What's happened?' I said. 'Lucy's pregnant.'

He sank to the floor, one potato wedged in between his oven-gloved fingers. It was black all over, except for a small spot underneath where it'd been resting on the oven tray. He stared at it, turning it over in his hand.

'Yes.' Was that all he could manage?

'Why didn't you tell me?'

He didn't answer, but carried on passing the potato from one hand to the other, his elbows resting on his knees.

'I can't believe it. It's over isn't it? That's the end for you and me. Why didn't you tell me? I didn't know what to say to her. She was so happy. She was smiling, beaming, she wanted me to be happy for her, and all I felt was complete shock. She might as well have told me you were dead.'

He dropped the potato and cradled his head with his hands.

'And she's happy about it. She's ecstatic. Your longed-for baby apparently. So where exactly, does this leave me?'

He cleared his throat, paused for a second and then stood up, putting the potato in the bin and taking off the oven gloves. He looked me straight in the eyes.

'Aren't you going to ask me how my exam went?' he said.

I'm sure my mouth fell open. 'Pete, listen to me, I'm going to speak very slowly. We need to talk about the fact that your wife is pregnant.'

'I don't want to talk about it,' he said, pushing past me out of the kitchen and into my room. I followed. He flopped down on my bed, sighed and ran his hands through his thick wavy hair. He looked irritatingly attractive, sitting there with a subtle frown on his face, like he was trying to work out some complicated algebra.

'Pete,' I said, calmly, taking a seat on the chair by my desk. 'We have to. I can't deal with this. You need to help me.'

'You think I can deal with it?' he said. 'You think it's easy for me? I didn't know she was going to get pregnant. I thought it was impossible.'

'Well that makes two of us! I didn't even know you slept together.'

'Please, I've just had a three-hour exam, followed by two pints of bitter. I'm exhausted and a little drunk. Can we not just have a nice lunch together and talk about this some other time?'

For once, I wasn't going to let him have his way – I needed some kind of decision to be made about my future. I didn't care whether it was bad news, I just couldn't stand not knowing what was going to happen to me.

'No we can't. Talk to me. What do you mean, you thought it was impossible?'

'I thought it would never happen,' he said. 'That's what the doctors told her. A one in a thousand chance, I think they said. I remember her coming back from the hospital. It was the day before we got married. I didn't know anything about it before, of course, I had no idea.'

I remembered the letter in their room, hidden underneath books about macroeconomics.

'You need to explain,' I barked.

'She asked me how much I loved her,' he continued, staring down at his burnt fingers. They had swollen slightly. 'I said of course I did. Then she told me she had some bad news, and that it might make me change my mind. She was pleading with me, begging me not to let her down. I asked her what it was, I told her it couldn't possibly be all that bad, and then she told me. She would never be able to have children. That she had this thing – endometriosis – and it was so bad they thought she'd never be able to have children... She started to cry, really softly, you know how she does, not a hint of self-pity, she was crying for me, because she was so worried that I would be devastated. She asked me if I still wanted to marry her. Said she'd understand if I didn't. I held her, I let her cry, I told her it didn't matter, that I loved her and everything would be fine. But all I could think of was you. I hated her, I was furious. It was too late to back out then, I knew that. How could I call the wedding off the day before? Imagine what people would think of me.'

I remembered the day before the wedding – the day I'd arrived in Newcastle. Lucy had met me from the train and I'd thought her eyes looked red, as though she'd been crying. Tears of joy, I'd assumed. So she hadn't come into Newcastle especially to meet me – she must have come from the hospital.

'It was too late,' Pete continued. 'I was trapped. And then you arrived. When I first saw you, and you gave me a hug and a kiss on the cheek, you looked so unhappy yourself. I just wanted to pick you up and run away with you. But there she was. In the corner, standing behind you. And there were all her relatives, and that awful Joe, staring at me, suspicious, not trusting me to take proper care of his bloody sister. Lucy. My whole life has revolved around her, ever since I was little. Of course I love her. She's like a sister to me. My mam doted on her, you see. "Watch out for little Lucy, won't you?" she'd say. I didn't have any brothers or sisters, I liked being her protector. And we fell into a relationship when we were just 13. Just kids. It all seemed so natural. She was my best friend, and she became my girlfriend. It would all have been fine, if I hadn't met you.'

He looked at me when he said that. I couldn't hold his stare.

'She always wanted to get married. As soon as we turned 16, she started mentioning it. And her infernal mother. Always dropping hints. Even Father Gerry. Everyone thought it was a good idea, a natural progression. They must have thought we'd been together so long, it was about time. They must have thought we were desperate to have sex.' He laughed cruelly. A door slammed somewhere in the building and we both looked up.

'Carry on,' I said, keeping my voice controlled.

'I put her off, I told her we should wait, but then I met you, and I got so confused. I just thought it was the right thing to do. All I ever wanted was to make my mother happy. Lucy was miserable without me. Every week I'd hear about how much she was missing me. She doesn't have a life, Emma, except for me. I am her life. She's so weak. And my mam always said that I must take care of her. And so that's what I did.'

'At the wedding, I was so confused. I didn't know what to do. I spoke to my father about it, and he told me to back out, that I was stupid. That I shouldn't marry some barren weakling. Some pathetic woman. He said that's what he had done and look where it had got him. And that's when I decided Emma, that I had to marry her.' He looked at me again.

'I didn't want to be like him. I wanted to make Mam proud. So I married her. And then I regretted it. Straight away. I got drunk. And then you found me. And we slept together. And I've been living my own personal hell ever since.'

'Pete,' I said, moving over to the bed next to him. I didn't know what to say, so I kissed him. He kissed me back, frantically, furiously. His kisses hurt, as though he was trying to punish me with pain, but I didn't care. I didn't care one bit. We had sex and then lay in silence in each other's arms, covered by my Ikea blanket, not bothering to get dressed.

There was nothing to say. Maybe Lucy would lose the baby, if she had endometriosis, if the doctors had thought it so unlikely she would get pregnant in the first place. I opened my mouth to ask, to explore the possibilities, but something stopped me. There was no point, she was pregnant, it was over, and we both knew it. We both knew the difference between right and wrong. We knew that Pete had to stand by Lucy, and their baby. He had to stand by the decision he made – he was her husband and that was his duty. He had made a promise before God and that was it.

As for me, I suppose I had got what I deserved. I'd driven my father to his death with my moralising, with my threats to tell Mum exactly what I'd seen. I'd meant it, and he'd known that, and he'd taken the coward's way out. If I'd listened to his excuses, allowed him to apologise, to make promises to put things right, instead of screaming and shouting at him, he might still be here today. To err is human, to forgive divine. I was so far from divine it was laughable. And poor, poor Dad. He'd gone to his death thinking I hated him, that I would never forgive him.

If he was looking down on me, what would he be thinking now? Would he be laughing at the irony of my situation, or crying that his daughter had turned out as weak as him? Hypocrite that I was, I'd followed his example – worse, followed *Mae's* example – and ended up in exactly the same situation as her. Pete might not be dead, but to me, he was as good as.

Divine retribution.

This was what I deserved; my place in life. Pete was too good for me, Lucy even more so. I'd stepped out of my boundaries for too long. We'd had our pleasure, we'd danced with the devil, and now it was time for penance.

There was no way back now. It was finished.

Chapter Twenty-nine

Pete, May 2006

They called her Lucy Moosey precisely because she wasn't a moose. Because she was the opposite: she was beautiful. While the others fought acne with overdoses of Clearasil and Oxy 10, her skin glowed with an unnatural clarity. Her hair was glossy and full, never greasy. She was an easy target. Jealousy, Peter realised, was something that possessed teenage girls, turning them into monsters. Lucy was too pretty and worst of all, too kind. She wasn't a geek. The geeks got left alone. She wasn't bright enough or plain enough to be ignored. She shone like a beacon and her beauty was her curse, her affliction.

He lingered in the doorway of the boys' toilets watching them as they walked past her. She was fumbling with something in her locker, appearing to ignore the passing taunts. Denise Richards, a buxom brunette with a family more dysfunctional than his own, was making her way down the corridor. He knew Denise hated Lucy more than most. This time, it wasn't because of her looks, but instead because she had the one thing Denise craved more than anything else, even though she might not admit it to herself: a stable family.

Peter looked at Lucy. As always, her head was down. She was so stupid, she almost deserved it. There would be only a few more seconds before Denise reached her. He felt the thrill of anticipation, wondering what she would do to her. His body ached for something physical. Denise was a strong girl. She could push Lucy against the grey metal lockers with a force enough to leave a dent in them, but he knew she wouldn't do that here. School wasn't the place for physical torment – it was hard to get away with. At school you had to be careful because whatever you wanted to do, whatever you did, it had to have the ability to be passed off as an accident. Words were intangible, effective weapons – provided no teacher was in earshot, they could reduce the victim to tears without leaving any proof for prosecution. Denise was smiling. She was definitely about to do something.

Peter shrank back into the doorway, allowing only his left eye to view the ensuing carnage. He steeled himself for his moment, no doubt only minutes away. Denise stopped next to Lucy's locker and leant her shoulder against it, one foot crossed in front of the other. She was chewing gum loudly, her mouth gaping open. The noise from her gob disgusted Peter. Denise was the very lowest of the low. He knew he should step forward now, prevent her from terrorising his oldest friend – his *only* friend – but he wouldn't. Not yet. He had plans, he would see them through.

'Alright Moosey?' Denise said. Lucy kept her head down, her hands pawing inside her locker in a pathetic attempt to appear distracted. She was so pathetic. Peter shook his head in frustration. Shearer, one of the lads from year nine, pushed past him into the toilets. Peter held his stare, knowing it was strange that he was here, lingering in the doorway, which made Shearer look away. Peter liked the fact he was regarded as a nutcase, that people were frightened of him. The whispers about the harm he'd done his aged aunt had blown themselves out of all proportion. It had only been one punch, but he'd become a legend. It took a particular sort of damaged soul to hit a 70-year-old lady, they seemed to believe. He'd even seen a sparkle of pride in his father's eyes when he'd reprimanded him afterwards. Paradoxically, it was this pride that made Peter regret losing his temper with Matilda. He didn't want his father's admiration – he never would.

'Oi, Moosey,' Denise said, her voice louder. 'I'm talking to you.'

Lucy looked up. 'Yes?' she said. Her voice wasn't shaking, not yet, but Peter could smell her fear. He knew her so well.

'I said,' Denise spoke slowly, as though Lucy were retarded. 'Are – you – alright?'

'Yes, thank you,' Lucy said. Peter wondered if she was giving full eye contact, or whether she was staring at Denise's chest like a teenage boy.

'Well,' said Denise. 'That's good, isn't it? Because I hear another member of the Nicholls family isn't.'

'Pardon?'

'Sally, isn't it?' Denise asked. 'One of your many minging sisters? Smells as bad as you do from what I've heard.'

'Sally? What's happened to her?' There was concern in Lucy's eyes. She cared so much – that was her problem. For a second, Peter felt confused.

'Oh I don't know exactly,' Denise said, the edges of her lips curling upwards. 'I just heard she got taken to hospital.'

'What?' Lucy rested her hand against her open locker.

'Yes. Broken thumb they think.'

'Sally? How?'

'Oh dear Lucy Moosey, you're not worried are you? I'm sure she'll be fine. It's easily done you see.'

Peter knew she was lying. He'd seen Sally in the playground just a few minutes earlier, playing Top Trumps with her friends. She was only a year seven. Denise wouldn't pick on a year seven. There were unspoken rules about this kind of thing. The year below was acceptable, but they were in year ten now, which meant seventh years weren't even on their radar.

'What's easily done?' Lucy said, raising her voice slightly. 'What's happened?'

'What's happened?' Denise asked, her tone light and mocking. She fiddled with her hair. Her lips were red – a blatant defiance of school rules.

'Tell me!'

'Well, you know, I'm not all that good at explaining things. Seeing as I'm so thick and everything. Not like your genius boyfriend.' Peter winced. His existence, his closeness to Lucy made her life harder, whereas it gave him more respect. They thought he was using her for sex, using her as a plaything, as entertainment, the same as they did. 'So since I'm so *stupid*, instead of me *telling* you what happened, how about I show you?'

The timing was impeccable. It was so quick, so efficient and unexpected, Peter had to give Denise some credit. He imagined the flash of realisation in Lucy's eyes, a mere microsecond before Denise slammed the locker door against her hand. But it was too late. She howled in agony.

'Something like that, I think,' Denise said, smiling.

Lucy just stared at her. The door sprang back open and she held her thumb with her other hand, tears exploding from eyes wide with pain.

'Yes, that'll be it.' Denise stared straight back. 'Ouch. Poor Sally.'

She started to walk away. Peter knew it was nearly time for his part.

'Oh, before I go,' Denise turned. 'Would you like some chewing gum? You know, chew through the pain and all that?'

Lucy said nothing. She was still holding her injured thumb in a protective cradle.

'Here you go then Moosey,' Denise said. She took the gum from her mouth, reached forward and stuck it on Lucy's forehead. It hung there for a few seconds, glistening with saliva, before falling to the ground.

Peter came out of the boys' toilets just as Denise was walking past. Lucy gasped with relief at the sight of him. He knew she was about to run and weep into his arms.

Denise saw him and flinched.

'What did you just do?' he hissed.

'Don't know what you're talking about.' She was too frightened to look him in the eyes and he loved it.

Peter pushed her back against the lockers.

'I said, what did you just do? To Lucy?'

'Get off me you freak!' Denise said.

Peter put his hands firmly around her neck. Her eyes bulged with fear. He saw Lucy approaching slowly.

'If you EVER touch her again…' he said, quietly.

'Get off me,' Denise babbled. He tightened his grip.

Lucy tugged on his other arm.

'Peter,' she whispered. 'It's OK.'

'I mean it,' Peter said, staring at Denise. He enunciated the words perfectly, ensuring tiny flicks of spit landed on Denise's orange cheeks with each one.

'I'm sorry,' Denise whimpered. 'It was a joke. I didn't know you were there. I didn't mean to…I'm sorry.'

Peter let go, satisfied. 'Just get lost,' he said. She fled without looking back.

He turned to Lucy. She was still crying, but her eyes were shining now. He put his arms around her and kissed the top of her head.

He knew this was the most significant incident of him standing up for her so far. Denise had been genuinely frightened and he was pretty sure she'd leave Lucy alone now.

Finally, after all these years of groundwork, he had become what he always wanted to be. Her hero.

Chapter Thirty

Emma, September 2011

Out of the tail of my eye, I saw her unmistakable treacle-coloured hair. I quickly ducked down the nearest aisle and tried to concentrate. I'd come in for some rice; the quick and easy microwaveable pouches, perfect for single people, but I didn't know where to find them. Morrisons was huge, and I hadn't been here for ages. I was in the baby stuff aisle, surrounded by nappies and bottles. I hurried towards the dairy products but it was, of course, too late.

'Emma!' she shouted. I hesitated and considered ignoring her, pretending I hadn't heard, but a chubby lady with hair scraped back into a ponytail looked up at me from the jars of baby food and motioned for me to turn around.

I turned. There she was, hurrying towards me. She was huge. Seven months gone. In the frequent dreams I'd had about Lucy in advanced stages of pregnancy, she was still beautiful, slim, with a perfect watermelon of a bump gracefully enhancing her figure. I'd had so many dreams about it. Sometimes I dreamt she was newly pregnant, and I saw her rushing out of the bathroom, buzzing with excitement and happiness, and straight into the arms of an equally thrilled Pete. Other times, she was feeling her baby kick her for the first time. Again, she ran to Pete, told him to put his hand on her stomach and feel the movement, and his face would light up too. But then the baby would begin to kick and kick and kick, harder and harder until foot-shaped lumps were springing up all over her swollen stomach, and both their faces would fall, masks of concern and fear, until she collapsed to the floor in agony.

Sometimes I even dreamt of the actual birth: propped up on her elbows in the throes of pain, her insipid smile plastered across her face even then, staring into Pete's loving eyes. I was like a sentient security camera, always watching but unseen myself. When the baby was finally delivered, with one powerful yet elegant push, the nurse congratulated her repeatedly on her beautiful child. I couldn't see the baby to begin with. The small bundle was first handed to Lucy, who smiled and cooed over it, before she handed it to Pete, who held it over his shoulder, stroking its head. It was only then that the baby's features were revealed, and I would discover that the baby had my face. I would wake up drenched in sweat.

But here, in Morrisons, standing before me on the brown and orange speckled lino, was a completely different Lucy. This Lucy was large, fat and very pregnant, with greasy hair and a puffy neck. A baggy, shapeless dress completely swamped her upper body but did little to disguise her legs, which were considerably larger than the last time I'd seen her. I suppressed the urge to smile with pleasure at the state of her.

'Hello,' I said. 'How are you?'

'Emma!' she said, leaning forward to hug me. 'Oh my goodness, it's so lovely to see you again. You look fantastic. How are you?'

'I'm great, thanks. You look well,' I said.

'I can't believe how long it's been since I've seen you. What have you been up to? What brings you back to Leeds?'

'Oh, well, I've been temping a bit, you know, before the new term starts.'

'What? I thought you'd moved back down south. Dropped out… I'm sure Peter told me… I would have been in touch. It's just, well, I was quite ill, you know in the middle of my pregnancy. I had all sorts of horrible problems, and I was in hospital for a while. When they let me out, Peter told me I had to start taking it easy so I haven't been out much. I haven't worked for ages either. I had no idea you were still here. I honestly thought you'd gone home.'

'This is my home,' I said, sharply. 'More than it is yours

anyway.'

She opened her mouth as if to speak but shut it again. The vitriol I'd believed was so well concealed, deep beneath the illusion of a personality, had erupted like a volcano. We stood there staring at each other, neither of us saying a word. And then, as ever, I began to feel sorry for her. She was finally realising that I wanted nothing to do with her, that I'd told Pete to tell her I'd gone back to Devon because I could no longer bear to see her. She'd spent the last few months believing these lies and now, confronted with me and my inability to hide my feelings, she realised that the truth was quite different.

I just didn't want to be her precious bloody friend. The words that had just escaped me told her more about me than ten months of fraudulent friendship. I hated her. She had what I so desperately wanted. She might be fatter, with bad skin, but she was having a baby with the man she loved, while I was walking around with a Pete-shaped hole in my life.

No, Lucy. I willed my thoughts to reach her somehow. *I'm not going to make this easier for you. Not this time. Why should I? You have everything I ever wanted, but you can't have me too. Not as a friend. Not even as an acquaintance to make polite conversation with in the supermarket.*

'I'm so sorry,' she began. 'so very sorry. I know…things were strange…for you and Peter. He's so easy to love. I am so sorry we hurt you. We never meant for…'

'Don't you dare!' I screamed. The chubby mum glanced at me nervously and scuttled off. 'Don't you dare feel sorry for me! You bitch!'

'Emma!' Lucy said, her eyes filling.

'You think you're so superior don't you? With your perfect little husband? You think, poor little Emma, she wanted what I had, she wanted my darling Peter. Poor Emma, she's never had much luck with men!'

'I never…I never thought that.' She stared straight at me,

swallowing back the tears.

'Do you know what? I had sex with your husband. Did you know that? Did he tell you that, your darling Peter? Did he tell you, that on the night of your stupid, pointless wedding, we slept together? I suppose he forgot to mention it didn't he? Didn't manage to slip that one in over the last few months of blissful marriage?'

'Stop it, please.' All I could see was the infuriating pity was still in her eyes. She didn't even believe me. She thought I was a crazy woman, ranting away, driven mad with jealousy.

'And not just on your wedding night. Oh no! We saw each other quite regularly, until you got pregnant. Pete used to come over to Clarence Dock after uni every day. I bet you thought he was in the bar or something didn't you? Well, he was with me. We were having a relationship behind your back. He only married you because he felt sorry for you. Because his mum liked you.' I noticed several people had gathered at the end of the aisle, watching us. I lowered my voice.

'Emma,' Lucy said, slowly. 'There are things about Peter you don't know. Please. Stop this. I'm going to leave now. I can tell you're upset.'

'I'm upset?' I hissed. 'You're the one who should be upset. You're the one whose husband has been cheating on you.'

She smiled at me sadly, and reached forward to pat me on the shoulder. I recoiled as though she had flicked acid at my bare skin. There were still tears in her eyes, but she looked peaceful. I was quivering with emotion, my heart pounding.

'I'll pray for you. I'm so sorry you're hurting like this.'

With that she turned and walked away, staring down at the floor as she left. People began to cough and titter nervously and dispersed to let her pass. I gazed after her, my vision hazy and blurred. The people at the other end of the aisle began milling about: some walked off, others came towards me. The woman with the messy ponytail indiscreetly peered down to see if the commotion had ended and seeing that it had, came back towards me. Back to the jars of Apple and Banana custard and Mum's Recipe Chicken and Vegetable Risotto. She looked at me nervously and I put my hands up to my face, suddenly self-conscious. It was wet with tears I hadn't even acknowledged I'd cried.

I wiped them away and started to turn on the spot, searching stupidly for some product on the shelf – anything – desperate to blend in again. They were all still looking at me – I could hear their whispers and coughs, I could feel their curiosity, invisible fingers were pointing at me from all directions, no matter how many times I spun round and round.

The aisle became a blur of faces, eyes, fingers, nappies, baby oil, feeding bottles, baby food jars. My ears began to hum and fill with water; the blood from my head fell straight down to my feet, like a tap turned on full. As I started to feel weaker, I bent down and knelt on the orange and brown floor, the splodges of colour starting to break free and run together, until I felt I was drowning in a sea of vomit-coloured paint. A sickening taste was rising in my throat and the humming was getting louder and louder.

'Are you alright?' The woman with the ponytail was kneeling on the floor beside me, her concerned eyes and fuzzy words boring through me like a drill through rock. I tried to look at her, to reply, but it hurt. I hauled myself to my feet and ran, away from her, away from all the baby food, away from the whispering faces and away from the orange and brown sea, seconds before it could consume me completely.

~

I ran out of the supermarket, down the Headrow, around the Millennium Square and took a side street off Woodhouse Lane. I paused for breath, leaning against a lamppost, staring around to make sure I was alone. It was quiet and shady in the street, and as I panted I began to cool down. I walked again, feeling calmer now, but I was still too hot. It was the most beautiful day I had ever seen in Leeds – clear, blue skies with a bright sun blazing away above me – but it irritated me, sweat dripped down my back and my hair stuck to the sides of my forehead like an Alice band. At least I knew where I was going. A short time later, here I was, here it was, towering above me and casting a reassuring shadow large enough to cool the whole street.

The Cathedral Church of St Anne's.

I looked up. The heavy door was shut. It was 2.15pm. Since Pete and I had stopped seeing each other, I hadn't been to church once.

Standing still made me hotter so I pushed open the door slightly, and peered inside. I felt like a child venturing into her parents' bedroom, even though this wasn't forbidden territory. The whole point of a church was the open-door policy and the fact that anyone was welcome, at any time.

It was so wonderfully cool and quiet inside. The traffic on the Headrow reduced to dull murmur; a reassuring white noise. I genuflected shyly and walked up the aisle. My flip-flop footsteps echoed on the smooth stone floor. Just before the altar, I stopped and looked up at Jesus. He was still miserable, tortured, frightening, intimidating disappointed. He was supposed to be loving too, but, as usual, I searched for an indication of this and found none. He was a broken man, completely destroyed, betrayed by everyone he knew, and I had never been able to find any sign of everlasting love for all mankind in his face.

Even so, I understood him. I knew how it felt to be alone, to have the people you believed cared about you betray you in the most devastating way possible. We were supposed to feel gratitude that he died for us, and love and admiration for his altruism. But all I'd ever found was pity. Pity that his life was probably the most miserable and wretched out of all human

beings – that was my overwhelming emotion.

None of it mattered anyway. I turned my back on the image of Christ and sat in the front pew. If this had been a film, a priest would have popped out of nowhere by now to counsel me. I would pour my heart out to him, all my worries and fears, my doubts and desires, and he would listen kindly and take my hand as he gave me the solution to all my problems. But no one came. I sat there for at least ten minutes and nothing happened. I felt nothing. The church was oppressively silent, without even a ticking clock to neutralise the atmosphere. I picked up one of the hymn books and flicked through it, trying to find a particular hymn that I liked, or at least one that I had played on the piano. There wasn't one. Then it struck me, the only religious songs I'd ever really played on the piano were carols. I began to hum Silent Night, then laughed at the absurdity of it.

Was this what it felt like to lose your mind? Nearly fainting in a supermarket, screaming at a pregnant lady, and then running through the centre of a city until breaking into an empty church, only to sit there alone and hum carols to yourself? I looked around the church for an image of Mary. She had a kind face. She didn't die in agony. She lost her son, but he became the son of God which must have been some consolation. Strangely I couldn't see her anywhere, not even on the stations of the cross. I could never remember which one she appeared on anyway. I ran through the various stages of Jesus's route to his death, but I couldn't recall at what stage Mary came to weep for him. Like me, Mary felt pity for him. Or maybe I was wrong, maybe she just felt pity for herself.

My thoughts wandered to Dad, of how much it still hurt that he had abandoned us. Despite the affair, despite the magnitude of his betrayal, what hurt the most was that he had given up on us so quickly, so easily. I hated that he had been such a coward. It had been more than eighteen months now, but the pain was still as fresh as ever. The anger had dissipated, faded to a

frustrated disappointment, and more than anything else, I just wished I could see him again. The morning he'd died, I'd stayed in bed too long, exhausted from the previous day's revelations and I'd missed our breakfast together. He'd left my bowl of cereal out waiting for me on the kitchen table. It was the memory of the cornflakes in the bowl, with the letter resting on top, which haunted me the most.

I reached for my handbag, took out my wallet and unfolded the note that was tucked inside, beneath my student union card.

Dear Emma
I'm so sorry to do this to you but I can't see any other way. There are too many problems, too many things to deal with and at least this solves one of them. My life insurance will sort out all our debts... I owe this to your mother. She's had years of rubbish from me, put up with my uselessness for too long, and she deserves some rest now. Things will be easier with me gone. Maybe not straight away, but in the long run. As for the other problem...believe me, I hate myself far more than you ever could. I'm so sorry that you had to find out. Not sorry for me, but sorry for you because I have to ask you one final favour. One last thing you can do to help your old dad out. Please don't tell your mother. There's nothing to be gained from telling her, it'll only cause her more pain.

Do it for her, if you don't want to do it for me. Love Dad

I stared down at his writing, of all that was left of him. I loved him and I missed him. I hated him too, for making me choose between him and Mum, for forcing my loyalties to lie with him. I loved him and I hated him, every day, although it did me no good.

I became cold, in my sleeveless t-shirt and skirt, but I was rooted to the pew. I stared down at my neat, unpainted toenails in my flip-flops.

I thought of Lucy, of my outburst. It was wrong. It was almost

worse than the betrayal itself.

I folded the note back up again and returned it to its hiding place. I wished my heart would just stop dead, right here and now. I concentrated on my breathing, trying to make it as shallow as possible, trying to stop my body from moving, trying to control even the slight quivers that come with being a living, breathing entity, but I couldn't. My hands shook, ever so slightly. I willed my heart to stop beating. I shut my eyes, screwed my face up tight in concentration and told it to stop. But it didn't. If anything it started to beat harder and harder, until I could almost hear it pulsating.

And then, from a different world entirely, came the triumphant chorus of Handel's *Arrival of the Queen of Sheba*. I flung my arms out in self-defence, as though I had been attacked. It took me a few seconds to register that it was just my mobile phone ringing. Not the Apocalypse. Not the Arrival of the Son of God. Not Jesus' Second Coming. Just someone calling my phone.

It was Joe.

'Hello.' My voice was croaky, the way it is when you haven't spoken for a while.

'Emma? I can't hear you very well. It's Joe.'

'Yes I know,' I said, my voice returning.

'What?' I could hear him perfectly well. 'Emma? I can't hear you. Can you hear me?'

'Hang on,' I said, getting up from my seat. 'I'm just going to go outside.'

I half-heartedly ran down the aisle and heaved open the door. The noise and heat of the road outside hit me and my eyes squinted at the brightness.

'Joe?' I said, loudly.

'Emma? That's better. Listen, is Pete with you?'

'Pete?' I asked. 'No, of course not.'

'Do you have any idea where he might be?'

'No. Why would I?' Perhaps Lucy had told him what had

happened in the supermarket. Although they didn't talk that often, considering. Joe once remarked that he spoke to me more often than Lucy.

'Just thought you might know.' He didn't sound cross, just agitated. 'Listen, Lucy's gone into labour, she's at Leeds General, and I can't get hold of him. You don't have any idea where he could be? Think Emma, please.'

I gripped a nearby lamppost. It was just after 4pm. My brain struggled to catch up. I couldn't believe I'd been in the church for two hours. And what was Joe talking about, saying Lucy had gone into labour?

'What? How can she have gone into labour? I thought she had a two months left. I don't understand.'

'She does. It's premature, and she's alone. Can you do me a favour, Em?'

I didn't reply, but he continued talking.

'Can you go round to their flat and check if he's there? You are in Leeds aren't you? When Lucy called me from the ambulance she mentioned she had bumped into you earlier today.'

'Yes,' I said, pausing. I could hear him panting on the other end of the phone, as though he was running. 'I saw her earlier. What else did she say?' I prayed she hadn't told Joe about my horrible scene.

'What?' he said. 'Nothing, nothing, just that she'd seen you. Go round to the flat and see if he's there and he's just turned his phone off or something. And then get to the hospital, as quick as you can. She needs somebody to be there, and if we can't find her bloody husband it will have to be you.'

'OK,' I said, not really comprehending. I paced up and down. 'What are you doing?'

'I'm walking to the station. I was in Newcastle anyway. I'm going to get a train straight to Leeds, but it'll still take me a couple of hours. Get to the hospital as soon as you can, won't you? She needs you.'

'Yes, OK, of course,' I said. Lucy needed me. Here was my chance to make it up to her.

'Great, thanks. Tell her I'll get there as soon as I can. See you later, bye.'

He didn't wait for me to reply before hanging up. I stood in the street, watching the crowds of people on Merrion Street, surging up and down with their shopping bags. I had to get to Lucy and Pete's flat. That's right. I stood for a second, trying to think, but I couldn't remember where they lived.

'For fuck's sake!' I shouted.

Then it came back to me. Royal Park Terrace. Number 7, my childhood favourite number. They lived at Royal Park Terrace. Number 28 bus, straight from Merrion Street. I walked towards the crowds, determined to make it up to her. I would do this one thing for her, and then I would get out of her and Pete's lives forever, and leave them to be happy. Them, and their baby.

Chapter Thirty-One

Emma, September 2011

The bus moved slowly. I stared out of the greasy windows, down at the people on the street below. I had no idea what I would say to Lucy. I could tell her that it was all a lie and that I had made it up because I was pathetic and jealous. Since she seemed to believe that anyway, I might not even need to say anything. I would ask her how she was feeling, hold her hand, and try to be encouraging.

There had been no sign of Pete at their flat, and I'd lingered outside for ages, peered inside the front windows and even knocked next door but no one knew where he was. I couldn't imagine a more miserable situation than going through a premature labour all alone. Lucy didn't deserve that. Lucy didn't deserve any of the things that had happened to her.

Lucy's labour could be my fault. I might have brought it on with my evil scene in Morrisons.

Beads of sweat continued to run down my face, no longer brought on by the heat but by my thudding heart. I rummaged around in my bag, looking for my phone, unable to find it among the junk – notebooks, my glass case, old tissues, chewing gum packets, screwed-up receipts.

'For god's sake!' I muttered. People looked at me: the crazy lady rummaging in her handbag. I couldn't cope with another public meltdown. Eventually, I turned the contents of my bag out onto my lap, and finally, there it was, hidden in the dark folds of the lining.

I knew Pete's number off by heart, but it had been so long since I had rung it. Many times, especially late at night, I'd lain in bed, watching my red alarm clock marking each minute, my phone in hand, poised to dial. I'd never rung him though – not even when I was drunk. That was something. I had broken things off with Pete when I'd found out Lucy was pregnant, which was the right thing to do. I wasn't all bad.

I hesitated for a few moments longer, but the bus was getting close to the hospital. I pressed the green 'Call' button. It rang for a minute, before switching to the generic voicemail message. I knew there was no point in leaving a message, as Joe would already have done that.

I got off the bus just outside the hospital. I'd spent more than a year in Leeds and yet I'd never been there. I followed the signs to the maternity department, to a reception area painted in pastel tones. There was a nurse sitting behind a large desk. She didn't notice me, so I leaned over slightly and gave a nervous cough.

'Excuse me,' I said. 'I'm looking for a Mrs Lucy Field.'

She looked up and smiled. 'Lucy Field,' she said, looking down at a book on the desk. 'Yes, she's in room four at the moment. But she hasn't given birth yet so I can't let you see her I'm afraid. Are you a relative?'

'No, no, I'm her friend. She's alone, isn't she? Is there no way I can go in?'

'Sorry, not unless you are her birthing partner or her other half. She has a midwife with her. She's in good hands, so don't worry. Take a seat, and I will make sure someone tells you as soon as the baby is born. What's your name?'

'It's Emma. Please can you just tell her that I'm here? She might want to see me.'

'Sorry, Mrs Field requested that only her husband be allowed in. We're still waiting for him to arrive. Please, have a seat.'

'You don't understand,' I said, feeling flustered, my right shoulder aching at the weight of my bag as I leaned on the desk. 'We can't get hold of him. He doesn't even know she's in labour. Please, I want to be with her.'

The nurse considered me for a few moments, as though she was searching for authenticity.

'I'm sorry,' she said, after a while, looking down at the desk.

'Rules are rules. I don't see what I can do. You've left a message for her husband I assume? I am sure he will get here soon.'

'Yes but we don't even know where he is. He could be miles away. Please, can you just tell her I'm here? So that if she does want someone with her, I can go in?'

'I can't go in there, I'm afraid. I will ask the midwife when she comes out, perhaps she can pass the message on. But it depends on Mrs Field's condition. Sorry, that's the best I can do, please take a seat.'

'What do you mean on her condition? Is she OK?'

'I can't tell you any more,' she said, her voice rising slightly. 'Please take a seat.'

I let out a whine of frustration and sat down in the waiting area. Dog-eared copies of *Practical Parenting* and *Junior* magazines lay untouched on a small chipboard coffee table. There were two men and a middle-aged lady sitting nearby. The men both looked sick and uncomfortable. The lady was muttering to one of them and he nodded in response, clearly not listening. Why weren't the men weren't in the room, watching their partners give birth? Perhaps they were squeamish. Perhaps they were reluctant fathers. I'd heard people say that some men couldn't stand to watch the women they loved in so much pain, but it sounded like a cop out to me.

I took my phone out of my bag, but I had no messages. It was nearly 7pm. Above the receptionist's head was a sign that read 'PLEASE SWITCH OFF YOUR MOBILE PHONE'S'. How could you trust people to guide you through the trauma of childbirth if they didn't even know how to use apostrophes correctly?

Half an hour later, I was still waiting. No one had gone in or out of Room Four. Then, finally, a doctor and nurse opened the door and disappeared inside. A few minutes after, Joe arrived. He didn't see me at first, and marched straight up to the reception desk, as I had done. He was wearing khaki shorts, revealing muscly legs. His face was red, and he wore a green fitted t-shirt.

The reception nurse smiled kindly at him and pointed to me. She probably thought I was his girlfriend or something.

'Emma, hi,' he said, sitting opposite me. 'What's going on? Any news?'

'No,' I said. 'They won't let me in, and they haven't told me anything.'

'No sign of Pete?' Joe asked, frowning.

'No. I went to the flat but there was no one there. I have no idea where he could be.'

'He must have got our mobile messages by now, surely? What's he playing at?'

'Maybe something's happened to him.' I asked, starting to worry. 'Perhaps he's had an accident.'

Joe rolled his eyes at me. 'What are you like? Don't be so melodramatic.'

'She's in room four,' I said, turning my head in its direction.

'Really?' He followed my gaze. 'I wonder if they'll let me see her.'

'I asked them to tell her I was here and that I'd go in if she wanted me to, but I don't know if they have. Perhaps you should ask? You are her flesh and blood after all. Not like me.'

'I don't think that will make much difference Em. Who would want their brother to see them in the throes of childbirth anyway? Come to think of it, who'd want to see their sister give birth? I'd rather have the bloody baby myself.'

The doctor who had hurried into Lucy's room just a few minutes before came out again, followed by a nurse. She didn't bother to close the door behind her as she left and as it slowly swung shut, I could just make out Lucy's shadowing figure lying on a bed in the middle of the room. I was sure I could hear her moaning. There was someone else in the room with her.

'What's going on?' I said, pointlessly to Joe.

He didn't reply but got up and walked towards the room. The nurse from behind reception saw him and got up, putting her hand on his arm when he tried to pass.

'Sorry, you can't go in there. Please, take a seat.'

'But my sister is in there. What's happening?'

'I don't know. But please, sit down. I'll try to find out for you.'

Joe looked past her, towards the door to Lucy's room. He didn't bother to argue, but turned and sat back down.

We waited for another half an hour, both of us watching the door intently. Neither of us attempted conversation. Eventually, the doctor who had rushed out of the room walked up to the nurse and whispered something to her. She turned and pointed towards us. I stood up.

'Hello,' he said, looking at me, and then Joe. 'I understand you are Mrs Field's brother and friend?'

'Yes, is she OK?' I asked.

'Please come with me, I'd like to talk to you in private.'

We followed him into a tiny room, which had a placard on the door declaring it the 'Family Room'. The walls were pale blue; there were a few fraying brown tweed chairs, a water cooler and some forgettable, faded water colours in cheap frames. I didn't want to sit down, so I hovered near the water cooler, while Joe and the doctor sat opposite one another.

'I'm sorry to tell you that Mrs Field has lost the baby.'

He came straight out with it. I had expected some kind of soothing warm-up, some words to soften the blow, something. Not just that statement. I suppose there was no way of softening a blow like that. Lucy's baby was dead, and no amount of pleasantries could lessen the impact of that news. *Mrs Field has lost the baby*. A strange gurgling sound burst out of my mouth. Joe looked furious. I bit down hard into the sides of my cheeks.

'The baby died in the womb sometime earlier today. When Mrs Field...'

'Lucy,' I interrupted.

The doctor smiled at me kindly.

'When Lucy came in she already suspected something was

wrong. We gave her a scan and could see that the baby's heart had stopped. I'm afraid there was nothing we could do but ease her pain and help her through the delivery.'

The colour had drained from Joe's face. 'You mean, she had to give birth to…a… dead baby?'

'I'm afraid so. We don't know why the baby died, but we can perform a post mortem to find out, if Mrs… Lucy wishes.'

'How is she?' I asked, finding my voice.

'She's fine, very calm considering and health-wise, she's being checked over but looks absolutely fine.' He paused and looked from me to Joe, and then back to me. 'I'm so sorry to have to give you this news. I hope you understand that there was nothing we, or Lucy, could have done to save the baby by the time she came in today. She's very tired, but you can see her if you wish.'

'Yes,' said Joe, standing up. 'I want to see her.'

'Of course. I'll let her know, and if she's feeling up to it then you can come through.'

The doctor stood too, and walked towards the door, turning the handle.

I lingered by the water cooler. 'What…' I said, pausing him. 'was it? The baby, I mean. Was it a boy or a girl?'

'It was a girl,' he replied, looking away. 'I'm so sorry.'

~

I crept into the room behind Joe. She was lying propped up against some pillows under a cotton blanket, staring up at the ceiling. He took a seat next to her, while I stayed in the corner of the room, my eyes fixated on an antibacterial lotion wall-dispenser, underneath a sticker that said 'STAY SAFE, STAY CLEAN'. Lucy's eyes flicked around at us as we came in but she didn't move. Her face was puffy and covered in shadows. Some of her hair was stuck to the sides of her head, while the rest of it made a messy display on the pillow. I wondered why she hadn't tied it up. It was warm in the room – too warm, and stuffy. I wanted to open a window but it might not be allowed. Outside the sun was low, but still strong enough to throw shards of light across the floor and the foot of the bed.

'How are you feeling?' Joe asked, softly.

She didn't answer.

'Is there anything I can get you?' he said, persisting.

There was a pause, I suppressed a sneeze and then finally she spoke.

'I want to have a shower,' she said, her voice dull and emotionless. 'I feel so dirty. But they won't let me get up.'

'You need to rest. I am sure you can have a shower soon. Have you slept?'

'Even the sheets are dirty. If I could just get up, they could change the sheets, couldn't they?'

'Have you asked them to change the sheets?'

She finally turned towards Joe, a wrinkled frown developing across her forehead.

'No,' she said quietly. 'I haven't asked.'

Joe smiled at her and reached forward to take her hand.

'Look who's here to see you. It's Emma.'

My eyes widened at the sound of my name. I stepped forward slightly, from the shadowy corner into one of the sunlight patches on the floor.

'Hi,' I said. 'I'm so sorry.' My eyes filled with tears this time. I was too tall, too big, too awkward, dominating the space. She looked so small and vulnerable. Hollow, defeated. Like Jesus.

'Hi,' she replied, her eyes dull and heavy. Perhaps she was still woozy from the drugs they had given her. Presumably strong painkillers had side effects.

'Where's Peter?' she said, and her voice came out stronger this time, like a moan.

'We don't know,' Joe replied, and he squeezed her hand as if to inject her with strength. 'We've left messages for him, but we haven't heard from him yet. I am sure he'll be here soon.'

'He's left me,' she said.

'Don't be ridiculous. He'll be here soon.' Joe looked back at me and raised his eyebrows slightly.

'No,' she said, her voice getting louder. 'He's left me Joe.'

'Don't be silly. Why would he have left you?'

I was hungry. I hadn't had any lunch, or dinner. The clock above a small basin in the corner of the room told me it was nearly 9pm. I stared at the lumps in the blanket that indicated the position of Lucy's feet.

'Because he wants to be with Emma,' she said, simply, shifting in the bed slightly.

'I think the drugs are affecting you slightly, Luce. Emma's here. She's not with Peter.'

She pushed herself up higher onto the bed, wincing with the pain of the movement. She looked straight at me for the first time. Her eyes were wide and bright despite the purple shadows outlining them.

'He's gone to find you Emma. He's gone to your flat.'

'What?' I didn't understand. I wanted to run away, but I was nailed down by the intensity of her stare. Joe smiled at me in sympathy and turned back towards her.

'Should we leave you to get some sleep now? We can come back later,' he said, sounding tired himself.

'No I'm fine. Please don't go.' She smiled half-heartedly. 'Emma, come over here and sit next to me, please. I want to talk to you.'

She sounded kind and content, not angry and disgusted as she had every right to. My mind had turned to sludge. I obeyed her and silently took a seat next to Joe, noticing that the sheet under the blanket was stained with blood.

'I phoned Peter. He was in town anyway, we were meant to be getting the bus back together. We'd been shopping for baby things.' She coughed and started to twist the blanket between her fingers, looking down at it as she spoke. 'We ordered a Moses basket from Allders. It was beautiful. Expensive, but Mam says they're much better for tiny babies than a cot. Peter had gone to pick up the shoes he'd had re-soled while I went to get some dinner. That's when I saw you Emma. I knew you'd spotted me too, and I saw you try to run away and hide. But I didn't understand why.'

'Lucy...' I began but she quickly looked up at me and her eyes narrowed at my interruption.

'I thought you were making it all up to hurt me. I thought you were lying. I've always known you've been in love with Peter since you met him. I'm not stupid. But I always thought it was a one-way thing. I assumed you were just jealous, trying to hurt me. But something in the way you looked told me perhaps there was some truth in it. I called Peter, and I told him what you had said. He didn't deny it. He said he was sorry, that he hadn't meant for me to find out like this. It wasn't particularly reassuring. He told me he loved you. Not me. You.'

Joe's mouth was hanging open slightly, and he turned to me.

'What have you done?' he said. 'What's going on?'

I didn't reply. I just nodded and willed Lucy to carry on speaking, knowing that only she would be able to calm her brother down.

'They were in love Joe,' she said. 'I don't feel betrayed. I think I had always known, ever since Peter first came back to see me one weekend after being in Leeds. He showed me a picture of you – you look so like his mam you know – and as he spoke about you, his face lit up. I always had my suspicions. But I didn't realise that you...' She gave a choked cry. 'You slept together after the wedding. Before I slept with Peter, *you* did. Do you know that in the eyes of God, that means you two are married? Not me and Peter, you and Peter? Didn't he tell you that?'

'No.' I shook my head. 'No.'

'It's true. You should be together. I think God looks upon you as married already. Poor Peter, he feels such a duty to me, but that's not how it should be. He should be with you. And now, I've lost my baby. You two can be together.'

'No,' I said. 'He's your husband, not mine. I'm so sorry. For everything.'

'Don't apologise. The first time you slept together – that was enough. After that, he was yours and you were his and there was nothing wrong in what you did. Except perhaps for deceiving me. But I know you didn't mean any harm.' She gave a small, sarcastic laugh.

'Listen,' Joe interrupted, sounding firm and controlled, but I could sense his fury under the surface. 'You need to get some sleep. You've just had a major shock. You don't need to think about this right now. We are going to let you get some sleep. Is there anything you need? Lucy? I can go back to your flat and get some things.'

'Please don't make a fuss Joe,' she said. 'I just want to explain to Emma and have a shower and some clean sheets.'

'I don't know what to say,' I said. 'Of course Pete loves you. We ended it as soon as we found out that you were pregnant.' As I said the words I corrected myself in my head. We ended it as soon as I had found out that she was pregnant. But there was little point in being brutally honest to someone who had just given birth to a dead baby.

'I know, and that's why I can forgive him. He never intended to hurt anyone. The opposite in fact. But it was God's will that you two should be together, don't you see that Emma? It was God's will that I should lose my baby, to enable you to be together. You have a sexual attraction, something we never had. That's why you should be together. That's why my baby died.'

'What you're saying is crazy!' I cried. 'Really. He loves you. I haven't heard from him for ages. What we did was wrong. You two created a life together.'

'My baby was always going to die. From the very first scan,

we knew she was in danger. She had a weak heart. Formed not from the union of love but from the union of duty. A weak heart can't survive. A weak love can't either. The doctors monitored me loads but I knew every day I woke up and felt the baby move was a blessing. And I'm grateful for that. And I'm grateful for your honesty earlier. I really am. I told Peter what you had said and his immediate reaction was that he should be with you. He went to find you. I went to the Millennium Square and sat for a while. And I knew that my baby's heart had stopped. I felt her die within me. She's gone to heaven, a better life. They induced me. It didn't hurt much really, because I was allowed morphine. They don't let you have that when the baby's still alive, I don't think. In case it hurts it.'

Even Joe was crying now.

'I'm so sorry,' I said. 'I'm so, so, so sorry.'

'It's OK, I forgive you. What's the sense in hating you? Or Peter? We can all move on from this. Somehow.' She gave a false smile.

Neither Joe nor I found anything to say to fill the silence. She was acting. Or perhaps it was the morphine. Maybe tomorrow I would come and visit her and she'd scream and shout and swear at me to get away from her, to never come near her again. I didn't want to leave the comfort of her serene smile and kind eyes. It was obvious that Joe, who I could sense was quietly seething next to me, was ready to rip me to shreds once we were alone. I wanted to stay on that hard black chair at her bedside forever.

She watched both of us and eventually spoke again.

'I'm getting quite tired now. I think I should get some sleep. Please will you ask the nurse to come and change the sheets? I couldn't bear to sleep in all this mess. I need the toilet too, but I think I'll need help getting there. Would you mind asking the nurse on your way out?'

'No, of course not. Of course I will. We'll come back tomorrow.'

'Thanks. And Joe, don't be too angry with Emma, or Peter.'

'OK, whatever you say.' He leaned over and kissed her on the forehead. 'And you promise to get some sleep please big sister.'

She smiled up at him one final time, and together, we left the room.

Chapter Thirty-two

Emma, September 2011

When I woke the next morning, the note I'd found pushed under the front door the day before was stuck to the side of my cheek. I was the only one who'd stayed on at Clarence Dock over the summer, and having the whole flat to myself was lovely.

Em,

I can't believe you told her but in a way I'm relieved. Everything is out in the open now. I immediately came to find you but since you're not in, I wonder if it might be fate. I need some space to clear my head, so I'm going home for a few days to stay with my father. I know it's wrong for me to abandon both you and Lucy but I feel I need to work out a way in my mind that we can be together. There must be a way through this mess.

Lucy says that you and I should be together, that in the eyes of God we are one. I'm so ashamed to admit I don't actually know the rules on matters like this. Perhaps there are none. I need to speak to Father Gerry, to get things straight in my head.

If she asks, please don't tell her where I am. I'm praying for all of us. I'll be back soon.

Pete x

I stayed in bed, kicking the covers back to allow fresh air to get to my legs and considered the note again. Last night I had been furious, unable to believe he'd disappeared, leaving me to deal with his poor wife. I knew he wouldn't have known that Lucy had gone into labour when he had written the note – he didn't like using his phone on the train and by the time he'd got his messages he would have already arrived in Newcastle. It was still hard to imagine him making polite conversation with his distant father over breakfast this morning. I had no idea where he was or what he was thinking, and my guesses were worthless.

I shivered. Joe might be in a different mood today – he'd been oddly understanding the night before when we'd left the hospital, saying he didn't think it would help Lucy if we fell out. When I tried to explain what had happened with me and Pete, he gave me a look to say he wasn't going to buy it and that he'd rather not even know, so I shut up. He was disappointed in me.

We'd agreed to meet at noon outside the hospital, to visit Lucy again. It was 8.30am, and I'd had one of those night's sleep where you are convinced you have been awake all night, but you can't have been because it's the morning and there's no way a whole night has passed.

I ate breakfast, washed my hair, put on some clean jeans and left the crusts from my toast on the windowsill outside my bedroom for the birds. Outside the window was more lovely sunshine, not quite as stifling as the previous day. I hoped the nurses had given Lucy my message that Pete had gone up to Newcastle. It didn't matter that I'd gone against his wishes – he hadn't known the full situation when he'd written that note.

Joe was sitting on a large sign outside the hospital when I approached, waiting for me. He gave me an undeserved half-smile.

'Lovely day, isn't it?' he said. He clearly hadn't gone home and seethed all night about my betrayal of his sister, but then, it just wasn't Joe's way. Perhaps the fact that Lucy was prepared to forgive me was enough for him – maybe I'd never have to face his wrath.

'Yes it is. Have you been in yet?'

'No, thought I'd wait for you.'

As we walked inside, he took my arm for a second and stopped.

'Emma,' he said, looking at me seriously. 'I have to warn you, if Lucy's not in such a forgiving mood this morning, then I have to support her OK? She's my sister. I don't doubt that whatever went on with you and Peter was more his doing but I still have to be on her side. You're both victims of him as far as I can see, but she's my flesh and blood.'

'Of course,' I said. 'I understand. But Pete…it's not all his fault.'

'Don't go there. As far as I'm concerned, it's completely his fault.'

We arrived in the maternity department to find a different nurse at reception. She looked really young. Joe explained we were there to see Lucy. She checked through the same big book as the nurse the day before, frowning and chewing the end of her pen. She flicked through a couple of pages and then flicked back again.

'Sorry,' she said, after a while. 'I can't see her name listed. I mean, she was here, but she discharged herself first thing by the looks of this. Hang on, I've only just come on shift, I'll just ask someone else.'

She rang somebody and explained the situation to the person on the other end of the line so quietly I could barely hear. I wondered if it was her first day. She seemed a bit nervous.

'I'm sorry,' she said, putting the phone down. 'It's as I thought, Mrs Field discharged herself this morning.'

'What?' said Joe. 'She can't have done. She only gave birth yesterday afternoon.'

'Sorry, you are?' she said, looking sympathetic.

'I'm her brother. She knew we were coming to see her today. I don't understand, I think you must have got mixed up or something.' He leant in closer and dropped his voice to a whisper, even though there wasn't anyone else in the waiting area. 'Her baby was born dead.'

'Stillborn,' I interrupted.

'Yes, stillborn,' he repeated. 'She was very upset last night, as I am sure you can understand. She was also very weak. There's no way she would have discharged herself. She could hardly even stand up.'

'Sorry sir, but that's what I've been told. I can get the doctor on duty to have a word with you if you like, but as it was quite early – 8am it says here – he might not know the circumstances of the situation either.'

'Are you serious?' Joe said, looking amazed. 'Come on, this is crazy. Yesterday she couldn't even get out of bed. You're telling me she just walked out of here on her own?'

'I don't know, as I said before, I wasn't here. I can only tell you what I've been told. Please, take a seat, and I'll get the doctor to talk to you when he's free.'

'Why on earth would they even let her out? Why didn't someone stop her?' His voice was loud. I felt my throat tighten.

'This isn't a prison, we can't keep patients in if they don't want to stay. I'm sorry, I will get the doctor to have a word with you right away.'

She looked at me, her eyes tinged with anxiety.

'That would be good. We'll wait over there. But please, can you get him to come and see us as soon as possible. We're both really worried about her, as I am sure you can imagine.' I took Joe's arm and guided him towards the seating area. I felt calm and in control for the first time in a while.

'Where the hell did she go?' Joe asked, staring straight ahead, his eyes fixed and unblinking.

'I don't know,' I said.

'I was at her house all night, and all morning, she never came back. So where the hell did she actually go? God, what happens if she collapsed in the street or something? She could be dead. Anything could have happened to her.'

'Now who's being melodramatic. Maybe she's gone to see a friend. Maybe she just wanted some time alone to think.'

'She doesn't have any friends in Leeds. You know that. Nobody but you.'

'That's not true, she knows some people at the library, where she worked. I've heard her talk about them.'

'She left the library ages ago. You know what Pete's like. He wouldn't let her have any friends that he thought weren't suitable. When I see him I'm going to knock him into the middle of next week.'

'I suppose you think it's my fault too,' I mumbled, in my smallest voice.

'Oh don't you start a pity-party for yourself. Not unless you really want to piss me off.'

I didn't say anything. After what felt like hours, a middle-aged Indian man wearing a white overall came towards us.

'Hello,' he said, taking a seat opposite us. 'You're Mrs Field's relatives, yes?'

'You tell me why she was allowed to leave the hospital this morning,' Joe began, angrily. 'Why she wasn't stopped? She was so weak, she couldn't even stand up.'

'I'm afraid I don't know any more than you do. She discharged herself at about 8am. I wasn't working this morning. Her notes say she was feeling fine but desperately wanted to be at home. Under the circumstances, I am sure whoever was in charge thought her mental state of mind was more important. She clearly had a horrific experience, but physically she was fine. I think perhaps when you saw her, the effects of the morphine were wearing off, that's why she might have seemed weak. But she was in good health, I can assure you. She was given an outpatients appointment for this afternoon. Just for a check up. There will be some unfortunate side effects for her – milk production… it's a shame. Someone will advise her, and there are good counselling services available on the NHS.'

I wondered why he told us all this in the waiting room. He should have taken us somewhere private like the doctor had done yesterday. It was disrespectful of him to blurt out this terribly confidential and private information in the middle of the reception. We were both consumed in a stunned silence.

'Well,' he said, getting up. 'I'm afraid that's all I can tell you. If there's nothing else, I must get back.'

'Wait!' Joe said, as the doctor turned his back. 'Did she say where she was going?'

'Yes. It says in her notes she was going home.' He patted Joe's arm and then walked away.

~

Outside, the sun was beating down hard on the concrete pavement. There wasn't a single drop of moisture left in the air. The brightness hurt my eyes after the cool interior of the hospital, but when I looked in my handbag my sunglasses weren't there. Joe tried to ring Lucy's mobile as soon as we were outside, but shrugged his shoulders in despair when it went straight to voicemail.

'How could she have gone all the way back to Cresswell? It's so far,' Joe said, kicking at some loose tarmac on the hospital drive.

'She must have done. She must have got a train first thing. Perhaps she went straight to the station,' I said. Lucy's departure was my fault. She had obviously got my message last night and gone to find Pete.

'You think?' he said, sounding calmer, considering the idea. 'Perhaps. I suppose she probably wanted to see Mam. I called her last night and told her what had happened: maybe she rang the hospital and asked to speak to Lucy and Lucy said she wanted to come home.'

'Yes, maybe your parents even drove down to pick her up?' I said, making my voice light and positive.

'Perhaps,' he said.

'I'm sure that's it Joe. She would have wanted to be with her mother – of course she would, that's natural. What a horrible situation to be in, stuck in Leeds with your husband nowhere in sight and no friends or family. I'm sure she would have wanted to go home. I'm sure that's it. I bet she's tucked up in bed right now, with your mum bringing her cups of tea and toast.'

'Yes I expect you're right.' He took his phone out of his pocket. 'I'll give Mam a ring.'

'Um…wait,' I said, controlling my tone just before it sounded like a shriek. 'Just wait a second. Just in case she's not there. You don't want to worry them, do you? I mean, your parents. In case she's gone somewhere else.'

'Make your mind up Emma. Where else would she go? She doesn't have any close friends back home either. Of course she's gone to Mam and Dad's.'

'Well, there is one other place she might be.'

'Where?'

I hesitated. 'She might have gone to find Pete.'

Joe stopped walking and looked at me. 'Is there something I don't know?'

'He left me a note yesterday afternoon, while we were at the hospital. He had come to find me after Lucy had told him... In the note he said he had gone home for a few days to sort his head out. He didn't know about the baby then, of course. He told me not to tell Lucy where he was. But…'

'But?' The little patches of red were forming again on the corners of his cheeks. They spread, like little red clouds.

'I had to! She had a right to know. I phoned the hospital and left a message for her. Just so she knew he was OK. Perhaps it was the wrong thing to do, but I thought she might be worried about him.' I watched the news sink in. The red clouds didn't get any bigger. It was so lovely that Joe's face was so transparent, such a clear indication of his emotions.

'It's OK. I get why you did that. Don't know why you didn't tell me though. So, in all likelihood, she's gone back to Cresswell, either to see him or to see Mam and Dad. Well, I'll have to go back too then. I don't think she's still in Leeds.' He looked to either side of himself, as if he might spot her walking along the street there and then. 'I'll have to go home.'

'Joe,' I said, a little cautiously.

'Yes?'

'I want to come too.'

Chapter Thirty-three

Pete, August 2009

It was the first time she had disobeyed him in for ages. She'd refused to come to the door when he'd called for her at the last minute, sure that she would change her mind. Refused, point blank. He hadn't even been treated to an apologetic, tear-stained explanation. She wouldn't see him and that was that. Joe, her immoral, idiotic brother, stood in the doorway, barring Peter from entering.

'She's too upset to see you,' he said, scowling.

The dislike was mutual. Peter knew it was Joe's influence that was stopping Lucy from coming with him today. Joe must have seen how upset she was last night, and persuaded her to stay at home. Joe was his only competition, and the only other man Lucy looked up to. Her father was a fat, lazy waste of space, and although she was fond of him, and fiercely loyal, Peter knew she'd always needed a stronger male role model. That was where he'd fitted in perfectly. Up until last year that is, when suddenly Joe had sprouted like an irrepressible beanstalk and was now only marginally shorter than Peter, and just as protective.

'Tell her to come down,' he said, scowling back at Joe. Who did he think he was?

'No. She's crying. She doesn't want to see you. You'll just have to go on your own.'

With that, the pipsqueak younger brother shut the door in Peter's face.

He turned and walked back to his own house. His father was already in the car, shaking his head with impatience. Peter climbed into the passenger seat, averting the irritated stare directed his way.

'Where's the lass then?' he asked him as they pulled out of the drive. 'Let you down has she? What a surprise.'

'She's not feeling very well,' Peter said. No matter how cross he was with Lucy, his unending fury towards his father would always win out.

'Not feeling very well,' his father echoed, in a voice laced with scorn.

Peter stared out of the window as they drove through Cresswell. It was hot, the hottest it had been for a few weeks now, and the sun broke through the car's windscreen visors and pounded at his forehead. He squinted and allowed himself to feel genuinely sad that Lucy, his Lucy, the only person in his life who actually mattered to him, couldn't be bothered to come with him today. It was so unlike her to put her own feelings first. He wondered if this was the beginning of a change. In just a few weeks, he'd be gone, away from Cresswell, settled in a city that she'd never even visited. Was she trying to distance herself from him already? He couldn't believe that she had so little strength, so little faith in their union. He'd reassured her, time and time again, that things would stay the same, forever. They'd always be Peter and Lucy, and his three-year degree in Leeds was nothing more than a brief interlude. A mere fraction of an inconvenience in their life-long story together.

Of course, he'd said all this, his voice powerful with passion, but he always forgot how well she knew him. Not as well as she thought she did, but still, perhaps she could sense tremors of insincerity in his words. She knew there were doubts, there were ideas bubbling away under the surface that she would never be party to. She didn't know what they were or what they involved, but she knew. He always had her down as weak-willed, naïve and trusting, but she was sharper than he often gave her credit for, and he reckoned she could sense that something wasn't quite right, even if she didn't know exactly what it was.

What was the point of her coming with him today, she'd asked him on the beach last night. There was no point. She didn't need to be there to see him open his envelope, to see his face light up as they both knew it would when his three As were confirmed. He would take pride in seeing his results, despite himself. He was impressed by his own achievements. He'd come from such trauma, from such a fractured start, that he always gave himself due praise for his application academically. It would have been so easy for him to have gone off the rails completely, but he hadn't. He'd stayed on the straight and narrow, worked hard at school, and was soon to reap the rewards for his efforts. Most importantly, he knew, wherever she was now, his mam was proud of him.

'Better not take long this,' his father muttered, wrinkling his forehead. 'Got a delivery in an hour. Could have done with going to the shops this morning too.'

'We can go on the way back,' Peter replied, his voice dull. 'It shouldn't take long.'

It was wrong of him, he knew, to want someone there to share his joy. It was selfish, narcissistic. But he did, he wanted someone to whoop with delight at his outstanding grades, and he knew his father would do the exact opposite. He would snort, mutter something derisive about it being expected, and they'd be on their way. It wasn't fair, he wanted praise. He deserved it. Lucy's decision to withhold it was cruel and spiteful. If only his mam had still been alive…

As always, a reflex kicked in, and he closed his brain off at such thoughts.

The car pulled into the school gates, swinging round before coming to a halt outside the entrance.

'Well, go on then,' his father said. 'And don't be taking all day about it.'

Of course, he could have received his results by post, like most of his classmates, and his father knew that. It would only have meant one more day's wait. This was the first time for a while that he'd asked his father for a favour. Not much of a favour either, but it would be held against him for a few days at least.

Peter hurried in the entrance. The school secretary was sitting at reception. He could never remember her name but she was slightly stupid, and had a habit of clutching injured seventh years to her bosom whether they liked it or not. Beneath a mass of grey curls, she smiled up at him.

'Peter Field,' she said, pushing her glasses up slightly. 'The first one! You are keen. Here you go, dear.'

She handed him a brown envelope with his name written on it. He paused, wondering whether it would be best to open it here, in front of an old bat he hardly knew, or in the car, in front of an old git he knew too well.

'Good luck,' she said, smiling again.

'Thanks,' he replied. Might as well get it over with, he reasoned, seeing as it was all ruined now anyway, without Lucy. He opened the envelope. There they were, as expected: three As. One for Maths, one for Economics, one for Philosophy. He would be going to Leeds. He stared at the piece of paper. It was thin, almost transparent, the marks printed in old typewriter-style letters. He tried a smile, but he'd never been able to force one, and it wouldn't come naturally.

He felt nothing.

'Well?' the secretary asked. 'Good news I hope? Got what you wanted? I know the head and the other teachers have always had such admiration for you. An exceptional talent, Mr Miller said.'

'I have to go. My father's waiting,' Peter replied. The lady's face sank in embarrassment, and she looked back down at the desk in front of her, at the rows of envelopes lined up expectantly.

He turned and left the building. Outside, the green Volvo loomed, its engine ticking over, his father's shadowy figure filling the space behind the steering wheel. The last thing he wanted to do was get in the car. He lingered for a few seconds on the steps outside the school's entrance. He still felt numb. Perversely, he wished he'd failed – at least then he knew he would feel something. Shock, anger, disbelief, frustration, whatever. Anything would be better than this gaping emptiness.

He walked slowly towards the car and got in. Before he'd even had time to do up his seatbelt, his father had pulled away, out of the school gates and back towards Cresswell.

'Well?' his father asked. Peter felt a flicker of satisfaction at the interest. 'Got what you wanted did you?'

'Yes,' Peter said, although it was a lie. This wasn't what he wanted at all.

It was Lucy's fault. She'd ruined the day. If she had been there, her happiness and admiration at her exceptionally intelligent boyfriend would have rubbed off on him. It would have infected him too, he would have felt it through her. He'd known for a long time that he was somehow incapable of normal feelings, the feelings other people had. The logical feelings that made sense to everyone else in the world: sadness at the news of a death, disgust at crimes against the elderly, love for animals. All these emotions, he seemed immune to. He only felt human when Lucy was there, when she was living and breathing life for him, giving him constant cues as to the right way to behave. He wanted, so desperately, to feel the way he imagined he should feel today, but he was impotent. Lucy had spoilt it all, just like she always did.

His anger grew. He would be going to Leeds now, without her. He'd wanted her to come too but a sense of familial duty, something he also failed to experience, prevented her. Her mother's illness had dominated conversations for weeks now. She couldn't possibly leave her mother. He would have to cope without her. Simply put, her mother was just more important to her than he was.

On the beach last night, she'd berated him, tried her best to manipulate him, calling him selfish for applying to Leeds in the first place when there was a perfectly good university in Newcastle. It had amused him slightly to watch her debase herself like that. She had pleaded with him, literally begged him, prostrate on the sand, kissing his feet in some bizarre desperate attempt to change his mind. He'd stayed calm, for a while, ignoring the mounting irritation growing inside him. Then, he'd lost it, called her selfish in return, saying she was boring, pathetic, that she would never make anything of herself if she stayed in Cresswell, with her siblings and her parents, for the rest of her life. His words had silenced her like a slap around the face, and she'd run off without responding.

It was how he felt though. That much he did know. She was being selfish: her mother might have been ill, but she had her father and the pestilential Joe to take care of her. Who did he have? Nobody.

Whatever happened now, it served Lucy right. She had brought it all on herself.

The car was speeding through Ashington. He wound the window down, stuck his head outside, and breathed deeply.

Chapter Thirty-four

Emma, September 2011

The train was relatively empty, but the air conditioning was broken, spewing out only intermittent blasts of cold air, and by the time we'd reached Darlington I nearly passed out from the heat. It was close to 5pm as we trudged along the long road Cresswell, and the sun was finally diminishing. I phoned the temping agency to tell them I wouldn't be in for a few days as I was visiting a sick relative. They didn't sound too convinced, but I didn't care anyway. I'd packed enough clothes for two days, but five pairs of knickers just in case. I had no idea how long I'd be.

Joe and I had run out of small talk on the train and so we walked along in silence. Joe seemed deep in thought as we strode up the long dirt track towards Lucy and Pete's houses. Lucy's was concealed behind a thick, high hedge on the right, while Pete's lay straight ahead, at the end of the track; large, stone and prepossessing. The rooms on the ground floor had their shutters drawn across, and the whole house was in shadow, grey and quiet, as though no one had been inside for years. In contrast, a bunch of colourful balloons, emblazoned with HAPPY BIRTHDAY, dangled limply from the gate into Lucy's front garden.

'It was Martha's fifth last weekend,' Joe explained, reading my mind.

'Oh,' I said. I had forgotten. It must have been hard keeping up with all the birthdays in that house.

We stood still on the track, unsure of which house to go into first.

'Let's try Pete's first,' Joe said, sounding a bit reluctant.

I nodded and we walked up to the entrance. I pushed the button for the bell, but couldn't hear it ring behind the thick, oak door.

'What are we going to say?' I said, my voice reduced to a

whisper.

'I don't know exactly,' Joe mumbled.

We waited for a few minutes but there was no reply, so I rang the bell again. Five minutes later it was clear that no one was at home.

'Your house then?' I asked.

'No,' he said. 'Not yet, let's go round the back first, see if they are in the garden.'

We walked round the side of the house and Joe opened the gate. The garden was empty and the lawn was brown. It had been months since I'd been to Cresswell and I'd forgotten how quiet it all seemed, without even the distant purr of motorway traffic a few miles away. The air was thick and humid, not dry as it had been in Leeds. It needed to rain. I turned towards the house. Black, dark windows looked down on us. The brightness made it impossible to see inside the house, even though the windows were just a few feet away. Perhaps Lucy and Pete were inside, watching us wandering around the garden. Perhaps Pete's father was in there.

There was a rustle behind us, and the sound, magnified by the silence, made me turn in surprise. In one corner, a deer had made its way through a hedge and looked at us, frozen, its eyes wide in terror.

'Look!' I said, turning and tugging at his arm, but by the time he had followed my pointing finger to the spot, the deer had vanished.

'Come on,' he said. 'They're not here. Let's try the beach.'

'OK,' I said, following him out of the garden.

It was the perfect day for a seaside visit and the car park near the ice-cream shop was full. People were packing up their things now and leaving, and lots of families stumbled past us, their arms full of spades and buckets and towels. The children all looked happy and excited, their cheeks glowing from the fresh air. It felt like the most unlikely place to find Lucy or Pete.

But there they were. We saw their silhouettes immediately, far along the beach, perched on some rocks. Pete was sitting at Lucy's feet, looking up at her. My heart started to beat more rapidly and I felt an urge to flee. They made an intense, striking picture against the disappearing sun. Lucy was wearing a dark ankle-length skirt, which billowed out around her. Pete looked like a tiny, thin shadow in comparison to Lucy. They were staring intently at each other, their conversation consuming them. I imagined them through the years, cutting the same enticing image, first as little toddlers, then as children, then teenagers, and now as they emerged into adulthood. They belonged here. They were as familiar with the bays and tides as I was with the thread veins on my cheeks. For as long as they had ever known, the beach had been there, the backdrop to their lives.

'Wait,' I said, pulling Joe back as he strode towards them. 'Do you think we should interrupt?'

'I want to see if my sister's OK. What on earth does he think he's doing, chatting to her out on the beach as if nothing had happened? She should be in bed.'

'But,' I insisted. 'Wait. Please, give them a few more minutes. Whatever they're talking about, it looks important. It looks serious. They have so much to sort out; we should leave them to it. Come on, at least we know she's OK. Why don't we get an ice cream? I could really do with a sit down, I'm completely exhausted.'

'OK,' he said. 'But only if you pay.'

'Deal.'

There was a long queue in the shop and the sign on the door said it should have shut fifteen minutes ago, but the lady behind the counter didn't seem to mind.

We took our rapidly melting cones to the bench at the edge of the sand and sat down. Lucy and Pete were still there at the southern end. I squinted to try to make them out more clearly. It looked as though Pete had turned around and now had his back to Lucy, so they were both facing the sea. It was starting to get cooler, and I felt the tiny pricks of the beginning of goose pimples forming on my bare arms. In contrast to earlier, when I'd been sweating on the train, I was glad that I was wearing jeans.

'I wonder what they're talking about,' I said, licking the sides of my cone.

'Hmm.' Joe didn't seem to be listening.

'Where do they go from here?' I asked. The waves trickled onto the shore and then dragged slowly back out to sea. It was hypnotic. I let my eyelids fall down slightly.

'I don't know,' Joe replied. 'I can't see them breaking up. They're both so religious. They meant it when they married for life.'

'Why aren't you religious?'

'I am,' he said. 'I believe in the religion of me, myself and I. Catholicism never held much appeal for me. And then there's the fact that the dirty old priest we used to have in the village encouraged me to go into detail about my wet dreams when I was 12 and 13. That put me right off.'

'Are you serious?'

'Oh yes, he loved hearing all the gory details. There's no one on this earth more sexually frustrated than a Catholic priest. They're not even meant to wank for Christ's sake. Bloody bound to send them insane.'

'I don't think that it's fair to say that. Not all priests are perverts. I've met quite a few really nice ones. And not being able to…masturbate, I'm sure it doesn't affect all of them in that way.'

'No probably not,' he said, lazily. He wasn't paying attention to me.

'What about Lucy then?' I asked, popping the last piece of my ice-cream cone into my mouth. 'Why is she so religious?'

'Luce takes after Mam. Mam's a religious nutter. But she's got a heart of gold, and Lucy takes after her in every way really. Suppose she would do, being the oldest daughter. Not so sure my Dad believes, but he goes along with it for an easy life. No harm in church on a Sunday. Don't get me wrong, there are many positive things about it, I just don't believe in all of it. But it's OK, because God loves me, and he's the forgiving type.'

I laughed.

'What about you though?' he said, turning to face me. 'Your family aren't religious are they? What made you suddenly see the light?'

'I don't know,' I said, thoughtfully. 'I think I was just lonely. And Lucy and Pete were so kind to me, and so… persuasive. It seemed like a good thing to do. It helped me, after my father... he died, it was a shock, I found it hard to understand. I wanted to be like them. They seemed happy, like they had this security, this secret knowledge that everything would always be OK because God was looking out for them.'

'But did it make you happy?'

'I'm not sure. Maybe. But then I found myself feeling superior to other people, which was awful. And then the thing with Pete started and it was all wrong. Going to mass, saying these prayers... I used to go to mass every day you know. But not since I stopped seeing Pete.'

'Catholicism asks a lot of people. That's it's fundamental flaw, in my opinion.' He ran his fingers through his hair and let out a sigh. 'The trouble is, we're only human. We mess up all the time. It's all very well God forgiving you, but what's more important is whether you can forgive yourself. Trying to live the perfect life, well, it's a recipe for depression if you ask me.'

'Yes. You're right.' I looked sideways at Joe, the pink sun casting a beautiful haze over his face. I couldn't believe he was younger than me.

The beach behind him had emptied. There was no one left now, except for the two shadowy figures at the far end. I turned my head in their direction, and realised that Lucy was walking towards us, trailed by Pete.

'Joe,' I said. 'They're coming.'

Joe stood up and wandered towards them. Lucy must have spotted us, as she suddenly seemed to pick up pace, and it looked as though she was running. Pete was being left behind. As she got closer, I saw her flushed cheeks and beaming smile. Her lips were moving, making the same shapes over and over again. As she came with a few feet of us I finally heard her.

'It's going to be OK!' she was shouting. 'It's going to be OK!'

She flung her arms around Joe's neck. He took a few unsteady steps backwards at the impact, but hugged her back.

'Oh Joe!' she said, panting heavily.

He held her at arm's length. 'Lucy, calm down. What's the matter?'

'Nothing. Isn't it an absolutely glorious day? I'm so happy to be home.'

I stood back a bit, unsure whether to walk away and give them some time together. But before I had the chance to decide, she had stumbled towards me and given me the same throttling hug.

'There's nowhere, absolutely NO WHERE like this on earth is there? The weather! I've never known weather like it, not here. Did you see all the children on the beach? They've gone now, but they were in the sea. Lots of them. Look at all the sandcastles they've left behind. I wish I had a camera.'

She stopped hugging me and took a few steps back. I noticed she was shaking. Perhaps she had been drinking.

'Are you OK?' I said, quietly.

'Of course. Fresh air and sunshine. What more could you want?'

'Sit down,' Joe said, looking concerned. He gestured towards the bench we'd been sitting on just before. A few drops of strawberry ice-cream were evaporating in the sun on one of the slats. 'You look worn out.'

It wasn't true. She looked amazing – her happiness, although bizarre and inappropriate, seemed entirely genuine. She seemed like the real her. This was what Lucy was like. This was why she had been named after the Latin word for light. I hadn't seen her look this radiant since her wedding day. She ignored his request and started to dance about on the sand. It made me want to laugh, but I suppressed the urge. There was something frightening about the way she was behaving.

'Lucy,' Joe said, again. 'You're making me dizzy.' He wasn't laughing.

Pete was approaching now, but hung back slightly, watching Joe. I looked at him, a miserable, pale-faced figure against Lucy's plump and glowing form. I didn't want him to come any nearer, and spoil the ridiculous but infectious delirium that Lucy was spreading. I tried to catch his eyes, to warn him off, but he was staring at the ground, glancing briefly at Joe from time to time.

'Oh Emma. I have so much to tell you. It's all going to be OK. It really is.'

I stared at her, watching her hair whipping about behind her in the stiff wind.

'What's going to be OK?' I said.

'You two. You can be together. As it should be. I have a plan.'

'Lucy,' Joe interrupted, sounding angry again. 'You have to come home now. And rest. Look at your top.'

I followed his eyes and saw what she saw now; two great stains on each side of the front of her yellow t-shirt. Her stomach bulged over the waistline of her skirt and the t-shirt, though large and loose, did not contain it completely.

'What?' she said. 'What?'

'The doctor said there would be side effects...with...milk. Lucy, you need to rest. You're coming home with me. Now.' Joe's voice was gentle but authoritative, and Lucy responded, folding her arms across her chest, looking ashamed.

I wanted to punch Joe then, for breaking Lucy's mood, for trampling on her freedom and spirit. She didn't speak any more, but followed us numbly back to the house. I looked around for Pete just before we left the beach, but he had gone.

We took Lucy up to her room, and got her into bed. It wasn't her room anymore, or her bed, since Joe had taken up residence in there after she had left for Leeds, but she didn't seem to care. She didn't speak again. I stayed next to her, stroking her hair, while Joe went downstairs. Desperately, I hoped he hadn't mentioned Pete's cheating, or my part in the matter. It would only cause more harm, and there was no need now.

Lucy didn't sleep, but stared at me with hollow eyes as I ran my fingers through her tangly hair. She had two freckles on her nose I'd never seen before. I whispered this to her, and she smiled in acknowledgement but didn't speak. I asked her if she wanted a bath, but she shook her head, so instead I went to the bathroom, found a flannel and soaked it in warm water, and washed her breasts as tenderly as I could. They were swollen and hard and her nipples were inflamed and encrusted with dried discharge. I wiped them as clean as possible, patted them dry with a towel and then pulled a fresh t-shirt over her head, and her eyes spoke her gratitude.

I sat with her in a peaceful silence and watched her fall asleep. Joe came in a little later with a bowl of soup and a slab of crusty bread for me. He asked if I wanted to come downstairs and watch TV with the rest of the family but I shook my head. When he left the room, I looked up and saw Ruth was standing in the doorway, a hanky pressed to her nose, her eyes bloodshot and her cheeks tear-stained. She didn't come in, but when her eyes met mine, she offered me a half-smile, and I knew Joe hadn't told her about my part in the betrayal.

I watched it grow darker and darker outside, until it was truly night, and the only light behind Lucy's window was the street lamp at the end of the track. I had stared out of the same window on the night of the wedding, watching Lucy and Pete get into the car that would take them to Rothbury for their honeymoon.

I reached over Lucy's bed to draw the curtains. She murmured and shifted positions, turning to face me, and opened one eye.

'What are you doing?' she said, sleepily.

'Just drawing the curtains, that's all,' I replied, as softly as possible.

'Leave them open, please.'

'Oh,' I said, pulling them back. 'OK.'

'I like seeing the moon,' she said, and on one side of her face, her lips moved to form a smile.

I looked but couldn't see the moon myself. 'Right.'

'Emma?' she said, her voice a whisper.

'Yes?'

'I have a plan.' She paused and her eyelids quivered slightly.

'I know you do, you said before. But you can tell me all about it tomorrow, is that OK? Because you have to sleep now.'

'I love you Emma.'

A cloud must have passed because suddenly the moon was in front of me, full except for a sliver missing on one corner, an imperfect circle casting a soothing grey light onto Lucy's bed.

'I love you too Lucy.'

Chapter Thirty-five

Emma, September 2011

When I woke the next day, it was bright again outside, and I was leaning with my head on the edge of Lucy's bed. There was a painful pounding on the side I'd been leaning on, just above my eyes. My neck was stiff and my shoulders ached. Lucy was awake, sitting up in bed, reading the Bible.

'Morning,' she said, putting the book down.

'Morning,' I said, stretching awkwardly. I had pins and needles in my hands. 'I can't believe I fell asleep like this. How are you?'

'I'm fine,' she said, smiling broadly. There was that same ecstatic look she'd had yesterday at the beach. 'And you?'

'Thirsty. God, my head aches.'

She poured me a glass of water from a jug that was sitting on her bedside table. I gulped it down.

'I've just got to go to the bathroom, I'll be back in a few minutes.'

'OK,' she said.

I met Joe in the hallway and fiddled with my hair, pushing it out of my eyes. I must have looked such a state. He was red-faced and panting slightly.

'Morning Em,' he said, wiping his glistening forehead with the back of his arm. 'Just been for a run. How is she?'

'She seems OK. I just woke up, haven't had the chance to talk to her much yet.'

'Mam has asked the doctor in Ashington to come over and take a look at her. Luce's going to hate us, but it has to be done. He's coming at 11, if you could mention it to her. Or do you think I should pop in and tell her?'

'I don't know. It's up to you. You could do.'

He looked thoughtful.

'What time is it? Have you seen Pete?' I asked. 'And where is everyone else?'

'Various places – friend's houses, Da's at work, Mam's in the kitchen downstairs, think a couple of the littluns are on the beach. As for Pete, no I haven't seen him. I guess he's at home. It's about half past nine. Anyway, I'm going to have a shower. It's all right, you can use the bathroom first, I'll wait.'

I squeezed past him and went into the bathroom. I didn't look as bad as I had anticipated. My skin was a bit greasy though, so I washed my face, and cleaned off my eye make-up, and borrowed a pink toothbrush, trying not to think about who it might belong to. I brushed my hair through with a comb I found in the glass with all the toothbrushes. I left fresh-faced and determined to do my best for Lucy, to help her through the next few days.

Joe was sitting on the floor outside the bathroom when I came out, with Martha on his lap, reading from a book, which had pictures of cats all over the pages. He read the lines of the cats in a funny voice, following each sentence with a deep purr. Martha was giggling. They both looked up for a second as I stepped past them, and Joe winked at me, but carried on reading.

Back in the bedroom, Lucy was still sitting in bed. She had changed her top, and brushed her hair too. She was reading from the Bible. She put it down as soon as she saw me, and patted the space to one side of her. I sat down obediently.

'We've got a lot to talk about, haven't we?' she said.

Was she now going to start shouting at me for having an affair with her husband? Maybe all her crazy behaviour was just a mask for how she really felt and she had been waiting until we were alone to tear strips off me.

'I'm so sorry,' I said.

'What for?'

'For everything. For being with Pete, for you losing your baby.' Tears would have lent gravitas to my apology. I tried, but none came. At the back of my mind, Pete's face was hovering. I tried to push it away.

'Emma, please. Not again. We've been through this. There's no need for you to apologise to me. Ever. I've told you, and I've told Joe, and I've told Peter. It's forgiven, it's forgotten, it's all in the past.'

'Well, that's very…' I paused, trying to find the right word, '…generous of you.' That wasn't what I meant but I hoped she'd understand.

'No it's not. I should be thanking you. You've given me the opportunity…look, things will be OK, I promise. I've thought of a way you can be together.'

'I don't understand,' I said, noticing the strange dazed smile she'd had yesterday on the beach start to creep across her face again.

'Listen.' She leaned forward. 'You remember what Peter and I taught you about sacrifice?'

'Yes of course.'

'About the importance of mortification. Of denying yourself things.'

'Yes.'

'Do you still keep a log, you know, of your daily sacrifices?'

My cheeks started to heat up. I'd lied too much already.

'No, not anymore.' Her face fell. 'Well, not written down anyway. I keep them in my head, of course.'

'Do you still make daily sacrifices though?' Her voice was pleading.

'Yes,' I said, honestly. 'I do. It's a habit I got into, it's hard to break.'

'What sort of things?'

'Well, I turn the shower to cold for five minutes after I've finished.'

'Emma,' she said. 'You know very well that's just a way to make your hair shiny. Not a mortification at all.'

'But it's cold,' I said. 'I don't enjoy it, it's horrible. The shiny hair is just an unexpected bonus side-effect.'

She was giggling now.

'Emma! You're terrible.'

'No, I'm smart. No reason for a mortification to be all bad, is there?'

'That's the whole point of them! Anyway, what else do you do?'

'I don't have sugar in my morning cup of tea.'

'Ever?'

'Well, not on most days. Sometimes, when I'm really tired or have a long day ahead, I have it.'

'Hmm. Anything else?'

I sighed. 'I use the discipline. Sometimes. Well, I used to use it a lot. When me and Pete were...'

She nodded but a trace of pain flashed across her face.

'That's the other extreme isn't it?' she asked.

'What do you mean?'

'Well, the discipline – that's corporal mortification.'

'Is it?' I asked. 'I hadn't really thought about it. It just seemed like a way of doing penance. It was a really bad sin, so I think it earned a really bad penance.'

'Yes, but I'm not talking about penance here. I'm talking about small mortifications, the daily ones.'

'OK, well I often crave chewing gum, or chocolate but won't have any.'

'Yes, that's the sort of thing I was thinking about.' She fingered her Bible, but didn't pick it up. 'How do you feel when you've done things like that?'

'Better,' I said. 'Obviously.'

'And you remember what Jesus did for us?'

I thought this must have been a rhetorical question, so I didn't reply.

'He died,' I said, after she didn't say anything else. I was bored, I didn't want to hear any more preaching, but it was my duty to listen to Lucy. She was, after all, grieving.

'He died,' she said, in a schoolteacher voice. 'Yes, he gave up his life so that we should be saved.' She turned her head towards a painting of Jesus of the Sacred Heart, which hung lopsidedly next to the window. The glass in the frame was smeared.

'We spend our lives trying to follow his example.' Her voice had lowered to a conspirational hush but her eyes were sparkling. 'All my life, I've never loved anyone more than God.'

'I know,' I said.

'I love him more than I love anybody. But that doesn't mean I don't love you, or Peter. Because I do. So much. And all I want now is for you two to be together.'

'But Lucy. You know how it is...I don't understand...'

'Hush,' she said, putting a finger to my lips. 'You don't need to understand. Not yet. Tomorrow. Just trust me.'

~

I left Lucy's room. Joe was no longer in the corridor, and there was no one else in my way as I ran down the stairs and out of the front door. I went round the Pete's. I wanted to see him. There was something about the way Lucy was behaving, something strange, unsettling. She needed help, therapy, something. I hammered on the door until Bert answered, grunting in my face.

'The southern lass. What do you want?' he said, staring down at me.

'Sorry,' I said. 'Is he there?'

'Yes he's here. Turned up out of the flamin' blue yesterday. Round the back.' He jerked his head in the direction of the side gate to the garden and shut the door in my face.

I went round the side. Pete was sitting under one of the large willow trees, reading something in his lap. His posture was exactly the same as Lucy's had been earlier that morning. When I approached, I saw that it wasn't the Bible, but a slim book entitled *Solemn Modern Benedictions*. I coughed to announce my appearance, because I didn't want to make him jump. He looked up at me for a second, then back down to his book.

'Now may the God of peace who brought up our Lord Jesus from the dead, that great Shepherd of the sheep, through the blood of the everlasting covenant, make you complete in every good work to do His will, working in you what is well pleasing in His sight, through Jesus Christ, to whom be glory forever and ever. Amen,' he read.

'Amen,' I said, automatically. 'I have to talk to you.'

'Of course, hang on a sec. I'm just finishing my spiritual reading.'

It was wrong to interrupt. I sat down next to him, but he put the book down anyway.

'What's the matter?'

I didn't reply. There was something about the way he looked at me. I was overcome. It was all too much – I just wanted to sleep. I didn't have the strength to deal with any of it. I was exhausted, sapped of all energy. The sun was strong on my face.

'Do you love me Emma?' he asked, coming closer, blocking the sun from my face with his.

My scalp tickled. His eyes looked like pools of liquid chocolate. I opened my mouth to reply, but he kissed me. I didn't respond. I felt as though I was made of stone.

After a few minutes, he pulled away.

'Come with me,' he said, standing up and offering me a hand. I followed him, as he walked to the edge of the garden.

'Look at all this,' he said, gesturing around at the garden, and towards the big, square house. 'It's beautiful isn't it?'

I nodded. If only I could sleep.

'All of this is going to be mine soon. My father's very ill. He won't last long. And I'm his only relative.'

He picked the pink head from a rose that climbed all over the back wall of the garden, and handed it to me. It was dying, the outside petals were wilting and brown and one fell off as I took it.

'I love gardening,' he said. 'You didn't know that, did you? That's what I love about you. We have so much to discover about each other. When we live here, I am going to make this garden the most impressive in the whole of Northumberland. My mother, you see, she loved to garden. These roses were hers. My father couldn't care less, but she loved to look after things, to watch them grow. I made sure he kept up her work once she died. It was a struggle but somehow the old git found the money for a gardener, so things haven't gone to pot. There's so much potential here, don't you think? You could have all sorts of different things going on in such a large space. It's half an acre. I'd have a wildflower area, like a mini-meadow in that corner, and a vegetable patch and herb garden near the house, and an arbour covered in trailing roses and honeysuckle. And we could sit under there, and read together. And I'd get you a piano, a proper grand piano, and you could have it in the big room over there, that looks over the garden. My dad doesn't even use that room. I could sit and listen to you play. It would be like nowhere on earth.'

Like nowhere on earth. The way Lucy had described the beach the day before.

'I'd make you happy you know. If you'd let me. We've been through so much together. You need to trust me. Trust us both. We've found a way. It's all going to be perfect.'

'OK,' I said. I frowned, tried to remember what I'd learnt about divorce, remarriage. Pete had always insisted there was nothing we could do; that there were no loopholes. So what was new? Annulment? I racked my brains trying to remember the ins and outs of it, but it was too hot and I was too tired and I just couldn't think.

'Come with me, there's something I want to show you.'

I followed him as he wound his way through some thick

shrubs at one corner of the garden. My flip-flops sank into the soft soil but it was dry and cool and the dirt simply fell away from my feet as I walked. Eventually, we came to a door in the wall. The handle was rusted and only traces of sun-bleached green paint remained on the woodwork. Pete opened the latch and pushed, but it took a gentle kick at the bottom for the door to open. On the other side was a carpet of stinging nettles, surrounded by monstrous pine trees. I hesitated.

'I'll carry you,' Pete said, and picked me up, before I had the chance to protest. He leaned over and kissed me again, and this time, I wanted him more than anything I had ever wanted in my life. I kissed him as though he was providing the oxygen that was keeping me alive.

I had missed the physical side of our relationship. It hadn't all been about our minds, about how I'd admired his intelligence, reticence and integrity. His body and face were the most appealing things I'd ever seen, and watching him move, speak and interact with the world was a pleasure in itself. Along with the sound of his breathing, I could hear the sea moving in and out on the sand, and the two were perfectly synchronized.

'We're going to be together. No matter what,' he whispered into my hair.

'Yes,' I replied. Perhaps we would abandon Catholicism. It was the only thing stopping us being together. The hows and whys and wherefores were irrelevant to me. I'd had more misery than anyone deserved over the past year. It was my turn. As I'd always believed it would, my turn had come. All that mattered now was Pete and I being together.

'Yes,' I said, my words thick with emotion. 'We're going to be together. No matter what.'

Chapter Thirty-six

Pete, September 2010

'You're leaving me,' she said. Her eyes began to glisten.

They were standing in Lucy's front garden. Upstairs, a curtain twitched and Peter caught her mother's eye at the window.

'The point is not that I'm leaving,' he said, 'but that you've decided to stay behind.'

'Decided,' she repeated, her voice quiet. 'You know it's not like that. I have to stay, Mam needs me.'

'And I don't?'

'It's not that simple.'

'Really?' Peter looked away. He wondered whether he should turn and leave.

'You could defer,' she said, her eyes widening. 'For another year. You could stay behind for another year, keep working at the factory. Just till Mam is in the all clear. Please?'

'She'll never be in the all clear,' he said, cruelly.

She stared at him. For a second, he thought she might be about to say something, something feisty and argumentative, but the flash of courage faded, and instead she began to weep. She sank to the ground, folding her arms across her legs, and placed her head on her knees.

Peter ran his hands through his hair. He no longer knew what he was trying to achieve. It was all so confusing. Should he put his arms around her, comfort her? No, not this time. He'd given in last year. He'd mollycoddled her enough, her vulnerability was beginning to bore him. It drove him onwards, towards outright cruelty.

'I would have asked you, you know,' he said, playing his trump card, the one he had reserved for months. It was what she wanted, so desperately. He would wave it under her nose, then snatch it away. 'To marry me. But now... I don't know if you care for me enough. Not as much as I care for you.'

'Peter...' she said. She was choking on her sobs, now. When she looked up at him, strands of her hair were stuck in her tears.

'It's always been about you,' he said. 'And your problems. What about me? I've spent my whole life rescuing you.' He was playing a game, spouting well-rehearsed lines, yet it struck him that the words were true and the realisation strengthened his resolve. 'You're completely selfish.'

'Please Peter, don't say that. Don't be so cruel. It's not my fault. You're so much stronger than me...'

'Look what I've had to cope with!' His voice became a roar. 'You've had it all. Two parents who love you...' He stopped himself, determined not to lose his cool.

'I haven't had it so easy,' she said, quietly. 'You know I haven't.'

'For goodness' sake!' he said. 'It's all in your head. It's over now, you left school years ago.'

'But it's still... please.'

'Don't think I don't know,' he sneered. 'This is emotional blackmail. You did the same thing last year. The one thing I want to do – go to Leeds, get away from my father, see something of the world. Not even the world, just another part of the country. But no, I can't. Because I know what you'll do, the second I'm gone.'

'What do you mean?'

'Stop the act. I know all about it. Pretending to your brother, to your parents, that it's my fault. Did you ever think how it feels for me? Knowing one day, you might go too far, knowing one day you might end up just like my mother?'

'What are you talking about?' she asked, weakly.

He took two steps forward and grabbed her wrists, hauling her to her feet.

'This,' he said, pulling back both sleeves of her cardigan. He twisted her arms round, so that her wrists were facing upwards.

'This is what I'm talking about!'

She squirmed in his grip, refusing to look down at the furrows that decorated her skin. Some were faded, almost white, hardened welts, others were narrow grooves, pink with newness.

'Don't,' she said.

'Did you think I didn't know?' he asked, still holding her wrists. Under his thumbs, her skin was going white. 'That you sit there, night after night, slashing away?'

'Please,' she said, although she was no longer wriggling in his grasp. The tears cascaded down her cheeks.

'Do you realise how easy it would be to go too far?' he asked. 'What do you use anyway? A razor? A knife?'

'Let me go, please.'

He stood back and dropped her arms. She pulled her sleeves back down. The expression on her face was one of a naughty child.

'It's September. It's been twenty degrees or so for the last few weeks. Did you never think I might wonder why you always covered yourself up? Is it the same on your legs? Shall we see?'

She shrieked as he lurched towards her.

'Get off me!' she shouted, stepping backwards until she was pressed up against her front door. As far from him as possible. 'Leave me alone. You don't understand.'

'You could end up killing yourself,' he said, quietly. 'You have no idea what that would do to me.'

There was a pause. He looked at her, wondering what she was really thinking. Her behaviour was wrong, he had every right to be angry with her. He'd kept her secret for weeks now, unsure how to let on that he knew. When he'd first realised, it had seemed like such a strange thing for Lucy to do. It annoyed him that he couldn't understand it.

What was she thinking? Did she really hope he'd never find out? It didn't seem possible and it seemed pointless. Why would anyone cut their own arms, hoping that no one ever found out? It was simple, straightforward attention seeking, which meant she must have wanted him to know – deep down, she must have hoped he knew. So why did she look at him now as though he'd seen her naked?

'I'm sorry,' she said, hanging her head. 'I always…offered it up...'

'Don't even try to pretend this is a mortification. It's not and you know it. It's wrong. You know how much your parents love you. What would they say if they knew? Imagine if someone sliced away at Sally's arms? How would you feel then? That's how I feel. Devastated.'

She said nothing.

He sighed. 'I'm sorry,' he said, meaning it. He had forgotten, momentarily, that this was what he wanted. He wanted her to be messed up, vulnerable. She was no use to him if she was strong and didn't need him. If she could cope without him then he no longer had a purpose and his life was wasted.

'I'm sorry. I shouldn't have shouted,' he said, gazing at her with sympathy.

She sniffed, pushed her hair from her face.

'It's just… I love you so much. You must realise that.'

'Yes,' she said.

'I want you to promise me, hand on heart, before God, that you won't do this again. I have to go to Leeds, you have to stay behind. It will be hard but I don't want you to do this to yourself. Ever. Do you understand me?'

'Yes,' she replied.

'Good.' He drew her towards him, buried his lips in her hair, and traced his fingertips over and over the bumpy, damaged skin. The sensation made him smile.

Chapter Thirty-seven

Emma, September 2011

My chips grew cold. Somehow, I had no appetite. It seemed too good to be true, this mysterious plan. Were they going to lie? Pretend they had never married? Were we going to run away together, somewhere nobody knew us? It wasn't possible. Real life didn't work like that.

'We'll rent a flat in Headingley, until we've finished our degrees,' Pete said, stabbing his with the plastic fork. Some fell to the ground and the seagulls arrived in seconds. 'Then, I'll do my MA up here and we can move into the house. The old man will be long gone by then. There's loads going on in Newcastle – you'll find a job no problem.'

I smiled cautiously.

'You're worried aren't you?' he asked. 'You're so quiet.'

'I just don't understand,' I said.

'Don't worry about it,' he said, after a while. 'We'll explain it all tonight. I told you. 9pm, on the beach.'

I thought of my dad. He didn't have religion as a barrier. If all he'd wanted was to be with Mae, he should have just left Mum. It didn't need to be so drastic. All this time, I'd seen him as a coward, but now I considered it again, I realised he was brave. Braver than me – I could never kill myself, I knew that. He must have found the idea of Mum's wrath so terrifying, to take such a risk. After all, no one knew what awaited you on the other side. It might be even worse.

'My dad had an affair,' I said. 'He ended up killing himself.'

'I know,' Pete replied softly. 'Lucy told me. You never talked about it though. I didn't want to bring it up.'

'It was my fault. I made him do it.'

Pete looked across at me. 'What do you mean?'

'I caught him. I came home from school early – skipped my

last lesson. General Studies. I was upset; I'd just heard that Ben – my ex – was definitely going out with another girl in my year. Dad was meant to be at work. They were in the kitchen…' I stopped speaking, remembered how repulsive the sight had been. And Lassie, poor silly Lassie, sitting in the corner in her dog bed, watching them. Doing it in front of her – it was disgusting.

'What happened?' Pete asked.

'He was…' I laughed. 'On the sofa in the kitchen.'

'With another woman?'

'With my aunt.' Pete breathed in sharply. 'Not my real aunt,' I added, 'my mum's best friend.'

'Jesus.' It was the first time I'd heard Pete swear like that. A venial sin: one for him to confess at the weekend.

'They didn't even see me. I ran off, back into town. I think I might have been sick. I don't remember.' That afternoon was a blur now. All I remembered was confronting Dad that evening, when he was out at the boat. I'd lingered by the river waiting for him. 'Later, I found him. I told him he had to tell Mum, or I would. He begged me not to. Then he got cross, told me I was his daughter and had to obey him. He slapped me across the face. It was the first time he'd ever hit me. But I still said I would tell Mum if he didn't. And I meant it.'

'So what happened?'

'I went home, and went to bed. I didn't speak to him again. And the next day, after breakfast, he went to kill himself.'

'How?' Pete asked, putting down his can of Coke.

'He threw himself in front of a train.'

I paused. That was one of the things I'd hated the most. That I'd always be known as the girl whose father had thrown himself in front of the 16.15 from Paignton. The daughter of the only man stupid enough to choose one of Devon's leading tourist attractions as his suicidal modus operandi.

Did he get steamed to death? The boys in Matt's year had said, knowing full well we were both in earshot. *Like a plate of vegetables?*

No.

I'd wanted to set them straight, to take them by the shoulders and explain he'd died just as revoltingly as any other person who is hit by a train, whether steam or diesel or electric. Squelched. Dragged along the tracks for at least a mile, his body shredded, reshaped, damaged beyond recognition. They'd covered the pieces of him with tinfoil before removing and returning them to my mother. The sight of the human-shaped coffin at the funeral had irritated me when a square box would have done. There was no point in trying to reassemble the bits. He'd never be presentable again.

Goliath. That was the name of the engine. It was the most powerful locomotive in the whole Paignton and Dartmouth Steam Railway fleet. It was almost funny. I often wondered if he'd known, if he'd planned it. Struck down by a Goliath – what a way to go! But he'd never been a trainspotter, and he'd had no time to plan, so it seemed unlikely.

'It's difficult you know,' I said, looking straight at Pete. 'I researched it afterwards. You have to get the timing just right. And there's no use doing it from a platform. You have to do it from a bridge, so that the train's going fast enough to kill you instantly.'

'He must have been very troubled,' Pete said, putting his arm around me. I rested my head on his shoulder. 'But it wasn't your fault. You must believe that.'

'I suppose. I don't know. I still don't have the answers. I haven't even spoken to my aunt about it.' I stared down at my chips. 'There was the debt too, of course. He was in a huge amount of debt. Nearly two hundred thousand pounds. When he died, his life insurance cleared it all, which was something. He was broke, and he was weak. I guess he couldn't face letting us all down. Especially not Mum.'

'So, did you ever tell her?'

'No. He wrote me a letter, he begged me not to. There didn't seem much point.'

'You should do. You should tell her the truth. If you still have the letter, you should show her.' Pete sounded serious, more serious than I'd ever heard him.

'What about your mother? Why did she kill herself?'

Pete shifted away from me slightly. 'She killed herself because of him. He made her life unbearable.'

'Your father?'

He nodded.

'We haven't had much luck have we?'

'No,' he said. 'I suppose we haven't.' A slow smile spread across his face. He reached over and kissed me. 'But don't worry, our luck is about to change.'

Chapter Thirty-eight

Emma, September 2011

I saw the fire before I saw them. The sun was in its final throes and the flames flickered on the sand, spreading a warm glow that drew me towards them. The first thing I noticed as I approached was the beer bottles. Several of them empty, littering the ground before them.

'Have you been drinking?' I asked, confused.

'Sit down Emma,' Pete said. 'You can have a bottle if you like.'

'No thanks.' I sat opposite them and looked across at Lucy. She was crouched with her knees drawn up under her chin. The sadness in her eyes made me uncomfortable.

'So, come on then. This big plan of yours?'

I cast my eyes back and forth between them both but neither spoke. Something glinted in Lucy's hand: a spoon maybe; something metallic. I looked again but Lucy tucked it away, underneath her skirt.

'What's going on?' I said. 'Why aren't you saying anything?'

'The rules of marriage are very clear aren't they?' Lucy said finally, speaking slowly.

'Yes.'

'I am married to Peter. And there's no way that you can be with him, while I'm still alive. Not in the eyes of God.'

I didn't answer her. My instincts were screaming at me that something wasn't right.

She continued. 'The only way you two can be together is if I'm dead.'

'Don't say things like that,' I said. My voice shook. 'I thought you… I thought you said you had a plan.'

'It's the truth,' she said, crossing her arms. 'And I do have a plan. An idea that no one else has ever thought of. Something completely original. The ultimate mortification,' she said, twisting her hands together.

And then, I knew what was coming. 'The ultimate sacrifice. My life.'

'Stop it!' I shouted, springing to my feet. 'This is your plan? I can't believe you're saying this. This is a joke, right? It's a mortal sin. You told me that.'

I looked across at Pete. He looked calm. Too calm.

'It's a mortal sin, if it's done for selfish reasons,' Lucy said, her voice monotone. 'If it's done because the person can't bear to live anymore, if they're a coward, looking for an easy way out. But I'm doing it so that you two can be together. God wants you to be together. It's what you want, too, isn't it Emma? What you always wanted.'

'Shut up,' I said, desperately. 'Shut up. Shut up. Shut up. Stop this. I don't want to be with Pete. Not like this. I don't want you to die. I never wanted any of this.'

'You won't stop me,' she said, coldly. It didn't sound like her. She sounded authoritative, pushy, irritated. 'You've had your way long enough. It's God's will that matters now. Not yours, or mine, or Peter's. And it's God's will that I kill myself, so that you and Peter can be together. And nothing you can do, or say, will stop me from following the path of the Lord.'

She didn't allow me any longer to argue. Quickly, she took the knife out from under her skirt, and when the blood on the palm of her hand oozed out, thick and scarlet, I realised she was serious. I lurched forward, tried to grab the knife from her, but Pete stood up, and quickly and calmly broke the bottle of beer he was drinking over my forehead. He told me to shut up. I fell, dazed, and didn't have the balance to try to stop him when he took some thick blue string out of his jacket pocket and tied my wrists and ankles together.

'Pete,' I cried, 'No, please, no.'

I looked over at Lucy. There was a fear in her eyes I hadn't encountered before.

'Sorry,' Pete said, bluntly. 'But you're a crucial witness. You have to watch. Or we would never be able to prove it was suicide.'

My head hurt. I felt my own blood run down my left cheek, spots of it landing on my white dress, the fabric sucking it up eagerly, creating perfect ruby polka dots. It was dark now. The sun had left, the moon was hidden, and the only light came from the small fire.

I looked again at Lucy. She ignored my sobs, my desperate pleas for her to stop. She ignored Pete's smile. Her eyes were wide but she continued in her gory mission. I was thankful for the tears that filled mine as I watched her – they blurred my vision. Those tears and the dimness of the firelight saved me. They told me that it wasn't real, that it was a dream. A horrible dream.

Wordlessly, she nicked at the skin around her neck, tilting her head upwards. The cuts here were shallow and superficial. I knew why. It all made sense now. She worried that if she cut her throat too deeply she would die within minutes, when that wasn't the point. The point was to endure a painful death, like Jesus. She wanted it to be slow and drawn out. Skinny red rivers of blood flowed down her neck, their passage easy over the smooth young skin.

After a while, she came to her chest, opening her shirt to reveal her black bra, wet from the milk, straining under her swollen breasts. She carved more deeply here, creating a cross, keeping the long cuts neat and accurate.

'Lucy,' I whispered, as my heart filled with horror. 'Don't...'

After she gouged the cross into her chest, a delirium seemed to take hold of her. She was fervent, excited and wanted to pray the whole rosary. Pete stood over me, demanding I pray with them. The string holding my wrists together scratched my skin. *Glory be to the Father, to the Son and to the Holy Spirit. As it was in the beginning, is now and ever shall be, world without end.* The words didn't stick in my throat as I had expected. I did it for her. Lucy was drawing strength from my cooperation.

Her body had become a work of art. A dedication. A sacrifice. She moved across her arms and legs in the same, methodical manner, growing weaker and weaker as more blood drained from her. Her breathing became shallow as the fire began to burn out. My eyelids grew heavy – it felt as though we had been on the beach for hours.

I couldn't tell the exact moment that she died. It wasn't like in films – there was no sudden last gasp of air, no dramatic final words. After she lost consciousness I watched her still, but I couldn't tell whether she was breathing. The moment when her heart finally stopped and her soul left her body – that moment I couldn't have picked out. Instead, after a time, I simply felt she was no longer there. Her presence had gone and the atmosphere of the beach was changed. It had become colder. Lucy was no longer there.

She looked even more beautiful than before, lying there dead. Her face was the one part of her body left untouched and the skin was still so perfect. It was the kind of skin that shouldn't exist in reality. Her hair was hidden behind her where she had slumped, and only her face stood out, a pure white mask, glowing in the moonlight that filtered through the broken clouds and fell onto her face in dramatic shards. Her eyes were still open, but their colour wasn't visible. They were black pits, contrasting with the milk of her skin. I stared at her face. It was expressionless. I wanted her to look peaceful, or happy, but she just looked dead. It was impossible to tell the ecstasy she had felt as she had taken her own life. God had wanted her, she believed. She was now an angel, a saint, a martyr. But slumped in the corner of a group of rocks, with the wind from the sea gently lifting strands of her hair, she looked like a doll – unreal, cold, lifeless.

I was frightened to look away from her, so I stared, unblinking, at her corpse, until my eyes were dry and sore. But I couldn't look at her forever. At some point I would have to turn away, and see the man who I now knew was responsible for her death. For a second I prayed to the very God I hated but would forever be linked to, begging him for the second time to stop my heart, but he was capricious as always and ignored me.

I heard a noise and turned my head. My neck was stiff, my head still pounding. The moon was bright now, the clouds had disappeared, and there, in the sea, illuminated by the white light, was Pete, head turned towards the sky. Shouting. His words were carried away by the wind, drowned by the waves. I crawled nearer, to hear him.

'I did it Mam,' he called. 'For you. He was wrong, the old man. I told you he was wrong.'

'Pete,' I screamed.

He turned, looked at me.

'Pete,' I screamed, again.

He came out of the water, making great, galloping strides. They were strides of joy, of exuberance.

'Pete,' I said one last time, before I exploded into sobs.

'We did it!' he shouted. His jeans were dragging, hanging from his skinny waist, weighed down by the water.

'Please,' I said, choking on my tears. I could barely breathe. 'Don't smile…not like that.'

'He said what my mother did was unforgivable,' he said, his arms outstretched, palms turned towards me. 'The worst sin you could commit. But he was wrong wasn't he? We've proved it, you and I. I told him, time and time again. My mother was ill. She didn't know what she was doing. Her suicide wasn't a mortal sin at all.'

'What?' I spluttered. 'What are you talking about?'

'He didn't believe me. He wouldn't even have her buried. Do you know what he did to her ashes?'

I stared at him, said nothing.

'He poured them on the compost heap. The compost heap! I

was eight years old. He dragged me into the garden, and told me to piss on her ashes. Piss on my own mother. He said there was no way. Under no circumstances was suicide forgivable. It would always result in the soul going to hell. No person who commits suicide deserved to be buried, he said. But we've proved him wrong!'

'Pete,' I said, pain coursing through my stomach. I dug my elbows into my sides. 'I thought…I thought you loved me. You wanted to be with me.'

He laughed. 'Oh Emma, of course I love you! You were instrumental. You were fundamental to the whole thing. I couldn't have done this without you. Don't you see? I never would have imagined it was possible before I met you. And you made it so easy. I thought it would take years. You made it so easy for Lucy to love you. For her to want to give up everything for you.'

I coughed. Sour vomit came to the back of my throat.

'But Lucy…How could you do this to Lucy?'

'She had it coming. It was all her fault. Don't you understand? The afternoon my mother drowned, I wanted to go down to the beach earlier. But Lucy wanted to finish the jigsaw puzzle first. We always did what Lucy wanted. If I'd only been there earlier. Just half an hour earlier. I could have stopped her. She would have listened to me. "You're the only ray of light in my life Pete," she used to say. I was her whole world. If I'd only been there half an hour before, I could have stopped her from doing it. But no, Lucy had to finish her puzzle.'

'It wasn't Lucy's fault,' I shouted. My body began to convulse. 'You can't blame her. She didn't know. It wasn't her fault. She didn't deserve this.'

'Emma,' he said, calmly. 'She got what she wanted. Look at her – she's a saint now! A martyr. You don't need to pity her. She died as she lived – holier than fucking thou.'

There was nothing more to say. He climbed over me, spread-eagled and stuck to the sand, and picked up his bag, filling it with the empty beer bottles we'd drunk from earlier. He didn't even look at Lucy's body. And then, he left us.

~

Before long, the sun had chased the moon away and I awoke to find myself lying alone on the sand, with lines of Lucy's congealed blood running down the beach and into the sea. There were birds. Everywhere. It hadn't occurred to me that they would find her body so quickly. I tried to stand and fell headlong into the sand, bloody clumps of it sticking to my face. I looked down, and remembered my feet were tied together. All I could think was that I had to get the birds away from her. I tried to wipe the stickiness from my eyes but my wrists were tied too. For a second, I didn't understand, and then the pieces of my memory began to fit together, and I screamed.

The sound echoed out along the empty beach but still they kept swooping down. Their pecking made a sharp, hammering noise and I wanted to cover my ears. There were so many of them that they concealed her entire body, and I couldn't even see what damage they had done.

I looked around. I was completely alone, except for the birds.

My forehead hurt from where he had hit me, and the dried blood that had run down my face was itching unbearably.

Where was Pete now? I wiggled my wrists desperately, trying to loosen the string. I would break them if I had to. Then, I spotted the glass lying by the ashes of the fire – glass from the bottle he'd used to stun me. I wedged a piece between my knees, wincing as it sliced into my skin, and sawed at the string until it came loose. I reached down and untied my ankles. Screaming, shouting, waving my arms, I ran towards the birds. They flew away, off up to a higher rock, where they all perched, watching me, waiting for me to leave so that they could come back and continue their feast.

I looked at what was left of Lucy. Her breastbone was exposed. I could see a startling whiteness in amongst the layers of red and brown and pink flesh. Her arms were a horrifying mess of shredded fibres and lumps of tissue, strips of skin flapping about in the breeze. They hadn't touched her face, not yet, but it was only a matter of time. I resisted the urge to vomit, and ran from the beach, up the road, and straight to her house.

Joe was coming out of the gate as I approached. The birthday balloons were still hanging from it; one now punctured.

'Emma?' he said, looking shocked. 'Are you OK? Where have you been? What happened to you?'

I shook my head, over and over and over. No words came. And then I collapsed.

Chapter Thirty-nine

Emma, September 2011

Joe was the only one who didn't blame me. Lucy's mother and the rest of her family didn't want me in the house, so Joe took me to a B&B near Morpeth, and stayed with me for a few days. We watched the small television in the room, and I ate endless slices of toast. He didn't ask me any questions, but he told me stories of the way Pete had behaved as a child, about his mother, how she'd had manic depression, and about his father's violence. He told me how Pete had been lied to and not told his mother had killed herself, and when as a teenager his aunt had told him the truth, he'd beaten her so hard she'd been hospitalised for weeks.

He told me about the note that had been found under Lucy's head too: a note I'd never seen, but that appeared to have been signed by me. The police had kept it, but the words were stuck in my head, and they went round and round.

Lucy Maria Fields took her own life in an act of pure altruism. Please ensure that her body is buried in consecrated grounds and pray for her soul's rapid ascension to heaven. Signed, Peter Fields and Emma Dewberry.

I managed to persuade Joe I'd had no idea Pete had left it, and that I'd played no part in their plan. His belief in my innocence was the greatest compliment I'd ever been paid.

'He's gone, you know,' he said, on the third day. He filled up the small kettle and switched it on. I sat by the window, my knees drawn up under my chin, staring out at the garden. I could just make out the blurry shape of sheep in the far distance. 'There's been no sign of him. Even his father has no idea where he is.'

I watched him pour sugar into my cup, acknowledging just how much I respected him and his utter stability, and the balanced way in which he viewed the world.

'I'm not surprised,' I said. I wondered if he'd thought past this point, past the realisation of his great plan. It didn't seem likely. His obsession must have been all-consuming.

'I hope he's killed himself,' Joe said. 'Because if he hasn't and I ever see him again…'

'I hope so too,' I interrupted. I didn't want to hear his threats. I didn't want him to say anything ugly or vindictive. He was untarnished, well-meaning, the mirror of his sister, and I couldn't bear to hear him go against himself.

He sighed, staring down at the cups before him.

'Are they going to bury her?' I asked.

'Yes, of course.' His tone was sharp, as though I had asked him something stupid.

'I'm glad,' I said, placatingly.

'With the baby,' he continued. 'Pete's belief that suicide victims can't be buried was nonsense. His mam wasn't buried because his father wouldn't have it.'

He handed me my cup of tea and I smiled my gratitude. Turning back to the window, I twisted my rosary ring around my finger, counting the bumps, remembering the words.

As we fell into silence, I thought of Lucy, in heaven with her baby, and prayed for them both, despite knowing my faith – the faith that makes people behave like monsters – had died along with her.

~

The next day, I took the bus into Cresswell after dinner and went down to the beach. Joe offered to come with me, but I wanted to go alone.

Walking along the shore, I imagined I saw Pete and Lucy's shadows everywhere. Pete's especially – I would never forget the image of his lanky form in the water, staring up at the moon. It was cooler now, and I crossed my arms and tucked my hands underneath them. I approached the rocks. The white police tent was still there. A group of children played around it, running in between the rocks, giggling hysterically. I stopped walking and watched them for a while, not wanting to go any closer.

I sat down. The sea was calm; the sun had begun its descent. I took my mobile phone from my pocket. To my surprise, I had a signal. It felt like an affirmation from the universe that it was the right thing to do. I watched the sea for a little longer.

In my mind's eye, I saw Pete standing before me on the beach, smiling, his arms outstretched, inviting me towards him. I stared at the mirage. In his kind, loving stance, I recognised nothing but his duplicity. I didn't cry. I felt liberated, peaceful, and when I blinked, he disappeared. Then I knew: my grief would always be reserved for Lucy.

When I thought of Pete, there was now only a vague sadness there, and a sense of disappointment, the feeling of being let down. Even those feelings were weak, every day supplanted a little more by pity for him and his wasted life. I accepted now that he was damaged, defective, inherently flawed. Without even realising it, he had followed in his father's footsteps, despite vowing his whole life to do the opposite. Just like I had.

But he had been right about one thing. Mum deserved to know the truth. I had kept Dad's secret for more than a year, and it had brought me nothing but misery. Not just for me, but for Mum too – my strange, distant behaviour had been a constant worry to her. It was time to end it. Here, on Cresswell beach.

My future would be free from lies. That much I was sure of. The New Year would bring a new millennium, the chance to start again. I had two years left at Leeds and I was determined to make them worthwhile.

I noticed the tip of something sparkling in the sand beside me, and I dug it out with my nails.

It was a fragment of coloured glass. Red, and as smooth as a pebble. I rolled it between my fingers a few times, and then, although I had no use for it, slipped it into my pocket.

The sun was nothing more than a pale orange glow spreading across the horizon. I stood up, breathing in deeply, and dialled the number for home.

Acknowledgements

Heartfelt thanks to:

My lovely agent Caroline Hardman, for all her editorial input.

The fab Lisa Clark and the rest of the team at Sassy books, for making this happen.

My first reader Becky Cormack, for her invaluable help and advice.

Lilly Millington, for teaching me all I know about Catholicism.

Richard Manley, who introduced me to Cresswell all those years ago.

Oliver Darley, for all the 'M/mams', and for his constant encouragement.

The original MsBers, who all had a hand somewhere in this book.

All who ride the Lifeboar, for keeping me company.

My family, especially Mum, Dad and Poph, for their love and support.

About the Author

Lotte Worth was born in 1981. She graduated from Leeds University in 2002, then completed a postgraduate diploma in magazine journalism. For the last ten years she has worked on a variety of lifestyle magazines and websites. She lives in south west London.

The Perfect Suicide is her first novel.

For more information on Lotte and her writing, visit her website www.lotteworth.com.

Hip, real and raw, SASSY books share authentic truths, spiritual insights and entrepreneurial witchcraft with women who want to kick ass in life and y'know...start revolutions.